The L

by

Ruth Saberton

Copyright

Notes from the author

In 2017 I was immersed in the world and landscape of First World War Cornwall while writing my novel The Letter. The characters and settings from this book remained with me for a long time afterwards and I always felt that there were more stories to be told from the world of Rosecraddick. Since The Letter has a very clear resolution a traditional sequel wasn't possible, but I began to develop the idea of a companion novella drawn from a short story I'd written much earlier on. This novella's plan remained on my hard drive as notes while I worked on my other books and life continued to be busy. I always thought I'd find a moment to return to it one day when I had a spare moment, but I could have never dreamed quite how this would have come about...

In March 2020 the Covid 19 pandemic took hold in earnest in the UK and as an asthmatic I found myself having to shield. As for everyone else, my life changed overnight and living so far away from my family I was consumed with worry and the very real fear of not knowing whether my loved ones would be safe or when I might see them again. Although I was lucky to be here in Cornwall, by the beach and surrounded by beautiful countryside, it was still a frightening and isolating experience. Suddenly I had huge amounts of time on my hands and writing became more than my passion and my livelihood; it became my escape and my solace.

During this time I found myself returning to the world of Rosecraddick and The Letter. As always in Cornwall the past was just over my shoulder and I began to think about the other stories that were just out of sight. I started to write my planned novella but as the characters' voices took hold the story grew and the narrative developed into a novel. This novel became The Locket as the book began to write itself in that magical way that some novels do. The sense of loss and uncertainty that I was feeling had echoes in the events of the early part of the twentieth century and the time before Covid 19 seemed a golden era just like the summer of 1914. This novel became a wonderful escape and I loved every moment I spent with the characters. Even though I shed a lot of tears at times it was still a world I missed when

I wasn't writing. A few old friends made surprise appearances but many new faces also appeared to take me with them on new adventures. My old Kodak Vest Pocket camera also decided it needed a starring role!

The Locket was completed just as the severest lockdown restrictions were being lifted in the UK. The timings have been so apt and I cannot be more grateful for this book because it helped me through a difficult time and transported me to other places when real life travel was impossible. It's a novel of love and hope and above all the resilience of the human spirit – again more echoes of what was happening in the wider world while I was working on the book. I wasn't expecting to write a novel but sometimes events take over the best of plans and if there is one thing I have learned from my experience of shielding and isolating it's been to take away the good things from these difficult months. Along with learning to slow down and appreciating my loved ones even more, writing The Locket has been one of the experiences I am most grateful for. (Learning to use Zoom, watching far too much TV and living in yoga pants– not quite so much!)

I really hope you enjoy The Locket. For readers who know The Letter - I hope you enjoy returning to that familiar world. For all those visiting Rosecraddick for the first time - welcome to beautiful and timeless Cornwall.

Happy reading.

Ruth
July 2020

The locket ...

... had slipped to the bottom of the box. Swaddled in a scrap of black velvet bald from touch and green with age, it was tucked beneath strata of yellowed newspapers and faded photographs and a lifetime's beloved detritus rendered meaningless by decades of turning seasons.

This locket was an ornate piece, a heavy oval of engraved silver dulled to tarnished blackness by the years. The delicate chain was twisted into knots and as tangled as a love affair. Treasured for a lifetime, it had rested for decades against a broken heart, as much a memorial of love as any treasure sealed within a pharaoh's tomb or carved effigy found sleeping in a countryside church.

Although the antique necklace had slumbered for almost half a century, the locket's clasp remained true and if the catch was ever sprung his much-loved face would still gaze out from beneath a whisper of glass. Unfaded by light and time, the sitter for this photograph remained forever young, his dark eyes as full of humour as they had been the second the shutter had closed. The light in them was bright, as though the person they had belonged to was still living rather than a relic from a sepia-tinted age when young men donned uniforms and fought through mud and misery before passing into history.

Although this face was erased from memory and the name last murmured by long-passed lips, nothing is ever truly forgotten. Houses sell and dusty boxes are hauled down from attics, but eventually all neglected belongings are sifted like flour as new hands lift out books and smooth curling photographs. The time was approaching when wondering fingertips would brush the worn velvet before sliding out this antique piece. Then daylight would caress the face once more and questions would be asked. At last the stitched-up silence would start to unravel.

Secrets, however long kept, will find a way to be uncovered.

Prologue

Emmy

Cornwall 1914

Rosecraddick Halt was an afterthought of a station. Built for the convenience of a wealthy family, as its fortunes and deliveries dwindled the halt stood half-forgotten at the end of a rutted lane until the occasional train appeared and the platform burst into a flurry of activity. The guard's whistle blew, dogcarts rumbled up and down the lane and carriage doors clattered. Silence fled as voices were raised above the hiss of steam, the lone porter cursing as he heaved cases in and out of the luggage compartments, and iron-shod hooves pawed the earth while passengers alighted and embarked. Handkerchiefs waved and farewells were called as the train departed, growing ever smaller as it retreated down the track, leaving the halt all alone to long for its return, as a jilted bride longs for her groom.

Today the halt was transformed and like everything in this strange and not so brave new world, it had been turned upside down. The frantic girl who had run all the way there without a thought for the brambles which clawed at her skirts could only stand and stare. Not since its heyday in the old Queen's time, when trains laden with delicacies for Pendennys Place had puffed in daily, had Rosecraddick Halt seen such activity.

Her hand pressed against her chest; Emmy Pendennys fought for control as panic threatened to overwhelm her. There were so many people! How would she ever find Alex in such a crowd? Or what if he had already departed and she was too late? Her heart raced beneath her ribs and it felt as though somebody was tugging at her stays, squeezing out all breath and hope. Alex couldn't go to war believing she was still angry with him. He had to know she loved him especially if … if …

No. That notion was unbearable. The war would be over by Christmas – everybody said so – and Alex would return to Cornwall safe and sound. Emmy refused to think any other way. She glanced about, hoping for a glimpse of his tall frame and bright hair. He couldn't be far. She would find him. There was still time to put things right.

A train was pulled in alongside the platform. Dragon-like, it bellowed smoke while waiting to gobble up the crowds of khaki-clad men. A brass band was playing 'Tipperary', the cheerful tune in keeping with the carnival atmosphere of bunting-festooned station but jarring with the sobbing of the women gathered to bid their menfolk farewell. Flags fluttered in the breeze and men posed for photographs. As Emmy elbowed her way through the press of bodies, her ears were stuffed with snatches of music and fragments of conversations, sounds stitched together into a strange patchwork of pride and sadness and scarcely contained excitement. Envious older men imparted orders and cheerful instructions about 'playing the game', as though sending their sons off to school rather than war, but mothers and sweethearts bit their lips and choked out pleas to take care and to come home soon. She heard the cries of 'Over by Christmas!' and 'For King and Country!', familiar words which echoed the patriotic sermons that Reverend Cutwell, Rosecraddick's fire-and-brimstone vicar, had been preaching every Sunday since war had been declared.

Each syllable filled Emmy with dread. This rhetoric might rouse the older men as they clapped their sons on the back and reminisced about the Boer War, but it did nothing to reassure her. How could it, when she saw every day how war broke a man? Sewed up his trouser leg and twisted him into a parody of what he'd once been as he was left alone to marinate in alcohol and bitterness? Where were the songs, the Union Jack pennants and the sermons about *that*? Her own father wasn't glorious in least. Not these days, anyway.

Emmy was still wild with anger at Alex for enlisting. He might talk about his duty and having a calling, but those were just words. How could such abstract concepts be more important to him than his love for her? He had chosen this over and above the future they had planned, and white-hot anger surged through her again. She doused its fire quickly. The embarkation orders wouldn't wait for her to calm down. She must find Alex and explain how terror had made her angry and sharpened her tongue. Emmy prayed he would understand and forgive her, for today was not a day to cling to hurt or pride. Her fear for his safety must be put aside. Nothing mattered except telling Alex she still loved him.

She pushed through a group of village girls all clustered around a swaggering youth she vaguely recognised as Dickon Trehunnist, the son of one of her father's tenant farmers. Broad-shouldered and handsome, he certainly cut a dash, but Emmy scarcely noticed because all her attention was devoted to finding a tall young man with red hair. She stood on her tiptoes and scanned the crowd, but from the depths of this uniformed ocean it was impossible to see much at all. Reverend Cutwell was head and shoulders above the villagers on a makeshift stage, and firing a salvo of 'Show the Hun!' and 'For King and country!' which had everyone cheering and clapping. Colonel Rivers, the Lord of the Manor, was at the vicar's right hand, with his grey head nodding at each thundered word. As befitted their standing in Rosecraddick, his family had taken their places alongside him, Lady Rivers ashen-faced, and Kit, their only son, utterly transformed from childhood playmate to a stranger clad in officer's uniform. Even Rupert, her dear and gentle friend who hated hunting and shooting and wanted to study Classics, would be here somewhere, preparing to join his regiment. This war had drawn him and Kit into its craw, just as it had Alex and all the other young men, and Emmy's skin crawled with dread.

Everything was changing. Nothing would ever be the same.

Unable to bear it, she ducked back into the throng, not wanting to draw attention to herself or attract a helpful chaperone. As she wove through scores of uniformed boys newly plucked from farms and fishing boats, Emmy vowed that once she found Alex she would tell him exactly how she really felt. It was what she should have done as soon as he'd told her he was enlisting, for they had never dissembled or played games. They were honest with one another even when the truth hurt.

When Emily Pendennys had met Alex Winter his dark-eyed gaze peeled away her birth and title and privilege and the world had shifted beneath her silk slippers. An unknown young man with russet hair and a shy smile had looked straight into her heart like somebody gazing into a rock pool and glimpsing, beneath the distorted reality of reflected sky and clouds, the hidden depths where shy sea creatures hid beneath rocks and curled their secretive selves into shells. Alex Winter hadn't doffed his cap or flushed when he'd realised who she was. Her status hadn't mattered to him, and Emmy had known at once that the handsome stranger shaking her hand and smiling at her was the person she had been waiting for all of her life. He saw through the tangle of hopes and dreams and fears. He saw *her*, not Miss Emily Pendennys, the heir to Pendennys Place and god-daughter of Lady Rivers.

The busy station melted away as Emmy's thoughts drifted to their second meeting. As though it was only yesterday she saw the smooth lawns and the wrought iron table piled high with cakes and sandwiches, and boasting an enormous silver tea pot. Lady Rivers presided over the scene, flanked by the Colonel and with Kit and Rupert positioned behind, dapper in their boaters. It made Emmy smile to think that although she must have looked prim and proper in her big hat and white dress her heart had been racing and her knees wobbling beneath the table. If you looked at the photographs from that afternoon closely enough it was possible to see that her eyes were a little wider than usual and her cheeks flushed, her attention trained upon the young man behind the camera – the young man hired to take photographs that day and who had already stolen the heart of the heiress intended for the Colonel's only son …

Oh, Alex, Emmy wanted to weep, if only we could have captured that day for ever! If only you could always be safe in that place where the band played ragtime and the sun shone! If only the leaves hadn't turned to gold and ochre, and the summer could have lasted for ever. But it was an impossibility and a childish dream, because time was already running out for them all.

A shrill whistle from the train jolted her back to the present and she pressed forward through the throng. She needed to tell Alex that she understood why he had enlisted and that she admired him for what he felt called to do. She had to explain that it was terror which had made her angry. She had to hold him tightly and tell him that she loved him. How she hoped he could forgive her for the things she had said —

Blinded by haste, Emmy cannoned into a woman who shot her a glare and cursed before gasping, "Oh! Beg your pardon, Miss Pendennys! I didn't see it was you!"

Emmy waved away the apology, barely noticing the woman's mortification, because there was Alex at last and the relief of seeing him was overwhelming. As always, he was standing slightly apart from the activity, an observer rather than a participant in the scene, fiddling with a camera, his kitbag abandoned at his feet. She shook her head in fond exasperation. Pictures, always pictures! Even now?

Then she laughed. Of course, now. Especially now!

"Emmy! You came!"

The joy in Alex's voice was all she needed to hear to know she was forgiven. Emmy flew into his arms.

"I'm sorry! I'm sorry!" she gasped, burying her face in the coarse material of his uniform jacket. "I didn't mean it. I was frightened, Alex. I didn't mean any of it. I'm so sorry!"

His arms tightened around her.

"I know, Emmy. I know. Of course I do."

"I love you," she choked. Her tears soaked into the jacket and she clung onto him as though he might drift away. "I love you so much and I was scared. I didn't mean those things I said."

Alex tilted her chin up with his forefinger and kissed away her frantic words.

"Shh, lovely girl, that doesn't matter. None of it does. You're here now, and that means everything. *You* mean everything."

"And you to me," Emmy choked, and Alex held her so tightly she could feel his heart racing beneath his jacket. Her tears fell faster. "I'll be counting the minutes until you come back. Do you hear me?"

"I hear you! And I love you too, no matter what happens, never doubt that. You're my world, Emmy. My everything." He delved into his pocket and drew out a heavy silver locket. "I wanted you to have this before I left, and I was going to give it to you the day we quarrelled. I guess I thought it could be something to …"

He paused as he sought for the right words. Saying the wrong thing felt as though it could be horribly unlucky.

"Something to keep close to your heart while I'm gone," he said finally. "I know it's not a ring, but will it do until the time comes when we can choose one?"

"Of course it will. It's beautiful," Emmy whispered. She touched the heavy silver case wonderingly. "Oh, Alex, it's the locket we saw in Truro, isn't it?"

They had taken the train to Truro one soft May morning. Alex had wanted to buy photographic supplies and Emmy had slipped away with him – easy enough to do when her father was drinking and the housekeeper overworked – and they had spent a wonderful few hours exploring the cobbled streets sheltering in the cathedral's shadow. Emmy had admired this very locket in the window of a jeweller's shop. Engraved with birds and hearts, it had rested against midnight blue velvet and it shone with a light all of its own. It was a beautiful piece, heavy and classic and with an ornate clasp. She'd thought you could place all kinds of treasures inside it and keep them next to your heart.

It had also been dreadfully expensive.

"The very same," he said proudly.

"But how did you —"

"Afford it? Simple. I sold my Graflex."

Emmy was shocked. "But you love that camera."

"I love you far more," he said. "Emmy, I wanted you to have something from me. Something special to keep, just in case."

He said no more. He didn't need to, and Emmy nodded.

"It's beautiful," she said. "Thank you."

He fastened it around her neck and kissed her forehead tenderly.

"I'll always stay close to your heart, my beautiful, wonderful Emmy."

A whistle blew from the platform. Voices were raised and the men began to move into lines. Time was running out.

"Alex, please be careful," Emmy pleaded, holding onto his lapels and no longer caring who from Rosecraddick might spot her with this unsuitable young man. "Please!"

"I'll be back before you know it," he promised. "By Christmas, that's what they say. We'll find a little tree and have a high old time, you'll see. It'll be here in no time. Only four months, my love. It isn't long."

Then he peeled her fingers away, lifting each hand in turn to his lips and whispering words of love and comfort. Emmy closed her eyes in defeat. Four months felt like a lifetime. She would die a thousand fearful deaths between that time and today.

He swung his kitbag onto his shoulder.

"I'll write," he said. "And send you my pictures. The time will fly."

She nodded. Language had fled.

A whistle blew again. Sweethearts embraced and names were shouted by officers as they called their men to attention.

Alex pulled a rueful face. "This is it. Don't come to the platform, Em. I don't think I could bear it. I'm not as brave as you."

"I'm not brave."

"You *are*. You're the bravest person I know," he said fiercely. "I love you, Emily Pendennys. Never doubt that. I love you and I will be home again. You'll see."

Emmy didn't feel brave in the slightest. She had to bite her lip to stop herself from calling him back, and hug her arms around herself rather than flinging them about his neck and begging him to stay. Instead she swallowed the misery balled up in her throat and gulped the tears away. She wasn't alone in putting on a brave face, because the halt was filled with women wiping their eyes and pretending their menfolk were off on a jaunt rather than to war, while their children waved and shouted farewells.

She watched Alex's cap bob about in the uniformed sea before he turned to wave one final time. Emmy waved too, blinking away tears, but when she looked again he was submerged by khaki waves and swept up in a riptide of marching men. She craned her neck, desperate for one last glimpse of him, but he was gone. Alex Winter had walked out of her life just as abruptly as he'd walked into it. Standing in the midst of the pressing crowd, Emmy had never felt more alone in her entire life.

She curled her hand around the locket and already she treasured it beyond all else. Until Alex returned, this locket, hanging heavily from her neck and resting against her heart, was the only evidence she had that a man with sunset hair, peat-brown eyes and a headful of dreams loved her.

Chapter 1
Alison
Cornwall

The empty bedroom undoes me. The door's ajar and late afternoon sunshine streams through the window, turning dust motes to twirling sparkles and highlighting smeared panes. 'I must clean the glass,' I find myself thinking, 'Jamie likes to look out when he's working at his desk.' But then, and with that familiar twist to the heart, I remember my son isn't here. I won't find Jamie sitting at his desk, chin in hand and daydreaming as he gazes across the garden, nor will I watch him frown as he pores over his college artwork. He's not to be found lolling on the bed, headphones clamped to his ears as he scrolls through his phone, and he isn't cuddled up with Cally as they watch movies and shovel in handfuls of popcorn. Along with a well-stocked fridge and a biscuit tin that's no longer self-emptying, each small absence is a sly ambush of hurt.

I pause, one hand on the door jamb and the other clenched tightly around the handle of my bucket. Full of cleaning equipment and a tight roll of black bin bags, it contains everything needed for the full assault I've avoided since the dreary December morning when Jamie hoisted his kitbag onto his shoulder and kissed me goodbye.

"I'll be back before you know it, Mum," he promised as he hugged and kissed me. "The time will fly, you'll see."

I'd nodded, but my words of reassurance and cheerful agreement were wedged in my throat. This wasn't the first time Jamie had been deployed on active service – he'd already completed one tour of duty in Afghanistan – but this didn't make saying goodbye any easier. I couldn't imagine anything ever would. Steve might remind me a thousand times a day that our son is highly trained professional peacekeeper, but his words have no more meaning than the rattle of empty tin cans kicked along a road, because Jamie is more than a soldier. He was my child. My precious baby. The thought of him stepping into danger is unbearable.

"It's nothing we haven't faced before," Steve had murmured into my hair that final morning as I lay wide awake in bed and hoping dawn was still hours away. "He's been in Kabul before and he knows the drill. You have to be strong for him, Ali, okay? This is what he does, and he can't be worrying about us. Our boy mustn't be distracted from what he's there to do."

"I know, I know," I said tetchily. "I just wish he wasn't going. I wish he'd never joined the bloody army!"

Steve rolled onto his back. I sensed his despair in the darkness and, although I couldn't see it, I knew a deep crease had settled between his brows.

"He wants to serve his country. You should be proud of him."

"I *am* proud of him." My words were strung tight with terror, each syllable a bead thrumming on an overstretched necklace which could snap at any moment and spill a thousand more words into the void, terrible words which could never be recovered and restrung no matter how much you tried. Fear does that to people; it sharpens tongues into samurai swords and slices those we love with language.

I couldn't say any more. I didn't dare.

I lay on my back, staring into the darkness. I wanted to leap out of bed, storm down the hallway and demand my son to explain to me why he wanted to be a soldier. I trembled as I suppressed the urge to snap on the light, rip him out of sleep and beg him to make me understand what drove him to place himself in such danger.

I couldn't understand it. How could I? I was his mother. From the moment the midwife placed Jamie in my arms my every breath has been taken with the knowledge that I have to keep him safe. I'd protected him. Cherished him. Held him when he was sad. Nursed him when he was sick. Laughed with him. Watched him blur from baby to toddler to serious schoolboy. There were a thousand milestones, a million moments of joy threaded with fear and a million million memories of tears and hurts and heartbreaks. We'd helped him through all these, Steve and I, and paddled our small family canoe through the rapids of exams and appendix operations and teenage angst. And then, just as I'd believed we were moving into calmer waters, Jamie announced he wasn't applying to university or taking a year out to travel with Cally.

No. Our son's heart was set on joining the army.

It had been a shock because we aren't an army family. We have no background in the armed forces, give or take the usual world war stories. We don't even have a great deal of interest in war films, unless you count Steve's love of M*SH, and Jamie never played *Call of Duty* or any other shoot 'em ups. We don't live in a military town, but in a converted railway station buried deep in the Cornish countryside. Jamie's childhood was spent swimming from the rocks in Rosecraddick Cove, sailing boats and climbing trees. He liked to read books and spend time walking our dog, Waffles, on the cliffs. He loved taking photos and sketching so if I'd ever been asked to predict a career for him I would have plumped for something creative – a journalist perhaps or maybe an art teacher. I certainly never expected he would set his heart on the military, and he never once breathed a word of his plans to me.

How well do any of us really know our children? We think we know them because we see them as *ours*, extensions of ourselves and such a part of us that they must surely think and react as we do. Oh, we might not believe this consciously, convincing ourselves they are individuals and all we want is for them to be happy and to follow their dreams – but what we really want is for them to follow their dreams on the proviso that those dreams are our dreams too, and the path they choose to tread the one we would pick for them. I defy any parent to not be sliced through by shock when their child reveals long-held secrets, and not be doomed to ask themselves over and over again, 'How did I miss that? What did I do wrong? Is it my fault?'

I tortured myself with these questions after Jamie announced he wasn't applying for university but had decided to join the army. I was stunned by his decision and spent weeks trying to get him to change his mind, but I might as well have tried to stop the waves breaking on the beach. Joining the army was what he wanted to do. It was what he felt he had to do. Steve was also shocked, but said he understood our son's choice and would often tell me about the various careers within the army, as though I'd feel better by knowing our son could be a chef or an engineer.

"It's not just front-line stuff, love," he said. "Jamie's going to see the world. Who knows where this could take him? The army can lead a lad in all kinds of exciting directions."

I knew all this and, intellectually at least, I understood why Jamie was excited – but I also knew his chosen path could lead him into danger. How could I not when the news was full of stories of IEDs and roadside bombs? Princes who fought in the dust alongside their subjects? Bullets would no more respect rank than they would care how precious Jamie was to me.

"He could be killed," I whispered, and Steve pulled me into his arms, holding me tight against his chest while I wept hot and angry tears into his shirt. He let me cry myself out without offering any words of comfort or platitudes and I loved him even more for this. My husband didn't lie or make false promises. He never had. He couldn't allay my dread any more than he could his own, but his embrace promised we were in this together.

"Jamie needs our support if he's going to do this," I said finally, stepping back and wiping my eyes on the back of my hand.

Steve nodded and behind his glasses his eyes were deep pools of sadness.

"He does, Ali. We can't hold him back. We've raised a fine young man and I'm proud of him."

"Oh, me too – but I wish he'd chosen to be an accountant," I half laughed, and half sobbed.

My accountant husband pulled an outraged face.

"Are you saying dealing with HMRC and untangling tax codes isn't dangerous? Because believe me it doesn't feel that way each January!"

The mood shifted and although I was wrung out and knew my dreams would still be filled with shadows, panic's grip loosened. After this I did my best to hide my fears from Jamie. I helped him with his application and expressed excitement when he was called for an interview, and when an offer followed I celebrated with him. Sometimes my eyes met Steve's over Jamie's curly head and I saw my own misery reflected there, but I never breathed a word of it to my boy.

It's a mother's fiercest instinct to keep her child safe, but when that child is an adult her hands are well and truly tied. I loved Jamie but loving people means giving them the freedom to make choices that break our hearts. When alone, I cried a great deal and I walked Waffles so often that his little legs must have worn down a few inches. Movement was the key to survival. I would stride out my fears, and my routes often took me to places that shimmered with a new significance that was both dreadful and comforting. The war memorial on the cliff path became a favourite spot and after a steep climb up I would sit there and catch my breath while Waffles chased rabbits. Here, where silvered waves stretched to infinity and melted into acres of sky, I found peace. I would study the columns of names carved into time-smoothed granite and before long I knew them by heart: Gem Pencarrow, Christopher Rivers, David Trehunnist … My own great-grandfather's name was here too, Rupert Elmhurst, who had been awarded the Military Cross in the First World War. Was it because of him that Jamie had been drawn to the army? We had never talked about my great-grandfather and I knew little more about him than that he had died barely into his twenties. I think my grandma visited the war graves when I was small, to see where her father was buried, but these memories are hazy and there's no one left to ask about all this now. No one who might remember.

Steve doesn't like the war memorial and he thought it morbid of me to keep visiting, but I found the place one of solace because of its timelessness. The view I surveyed was the one these men fallen had known. The same daydreaming church I looked at, tucked into swelling hills rising above the half-moon of beach, had seen them born and christened, and their grandparents and their grandparents before them, and it would see their descendants too. I liked this place. It helped me to see that my family and our story was part of something bigger.

It put everything into perspective to view it in the context of eternity.

These losses carved into granite were consigned to history books, and the slashing cuts of each death had been healed by the relentless turning of the seasons. I didn't know anything about the Ruperts or the Gems or the Richards, but their mothers must have thought of them and watched the waves rolling towards the shore. I was linked to these women who had given their sons so that I could walk here in peace. Here I had a sense of continuity, and sometimes I felt as though I teetered on the brink of understanding something infinite and far bigger than myself – but then the wind would shift and blow my hair across my face, or a gull might cry and the tantalising insight would slip hopelessly out of reach – if, indeed, it had really ever been there at all.

I would turn at this point and call Waffles. We might climb down the steep path to St Nonna's cove, where I would fling pebbles into the waves for a while, then head into the village before turning past Rosecraddick Manor and taking the footpath through the woods and home to Halt House. This is a popular route in the summer for walkers and those who wish to pay homage to Beeching's handiwork, but in the winter it's quiet, with the dank earth silencing my boots and the world soundless save the raking cry of a startled pheasant or rustle of undergrowth when deer take off. I find it strange to think that our quiet lane had once bustled with carts and carriages and the shrill blast of a train whistle splitting the silence. Nobody comes to the old station now except for us and holiday visitors. Steve and I bought the place when it was dilapidated and just bricks away from tumbling down. We put our heart and soul and every penny we had into transforming the place into a family home, and we've been so happy here. Hidden deep in the Cornish countryside and at the end of a sunken lane, it's been our sanctuary and the safe home we wanted for Jamie as he grew up.

How ironic that now he was a young man he'd chosen danger. He was facing it again with his second tour of duty. What if his luck ran out this time? How could I bear to endure the fear again? Would it be for years and years until he decided to leave, or worse?

"Ali, we can do this. We've faced it once before," Steve said gently.

His voice had been hesitant as though I was some hair-trigger device which could explode at any moment. Maybe I was. I felt even more afraid knowing this was Jamie's second tour of duty in Afghanistan. Surely the odds of something dreadful happening must be higher this time.

"I'm scared," I said.

Steve nodded. "Me too, love, but we have to be brave for him. God knows how, but we do. Maybe because we love him. Maybe that's how we do it?"

"Because we love him, we have to pretend we're fine?"

"I think so," Steve said. "Yes, exactly that."

The helplessness in his voice broke my heart and I knew he was as afraid as I was, but I was unable to offer any comfort. We lay side by side, as silent and as unspeaking as the effigies in St Nonna's, until the first chilly fingers of day split the curtains apart and it was time to get up, smile, and pretend all was well.

I managed it, I recall now, as I teeter on the threshold of the empty bedroom, though God only knows how. Although my heart was shredded by the imminent farewell, I cooked bacon sandwiches for breakfast while Jamie teased me about the size of the Christmas tree I'd picked, and Steve threatened to hack the top off it. Then Cally arrived to accompany Jamie and Steve to Bodmin station and I knew the sands of my internal egg timer were running out.

"I'll give you a hand, Mum," Jamie said, picking up his plate, but I waved him away.

"Go and spent some time with Cally, love. Dad and I'll sort this lot. It's about time he did some housework."

"See what I'm in for, while you're away?" Steve grumbled, catching the tea towel I threw at him. "There's safety in numbers!"

Jamie laughed and took Cally's hand.

"Let's leave them to it before they change their minds and rope us in!" he grinned.

As they wandered into the garden to make promises and say their private farewells, I saw how my son drew his girlfriend against him and my heart swelled. He was tender with Cally, always kind and considerate and I was so proud of the man I could see my son becoming. Already he was a thoughtful person who saw people for who they were in their hearts, and who cared about their feelings. The men he served beside, and the army itself, were lucky to have him. But how I wished they weren't taking him from me! And how I wanted to tell him not to go. It was torture.

I plunged my arms into the sink and let the sting of hot water replace the burn of panic. Slopping suds onto the tiles and oblivious to wet socks, I watched the young couple walking into the woods until my vision blurred and they shimmered into emptiness.

"I love you, my darling, brave Mrs Foy," Steve said, wrapping his arms around me and resting his chin on my head.

"Me? I've not done anything brave."

His arms tightened around me.

"You have, Ali. You're brave every day and you're brave right now. You'll be brave until the moment the car vanishes down the lane and even then you'll still be brave. You're the strongest woman I know."

I don't feel strong. My family is made up of strong women. From my great-grandmother who, so the story goes, raised her daughter alone after the First World War, right down to my own beloved mum who battled Alzheimer's with gritty determination, they put me to shame. "I'm a jelly."

"You're not, Ali. You're strong and selfless and I love you so much," Steve said. "We all do, don't we, Waffles? You've made this easier for Jamie and one day, when he's a parent, he'll understand just what it is you've done today."

He kissed me and went to load the car, a task which meant he was somewhere fighting his own battle with conflicted emotions. I busied myself with clearing up and told myself sternly that if Cally and Steve could be brave, then I certainly could be. The time would fly, this tour of duty would go smoothly and soon Jamie would be safely home.

All too soon the cases were stowed in the boot and we were saying our farewells. As I hugged Jamie, I found myself wondering what had happened to the little boy with scraped knees I could comfort with the promise of a biscuit? Who was this muscular stranger? Where had my baby gone?

"Take care, Mum. I love you," he said, and I kissed him one last time before the car door slammed and the engine started. Panic crashed inside me as a moth's wings beat against a lampshade, but I waved him off with a cheery smile until, and as Steve had predicted, the car vanished around the bend in the lane and I crumbled.

That was over two months ago. Two slow months of watching the nights grow darker in tandem with my own thoughts, and two agonising months of watching the news and the letterbox with a cold dread. Christmas came and went like something from a dream, our visitors checked in and out seamlessly and somehow it's the end of January and life has taken on a new normal. Steve goes to the office each day, Cally has returned to college and I do my best to pretend I'm not living in suspended animation until April.

January's always quiet in the holiday letting business. It's a month when Cornwall mirrors the rest of the world and hibernates. The blinds are pulled down on second homes, and crumpled cottages slumber until the spring arrives and visitors begin to appear in harmony with bluebells and primroses. But at this fallow time the beaches and coves are deserted save a few lone souls throwing balls for dogs or perhaps hiking gallantly along the coastal path, their walking poles spiking the muddy earth and their breath clouding the cold air. Down in Rosecraddick village the gift shops are shuttered, gaudy souvenirs dreaming of the time when they'll be dusted off and snatched up by eager hands. The pub is empty except for the usual cluster of local drinkers gathered by the fire, pint glasses in hand as they spin tales of fishing boats and smugglers, and even the village shop is shut after noon. When I walk Waffles through the deserted streets I am Demeter waiting for Persephone, a mother stumbling through darkness and frantic to snatch her child back from the underworld. When these black-edged thoughts swarm I turn and head for home, where chores and work help to push them away.

Without the distraction of visitors arriving and holiday apartments to prepare, I'm at a loose end and in danger of unravelling. Keeping busy is the key, apparently, at least according to my best friend Pippa, who is a dynamo of energy and the kind of person who can hardly bear to sit still. Pip checks on me with the intensity and slightly askance look of one assigned to defuse a bomb – Jamie's analogy, and one which made me laugh at the time, although I'm not quite so amused by it much at the moment – and I love her for her concern.

"You're always saying you have a million things to do and no time for any of them," Pip pointed out when we were Christmas shopping in Truro. "Pick one of those lists of yours and get started!"

My lists are a standing joke with my loved ones. I have always made endless lists, optimistically setting out all the wonderful tasks I will undertake one mythical day when I have enough time, but I always relegate them to kitchen drawers or the bottom of my handbag. Never mind the road to hell being paved with good intentions; in my case it's littered with neglected to do lists.

This time it'll be different, I tell myself firmly as I lean against the door jamb and appraise Jamie's bedroom. This time I'll stick to a list and work my way through it. These can be my daily routine orders, and today's number one is 'Dust Jamie's room and strip bed'. The cleaning things are liberated from the store cupboard and I'm good to go.

But I can't step over the threshold.

Jamie's leather jacket is draped over the back of his desk chair and a magazine is splayed open on the bed. The room still smells of him, that clean scent of young man tinted with the Bleu Cally had bought him, and although I know the mug on his bedside table should have been stowed in the dishwasher weeks ago I haven't been able to bring myself to pick it up because left there it still looks as though he's only popped out for a moment. It's probably quite insane, but pretending my son's still here is how I cope with the constant dread. If his room looks lived-in I can kid myself he's at Cally's or out walking. If I start to tidy and dust and clean I'm accepting he's not here, which feels as though I'm erasing him, something that terrifies an atavistic and superstitious part of me.

Dust motes spin and my head spins with them. The house feels poised, as though holding its breath and waiting to see what I will decide. Time slows. Even my blood feels sluggish. I am glued. Anchored. Statued. Frozen as under an evil enchantment.

The landline shrills and the spell is broken. Granted a reprieve, I shut the door and turn sharply to answer the call, relieved and disappointed as today's list swells the ranks of countless others that came before it.

Chapter 2
Alison
Rosecraddick

"How about decorating?" Pippa puts her mug down with an excited thump on the kitchen island, thrilled with her suggestion. "That's something you've been threatening to do for ages."

We're drinking coffee in the kitchen. After an hour we're three cups, and more ideas to distract me than I can count, down, and even Steve has abandoned his study to join us. He claims he needs a break from preparing end-of-year accounts, but I'm not fooled – Pip makes the best flapjacks and he's already snaffled two.

"That's a great idea, isn't it, Ali?" he says, reaching for his third and smiling at me hopefully. His tone rings with the forced brightness that you might use with a patient who needs chivvying to take medicine or a recalcitrant child cajoling into eating vegetables. Oh dear. Is this what I've become to my nearest and dearest?

"Maybe," I say.

"It is looking a bit shabby, love. We haven't touched this room for ages," adds Steve, his blue eyes narrowed critically as he studies the chipped paintwork and faded walls. My husband sees jobs to be done and I see them too, but for me these imperfections are precious. They are the strata of our family life laid down by years and laughter and tears. Each layer has significance and holds within it a map of how we came to be. Where Steve sees dirt, I see us. The Foy family. These marks chart our history.

"It's in need of a freshen up," Pip says.

I don't reply because I know I won't be decorating this kitchen any time soon. It would feel like painting over Jamie's childhood, and these days I need the memories and marks more than ever. Take those faint smudges by the window, for instance. These are the messy ghosts of starfish handprints, kissed onto the wall when Jamie was first walking and hauling himself up with such concentration I scarcely dared breathe and distract him. Those chips in the paintwork on the skirting board by the Aga are from a close encounter with Jamie's scooter when he was five. And that scribble behind the door isn't graffiti but a record of my boy's growth, a birthday ritual only stopping when I could no longer reach above him to record it. This habit has faded into memory but as I look around my home I see the geology of us. Ghost writing of proud decorators haunts the hidden plaster beneath, and greasy blutack spots are on the walls from when it had secured splashy nursery school paintings, long since hidden away with the milk teeth, baby shoes and certificates and assorted detritus of my son's childhood.

"Out of season's the perfect time. We could go and choose paint this afternoon, if you like?" Pippa says, already itching to select sample paints and peruse colour charts.

Steve sets his own cup down next to Pip's.

"No time like the present. Then we could move on and do the sitting room."

"Maybe," I say, and he deflates. Steve knows my maybe means no. I gather up the cups and yank open the dishwasher, preferring the clatter of china to his weary sigh. Steve sighs a lot these days.

"You need to do something, Ali. It's not good for you to be moping like this."

I turn around, stung. "I'm not moping! I'm running our business!"

"It's January, love. Nobody in their right mind holidays in Cornwall in January. There's nothing to do until the spring."

He's right. Most days I drift through our two letting units flicking a duster or check the bookings page and, finding them unchanged, scroll through Facebook unseeingly.

"You could always lend a hand at the manor," Pippa suggests. "I know the shop's closed but there's always something to do at the house and I could do with help stocktaking. Once we open again my feet won't touch the ground. You know how it is."

Pippa manages the gift shop at Rosecraddick Manor, childhood home of the famous war poet Kit Rivers. History is her passion and she's been part of the manor's restoration project from the very beginning.

"That's a good idea," Steve agrees. "I saw Matt Enys in the pub the other evening and he was saying they expect a bumper season this summer, especially after that Kit Rivers movie. I'm sure he'd be glad of any extra help."

Matt Enys is the lead conservation historian at Rosecraddick Manor and has put his heart and soul into saving the place where one of Britain's finest poets was born. I know all this because firstly we all know everyone here, and secondly because you'd have to live on the moon to not have come across the Kit Rivers story. Pip's always asking me to volunteer, and in the spirit of being public minded I have manned a room in the house while visitors peered into glass cases and sighed over the sad stories of young lives cut short by conflict. I can't bring myself to become any more involved because it feels a little too close to home.

"I know it's war-themed but it's all olden-day stuff," Steve says, reading my mind.

The First World War may have been fought over a century ago, and the mud and gas and gunfire heard from Kent consigned to history lessons, but walking through the place where one brave young man once lived, a sensitive and artistic young man by all accounts, and never destined to be a soldier, makes me feel as though I'm making links between the past and the present that I would rather remained miles apart. For the coachloads of tourists who stream into the village, Rosecraddick Manor is another spot to tick off on their itinerary and a pretty setting for a cream tea. For others it's a place of pilgrimage. For me it's a sombre reminder of war and sacrifice. The sepia faces may be faded, and Kit's story lent the glamour of romance by time's distance, but I cannot bear to spend too long in a house where all life stopped the day an entire generation of young men stepped onto the train. It makes me uneasy knowing that the last view so many of them ever saw of Rosecraddick is the same one I enjoy now from my kitchen window.

"Matt would be thrilled and so would I," says Pip, never one to give up. "You could tie it in with some research into your own family tree. That'd keep you busy and you'd be amazed how absorbing it is. I spend so much time on Heritage that Billy's threatening to dress as a Tudor to get my attention. Any excuse to wear tights!"

Steve laughs and I find myself joining in because the idea of Pippa's burly farmer husband in anything other than John Deere overalls is ridiculous, never mind tunic and hose!

"Trace your family, Ali! I'll help you! It'll be fascinating," she says.

"I'll wear tights if it helps," Steve offers mock-gallantly.

"I'm not sure family trees are my thing," I say gently, once we've stopped giggling. "I'm more about living for the future. Besides, my grandma was adamant no good ever came from what she called 'raking over the past'."

As soon as the words have left my mouth, I want to stuff them back in because Pippa's eyes are blue saucers.

"Why would she say that? Was there a scandal?"

I've often wondered this too, but my mother said it was more likely Grandma Ivy had been wild and crazy during the war years before she'd settled down and married the local doctor.

"It was crazy back then here in Cornwall by all accounts. There were handsome young GIs everywhere," Mum had explained to me when, armed with a school history project, I'd badgered her for information about my Cornish roots. "Grandma Ivy probably had a fine old time flirting with the American GIs, painting her legs with gravy browning to make stockings and going to dances. She wouldn't want people talking about *that* at church, would she?"

My grandmother had been a stern woman who'd worked as the dentist's receptionist and spent her spare time at WI meetings and arranging the flowers in St Nonna's. With her snow-white hair bullied into a bun and deep brown eyes which rarely twinkled, I couldn't even imagine her being young, let alone kissing GIs and worrying about stockings.

"Grandma danced with *boys*?" I was incredulous.

Mum laughed. "Don't look so shocked. She was young once, you know. We all were."

I hadn't believed her. When you're a child, grown-ups seem impossibly ancient and serious. They could never have been young, and they certainly don't have an identity outside the context of your own existence.

"You must remember my granny," is all I say now. "Did you ever meet a woman less likely to have a scandal in her past?"

Pip grimaces. "I was more afraid of your gran than fillings – and that was in the days before injections for drilling!"

"Well, there you are. My scary granny was a pillar of the community and a prude. Nothing interesting there."

"But wasn't her mother something to do with the Pendennys family?"

I think about this. Somewhere deep in the cobwebby recesses of my mind it rings a bell.

"I think there was a connection, but I couldn't say for sure."

Steve leans against the Aga and rubs his chin.

"I know I'm just a humble incomer to these parts, but who are the Pendennys family?"

Pippa whips around. Captive audience alert!

"They were important local landowners. This station was built just for them to have their more exotic and out-of-season fruit and veg brought up fresh from Covent Garden. How weird, Ali. Imagine if you were related – you've bought back your own station!"

"I'm sure I'm not related to the rich ones —" I begin, but Pippa isn't listening. She's far too busy already planning her research.

"The family built a big house here in the early nineteenth century. I think it was called Pendennys Place and it was the far side of the woods," she explains, waving her hand towards the bare trees hemming the far end of our garden, black bones against a sky picked bare of colour and already sinking into dusk.

Steve frowns. "I can't remember ever seeing it."

"It's not there any more. It burned down during the First World War, I think. It's Tim Ellis's land these days and he puts sheep on it sometimes. There's nothing left of the house. If you didn't know there had been a building there you couldn't really tell now."

My husband pulls a disappointed face. "And there was I hoping my wife had a family pile waiting to be claimed, and even a title or two. Oh well, back to the grindstone it is, then."

"She still might have. That's what research is for," Pippa points out.

Steve whistles. "Hear that, babe? You could have a stately home and a title and all sorts! Better join Heritage right now!"

Pip whips her iPhone from her pocket. "I can sign you up in minutes!"

"It could be interesting, love," Steve says, but what he really means is this might distract me from fretting over Jamie. I love him for trying, but not even a forest of family trees could do that.

Pip's finger hovers over the touchpad. "You don't know how lucky you are having unusual family connections. It would be so much fun!"

She's good, but I don't bite. Poring over old documents and computer screens isn't what I need. I'm not sure what is, but I'm certain it's something active.

"Much as I appreciate your joint attempts to occupy me, I've already got a few jobs planned," I say. "I thought I'd made a start sorting Mum's stuff and clearing the spare room."

Pippa looks disappointed but Steve punches the air.

"Home gym, here we come!"

"Craft room," I counter, although to be honest I don't really mind if he puts his kettle bells and weight bench in there to gather dust; it's got to be better than looking at the piled-up boxes which are all that remain of my Mum's possessions. She passed away just under two years ago and I've been intending to finish sifting through her things. Although she sold her cottage and moved into a nursing home before she died, Mum accumulated a huge amount of stuff in her seventy-odd years, some of it my grandmother's, and I've been putting off going through it because there's something sad about cherished keepsakes that have lost their meaning. What was treasure to Mum and Grandma Ivy is just junk to me.

"I'll give you a hand," offers Pippa.

"Because you think there may be an exciting artefact?" I tease. "Or because you want to help me?"

She grins. "Maybe a little of both?"

Having Pip help will definitely make the task less onerous, and it will be good to laugh together about some of the items we find and reminisce over others.

"Maybe we could send some of it to an auction? It might pay for a weekend away," Steve suggests.

"I can't imagine there's much of any worth. And before you say to just bin it, I can't do that. That stuff might look like junk to us, but it must have meant something to Mum and Grandma for them to have kept it all this time. I think there's even some of my great-grandmother's belongings amongst it all too."

"More likely they just shoved it out of sight like we did," he shrugs. "I thought your grandma fell out with her mother. So would she really have kept her things?"

Pippa leaps on this juicy morsel. "Did she? Why was that?"

I actually have no idea what caused the estrangement. I'd never thought to ask Mum about it because it was ancient family history and I'd been far more interested in ponies, and later on boys, to care much for elderly relations and family stories. How much do you question things as a child anyhow? You're the centre of your own universe and it's only now I'm older, far older than Grandma Ivy was when she fell out with her own mother, that I wonder what their disagreement was about. What could be so serious that it rips up the roots of love that bind a parent and a child? With Jamie far away and in danger, I have little patience for families who squabble and part through choice when I'd give anything to have my loved ones safe and with me.

"Who knows? My grandmother wasn't an easy woman. Why do you think Mum left home as soon as she could? It wasn't just for the bright lights of the city!"

I'd grown up in London, which was where my mother settled after training as a nurse, but my childhood summers had been spent in Rosecraddick where the sun always shone, and the days were filled with beachcombing and rock pooling. When my grandma died her cottage passed to my mother and became our much-loved holiday bolthole. It was scruffy and filled with chipped furniture and worn lino, a far cry from the smart sage paint and shabby chic furniture of my own holiday lets, but it had an enchanted air and I lived for each holiday, dreaming in my London bedroom of towering cliffs and broad skies and tanned fisherboys who flirted while they mended nets on the quayside. I loved to climb trees, ride horses and scrabble over the seaweed-iced rocks. I skinned my knees and scraped my hands but loved every freedom-filled moment.

"Your mum came back, though," Pip says, and I nod.

"I think she always missed home."

When we lost my father, I hadn't been surprised Mum chose to return to Cornwall, any more than she must have been when Steve and I quit the city to make our family home here. Cornwall with its wide skies, gorse-splashed cliffs and secret coves claimed by smugglers and lovers alike, calls to the heart, and once you're nestled there, it whispers to you for ever like the waves against the shore. My family come from this place and I'd felt the tugging of my own root system, burrowed deep into the soil and running parallel with the rich seams of copper and tin which lace the rocks below. Leaving London for Cornwall and buying the old railway station had felt as inevitable and as natural as the turning of each tide.

"It could be fun to have a rummage and see what's in her things. You never know. There could be some heirlooms from the Pendennys family!" Pip is still thinking about family trees and lost treasures, and Steve winks at me.

"I might go and have pint in the Sail Loft if you two are about to get stuck in!"

"Have two at least," says Pip. "There's a lot here! Maybe even some antiques."

"Mum didn't have much that was of any value," I point out, before my friend gets carried away and tries to involve me in her own version of Bargain Hunt.

"Except the cottage," says Steve sadly. Comparing similar properties on Rightmove has become his own personal form of torture. "I can't believe what poky little cottages sell for now. If only we'd kept it."

"We had to sell. Nursing homes don't come cheap," I remind him sharply and Steve nods apologetically. He knows the loss is still raw and the memories of seeing my funny, sharp-minded mother stumbling through the fog of Alzheimer's is as painful now as it was at the time. The loss of our family home was nothing in comparison even if my heart cracked a little when we sold it. Saying goodbye to the cottage and my mother was like watching the final act in the play of my childhood; the curtain had fallen for ever in front of Alison the daughter and much-loved child. It was a closing too of a way of life I'd thought would never end, spooling on in an eternal loop of shrimp paste sandwiches at the kitchen table, crabbing from the harbour wall and sand strewn across worn floorboards, simple pleasures I'd repeated with Jamie and ripples from a pebble tossed in generations ago that I'd thought would stretch into infinity for his children and theirs …

"It's nuts, isn't it?" Pip is agreeing with Steve. "Billy was saying only yesterday there's no way we could afford to buy our place now. Not unless he gave up farming and became an investment banker anyway!"

The conversation turns to the familiar lament about second homers and the sky-high price of Cornish property. I tune out and refill the kettle. The sky is rodent grey, and sullen raindrops splatter the monochrome world beyond the kitchen. On such afternoons more coffee is needed and maybe some biscuits.

I place the kettle onto the hot plate. While I wait for it to boil, and Steve and Pippa moan about celebrity chefs and incomers, I wonder what my grandmother would have made of the changes to Rosecraddick since the seventies. Grandma Ivy wouldn't recognise the smart fish restaurant in the high street, a butcher's shop in her day; and the coachloads of visitors flowing through the manor's gates would have amazed her. And what about her mother, my Great-grandmother Emily, who raised her child in an isolated farmhouse without the luxury of electric appliances? She'd had a hard life by all accounts, losing her husband during the First World War and her son-in-law in the Second. How had she borne the dread and the grief? I wish I could ask.

And who was she, this half-forgotten woman who has fallen through the cracks of time? What was she like? Suddenly, my interest is piqued.

Maybe Pippa's right and there is something in this ancestry business after all?

As the kettle whistles and fistfuls of rain hammer against the window, I come to a decision. It's time to make a start on sorting through the boxes. Jamie's room and the redecorating can wait a little longer. Once he's home, we'll go into town and pick out the colours together, and he and Cally can help me. It'll be something to look forward to. Something positive to plan for.

Until then it's time, literally and metaphorically, to ignore superstition and old mottoes, and lift the lid on my family's past.

Chapter 3
Alison
Cornwall

The spare room faces what was once the station platform and now serves as a terrace. In the summer months that's a sun trap where our holiday visitors gather at the end of the day to sip wine and bask in the last rays of evening sunshine. The tracks and the opposite platform were removed years ago and replaced with a lawn which stretches to the edge of the woods. The room is small and cramped but as I step inside, armed with bin bags, I imagine it clear and flooded with light. Perhaps this is symbolic?

"This is such a peaceful spot, but it must have been so different back in the day," Pippa remarks, leaning on the window sill and staring down into the garden. "You'd have had the hissing of steam from the trains and whistles and shouting guards back then. Think of all the comings and goings this place must have seen over the years."

"I don't think it was used very much at all towards the end," I say. In the summer we often have railway enthusiasts turn up who love to impart their knowledge. Some of them even have tales to tell about the pre-Beeching days and share misty-eyed memories of catching the train from Rosecraddick to London. One old lady said she'd waved her son off in 1940 from this very spot, a tear rolling down her lined face at the memory. He never came home, she said.

I push this memory away. I hadn't liked hearing it then, and I don't like recalling it now.

"What would your great-grandmother make of all this stuff shoved into bags?" Pip wonders.

"She'd probably ask why I've let all this junk pile up," I say, looking around and feeling overwhelmed. Now I remember why I've been putting it off for so long.

"She'd have had a servant to do it all for her, but you've got me!" Pip grins and bobs a curtsey. So, Your Ladyship, where shall I begin?"

There's a big box beneath the window sealed with gaffer tape. I have a hazy memory of Jamie packing this one for me when we moved my mother to the nursing home. We went through the cottage room by room, sweeping pictures and books into boxes and mummifying china and assorted knick-knacks in bubble wrap. Opening these boxes will be like unsealing a time capsule. Rediscovering the once familiar objects will be both wonderful and terrible.

I take a deep breath. "Start with that box by the window, if you like."

Pippa nods her blonde head and within seconds is ripping the tape away. As the lid falls open I'm shocked to find that the scent of Mum's cottage is also stored inside, a heart-deep familiar bespoke blend of damp, salt, and polish mingled with faint traces of Chanel perfume. The smell spirals me down through the years until I'm curled up on my narrow bed beneath the eaves, listening to the waves lap the beach and reading illicit Jilly Coopers beneath the covers with a torch.

Smell is such an evocative sense. Whenever I wander into Jamie's room he could be beside me. The scent of clean skin, his favourite aftershave, even the festering trainers shoved beneath the bed, are him distilled, just as this released air is the last gasp of a life and place long lost.

"Ready?" Pip asks.

I crouch down beside her and tear a bin liner from the roll. There. A statement of intent.

"Ready," I say.

The box is full of worthless treasures. Once I'm over the initial shock of seeing these old friends again, I have fun telling Pip the stories which accompany them, for this is where the worth of the items lies. The chipped china donkey that my father had brought back from a field trip to Spain. The seashell mirror I'd made when I was seven. The wedding photo of my parents taken in the sixties, Mum all beehive hair, bell sleeves and dark eye makeup, and Dad rocking a Beatles haircut. They're ridiculously young, twenty at the most, and as they beam out of the frame life stretches before them, brimming with possibilities and wonders. There's me as a chubby toddler in a red coat, strung between them and clutching their hands like a bright bead, while they smile proudly at the camera. Who took this shot? Mum? Grandma Ivy? And where have we all gone? I am in my middle years and this young couple are dead. Where did those people go? Who stole the years away?

My heart bounces in my throat. I miss them, my mum and my dad. I miss being their little girl. I miss the golden days of childhood, of bedtime stories and snuggling up on the sofa. Time is a cruel and sneaky thief. I might be in my fifties, but I want my family back. I need them.

They're not gone while they live on in you, I tell myself sharply as I place these pictures in my To Keep pile. Nothing is ever forgotten while I remember them – and then there's Jamie, and one day, I hope, his children too and then their children. On and on it will go. Jamie is the reason for all of it. He is the best of us.

As Pippa and I work our way through Mum's belongings, a task which proves slow as we spend more time looking at items than sorting them, the rain hammers against the windowpane and the trees are bent almost double by the gusting wind. The afternoon grows gloomy and I switch on the lamps, comforted by their pools of buttery light. By the time the trees at the end of the garden are lost in the darkness, Pip and I have emptied two large boxes and organised a pile of clothing to take to the charity shop, and are making inroads into the third box. The task has been absorbing, and curiously uplifting too. The more I do, the more I find that I don't want to stop.

While Pip makes tea, her chatter with Steve floating up from the kitchen, I turn my attention to an old shoebox tied tightly with frayed string. It seems that the knot has tightened over the years and as I pick at it, it seems reluctant to give up its claim on the box, biting into the cardboard and pulling itself tauter until my fingertips are sore and my patience is fraying with the string. Just when I'm on the brink of fetching scissors the knot surrenders and the string loosens. Triumphant, I lever the lid off and discover a treasure trove of old photographs, pictorial precious stones and pearls of the past to people like Pip. There are envelopes stuffed full, and as I tip them out I smile to recognise old faces and events. Some are brightly hued relics from the seventies and I recognise myself in various incarnations: a chubby baby in a violent orange romper suit held aloft by my proud moustachioed father; a five-year-old on Santa's knee in some department store grotto back in the days before safeguarding was even dreamed of; an eleven-year-old proud in school uniform; a teenager in full Bay City Rollers flares.

I laugh. Mum hoarded all these for so long, but I wish she hadn't! What *was* I thinking with that dreadful bubble perm? And how could I ever have dreamed a ra-ra skirt looked good with skinny legs like mine? I looked like an ostrich!

"What are you hooting at?" asks Pippa. She puts two mugs down on the windowsill and I hold up a picture.

"Recognise them?"

I've unearthed a polaroid of two girls in full makeup, shoulder-padded and hair-sprayed glory, pouting into the camera in the style of Madonna at her angry young woman best.

"Oh my God! That's never us?"

"It is. The disco at Rosecraddick village hall in 1985. You fancied a certain handsome young farmer, I seem to recall?"

Pip blushes. "I can't remember."

"Bollocks! You talked about nothing else all summer. I was nearly flattened by a combine when you decided to stalk him at work. That picture was taken at the harvest home disco when you finally snogged Billy!"

"I never stalked him. I just accidentally happened to be in the same places he was!"

"Like the grain barn? In your bikini top?"

"Here! Give me that!" Pip snatches the picture and cringes. "Good God! I'm amazed Billy came near me looking like that! Come on, then! What else have you found?"

I tip the contents onto the rug and we spread them out, laughing until we can't breathe at our outfits and hairdos. These photographs are the alluvium of friendship, the layers of who we are, the people who star in the story of us.

There are endless pictures. I find black and white snaps of my parents, and postcard-style prints of people I don't recognise in nineteen-thirties fashions. Maybe it's Grandma Ivy? Or her friends? I'll never know for sure now, because there's nobody left who might recognise them. Their identities are lost in time, and with them all the stories, both funny and sad. For the first time I understand why Pip and so many other people are fascinated by family history, because it's not so much raking up the past, as Grandma Ivy put it, as making sure people aren't forgotten or their stories lost.

"Who's this visiting war graves?" Pippa holds up a photo of an old woman wading through a sea of headstones. Her thick snow-white hair is pulled back into a bun and her face is heavily lined, but the eyes staring at us across the years are bright and filled with life. I've seen this before, I think, a long time ago at my Grandma's house.

"She's my great-grandmother. Emily Elmhurst."

"Are there any more of her?"

"No idea. There's a couple of envelopes I haven't opened yet, and that old suitcase. I was too busy laughing at our eighties fashion sense to get much further."

Pip is instantly distracted.

"We looked great back then. I might dress up for Billy and take him back down memory lane. We still have the grain barn and I can dig out my swimsuit, although I think it might kill him now to carry me in, bend me over and —"

I put my hands over my ears. "I don't need to hear this!"

"Fine! In that case let's have a look at those. They might distract me long enough to forget to tell you that when I read *Fifty Shades* Billy went and dug out some cable ties. He put his back out and we gave the book to Oxfam!"

As much as I adore Pip's husband, balding Billy with his love of overalls and wellies is hardly Christian Grey … I distract her by pulling a photograph from the envelope and Pippa falls on it excitedly.

"That's Rosecraddick Manor at the turn of the last century! Look at the ladies taking tea on the lawn! How amazing!"

She holds it up, a faded portal to a long-lost age when women dressed up for afternoon tea and men decked out in white suits and straw boaters stood stiffly behind them, staring unsmiling into the distance. The manor house is staged in the distance, a reminder of the family's wealth, and the sitters have been carefully arranged in front of it on the lawn beneath a cedar tree, in a tableau of pre-First World War high society captured for ever in film. An older man with a walrus moustache glowers at the lens, and the woman at his side is stony-faced. Even the two young men who flank them are serious-faced. Only the young woman seated at the table looks straight at the camera, and it seems to me that her lips long to curl in a wide smile. Being a parent, I know teenagers, and this one looks as though she's up to something.

Was this her? Emily? My great-grandmother?

"Don't people always look miserable in these old photos?" Pip is saying.

"The exposure was so slow that it was difficult to hold a smile for long," I tell her. Jamie loves photography and studied it at A level, and I remember him telling me all kinds of facts. "I think they thought smiling was bad form too, back then. They wanted pictures to look like formal portraits."

Pip jabs a finger at the moustachioed man in the centre of the scene.

"That's Colonel Rivers, and he was always miserable by all accounts, so I don't think we can blame the photograph. And the fair-haired boy behind the blonde woman is Kit Rivers."

"The war poet? You really think this is him?"

"I'm sure it is. I've seen enough pictures of Kit up at the manor. I don't know who the other lad is, though, or the girl. Perhaps she's your great-grandmother? The Pendennys family were friends with the Riverses. Can I take a picture of this for Matt? He'll know a bit more."

"Sure," I say. It'll be interesting to find out about the people in the scene. I'm already wondering about the identity of the girl. Is the tilt of her chin similar to that of the elderly Emily in the war graves picture? Or is my imagination starting to run away with me? In my longing to make sense of it all, am I finding similarities that doesn't exist?

We get down to work and the time flies by. When Pip's phone beeps, I'm amazed to discover it's past six o'clock.

"All okay?" I ask. Each time I have a text my feet practically leave the floor. It's not that I think it's Jamie – he doesn't communicate with us while he's away – but rather I fear it's someone with news of him. I'm on edge a lot of the time, which makes me realise just how much of a welcome distraction this afternoon has been.

She pulls a face while scrolling through the incoming message. "Just Billy wondering where I am. What he really means is 'where's dinner?', because he knows I'm here and he can't work a tin opener even though he can operate a combine. Typical. Just when it was getting exciting."

"You'd better get home before he starves. This lot'll still be here tomorrow," I say, and Pip nods.

"Yep, I'd better haul ass. Give me strength! I'd thought my cooking days were over when Clare left home, but apparently not." She pauses and inhales deeply. "I wish he'd take lessons from your Steve. Whatever he's making smells amazing."

Steve learned a long time ago that I can burn water and luckily for Jamie and me, he turned out to be a natural chef. Tonight, he's making Irish stew and the rich smell of tomato and onions drifts up the stairs. I glance down at the pictures carpeting the floor like autumn leaves, loath to abandon them even for supper. Something about their sepia world has drawn me in.

Maybe there's something to this family tree business after all?

Chapter 4
Alison
Cornwall

After dinner Steve opens a bottle of wine and settles down on the sofa, Waffles sprawls out by the woodburner and dreams of doggy adventures which make his legs and nose twitch. I pour a glass of red to carry up to the spare room while carrying on with my sorting. I'm like that hat in Harry Potter but with pictures, I think with a smile. How Jamie had loved those books when he was small. I'd read them aloud from cover to cover until the dulcet tones of Stephen Fry took over and rescued my vocal cords. If I'd realised how precious that time was and how fleeting, I'd have read every word more willingly and until my voice was hoarse.

"Are you sure, love? You don't have to do the lot all in one hit." My husband throws me a concerned look, puzzled because I haven't chosen to slump in front of Netflix as per normal. Although longing to watch DIY Car SOS or some other blokecentric show, he's alarmed by my sudden enthusiasm for clearing junk. He's probably worried it's a symptom of a breakdown or something

"I may as well carry on while I'm in the mood," I say. "Besides, I'm looking forward to getting my craft room."

"You mean the gym," Steve counters, and we laugh because this has become a family joke. My husband's idea of exercise is lifting a pint in the local, and any exercise equipment he buys in a fit of sudden enthusiasm quickly gathers dust or ends up on eBay. Jamie was keen on the idea for a while when he was into running, but later on he liked to train at college and when he joined the army there was no longer any need to have a gym at home.

But I'm not thinking about the army now and I push the dark thoughts back down. As I climb the stairs I'm thinking about the world of tea on the lawn, dogcarts and long summers of cricket and croquet when girls wore white dresses and held parasols. Apart from the contents of the glass in my hand, this afternoon's endeavours have proved the best way yet to silence the constant hum of terror.

While we ate supper, I thought about my family and tried to remember the stories Mum told me when I was small, but my memories are fragmented. I can stitch some of them together, but they form an uneven patchwork of anecdote and half-recalled tales. There was something about a house fire, I think, and somebody who died of flu. Or am I getting confused with Granny Ivy's husband who died in the Second World War? I wish I'd paid more attention, because there's no way of knowing for sure. Maybe some of the answers lie in these pictures or are tucked away in the other boxes.

Pip was right; this journey into my family's past is a great distraction. All through supper my thoughts kept drifting back to the pictures and the long-forgotten people framed within them, and I'm keen to see what else has been packed away. If I can pull some kind of narrative together from this cherished detritus, I can pass these family stories on to Jamie and the family I hope he'll make one day. My heart lifts because this feels like something useful I can do for him while he's away.

I sit on the floor with my back resting against the radiator. The warmth is soothing through my sweater, as though Mum's here, hugging me as I rummage through the last of her things. Although she was lost to me long before she died, slipping her moorings and drifting a little further into the mists with each passing day, the shock of losing her was still a blow. Although I'm a woman in her fifties and a wife and a mother, it hurts, it really hurts, to no longer be somebody's little girl, nobody's precious child loved unconditionally and comforted when the pain becomes too much to bear. That's the real reason why I've left all these boxes here for so long; once they have been tidied away then my mum has truly gone, and I can no longer kid myself I'm just storing this lot for her until she's better.

The room blurs. Grief is sneaky, creeping up on you in a game of grandmother's footsteps to poke you in the heart with his bony finger when you least expect it. Mum's been gone for several years but sometimes the smallest things – a breath of scent or a few notes of music drifting in the breeze – become wrecking balls which sweep me from my feet and leave me broken.

I gulp a mouthful of Merlot and put the glass down with a defiant thud. I'm not going to be submerged by loss this evening. I won't let it crash over me and drag me into the depths. I *won't*. I have a job to do. Feeling determined, I reach for the photographs, fanning them out onto the rug, and lean forward to study them.

There's no order to any of these pictures. Some of them are black and white countryside scenes, beautifully composed with the light catching trees or illuminating the ridges of corduroy plough. I'm not an artist, but the person who took these photographs was. The contrasts are striking, and the one of mist stroking the tangled limbs of winter trees is so beautiful and melancholy it makes me feel close to tears. No apps or Photoshop trickery when these were taken, only the skill of the photographer and the patience to wait until the perfect moment arrived to open the shutter. I admire the Eiffel Tower, skeletal in the early morning light, and the swelling breast of Sacré Cœur. Westminster Bridge at dawn, swathed in mist, is as breathtaking as in any sonnet. Rosecraddick Bay is here, too, captured from the spot where the war memorial now stands. I recognise the view at once, for there's no mistaking the tower of St Nonna's or the spreading cedar tree by the rectory.

This photographer was a local, then?

I turn the pictures, hoping they might be signed, but the reverse sides are blank. I place them to one side, curious as to who in my family might have travelled to France and taken them, before picking up the last picture. I'm expecting another beautifully framed shot of Montmartre or a landscape, but this final photograph is of an ivy-covered house, flanked by candled chestnut trees which flare against a goose-grey sky. With the curving drive and brick walls packaged in ivy, the house feels unmistakably English, albeit a relic of an England long since consigned to history books and Merchant Ivory films.

I hold the photo closer to the lamp. Do I recognise this house? Not at all, although there's something familiar about the sweep of the drive and those enormous chestnut trees. But those flower beds packed with roses fat as cabbages and the creeper-smothered brick building behind them are strangers. Are those thick trees smudging the background the woods beyond my own house, which I know so well? There's something about the density and the spread of these trees I feel sure I recognise, and if it was daylight I would surely see the same deep tangled pockets at the end of the garden. If I had to guess I would say that this photograph was taken less than a mile from my own front door.

Could this house be Pendennys Place, the mansion which burned down all those years ago? I've never seen a picture of it, but there might be something on the internet, or maybe Matt at the manor would know? It could be interesting to find out.

Fortified by another glug of red, I attack another couple of boxes. These aren't nearly as interesting, and mostly contain piles of parish magazines, WI pamphlets and the old newspapers Grandma Ivy hoarded. I smile fondly at reports of Mum as Rosecraddick's carnival queen, and my mind boggles over peculiar recipes from an era when rationing was still in place. By the time I've thumbed my way through piles of these, over an hour has passed and the radiator is cooling. I hear the chatter of the television downstairs punctuated by the rumbling of Steve's snores. All around me the house talks to itself, timbers creaking and floorboards shifting while pipes gurgle and chuckle. These are the sounds of home, the sounds I heard when I stayed up late while Jamie was teething or waiting for the scrunch of car tyres on gravel to herald Steve's safe return, and I sink into them because all is well. I'll make a start on the next box and do a bit more before calling it a night.

There's no logic or order to how my mother selected which belongings to keep. I sift through old school reports, boxes of buttons snipped from old frocks and shirts for a purpose known only to her, and a frayed patchwork quilt. A small leather folder, the sort used for artwork and sketches, has hidden beneath tangled skeins of embroidery silk. The light picks out tiny initials pressed into the thin leather, but they are so worn that it's impossible to decipher what they might be. I'd like to think it's an elaborate E and P, but this is probably just the dim light and my imagination.

Another lost identity. It's sobering how little we amount to in the end, and sad that without us to give them meaning our most precious treasures are little more than curiosities to be binned or kept, depending on a stranger's whim. I push these melancholy thoughts away. I'm making stories for Jamie; isn't that the intention and the purpose? I'm piecing together our family history and writing him firmly into it. Not depressing myself. Back to this portfolio, which closer inspection reveals is full of sketches. There are women in big hats, a piebald horse pulling a gypsy-style caravan, and several drawings of the same Victorian house I'd seen earlier, in the photograph. Whoever drew these was talented.

One sketch in particular catches my attention. It's a simple line drawing of a grey horse standing in front of the same house. A girl is sitting side-saddle, holding double reins loosely in one hand, and although her face is masked by the wide brim of a hat I have the strongest impression she's smiling down at the artist. Just as the lines on the page capture perfectly the power of the horse in a swell of muscled quarters and the flare of nostrils, so they also convey the laughter dancing over her lips and steely determination in the lift of her chin. This artist is captivated by her; the pencil lines stroke the lines of her slender body, linger over the fall of her habit and caress the curve of her cheek. It's no more than a sketch, yet so evocative I can almost hear the scratch of lead on cartridge paper and the swish of the horse's tail as it whisks away flies, and feel the sun on my skin.

I put the portfolio onto my Keep pile and continue shuffling through more photographs, which I suspect will mean more to Pippa and Matt Enys than they do to me. There is a blond-haired young man standing with a hound, a lone gypsy caravan in a woodland clearing, and a shot of two young men in full army uniform. I look twice at this, intrigued because they're not posed stiffly against a background as in other similar pictures I've seen in history books, but standing with their arms flung around each other's shoulders. Enlisting day? Embarkation day? There's no way of telling without an expert on hand, but their pristine uniforms, clear eyes and confident energy suggests this photograph was taken before the reality of war had sunk its fangs into them. The photographer's use of light and position distils the essence of each subject; the blond boy appears resolute, yet sadness shadows his eyes and plays around his lips; and the dark-haired lad stares into the lens as though challenging the photographer to portray him as anything less than resolute. It's a convincing act, and the truth is betrayed only by the glimpse of a clenched fist and flash of upper teeth worrying lips below a sparse and uncertain moustache.

It's an intriguing photo and definitely one for Pippa to explore, along with the last photograph in the batch, a more formal composition this time, and one familiar in terms of era and style. The sitter, a young woman, poses in front of a painted background of a castle, and is dressed from head to toe in white. Her slim hands clutch a posy of fat roses, several more are caught up in her dark curls, and more still are scattered at her button-booted feet. She leans on a parasol and gazes into the lens, every bit as prim and proper as a young woman of her class should be, and on my first glance at it I almost put the picture down without interest because it's generic. She is every pre-First World War young lady and none, all at once. This picture would be unremarkable except that she looks a lot like me.

It's a shock to see aspects of yourself in a stranger's face. She's a lot younger than me, of course, but I didn't always have wrinkles starring the corners of my eyes and silver threads in my own dark curls. Once – and it feels like five minutes ago – I'd looked a lot like her. I tilt the frame and examine the picture from all angles, taken aback to realise that the indignant way she holds herself, as though she's been forced into the dress and frogmarched to the sitting, is reminiscent of the younger Jamie when he'd been made to do something against his will. Tidy his room. Take out the bins. Put up with his mum when she's fussing. He'd tolerate it with good grace but underneath he was itching to rebel – just as I feel certain this prim and proper miss was. I know that stubborn chin and glower of old, because I see it in myself and I see it in my son.

This girl has to be my great-grandmother, Emily, I conclude, as I add the picture to the Keep pile. The similarities with my own face and Jamie's are undeniable. The period dress looks about right, too.

The television is still talking to itself downstairs, so while Steve snoozes I press on, figuring that the more I can get done tonight the better. Beneath another layer of yellowing newspapers is a brown box, battered around the edges and with the letters VPK embossed across it in swirling script. The paint must have peeled away a long time ago, but the elaborate loops still hold faint traces of silver, and I trace them with my index finger. The lid is held shut by a brass clasp and I hesitate to open it because it feels wrong. This doesn't belong to me. None of these things do. I'm like a latter-day Howard Carter. I'm a grave robber but with pictures and tat rather than pyramids and treasure.

"It's just junk, Alison," I say out loud, but my voice is thin in the watchful quiet. Even the house has ceased its dialogue with itself as though holding its breath and waiting to see what I do next. I flick the box open with a sharp huff of frustration at myself for dithering. An old camera nestles inside. An antique at last,

I lift it from the box, surprised by how light it is and how warm to the touch. It feels as though it's resting in my hands like a bird, all delicate bones and fragile tissue.

"Patented in the USA," I read, turning it so the lamplight catches the engraving on the plate circling the lens. "January 18, 1910. January 7, 1913."

This wasn't Mum's or Grandma's. Whose, then? Great-granny Emily? Did she take those pictures of France and the old house? Was she an amateur photographer? If so, I'd never heard of it, had never seen any pictures she might have taken. I've never heard that she travelled across Europe either. I'd thought she'd spent her whole life at Rosecraddick.

I hold the camera to my eye and peer through the lens, and the room swims blurrily into view. I lower it again and marvel that something over a century old can feel so modern in design and so oddly familiar. This antique camera, small enough to slip into a pocket, is not much bigger than my iPhone. Whoever owned it must have used it a great deal and carried it with them because the casing is worn shiny from touch, and it's dented in places too. Closer inspection reveals that the lens panel pulls out on a pair of concertina-style struts, and when I give it a tentative tug the whole section slides out as smoothly as though it had last been used only moments earlier.

The film seems to be loaded into the back compartment, and I'm tempted to spring it open to see if there's anything in it before imagining what Jamie might say if he was here.

"Mum! No! If there are any pictures inside, you'll ruin them!" he'd protest in alarm, prising it away from me and replacing it in its box. "Give this to somebody who knows what they're doing!"

Jamie knows a bit about cameras from his A level, and if he were here I'd ask him, but instead I'll have to consult Google. I tuck this find safely back into its case and give it pride of place on the Keep pile. Steve will be fascinated, because this is far more interesting than post-war recipes for jam and who won the prize for biggest marrow at the village fair.

Inspired by finding treasure I whizz through a bus ticket collection and old knitting patterns (all binned because I don't think stripy tank tops are quite my husband's style and even if I don't eat for a month a crocheted halter neck isn't going to flatter me) then pull out an battered tin of Quality Street, so old that it's hexagonal and features a regency soldier and his bonneted sweetheart. The tin is dented, and the lid welded so tight with rust and age that I break several nails attempting to lever it off. Flakes of rust drift to the floor and I suck my finger, sore where the nail's ripped too close to the quick. Pippa never once mentioned that family history was such a high-risk hobby.

But when I look inside the tin, all thoughts of sore fingers and torn nails flee. As I'd suspected, it's filled with more pictures, but these faded black and white images are a far cry from the elegant boulevards of Paris or elegant stately homes. I'm staring at graphic images of war, each one more harrowing and more dreadful than the last. Men drowning in mud. Plunging horses deep in mire and dragged under by guns. A boy with a shattered leg screaming silently into the lens. Armed men wielding bayonets stumbling through rain. A lone soldier ripping his comrade from barbed wire, oblivious to the lolling tongue and dark bloom of blood, as another cradles his head in his hands, face caved in and jacket dark with gore.

I drop the tin in horror and back away.

What are these, and why were they in my mother's possession? Each one is ugly and grotesque and powerful and true, now seared for ever in my mind's eye like a brand. Whoever stood behind this camera captured hell on his film. He peered into the deepest circle of hell and took pictures of it. He made a record of something that no one who sees it could ever forget. Now I know why the camera is so dented and why it lay hidden for so long.

My stomach rolls in a nauseating swirl of shock and pity and fear for my own boy. I can't stand to look at this, undoubtedly this photographer's finest work, because these pictures are my every nightmare. My deepest fear. Here on film my daily purgatory is laid bare.

I cannot bear to be near these photographs. I cannot stand being in the same room as them.

I scrabble from the floor. Pins and needles buzz in my feet and legs as I lurch from the room. I close the door behind me and hurtle down the stairs, not stopping to return and click off the lights or tidy away. These things can wait, because all that matters to me is fleeing from those photographs which lie spilled like blood across the spare room floor.

Chapter 5
Alison
Cornwall

"Are you sure you don't want a lift, love? The weather's wild."

Steve stands by the front door watching me wrestling with my raincoat, a task made ten times harder by Waffles, who spins around in excited circles. Coats mean walks and he can hardly wait to venture out, gales or not.

"I spent all day inside yesterday. Some fresh air will do me good," I reply.

My husband's eyebrows shoot upwards to where his hair used to reside. Outside the trees are doing a wild hula dance as a strong sou'wester pummels the Cornish coast. The sky is dark indigo slashed with manic slices of lemon sunlight, a vivid warning of heavy rain waiting to shotblast anyone foolish enough to venture outside.

"There's fresh air and then there's fresh air, Ali!"

I step into the porch and push my feet into my wellies. "It'll blow the cobwebs away."

"It'll blow *you* away, never mind the cobwebs."

I say nothing. After a restless night when I'd woken several times with a racing heart and with ragged nightmares flapping at the edges of my recollection, the idea of being blown away like tissue paper is very appealing, and if this gale blasts those images from my memory, so much the better.

After fleeing the spare room I'd poured another glass of wine and slumped beside Steve on the sofa. I'd hoped the warmth of the fire and burble of the television would soothe away the scenes of carnage, but the opposite had been the case, and my fears for Jamie, always slumbering, were wide awake and clamouring for attention. When I climbed the stairs for bed, I knew that sleeping would be difficult, and I tossed and turned until the small hours.

As soon as morning came I slid out from beneath my duvet and tiptoed into the spare room to sweep the pictures up and secure them beneath the lid of the old tin. Like the sins of the world released for ever more, there was no hiding from the contents of my own Pandora's box, but there might be somebody who knew what to do with it. I had to get these out of the house. They felt like curses. Unlucky. A bad omen.

While Steve showered, I googled Kernow Heritage Foundation to find the contact details for Matthew Enys, Pippa's boss and the main man at Rosecraddick Manor. I didn't ask Pippa, because I knew she'd want to know exactly what I'd found, and although it felt mean to leave her out of the loop I couldn't bear having to go through the disturbing pictures while she commented on them. She was always telling me how amazing Matt Enys was, so I was simply taking her advice, I told myself, as I pinged him a quick email explaining that I had some artefacts he might find of interest. When Matt emailed back within minutes I was impressed, and even more so when he offered to meet me at half nine at the manor. In the fashion of someone wanting to remove a voodoo doll from the house as quickly as possible I was keen to have the war photographs out of the halt. It may have been superstitious of me, but when it came to Jamie I wasn't taking any chances.

As I button up my coat, Steve watches me: "I'm working from home until lunchtime, love. If you need a lift back, just call me. Okay?"

"Okay." I kiss him quickly, pick up the carrier bag I've filled with items for Matt Enys, and open the front door. Waffles is fired like a curly golden bullet into the buffeting wind, and the door handle is wrenched from my grasp. The world outside is wild, and if we could glimpse the sea from Halt

House I know it would be battleship grey and flecked with foam.

My husband calls something after me, but his words are snatched away. When I turn to wave, a sudden squall of rain stings my cheeks and I see he's already closed the front door. The light from the kitchen windows shines warm and welcoming into the gloom and I almost turn tail because the dank path through the dark trees holds little appeal. Then Waffles shoots under the fence and vanishes into the trees and there's no turning back. It'll be drier underneath those, I tell myself as I clamber over the stile, and I'll dry off once I reach the manor. Unlike those poor boys tapped in the horror of trench warfare, a bit of rain and mud won't kill me.

The path is knotty with roots, and ivy scrambles across stumps and neglected piles of timber. I follow the worn track while the rain hammers the canopy above my head and Waffles dives in and out of the undergrowth, barking delightedly when he flushes a pheasant from the brambles. Against the stillness of the woods its waterfall of cries and flapping wings make me jump. The peace in here is usually a balm after cleaning the holiday lets, answering emails and solving the problems my guests bring to me, but today my nerves flutter and screech just like this hapless game bird.

Waffles bounds over to check I'm still here before tearing away once again. I tighten my grip on the carrier bag and continue on my way, doing my best to ignore the tin thudding against my calf and the bite of the plastic handles into my fingers.

This dense tangle of trees must have been managed back in the days when steam trains pulled into the station and girls in white dresses took tea on the lawn, but they are neglected now, owned by a farmer, and home to wildlife rather than woodsmen. I walk the paths most days with my dog, usually taking the sunken lane which leads into the village, but today I detour a mile or so to visit the place where the ruins of an old house list through the soil like architectural tombstones. Although nature has clawed back the space, green fingers prodding crumbling cement and forcing apart the remaining masonry, the faint scar of a drive can be distinguished beneath coarse grass, like a glimpse of seabed spotted in the depths of a rock pool. Rooks caw from the branches of the naked chestnut trees which claw the sky, sad carcasses of the leafy candle-bearing giants of the photograph.

Luckily for me there are no sheep grazing today and Waffles dives into the ruin, barking at some creature he's spotted in the thick weeds. I follow him, pulling up my hood and bowing my head against the rain. This is a spot I'd explored as a child, a wonderful place for games and dens and later on for smoking illicit cigarettes or making out with village boys, but as an adult I haven't meandered this way for years. Something about the place always dusts my skin with shivers, and as I kick my way through brambles and trace the outline of foundations I feel as though I'm trespassing.

The devastating blaze which destroyed the house which once stood here occurred so long ago that its cause is forgotten. The story went that the flames could be seen from Rosecraddick and by the time the villagers arrived with their buckets it was far too late: Pendennys Place was no more. It exists only in a curling sepia picture languishing inside my swinging Bag for Life and the faint foundation footprint in the grass. The cellars were filled in years ago, after the war and their use as a shelter, Mum said, and some scattered chunks of fallen masonry are still blackened from the intensity of the long-ago blaze. Not a great deal remains and I imagine what wasn't destroyed would have been gradually picked over and carried away over the following months, since the Cornish are a thrifty bunch. There are no gates or fences, and unless you knew that a house had once stood here few clues whisper of its existence. The spot feels empty, now the domain of woodland creatures and the scrambling ivy and ghosts.

I whistle for Waffles and with the dog at my heels pick up the footpath. Another mile through the woods and a short walk along a sunken lane slippery with mouldering leaves and mud brings us to the gates of Rosecraddick Manor. Even in heavy rain and with the wind whipping leaves along the drive, the old house is beautiful. Neglected for years, it's enjoying a renaissance with the renewed interest in Kit Rivers' war poetry. Freshly painted signposts direct me to the main entrance.

The manor's studded door swings open and a man wielding an umbrella leaps down the steps. Tall and wiry and with a long mane of raven-black hair falling to his shoulders, he reminds me of a bespectacled Ross Poldark.

"Alison Foy? I'm Matt Enys. Please come inside, out of this dreadful weather."

He places his hand in the small of my back and holds the umbrella above my head as he guides me up the steps, chivalric gestures which makes me feel like a cross between Demelza and a Jane Austen heroine. As he takes my coat and thanks me for coming over, I realise that Matt Enys is older than he first appears, with strands of silver threaded through the thick black hair and deep laughter lines ploughing the skin around his eyes when he smiles. A strong jaw shadowed with stubble and an earring glinting in the light thrown from the chandelier reinforces the Ross-ness, as does the open-necked white shirt and tight black trousers. No wonder Pippa has a crush!

"Welcome to Rosecraddick Manor," Poldark says.

I've visited the manor before but it's one thing to be inside a stately home when it's bustling and another again to see it empty. Everything about this vast entrance hall, from the six-foot-high fireplace dominating the far end to the glowing oak panelling, is designed to impress, even intimidate. Portraits stare down at me, and I shiver when I meet the cold eyes of the moustachioed man who had appeared in the tea on the lawn photograph.

"That's Colonel Rivers, Kit's father," Matt says, following my gaze. "Maybe not the most welcoming character, but it seemed only right to have him here to oversee the activity in his own house. Kit's far more friendly, which is why he's above the fireplace."

He indicates a full-length portrait of the boy I have already seen in so many of my photos. Incredibly young, he's dressed in riding breeches and a white shirt, and his eyes are bright. The pain which haunts them in the dreadful pictures I've bought for Matt to examine has yet to be inflicted, and I find I want to call up to this beautiful boy and warn him to be careful.

"I'd offer you a tour, but I'm afraid the rooms are closed for cleaning and cataloguing," says Matt, ushering me along a corridor looped with scarlet rope. "I thought we could talk in my office. I've managed to persuade Kernow Heritage to stretch to an electric heater so I don't freeze when the house is closed to the public, so you'll be able to dry out. I've a kettle too if you fancy a coffee?"

"I'm fine for coffee but I wouldn't say no to drying out," I say. "And please don't worry about the tour. I visited when the manor first opened."

"We've done a lot more since then. We've opened up the long gallery, put in the film room and expanded the gardens too. You really should come back and see it all again. Any time once we're back up and running, honestly. You really should."

His enthusiasm is so contagious I find myself agreeing that yes, I really ought to pay another visit. I don't mention that I can't bear to immerse myself in wars and death and loss, because Matt Enys doesn't need to know any of this.

As we talk we have diverted from the guided tour route and turned into a bare corridor lined with doors. Matt opens the first one with a flourish and steps back to allow me inside first.

"Here we are – the engine room!"

His office is a small room where packed bookshelves line the walls and windows overlook the same cedar trees which had once thrown cool shade onto the grass while the Rivers family enjoyed afternoon tea. One desk, set against the wall, is heaped with files and papers. The second, positioned in the window with a laptop and printer set up to face over the grounds, is no less burdened. Even the two armchairs which hug a much-ringed coffee table are drowning in folders and boxes.

"It's a terrible mess, I'm afraid," Matt says, with a rueful smile. "I'm not the best at being organised even though our volunteers do their best to try to sort me out. Jill used to be a head teacher and I drive her mad. The trouble is I tend to get so stuck into things that all the other bits mount up."

I'm not quite sure how to respond. It looks as though the place has been burgled.

"There must be an awful lot to do," I offer.

"Yes, yes, there is but that's all by the by." Matt sweeps a pile of papers and books from a chair and deposits it on his desk. "Please take a seat. And your dog too, of course."

I glance down at Waffles, no longer a golden cockerpoo but sludge-coloured.

"Are you sure?"

Matt pats Waffles, oblivious to the filth now coating his hands.

"It's only mud, isn't it, boy?"

Waffles flops at his feet with a grunt and I sit down, shifting when springs prod me in the backside. The room grows thick with the smell of damp dog, but Matt doesn't seem to notice; he's too busy rummaging in a box file he's unearthed from beneath a desk. He looks at his hands, as though surprised to see how dirty they are, and brushes them absently on his jeans before pulling out a sheaf of papers.

"I knew they were here somewhere! Here we are, the Pendennys family of Pendennys Place. I'm afraid I haven't got a great deal because they haven't been central to the work here – only as much as Emily Pendennys was supposed to marry Kit Rivers."

"Really? That's true?"

"Oh yes, although I think it was an unspoken assumption rather than anything formal. The two estates bordered one another, and it would have been very convenient, not to say profitable, for the Rivers family to acquire the land here. From what little I know, Emily was the last of her line; her brother was killed out hunting, and her father was badly injured in the Boer War and never remarried. I seem to recall the family had fallen on hard times by the early twentieth century, but even so your great-grandmother would have been the most eligible heiress for miles around. They'd made their money in India, I think."

I take this in while he continues to root around in the box. With his hair on end and wire glasses slipping down his nose, Matt looks every inch the academic and I don't want to interrupt him because I know he's got more to say. The man is a natural teacher and I can see why Pippa enjoys working with him. After only a few minutes in his company, this old house, and my own family's links to its past, are coming alive. It's strange not to glance outside and see Kit Rivers and his family out walking on the lawn or posing with my great-grandmother for a formal portrait. They feel so close, just a heartbeat away, and before I can think about it I reach into my bag and slide out the photograph of the girl in the white dress.

"I think this might be her. Emily, I mean."

Matt abandons the book and joins me, leaning over to inspect the picture with narrowed eyes.

"She looks like you," he says slowly, turning his head and studying me closely. "You have the same mouth and eyes."

I'm ridiculously pleased even though Emily looks so crotchety. "Do you think so?"

"Absolutely. I've never seen a picture of her, but I think we can now safely say this girl is Emily Pendennys. My goodness!" Matt shakes his head wonderingly. "How utterly incredible. She's part of the Kit Rivers' story – a small part of course, since as we all know it wasn't her he loved – but even so! To see her face and to know she was here at the same time as Kit and his family …"

He falls silent. Dust veils the air as a sickly ray of sunlight seeps through the clouds and trickles through the window.

"It's like catching up with an old friend after a lifetime," Matt finished quietly. "What a privilege."

He's so moved by this one picture that I'm suddenly worried for him when he sees the others. As the sunlight strokes his face and illuminates lines of middle age and life, there's something boyish about Matthew Enys, with his passion for Kit Rivers and the past, which is innocent and vulnerable. I want to protect him, and Jamie would laugh and say it's my mother hen side clucking around. He'd be right, but I don't know if I want Matt Enys to have to see the images that haunted my dreams last night and still drift before my vision like a grotesque mirage. If Kit Rivers is one of the young men in the pictures, maimed and dying and mired in horrors that my mind recoils from, how will Matt feel to be faced with this knowledge?

I'll come to those when I'm ready.

"She must have gone to a lot of trouble for this picture, although she doesn't look very impressed," I say.

Matt laughs. "It's some get-up. That poor girl's waist has been pulled in something savage, which must have been agony. Still, she needed to look the part if she was to find a suitable husband and save the family home. The

Pendennys family had the aristocratic lineage and the land, but they would have been pretty much penniless by the time this was taken. Her father, Julyan Pendennys, was a drinker and had been a gambler in his youth. By the start of the war the place was mortgaged to the hilt."

"So it was down to Emily to make a good match and save the place?" This is like something out of a fairy tale.

"I'd imagine so. She had the breeding, and the Riverses, for all their wealth, were originally a military family with aspirations. I imagine your great-grandmother and Kit Rivers would have known each other very well, being social equals and neighbours. If Kit's family had paid off the debts on Pendennys Place they'd have had control of the estate as well as the kudos of the match. Everyone would have been a winner. Here, have a quick look at these."

He hands me a piece of paper smothered in scribbles and lines.

"This is a rough family tree I put together when I was first here, and before it all went a little crazy with the Kit Rivers stuff. I had a bit more time on my hands then."

I study the branches of the sprawling family tree. Matt's writing is neat, but he's had to make it teeny tiny in order for everything to fit, and my eyes strain as I read. There are endless dates and names, some the same over and over again and branching into infinity, while others end abruptly. Some I recognise, like Emily Pendennys *b* 1897 *m* 1915 to my great-grandfather Rupert Elmhurst, the war hero. For others, such as Morvan Pendennys, my unfortunate great-uncle *d* 1907 aged 16, there's nothing beyond them, and my own grandmother's birth isn't even mentioned.

"I stopped at Emily, I'm afraid," Matt says when he sees me looking. "She's where Kit's story ends, and after that – well you know the rest."

I do. Like most people, I've read the book and seen the film. Kit's story really is history, his poems studied by academics and his life well documented thanks to people like Matt, but I feel sad that Emily has been lost, relegated to a footnote in the life of a literary giant. I wish I knew more. It feels wrong that the girl in the white dress is only remembered for not being loved by Kit Rivers the war poet. I wish there were things I knew about her for a fact rather than guesses based on a sketch and a handful of old pictures. Was she upset that Kit didn't choose to marry her? Did she miss her brother? What happened between her and Grandma Ivy? Why did they fall out?

I brush Emily's glowering face with my fingertip. Whatever the answers to these questions might be there is one thing I do know for certain; her blood flows through my veins, and through Jamie's too. Past, present and family future, we are all linked …

"I'm sorry I can't be more help," Matt says, "but Kit's letters don't tell us much about Emily. She's something of a mystery, and I'm not sure we'll ever know any more about her."

I don't like thinking of Emily as a bit part in someone else's story, and I'm sure there's more to discover, but my great-grandmother remains elusive, slipping back into the shadows where she holds her secrets close. There are so many questions that seem impossible to answer. Who drew the sketch of her? Who took the pictures? Did she want to marry Kit? Why is she so angry in the picture? There is a story here, I can feel it, and I'm disappointed Matt Enys hasn't been able to unlock more of it.

"I've brought more to show you." I hand him the picture of the Victorian house. "Is that Pendennys Place? I walked through the woods to where I think it was. The chestnut trees are still there, and there's a bit of the drive left beneath the weeds and grasses."

Matt examines the picture, a frown cross-hatching his brow.

"It could well be. I'd have to have a root through the archives and see what I can find. It's a beautiful house. What a tragedy it burned down."

"How did that happen?"

"Again, it's something I'd need to research." He gives me an apologetic one-shouldered shrug. "Mrs Foy, I hope Pippa hasn't been singing my praises too highly? I feel utterly useless."

"Alison," I correct automatically because Mrs Foy will always be my mother-in-law, and it makes me feel even older than her when attractive young men address me that way. "And you're nothing of the kind. Pippa was spot on, and I already feel like I've learned so much. I knew about Kit Rivers, of course, but it never felt real before. It was more like a history lesson."

Matt presses a hand against his chest. "This place makes you get it in here, I think?"

"Absolutely," I agree. Because it does. I pass him the photograph of the aristocratic party taking tea on the lawn. "That's here, isn't it?"

Matt stares at the picture.

"How extraordinary! That's the lower lawn right here." He points outside, and although the lawn is under attack from squalls of rain, it isn't difficult to imagine figures from the past seated there, sipping Earl Grey and eating cake. "That's Kit Rivers standing behind the table, although I don't recognise the dark-haired boy beside him. Oh! Emily's there too. Doesn't she look quite the lady, and far happier in this picture!"

"She looks like she has a secret," I say.

"Maybe she did? These are Kit's parents," Matt continues, pointing at the stern Edwardian couple flanking the tea table. "Colonel and Lady Rivers. You've already been greeted by him!"

"He seems rather unamused," I remark, and Matt laughs.

"Yes, he was a formidable man and by all accounts something of a bully. Kit looks like fun, though, and his friend has a really thoughtful expression. Whoever took this has done a wonderful job because you almost feel you know them and their personalities. They are beautifully composed, and the light is exquisite."

I'm pleased he thinks this. The talent of the mystery photographer is without doubt – the hellish scenes of war are among the most powerful things I've ever seen.

"Awful to think that war wasn't far away," Matt sighs, placing the picture on the arm of the chair and staring out beyond me to the gardens. "I never get over that, you know. It's like a dark storm cloud is on the horizon and people have absolutely no idea that life is on the brink of changing for ever. Kit is meant to have written a poem along these lines called 'The Last Summer'. He mentions it in his letters, but it was lost at the front when he was fighting."

"It was all such a dreadful waste," I say.

"Yes. You want to reach into the photograph and warn them, don't you? But you can't, and even if you could, you know they won't listen. They'll go off and fight regardless of any warnings because they know it's their duty."

Matt could be talking about Jamie. Maybe some things never change? We're doomed to repeat the past over and over again, the young men marching off to fight with high hopes and valiant dreams while the women wait at home to pray and hope and fear.

I hand him the picture of the two boys, pointing to the blond lad. "This is Kit Rivers, I think?"

"My goodness. Yes, yes absolutely – but I've never seen this before." Matt almost collapses onto the arm of my chair, taking the picture gently and holding it between thumb and forefinger, and staring at it as though unable to look away. "My God. How utterly, incredible to see this. He looks so young. They both do. So dreadfully and impossibly young and … alive."

"It's the same young man, isn't it? The one who's in the garden party picture?"

And the ones hidden in the tin, I add silently, but Matt can look at those alone because I can't face seeing them. They'll be historical documents to him whereas to me it's as though someone has photographed my worst fears.

"I think so, but I don't know who he is. This looks like enlistment day. Kit isn't thrilled, and neither is this fellow. Same photographer, I reckon. They must have been friends with him."

"You think they knew the photographer?" I hadn't thought of that. If Kit and this lad were friends with Emily it's likely she also knew the talent behind the lens.

I feel a tingle of excitement.

"I'd almost put money on it," Matt says. "This picture is really informal, but you'd expect them to have been posed if it had been taken in an official capacity. There's enough examples of those about. A good one is Dickon Trehunnist's enlistment picture; it's very serious, nothing like this. It's in the exhibition – I'll point it out to you."

"This was taken by a friend?"

"Perhaps. A gifted amateur or maybe a travelling photographer there for the enlistment day. There were quite a few of those about. They'd move from town to town and make their living taking pictures of those who could afford it. They'd set up for a few weeks wherever they could find lodgings; some even had caravans or barges. You'd be amazed where some of them travelled. Samuel Borne took pictures all around India during the Raj. It was incredible, what he was able to photograph." He flushes. "Sorry. I'm lecturing, aren't I?"

"It's fascinating. Lecture away!" I say warmly, and Matt needs no second bidding. As he talks about photographic history my mind scurries back to images of Paris and that odd shot of a solitary caravan in the clearing.

Whoever took these pictures was a nomad yet one who was close to Kit Rivers, close enough to have fought alongside him in the trenches. Did Emily come to know him? Did Kit introduce them? Were they friends?

I glance down at her picture and wish she could tell me. History is no longer a dusty subject filled with kings and castles and endless dates, but rather a world inhabited by people not so different from us and filled with questions we cannot answer. It's a riddle you need to solve. Now I really understand why Pippa finds this place so fascinating.

"So, sadly, I've no idea who this photographer was any more than I can say who this other young man is," Matt concludes, his eyes shining behind his spectacles. "Could be your great-grandfather? Didn't he serve in the war? Might he have enlisted alongside Kit?"

"It's possible. He died fighting in the First World War, and I believe he was awarded the Military Cross. I'm ashamed to say I don't know much about him at all."

He whistles. "Your great-grandfather must have been a brave man."

I've never thought about it this way before. Great-grandfather Rupert is a shadowy figure, dying when he was only just out of his teens, and I feel a prickle of guilt because yes, he must have been brave, and he deserves not to be forgotten.

"Grandma Ivy never knew him. She lost her own husband in the Second World War."

I turn icy cold as I say this. My family didn't have a lot of luck in these great conflicts; I'm praying it isn't some dreadful legacy.

Matt looks sympathetic. "Poor lady. Those were hard times. So, was your grandmother Emily's only child?"

"Yes. She didn't marry again. I guess her husband was the love of her life."

There's a lump in my throat as I look at the dark-haired young man, his gaze resolute and his fists clenched.

"Do you think this is him? Rupert Elmhurst, Emily's husband? Nobody ever really spoke about him. I imagine he's buried in France. There's a picture of her visiting war graves."

"It shouldn't be too hard to find out through the War Graves Commission," Matt says. "There's no mention of him or this photographer in any of the sources we have, but I guess there wouldn't have been. Kit's love affair was a big secret and his sweetheart wouldn't have met any of his inner circle. We don't know that much about his war either, since most of the evidence was destroyed, more's the pity, but I wish we did because it would really put his poetry into context. May I hold onto these for a bit?"

"Keep them, please. I've taken pictures of them on my phone."

Matt beams, genuinely thrilled. "Hey, thanks! Not a lot's known about Kit's earlier life, so this is an amazing find."

He's going to think he's won the lottery when I give him the rest, I think, as I reach into my bag and pull out the camera and the old sweet tin.

"Brace yourself. There's more."

"A Vest Pocket Kodak!" Matt takes the box and gently slides the camera out and whistles as he examines the concertinaed mechanism. "What a beauty! This must have belonged to our mystery photographer. They were really popular – the Soldier's Kodak was what they called it. Thousands of men took one of these to the front. See how it works? Look?"

I leave my chair, easier said than done because it's very soft and the rogue spring has caught in my jeans. I unhook it carefully while Waffles stretches and yawns. He's just dried off, his expression says, and he's not thrilled by the thought of moving. If a cockerpoo could use a phone, he'd be texting Steve and pleading for a lift home.

"This is one of the first ever portable cameras," Matt tells me, peering into the lens. "My goodness, what a find! It could even have film inside –

and the bellows still work! This must have belonged to our enigmatic photographer. Maybe he even took it to the war?"

"He did," I say.

Matt looks up from the fascinating workings of the camera.

"How do you know?"

"Have a look at what's in there," I gesture at the dented tin, "then come and find me. There's no hurry. Take your time."

Matt's grey eyes are filled with questions, but he doesn't argue. "I'll meet you in the café."

I pick up Waffles' lead, tugging the reluctant dog behind me. Just as I leave the office, I hear Matt gasp. If he truly wanted to know more about Kit Rivers' war I'd say he's got his wish. Black and white carnage. Blood and gore and deep, sucking mud. Barbed wire and rotting feet and death.

Maybe take care what you wish for?

Waffles and I walk through the empty museum. Rosecraddick Manor has been set up to look exactly as it would have done during the years of the First World War, and as I explore Lady Rivers' study and the deep crimson dining room it feels as though I'm an unwelcome intruder. Perhaps Kit and his parents are just a room ahead, or maybe Emily's behind me, her presence little more than the whisper of a gown across waxed floorboards or the sigh of a draught lifting the rugs in the long and shadowy corridors.

I follow the visitor trail past more empty rooms and through a gallery lined with glass cases exhibiting memorabilia from Kit's life. There are uniforms and diaries and pictures, amongst them that of a handsome young man, broad-chested and lantern-jawed, who stares at the camera with a gaze which even across a century is filled with confidence. A typed note beneath tells me that this is the same boy Matt mentioned, one Dickon Trehunnist, who was lauded in Rosecraddick for being the first to enlist. Was he brave? I wonder, as I peer closer. Did he, like my son, feel duty-bound to play his part? Or was he showing off to his friends and scoring points with the girls for signing up first? I guess I'll never know, but this proud pose, struck before a background of a drawing room, suggests he wasn't a shy and retiring young man.

The exhibits end, predictably, with a gift shop and tea room. Closed today, it's eerily still without ringing tills and hissing coffee machines. I take a chair down from one of the tables at the far end where the window overlooks a soggy courtyard. The cobbles beneath my feet and the intricate gullies suggest that this room was one of the stables in Kit's day, and as I sit at the table and scroll unseeingly through my Facebook feed I wonder whether Emily's grey horse would have ripped hay from the rack above my head. Had Emily stood on the mounting block outside? Or was she driven over there in a pony and trap so not to dirty her dress? I open up the photo library and study the pencil sketch of her and decide that she rode through the same woods I've trudged through earlier, maybe cantering along the tracks and jumping logs just as Pip and I once did. Emily might look the part, but the determined chin and the easy way her hands hold the double reins tell me she wasn't the type to be driven anywhere.

"There you are."

It's Matt, slightly paler-faced than earlier and with his hair standing in tufts as though he's been running his hands through it. Without saying a word, he lifts another chair down and joins me and for a few minutes we watch raindrops run down the windows like tears.

"Christ," he says finally.

I reach down and stroke the soft dome of Waffles' head.

"They're terrible, aren't they? In the true sense of the word, I mean."

"Absolutely. They're raw and harrowing works of absolute genius. Our mystery photographer had a real talent. There's no hiding from the pity of war with those."

"And are they of Kit Rivers?"

Matt takes off his glasses and starts to polish then with a serviette, but I know he's not seeing what he's doing but is years and miles away surrounded by mud and horrors; atrocities frozen both in time and now in his mind.

"Some of them, which makes this collection absolutely priceless. It's a wonderful find, Alison. Thank you so much for bringing them to me. I wish I hadn't seen them but I'm so glad I have, if that makes any sense?"

"It does. I can't bear to look at them."

Matt says nothing and suddenly I want to elaborate. There's something about him so gentle and so sympathetic that it invites confidences.

"My only son's serving in Afghanistan," I say quietly. "It's his second tour of duty."

This is usually the point in a conversation where the other speaker feels duty bound to tell me I must be proud/miss him, delete as appropriate, and I bifurcate, inwardly screaming while outwardly nodding and making all the right sounds. Nobody ever dares point out I must be worried sick because Jamie could be killed. They think it but they don't say it.

But all the hours spent walking alongside the shades of the First World War makes Matthew Enys unlike most other people.

"Those pictures are relentlessly graphic. All those boys being slaughtered. Seeing them must have felt way too close to home and utterly unbearable."

"Far too close," I agree. "I see those scenes everywhere now, and I don't want to. I have to put the reality of war out of my mind and do my best not to think about it at all, if that makes sense? Otherwise Jamie's job becomes unbearable for me. I'll fall apart if I let myself think about it."

"It totally makes sense. Kit talks about exactly that in 'Analgesia'. He wanted to numb his mind and distract himself in order to survive."

"And did he?"

"He decides not to. Kit chooses to feel everything rather than nothing. He concludes that not to feel is not to live: he may as well run into bullets as lose his sensibility."

"Kit never had a son fighting in a war zone," I say wryly.

"Yes, well …" Matt flushes, aware that his comments may not have been tactful, and I take pity on him.

"It's brave, given where he was and what was happening to him and his comrades," I add. "Keeping optimistic in the face of such awful odds is another kind of courage."

He brightens. "I think so, yes. These photos certainly give that poem, and so many of the others, even more poignancy."

"I'm glad they help."

"More than you can imagine. War photography was in its infancy then, so coming across these is an incredible find."

"There were war photographers in the First World War?"

"Absolutely! Newspapers were clamouring for pictures to illustrate dispatches from the front. It was all tightly controlled, though, because the authorities wanted to control the narrative. Their solution was to appoint official photographers like Ernest Brooks and do their best to ban the men from using cameras like the one you found. The army preferred scenes to be recreated or posed."

"Faked? Like those infamous *News of the World* shots?"

He laughs. "Don't they say there's nothing new under the sun? But yes, although 'staged' was the term used. There were strict rules regarding what could be shown but as we've seen it was impossible to control cameras, and soldiers continued to send pictures home."

"You think that's what our photographer was doing? Taking pictures to send his family? Would they want to see those?" My throat tightens at the mere thought of how it would feel to be sent something similar by Jamie. "Why would any young man want his loved ones to be faced with such things? Wouldn't that make it worse?"

Matt's dark brows draw together. "I agree. They're very graphic, and too well composed for lucky shots."

"Could they have belonged to another official war photographer?"

"No. These shots are too raw, and far from staged. I think they're the work of a professional photographer fighting at the front and trying to tell the truth of the conflict in the best way he knew. He wanted to convey the reality, and this was his means of doing so."

"Kit Rivers used poetry and this man used film," I say slowly. "They were doing the same job."

"Kit's in some of the pictures, here and at the front. They may have even been working together on something," Matt whispers. "This is incredible. It's a whole new layer to the story."

"But we don't know who he was, this photographer. He has no name. Nobody kept his memory alive."

"But we have his work, his incredible work, so he isn't lost if that remains. Nothing's ever forgotten, I promise you. You've brought him back to us, Alison, and I'll try my best to trace him for you."

But Matt Enys doesn't understand the unbearable ache of not knowing where a young man might fall and how he meets his end. I see rows of simple headstones stretching for miles and miles. Where does he rest? Is he at peace? And how have I ended up with what's left of his belongings? It has to be through Emily and my great-grandfather – but why has this never been mentioned? Why keep the camera and the pictures for over a century if they are meaningless? Something's missing.

Something important.

"How have his belongings ended up with me?" I ask, talking to myself, really, because Matt cannot know any more than I do. He can hypothesise, but the truth is somewhere in France, buried with iron and bones and bullets beneath fields of swaying poppies.

"Perhaps they were left somewhere when he returned from the war?" Matt suggests.

"I don't think he would have parted with them," I say, and he sighs.

"I agree. He went to great pains to take those photographs. Brooks suffered shell shock from what he saw, and I fear this man might have paid an even higher price. History's a mosaic of puzzles, and one of the things I love is doing my best to solve them. We have to use facts and guesswork and instinct to piece things together, and that's when the picture emerges. At least that's happened when we were researching Kit." He glances at his watch and rises from the table with a hurried scrape of the chair legs on stone. "Gosh! I've just seen the time. I'm afraid I have to scoot off to pick my daughter up for the orthodontist, but if you give me your number, I'll let you know what I can find out about your great-grandparents. And if there's anything on the film in that camera as well."

"I'm not sure I want to see it if there is," I confess.

"It's a big 'if' after all this time, but not impossible," Matt Enys says, "but you never know."

We leave the manor by means of a back door at the far end of the café. Matt setts alarms and secures locks, and as we walk around to the front of the house where the raked gravel drive loops around a neat turning circle of grass I imagine my great-grandmother arriving. Maybe this is where she met Rupert Elmhurst? Perhaps they fell in love here? The medieval manor house has a watchful air and there's a sense that time stands still, as though I've only just missed them walking by.

Matt offers me a lift home in his Defender but, and to Waffles' disgust – he loves car rides – I decline and instead take the path which leads into the woods, looping the site of what may have been my ancestral home before shadowing the path of the long-lost railway line. The rain still falls but beneath the trees it's little more than a soft patter. Waffles bounds ahead, leaping tangled roots and pausing to sniff delightedly at the foot of trees and knots of fallen branches.

Branches. Roots. Family trees. All of these are interwoven here and beyond. It's all here, laid out before me if only I knew where to look. I pause; something's just out of reach, something I can almost see is flickering caught in the corner of my eye. It's close, yet light years away.

I shake my head, perplexed because I have the strangest conviction that I've already found what I'm looking for. Which is odd, I realise, as I follow my dog along the soft muddy track and haul myself over the stile leading into our garden. Because until I'd opened my mother's boxes I hadn't realised that a part of me was even searching.

There's a shift. A lid lifts. Bright daylight trickles through cracks between newspaper, seeping through layers of playing cards and yellowed paper and mildewed books. The locket, alone and unloved in the bottom of the box, waits in its velvet swaddling while the papers above rustle, and cards slip and slide and resettle. The spine of a book cracks. The pages sigh. Muffled voices call. So close to liberation, yet still discovery hangs in the balance. It could be today or tomorrow or another lifetime away. The moment swings closer …

Footfalls recede and return. A cup chinks onto a surface. Boards creak. Even the rooks in the woods cease their cawing and the mice in the eaves pause.

Hands reach in. Items are lifted. Companions for decades, belongings are divided, examined and set asunder as their time together ends but, unnoticed and left until last, the pouch of worn velvet waits. The chain curls around the heavy silver locket like a cat's tail, prepared to settle back into repose or to pour like syrup into the first outstretched palm when the choice is made. Will it remain sleeping? Or will a wondering thumb trace the engravings and fingertips play with the clasp, urgent yet hesitant as they seek to open it?

As the years are sorted with each item sifted and every decade dusted down, the secrets hold their breath.

Not much longer now …

Chapter 6
Alison
Cornwall

"Yes, Pip, you were right, as always! Matt was really helpful."

I wedge the phone between my chin and collarbone while I give the bubbling soup a stir. Cally's due over to help with the last of the sorting, so in between deconstructing my visit to the manor and answering all Pippa's questions, I'm doing my best to prepare lunch without chopping off my fingers or scalding myself. It means a great deal to me that Jamie's girlfriend keeps in touch while he's away, and over the past few years we've become our own little support group. With both of us missing Jamie and anxiously awaiting his safe return, there's no need to explain or pretend. We understand each other perfectly.

"He's hot, isn't he?"

I turn the soup down before sliding bread rolls into the oven and shutting the door firmly, just as I'm going to shut a metaphorical one on this conversation. We're not fifteen any more, and running up huge phone bills while debating who's fittest, George Michael or Simon le Bon.

"I hadn't really noticed," I say primly, although of course I had – it would be impossible to not have been struck by those good looks.

Pippa snorts. "Fibber! You so did! He's lush and I totally *would*!"

I hop onto one of the stools at the kitchen island and slip the phone back into my hand.

"Would what?"

"*Would*. You know. *Would!*"

I raise my eyes to the ceiling. Pip loves teen slang. "Ah. And what would Billy make of that?"

"What's it got to do with Billy?"

"Oh nothing, except that you've been married to him for over twenty years!"

"Minor detail," says Pippa airily. "Anyway, everyone's allowed a hall pass. Bill's is Kelly Brook. If she ever comes along and fancies a balding middle-aged farmer, then he totally has my blessing for a one-off."

I'm not sure quite where this is going. Although Cornwall attracts celebrities who love to buy second homes here, they're mostly celebrity chefs rather than glamour models. And even if in a million to one chance Kelly Brook did choose to set up home in Rosecraddick I can't imagine farmer Billy would be her first choice.

"Aren't hall pass crushes meant to be hypothetical?" I ask doubtfully. "Celebrities rather than people you know?"

"Why? Who's yours?"

"I don't have one!"

"Bet you do," says Pip. "Not still Captain Kirk is it?"

"That was years ago!"

One of the worst things about having a best friend who's known you for ever is that they know all your embarrassing secrets from way back – and never forget them, either. Pippa's still teasing me about my bubble perm.

"Or is it Philip Schofield? Because I hate to break it to you, girlfriend, that ain't ever gonna happen now."

I start to laugh. "It's Jason Donovan, okay? But seriously, Pip, I don't think hall passes are real people you see on a daily basis, like your boss!"

"I'd have more chance with Philip. Matt's totally and utterly off the market," Pippa sighs. "Still, a middle-aged woman can dream."

"We're not middle-aged."

"We totally are, babes. We're older than Shirley Valentine was in the movie, and she was ancient!"

As Pip chatters on, I remind myself sharply how privileged I am to have made it far enough to see wrinkles, grey hairs, and my son grown up. Not many of the boys in those photographs made it into their twenties.

"All that aside, Matt's going to do what he can to find out a bit more about the photos," I tell my friend when she pauses for breath.

"If anyone can do it, he can," she says. "I can't wait to hear more about your mysterious photographer, and if he did snap Kit Rivers at the front. Oh! Hello, love! Did the zinc sulphate work on the foot rot?"

"I take it you're talking to Billy now?"

"Unless you've got a lame sheep I don't know about. Oi! Take your boots off! And those overalls! You're filthy! I'd better go before he destroys the place. Let me know if you and Cally find anything else exciting, okay? Love you."

"I can't imagine there's much left now —" I begin, but Pippa's already gone to shoo Billy out of her kitchen – and maybe into the arms of Kelly Brook. Smiling at this daft idea, I hop down from my stool and set the table. My heart lifts when I see Cally walking up the path to the back door to let herself in, just as she's done most days since she was sixteen, when Jamie, pink-faced and sweetly solicitous, first brought her home. Seeing my strapping son so gentle with this nervous girl was a privileged glimpse of the man and husband he would one day become; he was strong and kind, thoughtful and principled, and I couldn't have loved him more. I adore Cally because she sees in him all the wonderful things I do.

Maybe she'll be part of the family story one day I think as I open the door and give her a hug. It's strange because until yesterday family history wasn't something I'd given much thought to, but now I'm seeing it everywhere I look and making connections between past and present. From Emily to Grandma Ivy to Mum to me, and even to this slim girl chatting away while I ladle soup into bowls – we're all connected.

Cally and I sit down to eat, and I tell her a little about what I've found among my mum's things. When I come to the theory of a war photographer and mention the battle pictures, she looks stricken and her spoon clatters against the bowl.

"That must have been a shock."

"I could have done without it."

"I bet. It's strange Jam's nan never mentioned anything about them."

"She might not have known what was in there herself. The tin was really stuck shut, and it's mostly her mother's stuff, anyhow. Mum probably never got around to sorting it out, which is why it's been a bit of a double whammy for me."

"But didn't anyone ever talk about it? In my family everyone's always on about the olden days, especially my nan."

For Cally's generation the 'olden days' means about 1985. Her nan isn't much older than me.

I tear up a roll and butter it absently.

"Nobody ever talked much about the past in my family. There'd been a falling out at some point, I think. Her mother and grandmother didn't get on."

Cally stares at me across the kitchen island and I realise she's waiting for a story. Not having one to tell suddenly seems very odd.

"Why not?" she asks.

"I've absolutely no idea," I say slowly.

"Didn't you ask?"

"It never occurred to me. I suppose it didn't seem that important back then. Too late to ask now."

"Jam would be fascinated by this," she says.

I look up from my soup.

"Really?"

"Oh yeah. He's well in awe of the relative who got the medal. His great-

great-grandad, right? Jam told me all about it. He was a hero and saved a bunch of people in a battle."

I have no idea what Rupert Elmhurst did to win a medal, but it seems my son knows. Was it because of my great-grandfather's war efforts that Jamie was inspired to join the army? We don't even know if my great-grandfather wanted to fight or if he was conscripted. But has my son constructed his own narrative? Is he keeping up some family tradition that I didn't know about?

"I'm afraid I don't know much about it," I confess. "I can't even say what became of the medal. I hope it wasn't lost."

"It's in the Imperial War Museum. Your granny donated it when she was twenty-one," Cally says.

I put my spoon down, stunned. "Good Lord, did she? What else did Jamie discover?"

"That's about it. Jam wanted to know a bit about his great-grandfather, because he was a soldier too. Jam said he was never meant to be a soldier because he was at Oxford when the First World War started, but he gave it all up to fight. He must have been a really brave man to do that."

"Yes, I think he must have been. Goodness, Cally. I'm quite surprised. I wish Jamie had said he was interested in all this. I would have helped."

She shrugs. "He knows how you feel about him joining the army. I don't think he wanted to upset you. It wasn't a big deal, Alison. We got interested when we visited the manor and went to look at the names on the war memorial. My great-great-uncle's there too. Gem Pencarrow, he was called. He was only eighteen. A load of them joined up together and they left on the same day. In the film we saw it said they would have been really excited, like they were off on holiday."

I wonder if Gem Pencarrow is one of the boys in my photographs? So many of them are smooth-cheeked and horribly young. No wonder the war seemed a big adventure for them.

"We did the Kit Rivers walking trail last year," Cally explains. "Jam thought the memorial was fascinating, especially when Matt told some of the stories behind it. He said it made him think about friends he's lost."

We fall silent. I crumble my roll. When I glance at my plate it seems that each flake of crust is another part of my family past which has disintegrated and fallen away from what once appeared solid. It suddenly feels vitally important to catch hold of each detail and tether it with pen and ink.

"I'll write notes on whatever I find out for him to read at when he comes home," I say finally.

'When he comes home' is a mantra we repeat often.

"I think he'd like that," Cally agrees.

Once the dishwasher is loaded and humming away to itself, I make coffee and we head up to the spare room.

"Wow, you've been busy." Cally's eyes widen at the newly revealed bright patches on the carpets, ghostly reminders of boxes and bin bags. "It must have taken hours. Were you at it all day?"

"I got summit fever," I admit.

"My mum gets like that. She loves a good declutter, says it's good for the soul."

I'm not convinced this activity has done my soul any favours. My eyes feel gritty from my fitful night and my dreams will be haunted for ever as I carry those graphic images with me.

Cally perches on the window sill and tucks hanks of blonde hair behind her ears.

"What can I do? Whizz a hoover round? Carry some bin bags out?"

"In a bit. There's a couple more boxes left first and that tatty old suitcase. Why don't you give me a hand with those? We can go on sorting out what to keep and what to throw."

Cally springs to her feet and bounds over to the suitcase. Battered at the corners and dented, it's already in bad repair, and when she pops the catches open the lid's only just hanging on. The lining is stained and the faint smell of burning seeps out. She wrinkles her nose.

"Gross. Why would your mum keep this? It's falling to bits."

"No idea, love. She kept all kinds of strange junk."

She shuts the lid and the smell recedes. "Do you want to keep it, Alison? You could restore it like on The Repair Shop."

"Bin pile," I say firmly. "We can't keep it all. Come and have a look in this."

I kneel down and open up the penultimate box. It's light and I think it's full of clothing. Mum hated to throw fabric away and always had plans for patchwork quilts made from my old summer dresses and snippets of curtains. When we'd cleared her cottage, two of my father's Harris tweed jackets were still hanging in the wardrobe and wrapped in his scent. I'd buried my face in them, the scratchy fabric against my skin tugging me backwards through the years until I was a child once more and utterly bereft. Later on, when tearstained and wobbly from emotional time travel, I gently asked Mum if she'd kept them as a memento of my father she dismissed the notion outright and muttered something about wanting to make cushions. I never knew if she was telling me the truth, afraid perhaps to reopen a wound that was only just starting to heal, and by the final stage she was often confused. Now I'll never have an answer.

Whatever Mum's intentions may have been, I kept one of those jackets. It never became a cushion but hangs in our spare wardrobe and sometimes, when life feels a little too much to bear, I open the door to press my cheek against the tweed and feel safe again …

"Maybe we'll find some interesting stuff," Cally says hopefully, joining me to sit cross-legged on the floor.

"Don't get your hopes up. It's probably all jumble," I say as I pull out an old and threadbare silk kimono, something I can remember hanging on the back of Mum's bedroom door and a honeymoon relic. "See what I mean?"

But Cally's delighted with this find and jumps to her feet, holding the faded silk against her. "That's gorgeous! Can I have it if you don't want it?"

She waltzes around the room with the silk swirling, and I laugh.

"Be my guest! Help yourself to whatever you want, but don't blame me if your mum isn't happy!"

This sets the tone for the next hour or so and I unearth old hats and scarves and lurid cheesecloth sweaters. By the time we're almost at the end of the final box, Cally has acquired a huge pile of clothes, and the bin liners little more than old newspapers, a bunch of dried roses which shed petals like dead skin, the old quilt and a deck of mouse-nibbled playing cards. My work here is done.

"I think this calls for a coffee and some cake," I declare, gathering up the rubbish and admiring the room. It's bigger than I'd thought and, now that the storm has passed, is filled with watery sunlight. Steve can kiss farewell to his gym. This is perfect for a craft room or studio. I might have a go at painting again. I used to love art when I was at school.

"Can you grab those boxes and carry them down? It's recycling day tomorrow," I say to Cally, who's still cramming treasures into a bin bag she's snaffled for herself. I can't imagine her mum will be thrilled when it arrives back at their house, but my son's girlfriend is a budding hoarder.

She picks up the nearest box. "No problem. Oh! Hold on, we've missed something."

"Not more," I groan.

Cally delves deep and draws out a small package, her forehead creasing as she weighs it in her palm. It's a black velvet bag, the fabric so old it appears almost green, and she offers it to me.

"There's something in it. I think you need to look."

There are moments in life when you can sense that everything you know is about to shift, the past pivoting on the present and moving the future in a whole new direction. The hairs on the nape of my neck prickle and the air in the spare room is thick and heavy.

"Alison?" Cally prompts, holding the package out to me.

Reluctantly I take it from her, surprised by the weight within the fabric, and begin to unpeel the layers. I'm not sure what I expect to find within, but whatever it is it's been well protected – or well hidden, depending on your point of view.

There's a sigh of metal against velvet. Fine chain slides across my fingers like syrup. Metal rests in my palm, heavy and surprisingly warm. Instinctively, and as though they have done so a thousand times before, my fingers curl around it. Although it's dark with tarnish and the patina of years as I relax my grasp and run my thumb over the engraved surface, I know this piece was once beautiful and treasured.

Cally peers over my shoulder.

"A locket. Cool! It looks old. Like they'd wear in Downton Abbey."

I look at the ornate engravings, all elaborate swirls and flourishes, and feel the weight heavy and true. It's an expensive, if old-fashioned, piece.

"If it's from that era it could have belonged to my great-grandmother," I say.

The air in the room seems to shift as though agreeing.

"Is she the one whose pictures you gave Matt? Who knew the poet? From the house that burned down?" asks Cally excitedly.

"Yes. Her maiden name was Emily Pendennys, I believe, and later Elmhurst when she married my great-grandfather, the one with the medal you were talking about earlier. I think this belonged to her."

"A family heirloom," breathes Cally.

I tentatively trickle the chain through my fingers until the locket swings, pendulum-like, slicing the air and testing its freedom. We watch it as though hypnotised and as it spins, the light catches the reverse side and picks out engraved letters.

"Something's written on the back." Cally catches the locket so that I can see what has caught her attention. "It's faint but it's definitely there."

She's right. There is text, blackened by time and sleeping beneath the decades. I scrape tarnish away with my nail.

Alex,

Your wings were ready.

My heart was not.

One of the letters is wobbly, as though whoever engraved it had lost focus for a split second, but this doesn't detract from the simplicity of the words which keep an old grief raw, as though the passing of the years have done nothing to soothe the loss. Whoever this Alex may have been, my great-grandmother Emily kept him close to her heart for an entire lifetime.

But why, when my great-grandfather was called Rupert? Maybe I'm totally wrong and this was never hers at all.

"Are you going to open it?" Cally asks.

I nod. "Let's see what's inside."

The clasp is stiff and my fingers fumble before my nail finds the spot. There's a sharp click and the locket springs open, a tight clam of secrets forced open by my curiosity, and suddenly I have even more questions, all of which only have one answer ...

"Oh! How strange!" Cally exclaims, peering over my shoulder. "That looks exactly like —"

"Jamie," I finish.

The picture inside the locket, although black and white and rendered faint with time, is so familiar that if I hadn't known it was impossible, I would have sworn I was looking at my own son. The wide brown eyes, strong chin, dimpled cheek and mop of unruly curls are all Jamie's, and yet not his, either. Who is this stranger with my son's face?

"I don't understand," says Cally, puzzled. "Why does he look just like Jam?"

I think I know, and it's hard to articulate what I'm feeling. When I was child I used to have a puzzle that I loved playing with. It was a simple toy and worked by sliding square pieces about until you recreated a picture. The pieces were muddled up and I would spend hours moving them about, frowning because no matter what I did the picture was still wrong, making no sense at all even though the parts I'd rearranged had almost seemed to make meaning. Then, more by chance than by design, I would slide one random square into a new position, and it was done! The pieces slipped into place and the whole picture was complete and clear.

And this exactly is what just happened when I opened the locket. The final piece of a puzzle shifted and now I understand exactly what I'm looking at. I understand everything.

I search for the words to explain but before I can say a word there's a sharp blast from the doorbell, followed instantly by another and yet another.

Cally jumps to her feet. "Who on earth are you expecting?"

"It's probably DPD for Steve. I bet he's been ordering gym equipment," I say, starting to get up.

"I'll go," she says. "You look like you need to stay sitting down. You've gone a really funny colour."

Cally shoots out and I remain kneeling on the carpet with the open locket swinging from my fingertips. Jamie, who isn't Jamie, smiles up at me, voices rise and fall, the front door slams and two sets of feet thud their way upwards.

"You've got a visitor," Cally says.

Matt Enys is standing at the top of the landing, hair on end and face flushed as though he's been running.

"I'm so sorry to descend on you unannounced like this, Mrs Foy – Alison – but you weren't answering your phone," he pants. "I couldn't risk you throwing it out, so I had to come as soon as I realised."

I have no idea what Matt's talking about but it's obviously urgent if it's sent him tearing from the manor in such a hurry. Perplexed, I'm about to ask what the *it* he's referring to might be when his gaze alights on the small suitcase in my bin pile.

"Oh, thank God! It's still here!" He sags against the door jamb, holding his side and pointing to it. "May I? If I'm right, then this is huge!"

"I told you it was worth keeping," Cally says.

"It's priceless," Matt says.

"Help yourself," I tell him. "I'm afraid you'll be disappointed, though, because it's empty."

But he looks far from disappointed.

"If I'm right, that's just an illusion. Sorry, I'm not explaining myself very well, am I? It's all been a bit overwhelming. You hear about this kind of thing all the time, but you never think it'll happen to you. Lightning not striking twice and all that. I ran all the way from the manor because Chloe has the car. Can you believe it? Me? Running?"

"Catch your breath. Then tell me, slowly, what's up," I order, slipping effortlessly into mother hen mode. Matt does as he's told, shrugging off his gilet and lowering his lanky body onto the bed. I close the locket and slip it into my pocket, and fetch him a glass of water. When I return with a full tumbler Matt's breathing is less ragged, and he has laid out curling scraps of paper all over the counterpane which he's showing to Cally. Wound tight as springs, each faded coil is smothered in handwriting.

"They're letters written to the front by Alison's great-grandmother," he explains. "When I opened the camera to see if there was a film inside I found over twenty of these letters curled up and hidden away. The man it belonged to had treasured every single one."

"But no more pictures?" Cally asks, sounding disappointed.

"This is even better than that! These letters tell us everything about life at home during that time and the people here who lived through the war," Matt says, beaming. "They're a voice from the past linking everything together. Emily's voice. I've read them, Alison, I hope that's okay? I couldn't help myself."

I pass him the drink and perch on the window ledge while he sips. I daren't mention the locket because the poor guy will pop.

"It's absolutely fine, Matt. You're the expert, after all."

"But you're Emily's family, and this is first and foremost a family matter. A family secret."

I slip my hand into my pocket and close my fingers around the heavy weight of the locket, as I feel sure my great-grandmother must have done a thousand times, and I already know what he has discovered. I don't need letters to tell me what secrets my great-grandmother was keeping.

"What secret?" Cally asks. Her pretty face is confused. "And what's with the suitcase? If it's empty, I mean?"

"It isn't empty," he tells her. "Far from it. In one of her letters Emily describes exactly what's inside it and where. May I show you?"

"Please," I say.

He fetches the case and opens it tenderly, his fingers caressing the flaking leather as though reassuring it. The faint smell of scorching drifts through the room as his hands smooth the lining, coaxing the aged fabric to give up his secrets and pleading with it to yield before he tugs a little harder and the aged material gives way to the pressure. I feel as pang of shock as stitches rip apart and the lining falls away.

"You've torn it," Cally wails.

"I'm sorry, but this the only way I can dislodge these without damaging them. Watch."

And all at once, like a magician conjuring a rabbit from an empty hat, Matt is drawing handfuls of paper from the inside of the lining. What an ingenious hiding place! Nobody would have had any idea that tucked beneath the worn lining is a treasure trove of secrets. As Matt lays them out on the bed I see birth and death certificates, official sheets of thick cream paper covered with swirling signatures, deeds, newspaper pages and letters, tens of letters, millions of words which have stowed away and sailed through the years inside this threadbare lining. Cally and I watch in amazement as the loyal little suitcase surrenders the secrets it has guarded for over a century.

Deep in my pocket, the locket seems to grow heavier by the second.

"It's here. It's really here."

Matt retrieves the final envelope. Addressed in an elegant, slanting script, it rests in his hands while he stares down at it reverently.

"My God," he breathes as he opens the flap and draws out a sheet of paper. "The Last Summer."

"The missing poem you told me about? Kit's poem?" I'm staggered. "My mum had it all the time?"

He nods. "It suddenly occurred to me Kit might have sent it to Emmy when Rupert died. I realised she would have hidden it away with the rest of her precious things to pass on to baby Ivy."

Cally looks from Matt to me.

"Emmy? You mean Emily, Alison's great-grandmother?"

"Yes, sorry. She's become Emmy to me now after reading her letters and seeing the pictures. It was their last summer, you see: Emmy, Rupert,

Kit and —" He swallows, and I realise he's afraid of upsetting me by saying the wrong thing.

"And Alex," I finish.

Matt's mouth falls open, "How did you know?"

I take the locket from my pocket and open it, resting the case in my palm. The handsome young man my great-grandmother kept close to her heart for her whole life, this Jamie yet not Jamie, smiles at us through time and across the dusty years.

"Alex," whispers Matt.

"Alex," I nod. "He's the missing piece of the puzzle, and the one who photographed, and began, it all."

"He really did. More than he ever knew." Matt rises to his feet, swaying as though exhausted. "I need to get back to the manor to examine this properly and make some calls. Will you let me know when you've read the letters and looked at all these new pictures? No matter what time? I want to know what you think and what you want to do." He passes a hand over his face. "I don't think I'll be able to think about anything else. Have you any idea how huge this is?"

I do know. I've seen the tourists and watched the film. That my own family are entwined with the Kit Rivers story, that they have played their own part in literary history, is incredible; and tangled up with all of this is the truth about my own grandmother. Ivy's anger with her mother and our lost family history is contained within these tight epistles. Secrets are poised to leap out from the paper coils, and I won't rest until I've read every decades-old word. I'll read until the sun rises tomorrow if I must.

Once Matt has left, clutching the precious poem, and driven home by Cally because he looks too shocked to walk far at all, I collect up each curling letter and place them in a pile. The yellowed newspaper front page which shows the carcass of a house that had been engulfed in flames I lay on the bed, and then I sift through the photographs. There's a wedding photo of Emily standing beside the dark-haired boy who had been pictured in uniform alongside Kit. Rupert Elmhurst, the war hero, I think to myself, and he looks as serious here and as distant as a man who had seen the horrors of trench warfare might look. He certainly isn't a smiling groom, and Emily is pinched-faced and has dark smudges beneath her eyes. I put them aside and study the others. There's a chubby baby in a pram outside a pretty farmhouse I recognise from the edge of the village, all sage paint now and the second home of a wealthy Londoner, but rougher here in the black and white days and with a stooped old man and a plump woman flanking the gate. More pictures spill out – a girl on a pony, Emily leading a plough horse. An older Emily, with the elderly man haymaking. A little girl cuddling a chicken. Emily standing in a sea of war graves holding the little girl. Snapshots of the forgotten life which overlaps my own.

I carry everything downstairs to the sitting room and spread them out on the coffee table, before opening the locket once more.

"I'm ready to hear your story, Alex," I say.

Then I pick up the first curl of letter, smooth it flat against the table top, and begin to read.

Snapshots of the Past

1913–1918

Emily Pendennys' Sixteenth Birthday Photograph

Rowes' Photographic Studios

16th July 1913

Emmy Pendennys felt mutinous. Clinging to the bedpost while Henny
yanked at her stays, she gritted her teeth and did her best to focus on the
glorious day beyond her window. After days of rain scribbling out any view
and storms bruising the sky purple and navy, it was a welcome change to
see blue skies and sunshine. Misty and Hector were grazing side by side in
the paddock and Simmonds was toiling over rose beds, waging his endless
war on weeds and slugs. In the distance the sea was a sparkling blue smudge
in a dip between hills of deep and secretive green. Yes, it was a beautiful day
indeed, although one which still failed to raise her spirits.

Emmy sighed. She wasn't sure anything could, not when a girl was
trussed up like a chicken for the pot and trapped in a hot bedroom – and
on her sixteenth birthday to boot. She should be outside, walking in the
woods where nobody would notice or care if she abandoned her hat, kicked
off her boots and curled her toes into cool, damp grass. Better still, she
could be galloping Misty across one of the shorn fields with the wind
whipping her hair from her cheeks and his hooves digging into the soft
earth before his muscles bunched and they leapt over the bank to tear away
into the trees. After days of being cooped up in the house with Henny
looking over her shoulder and nagging about deportment and French verbs,
Emmy was itching to jump fences, both literal and metaphorical.

"Stand still, Emily! Breathe in!"

Henny pulled the laces so violently Emmy feared she would be cut in
two. Whalebone bit into her rib cage and her insides felt as though they
might burst as each tug forced more breath from her body. It was
becoming harder to breathe with each pull.

"Ouch! That really hurts!"

Henny shook her head. "I've never heard such nonsense in all my days. It's not nearly tight enough for this dress. You're making a dreadful fuss."

Pink-cheeked from her exertions, Henny lifted a chicken claw of a hand to poke a stray pin back into her bun. Emmy often imagined her head as one giant pincushion. The hair bullied back from a pale scalp was secured so tightly that it was no wonder Miss Henwood was always in a bad temper; she must have a constant headache. As she inhaled and opened her mouth to continue berating her latest charge, Emmy was already reciting the words she knew from bitter experience were forming on Henny's lips as surely as night follows day. It was her governess's catechism: 'The honourable Eleanor Banbury and her sisters …'

Any second now …

"The honourable Eleanor Banbury and her sisters would never dream of making such a fuss," Henny panted, placing her palm in the small of Emmy's back and resuming her task with the same brute force Simmons employed when tightening Misty's girth. "They were well-bred young ladies who knew how to behave themselves as befitted their station."

Emmy had never met the Banbury sisters, but she knew all about Henny's last charges, who were so 'saintly and well behaved they were right up there with Jesus and all the angels as far as she could gather. They never argued or answered back, muddied their hems or tore their skirts. Their school books had never seen a blot or a crossing out, and they certainly didn't know any bad language. Their hair was set each night in rags rather than knotting itself in wild curls, and their white-as-milk skin was a stranger to freckles. They sat nicely at the table, smoothed napkins across silken skirts and never spoke unless spoken to. They were paragons of virtue, from all accounts, and although Emmy thought they sounded dreadfully dull, were sorely missed by Henny, who found life at Pendennys Place something of a trial.

"You've laced it too tightly," Emmy protested. Was her face turning blue?

"Nonsense," puffed Henny. "It's not nearly tight enough. That dress needs a waist of no more than twenty inches. You're not used to it, that's all. Breathe in, dear, and do stand still!"

Emmy had never worn a corset, so she supposed Henny must be right. There hadn't been any need for one before. Growing up at Pendennys Place, she'd never been anywhere that had necessitated fashion. Sometimes she took tea at Rosecraddick Manor, home to her godmother's family, and if Papa was sober enough they would venture to St Nonna's on a Sunday or take the odd trip to Truro. When she wasn't under the eagle eye of the latest governess, Emmy spent most of her time riding Misty or roaming through the woods on foot, and Mrs Puckey, their housekeeper, wasn't interested in London styles. Neither was Simmonds, once Papa's batman and now the general jack of all trades. Emmy's dresses were mostly cobbled together from Mama's old clothes, and she quite liked this, feeling it brought her closer to the mother she had never known.

Henny continued to pull in the stays while Emily hugged the bedpost, hoping she wouldn't pass out. She wondered how long it would be before Henny concluded you really couldn't make a silk purse out of a sow's ear, as she often liked to sigh when she pored over Emmy's smudged handwriting Hopefully, not too long. She was sixteen now; surely this was old enough for her formal education to cease? It was something of a patchwork anyway, and unlike her friend Rupert, who had aspirations to read law at Oxford, Emmy knew she wasn't destined for university. Quite what she did want to do Emmy wasn't certain – but one thing she did know for a fact: it wasn't dressing up like a porcelain doll to pour tea, make polite chit-chat and find a wealthy husband.

Her godmother, Lady Rivers, had done her best to instil ladylike manners in Emmy, mainly because she had decided long ago that Emmy would marry her son in order to double the Rosecraddick estate acreage. Lady Rivers believed that young women of good breeding required a very precise skill set, including embroidery, dancing and a little French conversation – all talents which she believed, quite rightly, her god-daughter lacked. Sporadically a new governess would arrive at Pendennys Place and Emmy would have lessons and regular meals in the nursery, and drag a brush through her hair. Unfortunately for Lady Rivers these doughty spinsters tended to depart fairly swiftly, usually once they realised their salary, if indeed they ever received it, was not enough to compensate for living in the middle of nowhere, in a damp house with no electricity or indoor plumbing, and with a master whose temper was at best erratic and at worst absolutely terrifying. They would pack, and beg Simmonds to harness the dogcart to drive them to Rosecraddick Halt, and Emmy would be left to work her way through her father's impressive library and please herself until the next incumbent arrived.

If Emmy's father was in one of his sunny moods he might ask her to read to him, and they would spend a pleasant hour or two discussing Caesar's Gallic wars or swapping tales about hunting. These periods were like glimpses of sunlight between storm clouds and as rare and magical as summer lightning. They never lasted long before the dark spells descended once more, necessitating much tiptoeing and eggshell walking by everyone in the household. Simmonds would scrub the earth from his hands and brush horsehair from his breeches and become the batman once again, tending to her father behind closed doors, whence shouts and clatters punctuated the stillness like gunshots. Pendennys Place seemed to hold its breath during these times, and Emmy would scurry away to the woods or hide behind the library curtains with a book if the weather was bad and pretend she couldn't hear his screams and sobs.

Her papa was a great hero, everyone said so, and his terrible injuries dreadfully hard to bear for a man who had once been so strong and led men into battle. Mrs Puckey always said that if he sometimes became angry then it wasn't to be taken personally, but Emmy, often the recipient of a curse or a blow from a well-aimed book (losing a leg hadn't diminished Julyan's ability to hit a moving target) found this hard to believe. It was even harder not to feel hurt when he yelled at her to get out of his sight or said he wished she and not her brother had died.

"What use are you?" he would rage, face scarlet and lips flecked with saliva as he pounded his fist on his desk in time with each ugly word. "What use is a girl? Why couldn't it have been you with a broken neck instead of Morvan? Get out of my sight!"

Emmy would run at this point, but no matter how fast her legs carried her or how good her hiding place the words always followed her and so did the images of seeing her brother carried into the hall on a sheep hurdle, his neck lolling at an angle that had made her feel sick. She hadn't needed to hear her father's howl to know Morvan was dead. Sometimes when she woke up at night, her mouth dry and her heart hammering, she saw his glassy eyes staring up at the ceiling, the thin trickle of blood snail-trailing from his left nostril and the scarlet roses blooming in his white stock.

Morvan was gone at just sixteen, the same age she was today, and now there was only her left to bear the family name. As Henny tweaked ribbons and smoothed lace, Emmy wondered whether it was the corset after all that was choking her. The girl in the looking-glass peered back with troubled eyes, and Emmy thought her narrow shoulders seemed far too slight to carry such a weight. What if her father was right? What if the wrong child had been taken?

Mrs Puckey always said that the master didn't mean a word of it, and this was the drink talking. Simmonds tried to tell her it was pain and laudanum stealing his senses, but Emmy knew better. When he was drinking Julyan spoke the truth. He really did wish her brother had lived instead of her, and sometimes Emmy almost agreed with him because a son was far more useful to the estate than a daughter. A son could make his fortune. A son could take up his place in the army and win glory. A son could pay back the debts accrued from a lifetime of gambling and poor choices. But a daughter couldn't do much at all except marry, and Emmy didn't think she would ever do that.

No thank you. If husbands were anything like her father, Emmy would rather be a nun. Rupert had once offered gallantly to marry her if she was ever desperate to escape. Although she loved Rupert dearly, having grown up alongside him and her godmother's son, Kit, Emmy didn't want to marry him in the slightest. He was like a brother to her, as was Kit, who Emmy knew she was supposed to marry. Nothing much had ever been said about this; it was one of those things you just grew up knowing, but Emily had no intention of obliging, and neither did Kit. They'd shared some lessons, often attended the same parties, hunt balls and soirées, and she'd known him for ever – but marry him? Kit? With his nose always in a book and his talk of being a poet?

The mere thought was ridiculous.

Henny placed her hands around Emmy's waist. "They almost meet!"

Emmy pulled a face. "It's too tight."

"Stop fussing. It's a beautiful corset, and the petticoats are exquisite. You're a very lucky young lady."

"Mmm," said Emmy. The girl in the looking-glass gave her a doubtful frown.

"This dress, all the way from Paris too, and a visit to a photographer's studio for a birthday portrait," Henny continued, opening the large, flat box which Simmonds had carried upstairs and placed on the bed. "She's even sending the carriage. Your godmother's a very generous woman."

Emmy nodded while her reflection rolled impatient green eyes. Although this gift was undoubtedly generous, her everyday boots pinched and her dresses were getting too short, and she would have preferred something a little more practical. The corset was accompanied by an exquisite white dress, and like everything Lady Rivers had, it was beautiful and fashionable. Emmy could already see how the corset, worn over a delicate lawn chemise, skimmed the chest before falling down to the thighs in the latest style. With its extravagant lace, pink ribbons and beautiful embroidery the corset was a work of art as much as an undergarment and moulded her slender body into a curvaceous shape that was new and surprising. This was a dress to make Henny's proverbial sow's ear into a silk purse and, although a sixteenth birthday gift, far from unconditional. Emmy feared her godmother had decided the time had come to press for an engagement.

Her heart fluttered beneath the corset like a caged bird. What was she going to do? The last time she and Kit talked about this issue had been months ago at the hunt ball. They'd danced together as they had always done since they were small, but Emmy had been acutely conscious of Colonel and Lady Rivers watching them closely.

"Oh Lord, Ma's got her matchmaking face on," sighed Kit. "Don't look so worried, Emmy, there's no way I'd ever marry you. You're far too active. I feel exhausted just watching you charge around."

"I don't charge around," Emmy protested, but Kit had laughed.

"You most certainly do. You're always stomping through the woods or galloping about on that mad horse of yours. No, when I settle down it's going to be with a girl who likes books and poetry as much as I do."

Emmy understood. Everyone agreed that Kit Rivers was brilliant. He spent a lot of his time reading, and as much as she loved books Emmy far preferred being outside to sitting still. She wasn't sure what kind of man might want to marry a girl like her. Maybe she wouldn't marry at all but would make her own fortune or travel the world. Quite how all this would come about Emmy wasn't sure, but she was certain she wasn't destined to become the next Lady Rivers. However, she was beginning to feel uneasy. Kit was a determined young man, but he was also very sensitive, and although Colonel Rivers wasn't quite as volatile as Julyan Pendennys he was certainly a bully. Kit was already torn between his longing to study at Oxford and following in his father's military footsteps, and so Emmy feared her friend might crumple under any further pressure. Then it would be down to her to refuse.

Emmy hoped she was brave enough to do so. When Lady Rivers turned her blue gaze on you the temperature plummeted by several degrees and her icy temper could cause frostbite. She was not a woman easily crossed. And if Emmy did defy her godmother and refuse to marry Kit, what then? She had nothing of her own and no real education to speak of, because everybody knew education wasn't important for a well-bred young woman, no matter what the suffragettes might argue. Emmy had learnt early on that her sole purpose in life was to marry well. There was no need to go to university to find a suitable husband when your family name and estate featured in Debrett's, even if the money was long gone, and every now and then another picture vanished from the drawing room or a first edition-shaped hole would gape on a bookshelf like a tooth pulled from an increasingly gappy mouth. Although Julyan sometimes enjoyed discussing his books with Emmy, he believed she didn't need to know about Latin or French verbs or geography; she just needed to marry well. Besides, she could sit a horse well in the hunting field and had a pretty face, which he said was all a man really cared about in a wife.

As Henny chatted away about photographic studios and birthday lunch at a hotel, Emmy reflected on just how different her life might have been if Morvan had lived. How was it possible that one horse pecking on landing could change everything? Her big brother had shared Emmy's dark hair, green eyes and love of adventure, and had been her protector when their father rumbled his bath chair along the bottom corridor, yelling out in rage. They would have shared a tutor, and she might have even gone to university. Perhaps she could have even been a veterinarian? Emmy loved animals and Simmonds said she had the magic touch with horses, while the local hunt master sang her praises regarding the hound puppy she'd nursed back to health. But women weren't supposed to have dreams, unfair as this seemed; they had to do their duty. This was their lot in life.

Emmy needed air. Being a girl was smothering.

"Away from the window, Emily!" cried Henny, shooing her away in horror. "You're in your undergarments!"

"We're miles from anywhere!"

"That's by the by, young lady. Mr Simmonds is in the garden!"

Emmy laughed at this because Simmonds didn't count. Simmonds was practically family. He'd fished her out of ponds, taught her to ride and helped to bury her brother, and every day he performed duties for Julyan that most people would baulk at. But Henny wouldn't understand this. As far as she was concerned Simmonds was just a servant – and worse, a man, so not to be trusted.

"Lady Rivers' carriage will be here any moment, and I can't imagine your godmother will be pleased to see you hanging out of the window in your shift! Away from there!"

Taking pity on her governess, Emmy did as she was told. It might be her birthday, but it was clearly a day for taking orders. Wishing she could be out in the garden with Simmonds, pulling up weeds and listening to him explain what was best planted where, she turned away from the window. The corset rendered movement difficult and breathing even more so. No wonder her godmother was always reaching for smelling salts.

"My, this is absolutely splendid," Henny breathed, sounding envious as she lifted the white silk and organza gown from its box. Maybe she was envious, Emmy realised with a dart of pity on her governess's behalf. In her late fifties, her thinning brown hair shot through with silver, and a shapeless frame hidden beneath dung-coloured gowns, Henny was as likely to wear a dress like this one as Emmy was to fly to the moon. Did dour Miss Henwood secretly dream of balls and parties? Had there ever been a young man who had swept her off her feet? Who had she been before she had become so old?

Emmy hadn't thought about this before. Pondering such notions made her feel kinder, and she allowed Henny to help her into the dress without a single complaint. The twenty pearl buttons at the back of the gown were fastened, her stockinged feet slipped into elegant white button-boots and her dark hair topped with a huge cartwheel of a hat. When Henny stood back to admire her handiwork, Emmy scarcely recognised this stylish young woman in the mirror with her hourglass waist and swelling bosom. She didn't look anything like herself. She didn't *feel* anything like herself. How she wished she could shed the whole lot like a snake its skin and escape into the woods to listen to the birds and find herself again.

Emmy glared and her reflection glowered back.

"You'll get stuck like that if the wind changes," warned Henny, draping a shawl around her shoulders.

"Good," muttered Emmy. Maybe then she'd be left in peace rather than dressed up and paraded around like a china doll.

With Henny grasping her elbow in the manner of a gaoler escorting a prisoner who might make a break for freedom at any moment, Emmy descended the sweeping staircase. She could barely move a step without wincing and there was no possibility of being able to walk freely or run dressed like this, which she supposed was the point. Demure and dainty, dressed in white and clad in the latest Parisian fashion, she was everything a well brought up young lady was supposed to be.

The impressive entrance hall, a cavernous space with vaulted panelled ceiling, busts of long dead Romans skewered on plinths and vast marble fireplace all chosen by Emmy's grandfather to impress visitors and illustrate his vast wealth, was dark even on such a sunny day. Emmy glanced about in case Julyan was wheeling his chair through the shadows to wish her a happy birthday, but only Mrs Puckey was present to hold the front door open.

"You look lovely, Miss Emmy," she said. "Don't get that lace mucky, now! It'll be the very devil to get clean."

"Miss Pendennys won't be going anywhere she might get dirty," snapped Henny, propelling Emmy past the housekeeper and into the sunshine. She was always impatient with the staff, finding them too informal and lacking the respect she felt her position ought to command. She had tried to assert her authority, but, aware her reign at Pendennys Place would be short, Mrs Puckey and Simmonds politely ignored her and continued as always.

Mrs Puckey, to whom it usually fell to scrub the grass stains from hems and mend the thorn tears in skirts, gave her a knowing wink. 'I know you're still under there, my girl!' it said, and Emmy instantly felt better. Mrs Puckey was also making saffron buns especially for her birthday tea, so all was not lost. She took a deep breath, squared her shoulders and walked into the sunshine where Lady Rivers was waiting in the carriage with her smartly liveried groom. A few hours and this would all be over.

Emmy had forgotten how a few hours with her godmother could feel like a lifetime. The ride into town would have been pleasant, watching buttercup-dusted fields rolling by and the sea playing hide and seek in the valleys, but in the unaccustomed corset it was hard to think about much at all except breathing, and under her godmother's critical eye she had to sit up straight with her gloved hands neatly folded in her lap. While Lady Rivers spoke about hats and the latest society gossip, Emmy nodded in what were hopefully the right places while daydreaming about cantering Misty through the shorn wheat fields. What wouldn't she give to feel the wind on her cheeks and blowing through her hair! Henny had done a sterling job of pinning the hat and roses into position, but in her enthusiasm she had pulled Emmy's hair so tightly that her head ached and the pins bit into her scalp. A headache nibbled at her temples and it took all her willpower to keep her hands in her lap rather than ripping off the hat and tossing it away to sail over the hills and out to France.

Although the breeze was cool, the heavy dress stuck to Emmy's legs; sweat prickled from her shoulder blades, and the sleeves clung to her skin. Even her feet felt hot and bothered. It seemed very unfair to Emmy that on her own birthday she should have to endure such torture, but nobody ever thought to consult her about what she wanted. As Lady Rivers described the garden party she was holding the following month, Emmy had the horrible suspicion that she had stepped into her future life, a never-ending carousel of smart engagements and social gatherings where she would be dressed up, paraded around and expected to make polite chit-chat.

It would be totally and utterly unbearable.

Emmy's temples pounded more with each hoofbeat, and beneath the lace and silk and whalebone resentment and fear simmered in her heart. By the time the carriage was rattling over the cobbles at the edge of Bodmin, she had to grip her hands together very tightly to stop herself from crying. Luckily, life with Julyan had taught Emmy something about willpower – it never did to cry when he was angry because tears only made him worse – so she always focused very hard instead on riding Misty through the woods, closing her eyes and imagining the cool depths at the heart of the trees and the muffled thud of hoofbeats upon the damp earth. Maybe she could even persuade Simmonds to let her ride astride in father's saddle? Then she could dare herself to jump the big ditch at the farthest end where the trees met Halt Lane. Flying through the air with her fingers wound in the silvery mane and her stomach swooping with that wonderful blend of terror and excitement was the best way Emmy had ever found to escape all her troubles. Faster and faster she would go until the fence was almost upon them …

"Town at last, Emily dear."

Emmy opened her eyes, leaving fences and horses far behind, and discovered that the carriage was bowling along Fore Street. The town was busy; a delivery dray was unloading barrels at the inn, the fishmonger's cart was piled high with gleaming fish, and a cluster of twittering ladies gossiped outside the milliner's shop, looking like exotic birds in their new plumed hats.

"I must visit that establishment after luncheon. They have a French milliner and she makes exceptional hats. You'll need one for Ascot," said Lady Rivers thoughtfully, and Emmy's heart sank. More prodding and more discussion on the latest fashions and styles. She could scream.

The carriage drew outside a smart granite building. A sign above the door declared this to be M. A. Rowes Photographic Studio, and the bay window was crammed with framed pictures showcasing people posed in front of the wonders within. A chemist's shop huddled apologetically next door, and as the groom halted the carriage Emmy saw a young man stagger out with his arms filled with jars and bottles. He was so intent on carrying this load without incident that he didn't notice the carriage as he backed into the studio door and almost collided with the moustachioed proprietor on his way out to welcome Lady Rivers.

"Any breakages will come out of your wages," he barked. "And use the back door! The front entrance is for our customers."

"Sorry, Mr Rowe," said the young man, although he didn't sound anything of the kind, and Emmy recognised the tone of voice she used when Henny chided her for scuffing her boots or forgetting her hat and allowing the sun to freckle her nose. Sensing her looking at him he smiled, and her heart turned over because it was the smile of a kindred spirit as trapped as she was. When he vanished into the shop Emmy felt as though an ally had been taken away.

"I do apologise, Your Ladyship," Mr Rowe was saying. "Staff are meant to use the tradesmen's entrance, but Winter is new to our establishment."

Lady Rivers sniffed, unimpressed. The servants at Rosecraddick Manor turned to face the wall when family members passed by and she often complained the house was too old, otherwise service corridors would have been added so the staff could be scarcely seen at all. When Emmy had relayed this detail to Mrs Puckey, she had snorted like Misty.

"When I have an army of undermaids to give me a hand I might think about worrying who sees me go about my work," she scoffed. "Until then with only Rosie to help, and her living out too, I haven't got time for such shenanigans! Face the wall and hide away, indeed!"

The young man with the sunset hair didn't seem the kind to face the wall either, Emmy thought, as the groom helped her from the carriage. She liked the way his dark eyes had crinkled when they caught hers, as though they were sharing a secret joke. 'Isn't this ridiculous?' they seemed to say. 'Whatever will they think of next?'

"Welcome to my humble establishment!" Mr Rowe cried, practically genuflecting. "May I offer you refreshments? Tea? Lemonade? We have some wonderful ginger cake."

The air was thick and warm. A hefty sun blazed down from an ink-blue sky. Emmy longed for a glass of water, but Lady Rivers waved the offer away with a gloved hand.

"That won't be necessary, although I do wish to freshen up after the journey."

Emmy winced for Mr Rowe, but he didn't seem to mind the disdainful tone and was almost tugging his forelock as he called his wife to attend to Lady Rivers. Titles affected folk in odd ways; Emmy was under no illusions that were Papa not a Pendennys there was no way the butcher, baker and all their other creditors would be quite so forbearing. She also suspected that her godmother, Christian duty or no, wouldn't have been as attentive either.

Lady Rivers was escorted to the powder room, Mr Rowe's wife flapping around her nervously, while the photographer vanished to make his preparations. Emmy trailed behind and did her best to ignore the headache beating against her eyes like waves breaking on the beach. She was glad to be alone for a while to fan her face and gather her thoughts.

She wandered into a large room with three walls covered in pea-green paper with a swirly pattern and the fourth heavily panelled in mahogany. It was windowless and dark, with rich Turkish rugs carpeting the floor, a monstrous chandelier suspended from the ceiling and an ornate carved fireplace at the far end. Closer inspection revealed this to be a prop, for posing beside she supposed, and the once fine carpets were threadbare. This part of the studio looked exactly like the drawing room of a fashionable house with walls smothered in portrait-sized prints of previous sitters, and as she explored further Emily realised that even the stately busts on the plinths were made of plaster and the ornate golden furniture not gilt at all but covered in gold paint. Dusty potted palms sulked in dark corners. Wax fruit glistened in bowls. A stuffed canary perched inside an ornate white cage. This room was little more than a wonderful illusion, a stage set where people could step outside ordinary life to gaze into a lens and become whoever they chose. Photographers captured dreams and sprinkled a little glitter onto the ordinary men and women who stepped through its doors.

Who would she be if she could choose, Emmy wondered, as she studied pictures of demure young women and gallant hussars. Had any of these sitters felt as hot and as impatient as she did at this moment? Life was outside of this stuffy room and Emmy longed to turn on her heel and run straight towards it. Of course, even if she wasn't trapped in the corset this would have been impossible because she was laced tightly here too, if by duty and gender rather than pretty pink ribbons. Even if she fled right this very minute, where would she go and what would she do? Emmy was as caged as the stuffed canary.

She sighed and fanning her face with her hand turned her attention to the far end of the room where panoramic scenes mounted on rollers waited to be wheeled into position. There was a variety to choose from, and her eye was immediately caught by a dramatic landscape where clouds chased shadows over rolling hills and distant castle huddled against granite and moor. Or how about the desert scene, like something from Arabian nights? A clothing rack heaped with all manner of costumes from brocade cloaks to fringed scarves to feathered hats stood beside it, and there was a box of props, too, with treasures spilling out. Stepping closer to inspect it, Emmy saw swords, stuffed pheasants, baskets crammed with paper flowers and even a stuffed Irish wolfhound with mad glassy eyes. She laid her hand on its wiry head and imagined posing beside it, staring into the distance in front of the castle background.

Maybe this could be fun after all?

"He suits you."

Emmy started. Turning, she saw the young man standing in the doorway. Winter, she recalled.

"Sorry! I didn't mean to startle you. I was just coming to collect some plates for Mr Rowe and saw you admiring Paddy," Winter explained, scooping up a box from the table by the stuffed dog. "That's the wolfhound's name, Paddy. He's a big favourite. You should definitely have him in your portrait. You could be Diana the Huntress."

He smiled at her, tucking the box of plates under his arm, and Emmy smiled back. There was something about his dark eyes which made it impossible not to smile; they were so filled with humour and life, as though he was sharing a joke with her that nobody else was in on. Of course, he oughtn't to have been speaking to her at all, Emmy being a well-born young lady and a customer, but this didn't seem to matter in the slightest to Winter. He must surely have known who she was, but there was no deference or forelock-tugging. Instead he spoke with an ease that was quite intoxicating. Perhaps it was being in this odd room, surrounded by props and artifice, that freed her from the strictures of what was proper and made speaking to him come so easily. As though she was no longer Emily Pendennys, but had slipped into playing a new role?

"They won't let me do that," she told him. "My godmother wants a formal portrait, so I expect I will have to hold flowers or a book."

"And what do you want to do?"

Emmy stared at him. He might as well have been speaking another language.

"I beg your pardon?"

"I said, what would you like to do? If you could choose?"

He held her eyes with an intense gaze that made the floor ripple beneath her feet. It made no sense whatsoever, but Emmy knew that this stranger could see straight into her soul. Into the very essence of her. She ought to have been offended, or at the very least reprimanded him for being so impertinent, but she found she didn't mind at all because as she stared at him all she could think was, 'Oh! It's you! There you are at *last*!'

"If I could choose I'd be outside and not here dressed up like a china doll," she said, and he laughed.

"It must be sweltering in all that lot. I have to admit I'm always glad to be a chap when I see how much effort it is for women to dress."

He was wearing a simple white shirt, a cap rammed onto his chestnut curls, cord trousers and scuffed brown boots. His shirt was unbuttoned at the neck, and she glimpsed a triangle of skin the colour of warm honey. She pulled her eyes away, feeling a little giddy.

"My godmother commissioned a picture for my birthday."

He nodded. "Ah, yes. Mr Rowe has talked of little else for days. I should wish you many happy returns, but you look as though you're not feeling very happy at all."

There was a knot suddenly in Emmy's throat, as though the lace ruffles around her neck had been pulled tight. Nobody ever thought to ask whether she was happy. She supposed this was because it didn't really matter whether she was or not.

"You rather look as though you'd like to run away," he added, and Emmy's eyes widened. Had he been reading her mind? Like the woman who did the parlour tricks which Mrs Puckey swore by?

"I can't say I blame you either," he continued, "because it's a glorious day. If I was taking your photograph, I'd suggest being outside to make the most of the light, maybe down by the water where sun dapples the surface. At this time of year there's a radiant quality to the light which would make a wonderful contrast with the shadows, and your skin would shine like pearl against the darkness of your hair. Your face is the golden ratio personified. It would be breathtaking. Perfect."

Emmy stared at him. Breathtaking? Perfect. Her?

Winter flushed. "Sorry. I didn't mean to speak out of turn. I can get a little carried away sometimes when I think about composition. In fact, I'm often told I talk far too much when I get onto the subject of photography. It's my passion and my livelihood, I'm often told, which makes for dull company."

Now Emmy felt as though she was seeing into *his* heart. Like someone peering into the depths of a rock pool she pictured herself suspended above the shimmering meniscus, her eyes huge and her skin spectre-pale, before she reached her hand into the mysterious depths where shy fish and glittering treasures lay hidden. And somehow she knew that there would be treasures there amid the knots of mermaid's purse and kelp and bones. Treasure and danger and beauty and possibilities …

"Oh! You're a photographer? I thought you were —"

Now it was her turn to feel her face flame.

Amusement teased his lips into a smile.

"Please, go on. You thought I was?"

"A shop assistant?" Emmy offered, hoping he wasn't offended. She wasn't sure what she had expected, but nobody had ever spoken to her like this. Kit recited poetry that he was working on and it was clever and scanned and used all the right feet, but this young man had made her see that photographs could be poems too, composed of light and shade and angles.

"A shop assistant?" he said thoughtfully. "Well, yes, that's true. I am a shop assistant in a manner of speaking. I assist Mr Rowe. In his photographical shop. A man has to earn his crust somehow. I've learned a great deal here."

He paused, as though trying to decide quite what this might be, and Emmy said nothing. She watched him reach for the words and thought that he was clever and fascinating and also very handsome. Red hair brushed his shoulders and honey skin, his eyes were bright with intelligence and kindness, and he radiated an energy that spoke of a love for life and learning. He seemed to glitter, and she didn't think she had ever met anyone who was so wonderfully and totally alive.

"In truth, I'm just a stand-in," he confessed. "Mr Rowe's son usually assists him, but he's recovering from a broken wrist. I'm a travelling photographer and that can be a hand-to-mouth existence, so it seemed serendipitous that when I arrived here there was work for me at his studio."

"A travelling photographer?" Emmy was intrigued. She'd never heard of such a thing.

"Indeed. I've had a passion for photography ever since I was child. My father used to dabble a little in his spare time and taught me. It's all I ever wanted to do, so I did! 'Take charge of Fate before it takes charge of you,' Pa used to say, and when he died I used what money he'd left to set myself up. I intend to travel the world."

"All of it?" she asked. She was teasing but Winter was serious.

"That's my dream. Venice at dawn. The desert sky. Even the pyramids. I intend to see and photograph it all. Can you imagine?"

Emmy couldn't, but it sounded wonderful, and her corner of Cornwall suddenly felt very small. How glorious it would be to see those sights! Rupert had visited Paris and had told her all about the Eiffel Tower and an ancient cathedral which dreamed away the centuries while the Seine flowed by, and she had longed to see it for herself. Emmy supposed that speaking to this young man was probably as close as she would ever get to this.

"Have you travelled far?" she asked.

"Not yet. I did spend some time in France and Spain before my father became unwell and I needed to return home, but once I've earned enough money I'll set off once more – and this time I'll have all my equipment and my studio with me. Maybe I'll even publish my photographs as a book:

Around the world with Alex Winter rather than Phileas Fogg! On a serious note, though, most of all I want to use photography to tell the truth and help people understand things. I truly believe that a good photograph can change hearts and minds."

His eyes shone as he spoke, and she thought how marvellous it must be to have such a passion and to know exactly what it was that you wanted to do with life. How wonderful to have a dream and grab hold of it with both hands, to wrestle with it and make it happen! The mere thought of the narrow path she would have to tread if Lady Rivers had her way felt as restrictive as the corset.

"Goodness," was all she could say.

He ran a hand through his hair and his face grew pink.

"I'm babbling. Sorry."

"Not at all; it's fascinating," Emmy said quickly. She wanted him to keep talking, but most of all she wanted him to stay with her. "But how do you develop your pictures?" She waved her hand at the assortment of furniture and props which crowded the room. "Or keep all these things?"

"I have a mobile studio in my old wagon. Since I don't have a chandelier or a stuffed dog there's space enough," he smiled. "A couple of top hats, a fan and a few painted backdrops are enough for my customers. They're not fine folk like yourself, but they love the magic of having their picture taken. They can become anyone then, and look as grand as they could ever dream of being. People often yearn for more than they have, and pictures can give them that, just as pictures can also show us truths we don't always want to acknowledge."

Emmy considered this. It made perfect sense. Why else would Lady Rivers want a portrait of her dressed up in this beautiful gown which made her look nothing like herself?

"So photography can be both a mirror reflecting the world or a trick looking-glass that distorts it," she offered slowly, and he nodded, delighted with this answer.

"Yes! You understand perfectly! My God, that's a *brilliant* way of putting it. A looking-glass! *Exactly*!"

They smiled shyly at one another, and then he held out his hand, a flush colouring his cheekbones.

"Forgive me, Miss Pendennys, I should have introduced myself. Alexander Winter, travelling photographer at your service."

"And magician," she added, and Alexander Winter blushed a little more.

"Ah yes, that too. Forgive me! I can get a little carried away."

They shook hands and as his held hers Emmy was filled with the strangest longing to never part company with Alexander Winter; everything within her recognised that the quietly spoken stranger shaking her hand was the person she had been waiting for all of her life. She hated seeing her fingers slip from his, because what if this stranger were to drift away? Time seemed to hold his breath as they smiled shyly at one another, and even the world stopped turning for a moment or two.

Everything had changed, she thought. Everything.

"It's nice to meet you, Mr Winter," she said. Never had 'nice' felt like such an inadequate word.

"Alex, please. And it's a pleasure to meet you too, Miss Pendennys."

Her hand rested in his. It fitted perfectly.

"Emmy," she said, and he nodded, the dark eyes which held her suddenly serious.

"Emmy," he echoed.

"Winter! Winter!"

An impatient summons broke the spell and Alex Winter released her fingers.

"I think I may have taken too long," he sighed.

"Will you be taking my photograph?" Emmy snatched at the possibility, but he shook his head.

"A lowly replacement without formal training let loose on such esteemed customers? I think not. I'm needed to run errands this morning, and Mr Rowe has a list of jobs as long as his face. There's no likelihood of my being allowed behind a camera. I would have loved to take your picture. You have a fascinating face. Beautiful. The camera will adore it."

Emmy knew she was no beauty. Her hair was too curly, her mouth was too big for her face and her skin had the most unfortunate habit of toasting in the slightest ray of sunshine. How many times had she stared into the looking-glass and sighed to be so dark, with her limbs a tangle of bones and angles? It was far more fashionable to be curvy and golden, as Henny was constantly reminding her. If this had been any other young man she would have assumed he was either teasing her or making some strange attempt at flattery, but the regret in Alex Winter's voice was tangible as salt in the wave-licked wind. Her heart fluttered.

"When I return from my errands I'll develop the photographs, and I promise I'll do my very best with them," he promised. "I'll do my utmost to ensure you have a splendid portrait."

Emmy started to say that she would very much like him to take her photograph instead of Mr Rowe, but Alexander Winter was already stepping aside for Lady Rivers who, skirts hissing behind her, sailed into the room with Mr Rowe scuttling in her wake.

"This one," she ordered pointing at a background of a garden and not even acknowledging Alexander who, with a small nod of farewell to Emmy, backed out of the doorway. "And a bouquet of roses. Fresh ones, not these paper monstrosities."

A fleeting look of horror crossed the photographer's face.

"You do have fresh flowers, I take it?" Lady Rivers' voice was so cold that Emmy was surprised the poor man's nose wasn't frost-bitten. Emmy toyed with the notion of suggesting Paddy the dog instead but decided against it since her godmother was not famed for her sense of humour. How she wished her new friend was still present. She felt certain he would be able to defuse the situation.

"Begging your pardon, Your Ladyship, but we tend to use silk or paper. That way the blooms don't wilt, and they photograph more crisply too."

There was a pause as Lady Rivers considered this.

"They look a treat in photographs," added Mrs Rowe. "Lady Robartes held them in her portrait."

Lady Rivers was mollified. "Very well. You may continue with these."

"Could Mr Winter assist? He appears very knowledgeable," Emmy said to Mrs Rowe as the photographer's wife tidied her hair and pinned the hat securely, while the background was wheeled into place with several potted palms arranged to Lady Rivers' exacting standards.

Mrs Rowe's thin eyebrows leapt towards her tugged-back scalp. "I hope Winter wasn't making a nuisance of himself, Miss?"

"Not at all," Emmy said swiftly. She didn't want to get Alex into trouble with his employer. "I asked him a question about photography. I was most impressed."

Mrs Rowe's eyes, the same harsh green as unripe gooseberries, flicked towards her husband and Lady Rivers, who were still engrossed in a discussion regarding the choice of background. Leaning forward on the pretext of adjusting the hat, she whispered, "And not just with his knowledge of photography, Miss?"

Emmy wasn't quite sure what to say. The comment was impertinent but also warm and amused. Fortunately, Mrs Rowe didn't seem to require a reply as she continued to tweak curls and smooth skirts.

"He's a handsome lad and no mistake. You should see the shop girls twitter when he walks by! Not that Alex seems to notice. His head's well and truly in the clouds; I've never come across anyone with such a passion for the camera. He won't be here long – more's the pity! We've had far more ladies book sittings with us since he's worked for us!"

Emmy wasn't surprised to hear this, but the dart of jealously she felt took her aback. She didn't much like the idea of shop girls and middle-aged ladies giggling at and admiring Alex Winter.

Mrs Rowe leaned forward to tuck a final hairpin into place, adding very softly and with a note of warning in her voice, "His late father was a Methodist minister and he's a good sort, but he's not for the likes of you, Miss. He's only here to work in the darkroom and run errands, not speak to his betters in the studio. You'll get him into all sorts of trouble with my husband if you mention he's spoken to you."

It was desperately unfair, but Emily knew this was how society worked. A Methodist minister's son was no more her social equal than Mrs Rowe or Mrs Puckey. As far as Emmy was concerned, though, this was nonsense, because they were all people, so all worthy of equal attention, but she knew Lady Rivers wouldn't see things this way – unlike her son. Kit often said this wouldn't always be the way of things and Rupert agreed. She'd listened often enough to the two of them discussing the matter, and both young men were adamant that a time was coming when intellect and character would matter far more than an accident of birth. Unfortunately that time was yet to arrive, although Alex Winter hadn't appeared in the least intimidated by her superior social status or even seemed conscious that he was crossing boundaries by speaking to her. It seemed that swept away by his passion for photography, nothing else had mattered.

"I understand," was all Emmy said.

"Do try to stand up straighter, Emily dear," called Lady Rivers from across the studio. "Come here and hold these travesties of roses. Mr Rowe's ready to begin."

Emmy did her best to enter into the spirit of the exercise, but the room was hot, the corset felt tighter by the second, and the headache pressed against the base of her skull. The sooner this was over the better. She was also trembling with a curious energy, her every nerve jangling like the bells in the servants' hall. Would Alex Winter reappear after his errands were run? What if he didn't? She might never see that intriguing young man again.

While Emmy fretted and kept sneaking glances at the door, Lady Rivers presided over proceedings from a gilded chair, appraising the composition of the portrait through critical blue eyes. The photographer's nervous wife arranged the folds of Emmy's skirts and tweaked the position of her hat while Mr Rowe tried out a variety of poses, none of which met her godmother's exacting standards. With every minute that passed, Emmy's headache grew worse. She felt as though she was breathing thick, hot soup.

If only Alex Winter was taking the photographs! Emmy was sure he would have made everything work so perfectly. He made her feel as though she was the only person in the room that mattered. He had made her feel beautiful. Exquisite. Alive. Although she was hot, Emmy's skin was dusted with gooseflesh at the memory of that dark-eyed gaze sweeping across her face. She could scarcely think of anything but their chance meeting. Surely this was Fate?

'Take charge of Fate before it takes charge of you,' Alex had said, and the words reverberated through her blood. So far Fate had bounced Emmy Pendennys back and forth at whim, and she feared it would continue to do so, lacing her into its design just as Henny had laced her into this corset, unless something changed and she took charge of it.

Emmy had to see Alexander Winter again. She *had* to.

But how, when he was just a photographer's assistant and she was a

Pendennys? And a girl. If she saddled Misty and rode to town alone to see him there would be a scandal, and if Henny accompanied her it would be pointless. Maybe Mrs Puckey could be persuaded to visit Bodmin? Simmonds would be happy to drive them if there was a pint of cider waiting at the inn for him while they shopped ...

Emmy's mind was working with a speed and enthusiasm Henny would never have imagined possible. The sooner her photograph was taken the better.

"Turn your head to the left, Miss," said Mr Rowe, positioning the camera. "And relax your mouth a little. Tilt the parasol to the left."

As Emmy struggled to find solutions and make planes, the headache intensified. It was beating her hard now, a black bat of pain hammering the anvil of her skull. The room swayed. She leaned heavily on the parasol and gritted her teeth.

"That's better. It looks more classical," she heard her godmother say, and then, "Emily! Do stop scowling, dear!"

Emmy did her best. She wasn't scowling. It was simply that the room was very hot, her heart was beating very fast and her headache was growing stronger by the second.

"If you could keep very still, Miss," said Mr Rowe. "I'm going to expose the plate now."

He vanished under the camera cloth, pulled away the lens cover and began to count.

"One. Two. Three."

Emmy swayed.

Lady Rivers leant forward. "This won't do at all. Emily, dear, you must stand still. I never knew such a fidget in all my life."

"Four. Five. Six."

Emmy straightened her shoulders and glared into at the camera, all her focus on standing up. The rug rippled beneath her feet and suddenly the room receded, Lady Rivers growing smaller and smaller, and the heat of the room was pressing against her face like a smothering hand.

"Emily! Stop scowling!" she heard her godmother say.

"Seven. Eight. Nine. Ten."

Lady Rivers was speaking but no sound was coming from her lips. There was a buzzing in Emmy's ears. She gripped the silk roses and tried to rip her thoughts away from the pressing heat and the blackness at the corners of her vision. Maybe if she thought about Alexander Winter's smiling eyes she might feel better?

"Eleven. Twelve. Thirteen."

The edges of Emmy's vision began to dance and blur. She gritted her teeth and stared into the camera, every sinew and muscle straining to keep upright. The whalebones bit into her ribs and every breath was a struggle. Henny had laced it far too tightly.

"Fourteen. Fifteen. Sixteen."

Emmy's jaw clenched. The darkness was creeping closer. She wasn't sure how much longer she could stand. The corset squeezed tighter and tighter.

"Done!" cried Mr Rowe, from beneath the covers. "Although you looked a little anxious. We may need to do another."

"We most certainly will. That will never do," sniffed Lady Rivers. "Emily, shoulders back, dear! And stop scowling. A lady never scowls."

But Emmy, overwhelmed by a tidal wave of pain, swayed as the room lurched and the carpet bucked. Her last thought before the darkness swallowed her was that if this birthday portrait wouldn't do, perhaps a man with sunset hair and earth-warm eyes could be hired to take another.

Manor Garden Party Photograph

4th August 1913

Rosecraddick Manor

"I think it's a charming picture. I can't imagine why Mama's taken such exception to it!"

Kit Rivers, his eyes bright with mirth, set Emmy's birthday photograph down on the sideboard. Even graced with an elaborate silver frame, the image within couldn't be described as anything other than … unfortunate. With eyes screwed up, lips pursed and the roses all but crushed in her fists, the young woman in the picture glowered from the frame like a modern-day Medusa. It was hardly surprising that Lady Rivers was unimpressed. So much for Alex Winter's belief she would photograph beautifully. Emmy really hoped he hadn't been the one to develop the picture.

"Don't be rotten," she said. "I wasn't feeling well that day. Henny got quite carried away with my stays and I fainted."

"Truly? I thought this pose must be quite the latest fashion, a young lady looking as though she wants to throttle the photographer. All the mamas will be clamouring for something similar. This is the expression, I believe?"

Kit pulled a face and Emmy couldn't help laughing. Fighting to remain upright while the room whirled around you did not make for a flattering photograph. Kit, who had walked over to Pendennys Place to deliver the picture, had unveiled it with a flourish, and to his credit had managed to keep a straight face until Mrs Puckey saw it and shrieked with horror. Then they had both laughed, and even Emmy had seen the funny side. Nevertheless, she banished it instantly to the drawing room where, since few visitors chose to brave the rutted drive or Julyan Pendennys' temper, it would hopefully remain unseen until she could lose it. Imagine if in a hundred years' time people saw this photograph and thought this was what she really looked like?

"How am I doing?" Kit asked, imitating her pose and gurning over his shoulder. "Am I close? Shall I try this when Mama next decides to have my photograph taken?"

It was all very well for Kit to be so amused; everyone in Rosecraddick knew he was the apple of his mother's eye. Besides, he wasn't the one who'd been berated by Lady Rivers for an entire carriage journey home. Fainting while having her photograph taken had not endeared Emmy to her godmother. Not only did such weakness show a distinct lack of backbone, but the much-anticipated luncheon had been cancelled, as well as any hope of a trip to the milliner. Lady Rivers was most put out and had not been afraid to make her feelings clear. If Emmy hadn't already known there was no way she could ever marry Kit, the thought of living at Rosecraddick Manor under his mother's flinty gaze would have made her think twice.

At the studio, once Mrs Rowes's smelling salts had coaxed her back into consciousness, Emmy had rested on one of gilt chairs, her head hanging between her knees as she did her best to breathe in and out as slowly as possible. As she concentrated hard on her breath and the toes of her boots, Lady Rivers scolded her for not eating enough breakfast.

"I *did* eat breakfast," Emmy protested, hardly trusting herself to speak without fainting again. "It's my corset. I can hardly breathe."

She stole a look up through her lashes at Mrs Rowe who had been muttering under her breath that it was laced exceedingly tight and that it was no surprise so many young ladies swooned, but the photographer's wife swiftly arranged her features into a blank expression and Emmy sighed. There were no allies here, and although she would have liked nothing more than to see him Alex Winter had vanished on his errands.

"Nonsense, Emily," snapped Lady Rivers, quite unmoved by her goddaughter's plight. "And complaining isn't becoming in a lady. Fortitude is what is required. Fortitude and duty. Believe me, a corset is the least of a lady's complaints."

Emmy didn't argue, she couldn't spare the breath; but as she perched stiffly on the chair with her head drooping like a tulip after heavy rain, she decided she really didn't want to be a lady. She'd much rather take control of her own destiny as Alex Winter had done, and see the world. If only she could hitch Misty to a wagon and set off. Wouldn't that be something?

Of course, such a notion was an impossibility. A daydream. Emily would never travel far at all, and her life was already mapped out for her. Marriage to a suitable husband and a household of her own to run. Children. Old age. Death. And in between, countless social engagements when she would be expected to nod and smile and wear the right dress. As she fought to come to, Emmy knew the tightness in her chest had nothing to do with her stays and everything to do with the sensation that these walls were closing in around her. She knew there were suffragettes and female surgeons and clever young women who went to university, but these felt like creatures from another universe, as wonderful and as remote as the stars. Here in Cornwall, buried deep in the world of Pendennys Place and Rosecraddick, it truly seemed as though all roads to other places were closed.

Tears of frustration pricked Emmy's eyelids. Meeting Alex Winter had changed her. His stories of travel and his dream of telling the truth through his lens had been like opening a window on a stuffy day and breathing in cool salt-kissed air from a wide and endless ocean. Trapped in the hot studio, she ached for the open stretch of the beach, to walk over wet sand and trace the shell line along the beach before turning towards the water, kicking through green and purple weed before running all the way through the tide pools to the ocean and the brine-trapped sky. What lay beyond that water she could only imagine, but it must surely be preferable to what was mapped out for her? All these thoughts whirled through her mind, but under Lady Rivers' cold scrutiny she didn't dare reply that a world of duty and corsets and afternoon tea was enough to make her scream or that she never wanted to understand the future her godmother was showing her.

Eventually, the world stopped cartwheeling and Emmy was deemed sufficiently recovered to be helped from the photographic studio and into the Rivers' carriage. As the groom gathered up the reins and clicked to the horses, she cast a hopeful glance across the bustling street for a glimpse of conker-bright hair but was disappointed.

This disappointment and an uneasy sense of being trapped stayed with her. Alex Winter had vanished from her life as quickly as he had entered it and Emmy had felt flat ever since. Even when Miss Henwood predictably departed for a new position and her father was laid low and kept to his rooms, any freedom gifted to her was tinged with melancholy. Left to her own devices, she struggled to recover her usual exuberance, but even riding Misty through the woods didn't lift her spirits. Emmy's world felt newly narrow, and each passing day only brought her closer to a future which filled her with unease, a future where she would slowly shift into another woman who would gossip, play bridge and want little more in life than a new hat. Emmy had never had any intention of settling for this, but until she had met Alex Winter she'd no idea just how much more she'd wanted. Their conversation, although brief, had changed something fundamental within her.

"What do you want to do?" he had asked, and lost in the strength of his dark-eyed scrutiny Emmy understood he already knew exactly what it was she longed for and had recognised it in her from the moment he stepped into the studio. She didn't need to explain anything to Alex Winter because he already knew what she wanted.

He knew her.

And now he was gone. How could it be that you could feel something, recognise it with such utter certainty, only to lose it for ever?

The only bright spot on Emmy's horizon was that she hadn't heard from her godmother since her birthday, and she had become increasingly hopeful that the threatened invitation to the Rosecraddick Manor garden party had been withdrawn – a hope dashed this morning when Kit had arrived at Pendennys Place to deliver both her photograph and the invitation. Printed on beautiful thick card and tucked inside a cream envelope embossed with the Rivers' family crest, it was less of an invitation than a summons. Emmy appreciated that receiving this missive was a much coveted honour in the neighbourhood, but as she glanced at the smug cream rectangle, propped up on the mantelpiece beside a clock which had never ticked or chimed in her memory and would probably be the next item whisked away to a sale room, her spirits sank even lower.

"How does this expression look? Shall I try this when Mama next decides to have my picture taken?"

Kit's cheerful voice sliced into her reverie and Emmy couldn't help smiling. Her old friend was doing his best to cheer her up and his kindness spoke volumes about him – especially since Kit's lot was not a great deal happier than her own.

"It's most fetching! Every mama in the county will be desperate to introduce you to their daughter."

He sobered up straight away. "No thank you. That sounds exhausting."

"Then prepare to be exhausted. Surely matchmaking's the purpose of the garden party?"

"Not this time. Mama has limited herself to inviting a select few. You and your father, Rupert and his parents, the rector, the Dalby-Smyths and a couple of others." He gave her a small and apologetic shrug. "You know why."

Emmy did, and they exchanged a look of mutual sympathy. How much easier it would have been if she did have feelings for Kit, and he for her. Kit was kind and clever, and brimmed with an enormous passion for life and all its wonders. He was also very handsome with his thick golden hair, intelligent green eyes and easy confidence. When Kit Rivers was in a room everyone gravitated to him, longing for the sunlight of his attention and basking in it once it arrived – as it invariably did, as Kit would never dream of leaving anyone out, no matter how humble or insignificant others might deem them. He was the cleverest person she knew, even brighter than Rupert, who was going to read Classics at Oxford, yet Kit never boasted or made you feel foolish in comparison. He was unassuming, modest and generous. But Kit Rivers didn't shine for her the way that Winter had, nor did her pulse race when she thought about him, and Emmy knew that he never would.

The human heart was a strange thing. It didn't behave as it ought to, that was for sure, and Emmy knew that no matter what his parents might have decided Kit could no more bow to them and betray his own integrity than he could stop writing his poems. Any girl he fell in love with would have literature and verse flowing through her veins and possess a heart every bit and brave and poetic as his. Whoever this girl might be, the one who would complete Kit Rivers, Emmy knew beyond all doubt it wasn't her, just as she knew Kit would never fill that space in her own soul.

"If only Ma and Pa'd had another a son before me," he was saying quietly. "I think I would have made a marvellous spare. I would have very much liked not being the heir."

"Because you would be free to choose your own fate."

Emmy wasn't asking a question. This was a fact, and one she understood better than most, for if Morvan had still been alive the burdens of the crumbling Pendennys estate would have been lifted from her shoulders and she too would have been free.

Kit sighed.

"Yes. Imagine that. If I was a second son I could do something worthwhile with my life. No duty, no army, no traditions to follow, no heir to beget, and only myself to please. No more garden parties and soirées and dinners, making polite conversation with a privileged few, people who have seen little of the world yet seem to own it all and know all there is to know about everything. I could turn my attention to speaking truth and finding ways to share that through poetry. My God. I'd be free to choose indeed."

Kit's passion and energy and longing to bring his vision to fruition spun Emmy back to her chance meeting with Alex, another young man who dazzled all around him with the brightness of his dreams and his passion for life.

"Oh! You sound just like —"

She stopped just in time. Her cheeks flared guiltily.

"Who do I sound like?"

"Nobody," Emmy said, suddenly self-conscious. "Nobody."

"Doesn't sound like nobody to me. And judging by the way you've turned the same colour as the carpet, I imagine it's somebody who's made quite an impression on you – which rules out Rupert or Simmonds! Come on, Emmy. Who is he?"

She turned and walked to the window in order to avoid her friend's questioning gaze. It was a glorious day, the chestnut trees adorned with white candles, and through the grimy glass it was impossible to see that the lawns were too long and pitted with moss or that the windows of the conservatory were patched and cracked. She rested her forehead against the cool pane and felt surprised not to hear a sizzle.

"Just somebody I met briefly."

"He made quite an impression on you, I think?" he said.

Emmy was brimming with the need to tell somebody about Alex

Winter. Misty was a good listener but a hopeless conversationalist; and although Kit's path had diverged from hers at many points from the time he had left for prep school and started socialising with far more exalted folk than housekeepers and gardeners, he was the closest thing to a best friend she had. Emmy knew he wouldn't judge her for speaking so openly with a young man who was so far below her, because Kit never judged people this way.

"Yes. Yes, he did."

Kit said nothing. He didn't prompt or nudge her for more, unlike Mrs Puckey who was always niggling her, or Rupert whose sad spaniel eyes and hopeful expression often guilted her into spilling secrets. Kit's still patience invited absolute confidence. In the past he had listened when she told him about her father's violent outbursts and although Kit never said as much she knew he understood and sympathised.

Words began to flow like the first trickle of meltwater from a thawing river, as Emmy told him about the chance meeting with Alex Winter. Without fully disclosing the way this stranger's intense gaze and passionate words made him seem more alive than anyone she had ever met, or betraying just how much he had consumed her thoughts ever since, she described how Alex spoke to her as though her thoughts and opinions and dreams really mattered, and how he had listened carefully to what she said without diving in and smothering her opinions with his own. Kit laughed at this but didn't interrupt, listening intently as she recalled Alex Winter's delight when she had understood his vision for the truth-telling that good photography could achieve. It had felt as though there was a tie between them, she finished sadly, and although it made no sense at all everything felt different now.

Everything.

But most especially her.

"This chap sounds extraordinary," said Kit when she had talked herself to a standstill. "A travelling photographer and philosopher? I'm not surprised you were so struck by him. He embodies freedom and exploring dreams, doesn't he? Imagine the places he'll visit and the photographs he'll take."

It was a relief to have spoken about Alex and to hear Kit say his name out loud. If it hadn't been for her birthday picture, Emmy might have started to fear she had dreamed the whole episode. It had certainly taken on an unreal quality.

She nodded. "Imagine."

"Alex is a man with vision," Kit continued, hands buried deep in the pockets of his sports jacket and his gaze still fixed on the garden, "and from what you say, he's not afraid to follow his heart or do what he believes is right. He's someone you instinctively felt you could speak to openly and about anything. Even though that made absolutely no sense. You felt as though you recognised him."

She swallowed the sudden sadness. "Yes."

Kit gave her a thoughtful look. "I think you may have fallen a little in love with him?"

Emmy laughed, but it was an awkward sound, unconvincing even to her own ears. Shaken, she turned away from the window. Was Kit right? Was she a little in love with Alex Winter? Surely not. A romantic and a dreamer, always with his nose in a book, this was Kit's poetic soul speaking.

"I don't know about that! I couldn't have spoken to him for more than five minutes."

Kit turned away from the window. He looked wistful.

"Romeo didn't speak a word to Juliet before he fell in love with her, so I don't think the length of a meeting is an issue. Someone special comes along just once in a lifetime, and that's if we're incredibly lucky. You only need to read Shakespeare or Keats to know that much."

Emmy thought she ought to have studied harder. Maybe Henny was right, and less time in the saddle and more time spent in the schoolroom might have been a good thing?

"I wonder if there's another soul to match mine? And if there is, will I ever meet her?" Kit was saying, half to himself. "I must confess, I'm a little envious of you, Em."

She shrugged. "Don't be. I'll never see him again."

"You don't know that."

"I do. He's a travelling photographer and even if he wasn't, I'm supposed to …"

Her voice tailed off and she looked at him miserably

"You know what I'm supposed to do. What *we're* supposed to do."

Kit waved a hand dismissively. "We both know that won't ever happen."

Emmy nodded but no matter what Kit might say she still feared the power his parents wielded. Lady Rivers had set her heart on uniting the Rosecraddick and Pendennys estates a long, long time ago and she was not a woman to accept defeat.

"I know," was all she said, in a small voice.

"Tell me, did this Alex have red hair?

Emmy stared at him. "How do you know that?"

"Didn't you realise I have mind-reading skills?" Kit deadpanned before taking pity on her. "I'm teasing. A young man of that description delivered your photograph to the manor. I was reading up in the tower and I saw him walking down the drive, looking a little lost and rather dishevelled. He must have taken the train to the halt then had to follow the path through the woods, poor fellow. I thought at the time that was a hike above and beyond the call of duty when the post would have sufficed, but now I realise why."

He paused for dramatic effect.

"Why?" Emmy asked.

"He was hoping to see you, silly goose!"

An unexpected surge of hope made Emmy's head swim. She gripped the back of a winged armchair so tightly that her knuckles whitened.

"Do you think so?"

"I do," said Kit. "It's exactly what I would do were I in his shoes. I wouldn't give up if I thought I'd met my soulmate. I would do everything I could to see her again. Petrarch would. Or Romeo!"

Emmy laughed in spite of the hope blossoming in her heart. "I never said he was my soulmate. You read far too much poetry, Kit Rivers!"

"There's no such thing as too much poetry," he said staunchly. "Although, fair enough, have it your way, Miss Most Unromantic Emily Pendennys. Maybe it was simply Alex's job to deliver the picture since he runs errands."

There was a beat of silence while they considered this. Emmy decided she preferred Kit's original hypothesis.

"If you want to see him again, why not return to the studio for another photograph?" Kit suggested. He crossed the room and picked up the silver frame, brandishing it at her. "Let's be honest; you could do with a more flattering picture!"

This idea had crossed Emmy's mind. Knowing there was no possibility of visiting Bodmin unchaperoned she'd raised the idea of a trip to town with Mrs Puckey, who always enjoyed a meander along Fore Street with her straw basket over her arm in search of ribbon at the haberdashery or a twist of barley sugar from the confectioner. But Emmy had met with little success.

"None of the shopkeepers there will extend credit or issue standing orders for this estate," the housekeeper had pointed out, rolling pastry violently as though venting her frustration with this situation on the future pie crust. "So, unless you can persuade your father to settle our outstanding accounts, we'll have to make do with the village. Fortunately, your family name still counts for something there or we'd all surely starve."

If the Pendennys estate owed money to most of the shopkeepers in Bodmin, Emmy didn't hold out much hope of Mr Rowe extending credit for another photograph. Neither did she imagine her godmother would wish to repeat the costly experience, and her father certainly wouldn't pay.

"We can't afford another portrait," she said quietly.

"Oh," said Kit. "Right."

"You must see I have no choice in almost anything at all." She pressed the heels of her hands into her temples as though attempting to rub away the frustration. "You're lucky you're a man, Kit. You don't have to be stuck even if you think you do. You can take hold of fate before it takes hold of you."

"You're right," he said slowly. "I can. I absolutely can. And I think I will."

"What," said Emmy, "is that supposed to mean?"

"It means that I'm going to take hold of Fate and give it a jolly good shake!"

Emmy was on the brink of demanding he explain this when a breathless Mrs Puckey arrived in the drawing room, apologising for being in the garden picking peas when Kit arrived and asking whether he wanted tea. Kit declined, saying he needed to be back at the manor for luncheon, and as Emmy showed him out he looked exceedingly pleased with himself.

"What are you looking like that for?" she demanded.

"Like what?"

"Like you're plotting something."

"You *do* have a suspicious mind," Kit said, shaking his head sadly.

"Now, don't forget the garden party, will you? Mama will be expecting a reply."

Emmy rolled her eyes because there was little hope of her forgetting. The whole neighbourhood was in a tizzy about who was and wasn't invited. She'd even overheard Rosie complaining to Mrs Puckey that Miss Emily's lack of an invitation reflected badly on them, the servants.

Once again the honour of Pendennys Place rested upon Emmy.

"Please tell Lady Rivers I'd be delighted to accept," she said.

"You're a dreadful fibber, Emily Pendennys. Just promise me one thing?"

"And what might that be?"

Kit leaned forward, his mouth close to her ear, and said, "That you won't lace your corset so tightly that you pass out this time. You'll want to be conscious for this garden party."

In Emmy's experience, such occasions were torturous at the best of times. Surely unconsciousness was better?

"What are you talking about?" she asked impatiently, but Kit just smiled, tapped the side of his nose with his forefinger and said, "Trust me!" before leaping down the front steps and scattering gravel as he landed on the drive. He turned to wave before vanishing through the gates, and Emmy stared after him, perplexed. Kit could be enigmatic, often caught up in his own world of poetry and imagination, but these moods were usually accompanied by long silences and weeks where she saw nothing of him as he worked on stanzas and feet and heroic couplets. This surge of energy was most unusual. What was he up to?

She shook her head and closed the front door, turning down the tiled passageway which led to the kitchen. It was time for her to take Julyan's luncheon tray up to his study. Kit's enigmatic comments would have to wait. Emmy knew that by the time she had screwed up the courage to peek around the study door (you never quite knew if a book or a paperweight might come flying towards you on a deadly trajectory) Kit's words and the garden party, along with the estate's debts and marriage, would be the least of her problems.

It was a puzzle for another day.

It seemed that even the Cornish weather didn't dare disobey Lady Rivers. After a week of heavy rain, seven long days when the skies were washed of colour, when trees and bushes cowered beneath the watery assault and Pendennys Place was filled with a percussion of pings and plops as leaks dripped into the buckets, the morning of the garden party dawned sunny and warm. The fat roses in the garden turned their faces upwards and the horses no longer huddled into the hedges or turned their rumps to the wind but cropped the grass happily and whisked flies away with their tails. Emmy, who had been quietly praying that her godmother's gathering might be postponed, resigned herself to an afternoon of meaningless chatter.

"Away with the long face. A garden party will be lovely," Mrs Puckey scolded as she shooed the gloomy Emmy upstairs to change. "I've drawn a bath and laid out the garden party outfit your godmother's sent over for you."

Emmy pulled a face. She did not have happy associations with clothes supplied by Lady Rivers. Kit's instruction about not fainting was still playing on her mind. She had replayed their conversation many times and still not managed to make any sense of it, but she hoped Kit hadn't breathed a word about her meeting with Alex. She hadn't forgotten Mrs Rowe's warning, and the last thing Emmy would ever want to do was get him into trouble when he had been so kind.

She sighed. It was alarming how often she still thought about their meeting, and the long rainy days had only intensified her feelings. As she watched the raindrops trickle down the panes she had relived every word and almost driven herself to distraction wondering whether Alex Winter really had chosen to deliver the picture himself in the hope of seeing her. Kit had thought so, but Kit had the heart of a poet and was an unusual young man. He saw the world differently from most; to him it was a beautiful place filled with wonders and possibilities and where people were intrinsically good. She touched her cheek, sore from a close encounter with a well-aimed book, and decided that it was hard to share this view when Julyan Pendennys was your father ...

"Simmonds will be waiting with the dogcart at half past two," added Mrs Puckey, flapping a reddened hand in her direction. "Don't drag your heels, Miss. Chop! Chop!"

Emmy dutifully bathed and dressed – this dress, thankfully, allowing her more latitude in the matter of stays – and gathered her thick curls at the nape of her neck with a green ribbon. Thank goodness she didn't need curl papers or Mrs Puckey wielding a hot tong, she thought before ramming the hat on top and skewering it in place with a jewelled hat pin. What a bore that would be, and what a waste of time. Bad enough that she had to dress up in white and forgo a walk through the woods, something she badly needed after days of being cooped up indoors, but to have to spend hours having her hair bullied into ringlets would have been unbearable.

This will do, she decided as she caught sight of her reflection. The dress was demure and pretty, and the girl wearing it looked every inch the perfect god-daughter even if inside she was grinding her teeth. The garden party would only last a few hours. With Kit and Rupert present, she could endure it.

Simmonds had polished the dogcart and given the harness a buff, and as Misty trotted along the sunken lane, his polished hooves spitting up gravel and splashing through puddles, Emmy's spirits lifted. Lances of light sliced through the leaves, the air was soft and smelt of grass and earth, and the whole world sparkled as though Lady Rivers had arranged to have it washed especially for her gathering. It truly was a beautiful afternoon. The world was drying out after its lengthy soaking and it was hard to feel dispirited when the sun was shining and Misty's dappled rump was swaying from side to side. She tugged the pin from the hat and pulled the ribbon from her hair.

"You'll be for it if Mrs Puckey finds out about this," tutted Simmonds.

"But she won't find out, will she?" Emmy said. "Not if you don't tell her."

"'Tisn't none of my business what ladies wear on their heads," he sniffed, but she could tell by the way his moustache twitched that he was smiling. Simmonds had been turning a blind eye to Emmy's exploits for years, although when he'd caught her attempting to ride Misty bareback he had taken exception. Hats off he could handle, but some rebellions were just a little too much.

Rosecraddick Manor was bathed in honeyed sunshine as the dogcart swung through the elaborate iron gates and bowled along the immaculately raked drive. It was a beautiful building, aged and mellowed in a way that Pendennys Place, with its towering edifice of startling red brick, would never be, and as Simmonds drew up at the far side of the turning circle Emmy admired the immaculate flower beds with their patterns of lilac and pink flowers. Two liveried footmen flanked the front door, and once Simmonds had reined Misty in to a halt one of them stepped forward to assist Emmy then the second guided her into the great hall, where a maid took her shawl and offered her refreshments.

Flute of champagne in her hand, Emmy stepped through the hall and out through the drawing room onto the terrace, to be formally greeted by Lady Rivers. Then, standing near the balustrade she drank in the scene, marvelling at the lengths Lady Rivers had gone to. Emmy had visited the manor many times and the beauty of the place never failed to make her breath catch, but today the garden was especially lovely with the cedar trees casting cool pools of shade over a lawn rendered emerald by the rains of the past week and the ornamental beds bright with blooms. Alongside the walled garden a marquee had been erected, festooned with lilac and pink bunting which fluttered in the breeze and lent the scene a festive air. Inside were tables, each laid with delicate lace cloths, bone china teacups, silverware and cakes on stands, and decorated with vases crammed with pink and lilac roses and foaming baby's breath. A piano had even been carried out so a four-piece band could accompany the scene with the more refined tunes from Gilbert and Sullivan's operettas.

Ladies in pastel hues and large hats perched on top of elaborate hairdos flitted through the scene like butterflies, and a group of cream-suited men sporting boaters conversed loudly. Footmen bearing silver trays hovered around the guests and carried platters piled with sandwiches and cakes to the white wrought iron tables; and from the far side of the lawn emanated the smack of mallet against balls and the ripple of voices rising and falling amid the buzz of excited chatter.

Soon Emmy would step forwards and join them, but for a moment it was pleasant to be an observer. If she were a photographer like Alex Winter, what truths could she tell about this scene? Maybe that the vicar, the fearsome Reverend Cutwell, in awe of Colonel Rivers and standing a respectful few steps behind him, was pretending to be a part of the conversation by nodding at intervals but saying little? Or perhaps that the handsome footman was making eyes at the mayor's young wife? Maybe that Lady Rivers, wielding an enormous parasol as she strolled among her guests, only held court with the favoured few who leaned forward to hang upon her every word? Or would she photograph the girl with tangled dark hair who stood alone and observed them all? What would the truth be about that solitary figure?

Emmy raised a hand and shielded her eyes against the sun as she sought to distinguish Kit amongst the throng. She could do with an ally, but there was no sign of him anywhere. She swirled her drink and resigned herself to making small talk.

"I've been looking everywhere for you! I thought you'd decided not to come!"

Rupert Elmhurst stood at her side. As always, his dark hair was standing up on end giving him an air of surprise, and his suit was already crumpled and grubby. Even his boater looked as though it had been sat on, and knowing Rupert as well as she did Emmy guessed it had been. For such a clever young man – one of the most brilliant legal minds in the land according to Kit – he was utterly chaotic. As he leaned his elbows on the lichen-speckled balustrade, the champagne in his glass sloshed onto his shoes and splashed his trousers. Without saying a word, Emmy took the glass while he plucked a handkerchief from his waistcoat pocket and dabbed the fabric frantically.

"Damn! I didn't get *you*, did I?"

"No, you missed. Want to try again?" she teased, and he grimaced.

"Lord, you know how clumsy I am. Bound to get you at some point. I must stay away from any curried fowl!" Rupert folded the hanky up and mopped his brow. Even with the breeze his face was flushed pink, and Emmy took pity on him: poor Rupert was even less comfortable at these gatherings than she was. Tucking her arm through his, she steered him along the terrace, nodding at the other guests and hoping her godmother wouldn't descend on her. The moment she did so, Emmy would be obliged to sit with the colonel and his wife and make polite chit-chat to their guests. All she needed was a sign which read 'Our Son's Intended, and Heiress to the Estate Next Door' and their work was done.

"At least Ma and Pa are having a wonderful time." Rupert pointed to the marquee where the Elmhursts, wedged into wicker chairs, were consuming their own body weight in sandwiches and cake. Stuffing the handkerchief back into his pocket, where it bulged and fought to escape, he added tactfully, "I assume your father was indisposed?"

Emmy laughed darkly. 'Indisposed' was a polite way of putting it. The damp weather always caused her father's bones to ache and his injuries to plague him even more than usual, which resulted in heavy consumption of what remained in their cellars. His temper was black, but at least he kept to his rooms when in this state. She hadn't seen him since he'd thrown the book at her head, and Mrs Puckey hadn't mentioned his invitation to the garden party.

"Indeed he is," she replied, and her hand must have strayed to her cheek because Rupert frowned. Julyan Pendennys' temper was notorious.

"Did he do that?"

"Not intentionally," Emmy said. It was hard to explain, but Rupert, who was from Rosecraddick, knew enough of Julyan Pendennys to understand.

"Shall I be your knight in shining armour and whisk you away? Marry me, and you can escape him!"

She squeezed his arm. "Don't be silly. You don't want to marry me."

"I don't want to marry at all, but if I have to I'd rather marry you than anyone else," Rupert told her staunchly. "I'll fight Kit for your hand! I shall be your knight and protect you!"

This was a game they had played since childhood, but now they were older the joke had serious undertones. Emmy knew that Rupert no more wanted to marry her than Kit did. He claimed to never want to marry at all, and sometimes he looked so wistful and so sad that Emmy wondered if there was a secret love hidden away at Oxford. The wife of a don, perhaps? Or a society lady as far above him as the stars? It must be somebody out of reach, anyway.

"Kit wouldn't fight you for me," was all she said. "He'd be relieved, and tell you to help yourself!"

"Lady Rivers would combust if we married. It would be almost worth it to see her face!"

"How romantic you are," she remarked, and Rupert laughed.

"I've never been called that before!"

They reached the far end of the terrace and descended the elegant flight of steps which led to the lawn. The grass beneath Emmy's kid boots was springy, and she longed to kick them off and run across the lawn barefoot instead of having to hold her friend's arm and take the tiny steps necessitated by her skirts.

"Where are we going?" she asked Rupert as they passed the marquee. There was another set of steps here which led to a lower garden with yet more manicured lawns and another stately cedar tree. It was from this spot that the best views of the manor were to be glimpsed, and the setting for several of the paintings which graced the great hall.

"To find Kit. He's arranged a surprise for his parents and asked me to let you in on it. He also said to make sure you don't pass out this time. Should this mean something?"

Emmy was about to offer an explanation but Rupert, waving at two figures standing at the far end of the lawn, had lost all track of their conversation.

"There's Kit! Hello there! I've found her."

Emmy squinted against the light. Two young men were silhouetted against the glare, one positioning a table and chairs with great intent while another stood in front of a camera, adjusting the position to his satisfaction.

It was Alex Winter.

Emmy blinked in case it was the brightness playing tricks but when she opened her eyes Alex was still there. He was deep in conversation with Kit, as though being at Rosecraddick Manor was the most natural thing in the world.

There was a falling sensation in her stomach and her hand slid from the crook of Rupert's arm. As Alex straightened up from the camera their eyes met, and she knew that his expression of absolute joy was reflected in her own smile. The tangled fears that she might have dreamed the whole episode or imagined the invisible tie between them unknotted in a heartbeat, because it was plain that whatever linked her to this extraordinary young man was as real and as solid as the ground beneath her feet.

"Kit's hired a travelling photographer to record the garden party," Rupert explained, beaming at Alex. "That's the surprise. We're all going to have out portraits taken by Mr Winter here! Won't that make this a garden party to remember?"

"Yes," Emmy said, still holding Alex's gaze. She already knew she would never forget it.

"Emmy! Here you are!" Kit, final chair set down, kissed her cheek and flung an arm around Rupert's shoulders. "May I introduce Alex Winter, a photographer I was lucky enough to stumble across when I was in town last week? He's kindly agreed to take some pictures this afternoon." Giving her a ghost of a wink, he added, "I do hope you took my advice and can breathe a little more easily today?"

"Yes, I took it. Thank you," Emmy said. As she held out her hand to Alex, she felt as though she was in a dream. "We've already met," she heard herself say as his fingers closed around hers. "Hello again, Mr Winter."

As his fingers tightened on hers she heard his sharp intake of breath at the rush of heat between them.

"Miss Pendennys! What a wonderful surprise to see you again."

There are times when everything changes, moments when a parallel universe spins away on a new and wonderful course and life alters for ever, and Emmy knew this this was one such. As Alex raised her hand to his lips she knew that when her eyelids closed for the final time she would relive this memory. She would feel again his soft mouth brush her skin, hear the trembling call of wood pigeons from the woods and relive the pure joy of knowing she had come home after a long and lonely journey.

"You know one another?" Rupert asked, looking from Emmy to Alex in bewilderment.

"We spoke when Miss Pendennys visited Rowe's studio in Bodmin," Alex explained. He lowered her hand but still held it tightly, seeming unable to believe she was really present.

"That's where I had my birthday photograph taken. Mr Winter's employed there," Emmy added, since Rupert was still looking mystified.

Alex shook his head. "Not any longer, alas. I spent a little too much time running an errand one afternoon and not long after that incident Mr Rowe decided I was surplus to requirements." He smiled at Emmy, a conspiratorial smile which left her in no doubt what errand this might have been, before glancing down and noticing that he was still holding her hand. As his fingers fell away, she wanted to press the back of her hand to her mouth and seal his kiss against her lips. The spot his lips had brushed tingled.

"That's jolly bad luck." Kit was sympathetic, but Alex gave a philosophical shrug.

"That's the way of it in my game. It's back to the open road for me, or it will be once I've earned enough to set off. I'm without a horse at the moment."

"Horse?" echoed Rupert. He seemed more confused by the minute. Emmy took pity on him.

"Mr Winter is going to travel the world with his horse-drawn studio and use his camera as a mirror to reflect life. Photography is a way of showing people truth and changing their hearts."

"You remembered!" said Alex, and she blushed beneath the intensity of his delight.

"Of course. How could I forget?"

Rupert stared at them. "You two must have had a right chinwag."

"I'm afraid I took up far too much time of Miss Pendennys' time," Alex said, still smiling at Emmy and not looking sorry in the slightest. "It was terribly bad-mannered of me."

"Not at all," she said. "It was fascinating."

"Clearly," said Rupert.

"It sounds fascinating to me, too," Kit said. "I aim to tell the truth through poetry, which sounds rather pi now I hear it said out loud! I must confess I have a way to go yet with my verses."

"Don't listen to him. He's very good," Emmy told Alex.

"Don't listen to her," Kit countered. "She hasn't read my work since she was ten and I thought rhyming 'dove' and 'love' was a feat of literary genius. Then she asked me what rhymed with 'Parliament', and I haven't dared show her a line since. Emmy's a stern literary critic."

"You do sound a rather hard taskmaster, Miss Pendennys," said Alex. "Should I be afraid to take your photograph? Mr Rowe struggled, I believe?" He dark eyes sparkled with mirth.

"I imagine you're up to the challenge," she replied. "Unlike Kit and his poor attempt to rhyme the only word I ever asked for!"

Kit pressed his hand against his chest. "Wordsworth and Keats never had to suffer such disrespect!"

"One day you'll be up there with them. You mark my words. Everyone will have heard of Kit Rivers," said Rupert loyally.

"Then schoolchildren will hate me," Kit laughed.

"They'll loathe you," Emmy agreed. "Especially if they have to learn your longer poems by heart!"

"So, you're a poet, sir?" Alex asked Kit.

"A very poor one," Kit replied. "Like you, I believe that we can speak through art and even change the way people see events and each other. I've always thought this was my calling – to tell truths through words, however unpalatable those might be or however high the personal cost of writing it."

As Kit spoke, Emmy felt cold to the bone, even though the sun was beaming down powerfully. It seemed to her that she was watching their conversation take place from a faraway vantage point, one from where she could see the scene as though it was set on a stage, and she was powerless to call out or participate. All the players were in position; two young gentleman in suits and boaters, a dark-haired girl in bright white, and a handsome young photographer who, although in shirt sleeves and patched cords, still commanded all eyes. She heard the bubbles of conversation rise and pop like soap bubbles as their lines were spoken, but the meaning of the words barely registered. How would this play end? With tears or with laughter?

"That's exactly it!" Alex agreed, nodding. "People might not like what you have to say, but truth-telling never made a man popular. I'm moved by Matthew Barry's photographs of the American Civil War, but his work is disturbing and not at all pleasant viewing."

"Maybe we'll work together one day," Kit said thoughtfully. "Your pictures could illustrate my words."

As Kit made this suggestion Emmy felt as though the sun had plunged behind the darkest of clouds. She rubbed her bare arms as though she could smooth away the strange unease with the goosebumps, and wished she had kept her shawl.

"You'll have to hurry up if Mr Winter's off to travel the world," Rupert, ever the legal mind, pointed out.

Alex held up his hands. "No need to rush the muse on my account. I have a wagon, it's true, but no means of pulling it since Apache, that's my dear old horse, pulled a tendon. While he rests I'll be earning my crust another way. Or selling my cameras."

"But you need them for your work," Emmy objected.

"True, Miss Pendennys, but old Patchy and I also need to eat. I may sell my Graflex camera."

"You've got a Graflex?" Rupert said, impressed. "How on earth —?"

He stopped abruptly, mortified.

"I mean …"

"How did somebody like me come by such an expensive camera?" Alex asked with a grin. "Don't apologise, sir, it's a perfectly fair question! The answer is, it was actually very simple once I'd robbed a bank … I'm joking of course. The rather less colourful truth is my father left me a small inheritance and I put a portion of this into my cameras and the rest into my darkroom and travelling."

"You followed your dreams," Kit remarked. He looked wistful. "That's not always easy."

"No, indeed." Alex turned back to his camera, twiddling the lens. Over his shoulder, he added, "My father wanted me to go into the Church and is probably spinning in his grave, but somebody up there must be looking out for me because I almost took the Titanic to America."

"Pa lost friends on that ship," said Kit, shaking his head. "Dreadful. You were fortunate."

Alex unwound a rolled-up sleeve to polish the camera lens.

"I certainly was. I had an offer of work which I couldn't turn down, and when another lad offered to buy my ticket, I couldn't say no. I often think of him taking my place and wonder what I was spared for. It keeps me awake some nights."

"It makes you think, doesn't it? How absolutely everything can change for ever in no more than a heartbeat," Kit agreed quietly.

Alex straightened up. "It does indeed."

His warm eyes sought Emmy's, and the message in them couldn't have been clearer. She wished she could tell him everything had changed for her too.

All four fell quiet. The loss of life on the luxurious ocean liner had been shocking, and that Alex Winter had escaped the same end only by a quirk of fortune seemed hugely significant. Emmy wondered whether he had been spared so he could meet her. She liked to think so.

Alex tipped his head back and squinted towards the sun, which was slanting honeyed rays across the lawn and tempting the cedar tree into casting shadows of hunter's green over the lawn. Emmy loved the way the butterscotch skin of his throat tautened over the muscles of his neck in a perfect contrast to the bright white linen of his shirt. If she'd had a camera of her own she would long to capture him like this, so intent on his appraisal of the light and shade as he measured and judged it before catching time for ever like a firefly in a jar, eternal images to light memory.

"The light will be perfect in half an hour. The sun will be a little lower and the shadows will begin to lengthen. A soft pearlescent light will be beautiful."

"Marvellous," said Kit. "Tell me what you'd like me to do and then I'll fetch Ma and Pa."

As he and Alex discussed the best positions for the sitters, talk ebbed and flowed easily, and standing back a little in the shade of the tree Emmy allowed herself to study the photographer. She had never been so aware of another person's proximity and she gorged herself on every detail of him, memorising the curl of his hair against the nape of his neck and the warm accents of his tanned skin. Now and again their eyes would meet and she knew his thoughts were running in tandem. They shared a secret, a private code that nobody else would ever break, and they were linked by surprise and wonder.

It was all new and delicious and utterly terrifying.

"Will you still go to America?" Kit asked Alex. "I must admit I'm a little put off ocean liners."

"Not for a while. I have my wagon so I can travel across the Continent, which is a good place to start," Alex said. "Paris is wonderful and I long to see Florence, but before any of that I just need to earn enough to keep Patchy in oats through the winter."

"There's always work about at this time of year," said Rupert. "I'm sure you could find something to tide you over, and it would be a dreadful pity to sell your cameras. There's bound to be something at the manor, don't you think, Kit?"

Kit's eyes flickered to Emmy. He would know that hope had flared in her heart at Rupert's suggestion and she understood his poet's soul must be torn between the romance of this situation and the rules of propriety. Kit would never encourage her to behave inappropriately or to hope for more, yet she could tell he sensed a kindred spirit in Alex and felt sympathetic to his plight.

"Possibly," he said carefully.

Alex looked thoughtful. "I wouldn't want to impose. Besides, my old wagon is hardly a thing of beauty."

"You could set up camp in the manor wood where nobody would ever need to see," Rupert suggested. "You could give us a few photography lessons while you're here and earn some more funds that way. I've been meaning to get one of those pocket Kodaks for a while. I'm fascinated by photography."

This was the first Emmy had ever heard of Rupert's interest in cameras. Kit, catching her eye, raised an eyebrow.

"The Vest Pocket's a very good camera," Alex said warmly. "I have one myself, and I use it a great deal. I'd always keep it over the Graflex because it's so versatile and easy to use. When that's gone the Vest Pocket'll be my workhorse."

"You mustn't sell your camera!" Emmy cried. It seemed dreadful that he might be forced to part with the equipment that made his work possible.

"That's my absolute last resort, Miss Pendennys," Alex promised her. "I'm pretty resourceful, and I'm sure I'll find some work before that has to happen."

Emmy threw Kit a pleading look.

"Kit, this is all my fault. If Mr Winter hadn't got lost delivering my photograph and taken so long he would still have his job. Oh, Kit! Imagine how you would feel if you had to part with your copy of Keats or your notebooks? It would be unbearable! You must be able to find something for Mr Winter on the estate?"

Poor Kit had a tender heart and didn't stand a chance against this onslaught.

"I could have a word with our estate manager. It may be that he has a few week's work, if that would help?" he offered. "The gamekeeper could do with a hand, too, preparing for the shoot."

Emmy's heart rose. Kit, dear Kit, was offering a way for Alex to keep his camera and, even more importantly to her, stay in Rosecraddick for a little while. Her chest ached with hope, and she didn't think anything had ever mattered more than what Alex might say next. The whole world appeared intent on his answer; even the plump bumble bees working their way along the lavender bushes seemed to stop humming and the breeze to take a pause from ruffling the green frills of the cedar tree.

"Well? What do you think?" she prompted Alex, who hadn't replied.

Alex exhaled slowly and Emmy realised that he knew, as she did, that his answer was about to change everything. She held her breath, willing him to accept.

"I think that perhaps you don't need to travel the world to find yourself in exactly the right place," he said finally, holding out his hand to Kit. "Thank you, sir. It's very generous of you to offer to help."

"You may not think so once you've met my father," Kit warned as they shook. "And talking of Pa, I'd better fetch my parents to be ready for when the light's just as you need it. Emmy, that champagne must be warm and it's terribly hot in the sun. Why don't you wait in the shade while I fetch the others? We don't need another fainting episode while you have your photograph taken – Mama would combust! Rupert, come with me and fetch some cold lemonade for Emmy, would you?"

Rupert, unused to playing the footman, looked rather taken aback but didn't argue. He never did with Kit.

"Righto," he said cheerfully. "Lemonade it is."

The two young men departed in the direction of the house and Alex and Emmy were left alone. The air between them sparkled like the bubbles in her tepid champagne and she knew she wanted to hold onto this moment for ever and freeze it in her mind as a mental snapshot of a perfect summer's afternoon; music and laughter drifting on the breeze, the whisper of her skirts across the grass as she walked towards Alex, and the swelling certainty that just as Fate had turned this man away from a doomed ocean liner so it had brought him here and to her. Now, it said, make of this what you will!

"It's wonderful to see you again," Alex said softly.

"I didn't expect to see you again," Emmy blurted at the same time, suddenly shy. "I thought ..." her voice faltered, and she took a deep breath as she sought the words to tell this almost stranger how this thought had filled her with an inexplicable sadness. "I was afraid we would never cross paths again and it didn't seem right."

She knew her words would show him how bleak this had made her feel and that this openness left her vulnerable, as exposed as a soft-bellied crab scuttling across the sand as oystercatchers worked the tideline, but she wanted to be honest. Why pretend? In a matter of moments Colonel and Lady Rivers would arrive with an entourage of footmen and maids, and there would be no further opportunity to speak alone. This brief shade-dappled interlude was all they would have, and these fleeting minutes – minutes which offered a small respite from the world of tea and chatter – must not be squandered by playing games.

"I feared so too," Alex Winter said quietly. "I couldn't stop thinking about you, Miss Pendennys – Emmy. It makes no sense, and forgive me if I'm speaking out of place, but I just couldn't accept that one meeting was all it would be, and I confess I came here to deliver your photograph in person. I must have walked for at least an hour; I was so lost. When I discovered you didn't live here after all I was almost beside myself."

"You shouldn't have taken the trouble to come all this way. Not for a photograph," Emmy said, and Alex burst into peals of laughter. It was a lovely sound, warm and joyous and utterly contagious.

"Lord! I didn't do it for a photograph! And certainly not for *that* one!"

She fought to keep a straight face. "Don't you like it?"

"Do *you*?" Alex's look of abject horror made her giggle.

"No! It's hideous. My godmother was furious. I've hidden it in the drawing room."

"I would have hidden it in the dustbin," he said fervently. "While I was in the darkroom developing it, I told myself that I had to do whatever I could to put things right, although I knew that was just an excuse to see you again. Then, when Mr Rivers ventured into the studio requesting a photographer for his mother's garden party, I couldn't believe my good fortune. I've been praying you would attend today."

Emmy sent Kit a silent 'thank you'. Her dear friend surely had the kindest heart of anyone.

"So, you came here today to see me?" she asked, wondering if this was flirting.

A smile curled his mouth. Emmy thought it was the most beautiful mouth she'd ever seen.

"It's hard to say what swung it for me; the chance of seeing you again or keeping Patchy in oats!"

Definitely flirting! She caught his smile and returned it.

"I would say the answer's obvious. Your horse must eat."

"Yes, he must, but the truth is I was longing to see you again." Alex took her hand, drawing her towards him and suddenly serious. "Emmy, promise me you won't vanish again?"

Emmy tilted her chin to look up at him. Something deep inside her was trembling as the world she had always known tipped upside down.

This was more than flirtation or game-playing on a sunny afternoon. This was everything.

"I promise," she said softly, and in the stillness of the afternoon her words were a vow. "I won't vanish a second time."

He raised her fingers to his lips and kissed each fingertip in turn. The touch of his lips against her flesh was reverent and almost chaste, yet it made her feel molten and giddy. Something sacred and unbreakable had just been sealed between them. A promise had been made that would remain with her for ever, just as the lengthening shadows, wrought iron tables and elegant garden scene would soon be captured on film in a timeless image that would always remind her of this moment.

Excited voices rippled the stillness, heralding the arrival of the Rivers family and their guests, and the solemn atmosphere shifted back to sunshine and champagne. Alex pressed her fingers and released them, but his dark eyes were lit by her words and she knew her cheeks were flushed. While glasses chinked on wobbling trays, Lady Rivers scolded a maid, and liveried footmen set the table with cakes and sandwiches and an enormous silver teapot, Emmy watched Alex switch into professional mode as he arranged his subjects and directed each one into the perfect position. She loved the way he could measure light and composition, moving people and tweaking the angle of a shoulder or the tilt of a hat brim until the frame was literally picture perfect.

"No wonder you fainted, Em," Kit grumbled as Alex abandoned the camera for the umpteenth time, to angle him towards his parents.

"Ready?" Alex said, poised to dive beneath the drapes. "Everyone please stay still."

Emmy hoped the camera wouldn't be sensitive enough to distinguish her trembling as sat beside her godmother, loose curls tumbling over her shoulders and with her eyes fixed on the man behind the camera. This time she was not about to faint, and when she was an old lady, older than even the old Queen had been, she would show today's photographs to her grandchildren and tell them that although the girl in the white dress might look demure and proper, her hands had been shaking and her heart turning cartwheels. They would laugh, of course, and not believe a word of it, for what did old folk know of such things?

"Ready?" Alex asked.

The shutter closed and the scene moved from the present to the past, as the photograph was taken which marked for ever the day when Emily Pendennys' life truly began.

The Wagon

Rosecraddick, August 1913

The sun was high above the wooded hills, gilding the long grass on the unmown lawn, toasting inland seas of rippling wheat and drenching the wild garden with light as thick and rich as honey. Skylarks spun and trilled in the cloudless blue, and the scent of baked earth was warm and rich and tinged with salt. Bees droned from the flowerbeds as they bounced from rose to rose, and high in the chestnut trees the conker cases swelled green and secretive as they waited for the summer leaves to yellow and flutter to the ground. Until then they too would drowse in the warmth, just as Rupert drowsed on a tartan blanket, battered fedora pulled down over a pinkening nose, and Kit sprawled on in a stripy deckchair with his head bent over a book as he made notes. His pencil scratched over paper and the woodpigeons' calls trembled from the woods, it seemed to Emmy that on this August afternoon the whole world was dozing through a golden summer as endless as it was corn rich and pollen heavy.

This was what happiness felt like.

Since Lady Rivers' garden party, everything had become more glorious. The colours were brighter. The sky bluer. The sun shone with benign warmth and even the sunsets were more vivid and beautiful. There was magic in everything, from the countless greens of the canopy of leaves to the simple joy of catching a glimpse of Alex working in the garden while she drank tea and ate cucumber sandwiches with her godmother. It seemed impossible that only a few weeks ago she hadn't even known there was an Alex Winter in the world when now she couldn't contemplate the thought of one without him. Everything had changed.

Everything.

After taking their photographs, Alex was preparing to pack away his camera and equipment when several other guests drifted down to the lower lawn, delighted to discover a photographer and clamouring to have their own pictures taken. Emmy would have liked nothing more than to watch him work and hopefully snatch another exchange, but he was so popular she knew there was little chance of another conversation. While the gentlemen spoke to him and whispering ladies cast admiring glances his way, Emmy was shepherded back to the marquee to spend the rest of the afternoon making small talk and nibbling cucumber sandwiches – neither of which was easy to do when her heart in her mouth and her mind on the other side of the garden. She was terribly distracted, and several times Rupert threw her a puzzled look when she answered someone's question with a totally unrelated reply. It was impossible to hold the thread of a conversation when all she could think about was Alex. Her thoughts kept drifting back to him, and she barely registered the conversations taking place around her – which was no bad thing when Reverend Cutwell embarked on a monologue regarding the evils of women's suffrage.

"Such behaviour is damaging, unseemly and against the nature of God," he droned, gimlet eyes bright with righteous indignation at the audacity of Mrs Pankhurst and her acolytes. "A woman must be guided by her husband in all things, and only through marriage or good works she will prove her value. Wouldn't you agree, Miss Pendennys?"

Emmy, peering over his shoulder in case Alex ascended the steps to the upper lawn, hadn't heard a word. Floundering, she flung a helpless look at Kit who took pity on her by steering the conversation to cricket, another of the vicar's passions and one the Reverend was equally delighted to discuss at length. There was another dangerous moment when Lady Rivers asked Emmy to pour the tea and she almost missed the cup, but apart from this she was confident nobody noticed how her hands trembled or that she struggled to sit still.

It was the sweetest torture to be so near to him and yet so far. As the sun slipped behind the manor's gabled roof and the shadows lengthened across the lawn, Emmy realised that at some point between the teapot and the vicar she must have missed seeing Alex leave, and she felt disappointed but no longer afraid she would never see him again. How could she be after what they had promised? Emmy hoped that Kit had managed to arrange some employment for Alex. If not, keeping her promise could prove rather tricky.

Kit, as good as his word, found the estate manager, who agreed that more help would be useful in the grounds. While the guests sipped tea and ate cake, a groom was dispatched with one of the heavy horses to fetch the wagon, and by the time the last carriages and motor cars had departed through the manor's gates, Alex Winter was setting up camp in a woodland clearing. When Kit, driving Emmy home in his father's smart Rolls Royce, told her this, she flung her arms around him.

"Thank you!"

"Careful! I'll crash," he warned as the car swerved. "And don't get too excited – it's only for a couple of weeks while his horse rests. No offence, Em, but it strikes me that Alex Winter is far too talented and ambitious to stay here for long. He wants to travel the world."

"Yes. I know."

Emmy raised her face to the sky, loving the rush of cold air on her flushed cheeks as the car sped along the lane, dipping down the hills and surging up the steep-sided valleys. Kit was right; Rosecraddick was too small for a man like Alex Winter, but she already knew he wouldn't want to leave without her. They were destined to travel the world together, and her stomach twisted with excitement.

"I'm not sure I should have hired him today." Kit changed down a gear, guiding the car around a sharp bend, and Emmy looked at him in surprise.

"Why? I thought you liked him?"

"I do. I like him very much indeed and I can see you do too."

"Was it that obvious?"

"Only because you were the colour of Killjoy Cutwell's nose every time you looked at him!"

She sloshed him on the arm. "I was *not*."

"All right – you were very restrained, actually. I only knew because you told me."

Emmy was relieved. "I thought so. Red-faced, my foot! Rupert would have said so if I had been."

Kit laughed. "Rupe wouldn't notice what a girl was up to if she turned cartwheels and sang the national anthem! That's a given!"

"What's that supposed to mean?"

"Rupert and girls," said Kit, as though it was obvious.

Emmy frowned. She had no idea what he was talking about.

"I thought there was somebody at Oxford?"

"There may well be, but I'd be surprised if —"

A pheasant shot across the lane and Kit had to stand on the brakes, jolting both the occupants of the car and the conversation. The change of pace seemed to check him, and although Emmy waited, Kit said no more. She shot a questioning glance at him but beneath his hat and goggles it was hard to gauge what her friend was thinking. The subject was clearly closed.

Anyway, never mind Rupert. She wanted to talk about Alex.

"If you and I both like Alex, why do you think it was a mistake to hire him today?"

"Because I can see how you feel about him," said Kit.

"But that's a good thing, silly! When we talked before you said I was lucky to have met somebody like Alex. You said you were envious."

"I am."

His gloved hands gripped the wheel tightly and she laid her own hand on his arm.

"It's the kindest thing anyone has ever done for me, Kit. I will never, ever forget it and I will always be thankful."

"I hope so," said Kit, still sounding doubtful. "At least you'll have a decent photograph now, so I suppose that's something."

He turned a corner, breaking through the tunnel of trees and into the early evening sunshine where the gates of Pendennys Place, listing as drunkenly as her father on his crutches and equally past their glory days, loomed ahead. The car swept through them, bouncing along the rutted drive and paused at the bottom of the crumbling front steps. Kit pushed his goggles up and turned to Emmy.

"Look, I do like Alex, and I can see why you do. He's intelligent and charismatic, and although I'm no judge I'm sure he's very handsome, because all the ladies were most taken with him, even Mama!"

Emmy laughed. "She was rather keen to have him take her individual photograph! Oh Kit, do stop looking so worried."

"But I *am* worried. Even if in another world he and I would have a great deal in common, Alex Winter isn't a gentleman. Your father wouldn't think he was a suitable match for you. This is going to be trouble, Emmy."

"Whatever happened to 'rank doesn't matter' and 'the day is coming when everyone's the same'?"

He sighed. "Unfortunately, that day's yet to dawn. It's coming, but I'm not sure when or how. Something big will have to happen to bring it about – something that will change society and even the world – but until then you know as well as I do how these things work. Especially for a woman."

"It's not fair," Emmy said bitterly.

"I know it isn't, but it's how things are – for now, anyway."

Emmy scowled down at her lap. Her hands, hidden in her shawl, were bunched into tight fists. Nothing was fair when you were female, it seemed. Mrs Puckey always said such was a woman's lot in life and that this was to be borne and not argued with, a sentiment which made Emmy want to scream. Mrs Pankhurst and the suffragettes didn't hold with such views.

Maybe they would cause the changes Kit dreamed about?

"So, what would you do now if you were me?" she asked him. "Walk away and do what everyone expects of you? Ignore what your heart tells you and do your duty?"

Emmy already knew the answer to these questions. She knew that when Kit Rivers gave his heart it would be to the one woman his soul belonged with. Whether she was a queen or a scullery maid, it would make no difference to him. Kit was a romantic and a poet. Nothing else would matter to him except love.

He spread his hands helplessly.

"Well then," Emmy said.

Kit rubbed his face with his gloved hands.

"Emmy, you know what I would do, but it's different for a man. You don't need me to explain why. Look, how about I ask Ma to have some more photographs taken? You could join us, and Rupe's keen for a photography lesson or two; maybe you can share these? See Alex that way and with us as chaperones? Or you and I could take a walk through the woods and visit Alex while he's still here? Mama would be thrilled to see us about together, which would put me in her good books, and this way everything will be very respectable."

Emmy nodded but although it was typical of Kit's thoughtful nature to consider her reputation there was no way she intended to have anyone accompanying her the next time she saw Alex Winter. Their first two meetings had been gleaned from snatched moments, and the next time they met she was determined they would speak without interruption. Kit had barely driven away through the peeling gates than Emmy was working out how she could see Alex alone. As hugely fond of Kit Rivers as she was, Emmy neither wanted nor needed him as her chaperone.

Although she was almost bursting with impatience, Emmy waited until the next afternoon before taking the path to Rosecraddick Manor. She had told herself she was simply enjoying a walk through the woods, but her racing heart had known the truth; she was seeking out Alex Winter and without a chaperone – something which could get them both into huge trouble. After several hours of watching her fidget and drift about the house, Mrs Puckey had packed Emmy off outside to get some fresh air and Emmy thought that if it so happened that she were to wander by the clearing where his caravan rested, then nobody could blame her or him. It would look like a chance encounter.

It was a glorious day and as she walked through the woods it seemed to Emmy as though everything in nature had become more splendid. The colours were brighter. The sky bluer. Even the birds were singing their hearts out especially for her. She had walked this way a thousand times, climbing over the stile and kicking her skirts out of the way impatiently as she ran, but today the route felt different, twisting a little more and plunging deeper into the cool heart of the trees as though seeking to conceal her. She felt excitement and nervousness build inside her like the gathering of the spring tide, emotions which powered her forwards and to what she knew must be her destiny.

If Emily Pendennys had been born for any moment then this was surely it.

It was only a short walk through the woods, but each footstep took her further away from the girl she had been and a little closer to the woman she would become. The shadows beneath the thick canopy, green and deep, seemed to shift and breathe like waves as though she was walking through the landscape of a strange dream. Beneath Emmy's feet roots and brambles snatched at her as though wishing to imprison her like a fairytale princess, but she kicked them away with the toe of her boot. The dense tangle of undergrowth wouldn't stop her any more than Kit's warnings. This was her time, and she was ready for the next step.

A fork in the path offered a choice; right for the village and the manor – or left, deeper into the trees. Without hesitation her feet turned left and there it was, appearing like a mirage in the grassy clearing and shocking in its brightness. The abruptness of the revelation stopped her in her tracks, and she stared at the pea-green wagon with jolly red wheels and 'Alexander Winter: Travelling Photographer' painted proudly on the side. He was here! Alex Winter was really here! This was the mobile studio, the alchemist's den where Alex worked magic to conjure faces and scenes from film and secret chemicals. It was his studio in miniature where a top hat or a plumed fan could transform humble folk into gentry and where painted backgrounds whisked them away from Cornwall and to Paris or Florence.

So, it was here that Alex Winter slept and ate and dreamed of travelling the globe. Did he dream of her? Would there be a place in this world for Emily Pendennys? For a moment she was uncertain, her mouth dry with the enormity of what this could mean for them both, and she almost turned tail. The faded curtains were closed at the tiny window, and the door at the summit of four small steps was firmly shut. He would never know she'd been here. She could run home now and pick up the threads of her old life and nothing would change. Yet how would she ever live with not finding out what else there could be? How could she walk away from this? Emmy knew that she couldn't turn back now. There was no choice in the matter, and sense and logic and propriety didn't even come into it.

The heart has no room for such matters.

She pulled her shoulders back and walked into the clearing, mind made up. A piebald horse, tethered and champing the grassy clearing, looked up and whickered in greeting.

"You must be Patchy. Is your master home?" Emmy asked, as she scratched his hairy neck. "Should I stay and see him? Or is it better for us both if I leave right now?"

Apache stamped his foot and swished his tail in answer. Then the caravan door swung open and the decision, if it had ever even been one, was made for her. All the knotty complications, the million million reasons why she ought not to be here unchaperoned, unravelled like knitting because at the heart of it all was the man smiling down at her. At the heart of it all there was only love, and that was the simplest and most powerful reason of them all.

"Emmy!" said Alex Winter and the delight with which he spoke her name told Emmy she was exactly where she was always meant to be.

His hair was caught back from his face with a strand of leather, and he was wearing a white shirt and simple cords. Everything about him was gilded in the sunshine, and her breath caught.

"Sorry, did you knock? I was working and I get so wrapped up in what I'm doing I can't hear a thing. Time does strange things when you work alone in the darkroom."

She shook her head. "I've only just arrived. I was admiring the wagon."

"And making friends with old Patchy, I see." Alex leapt down the steps to join her in rubbing the horse's neck and scratching his withers. "He likes you."

"He's a handsome boy," Emmy said.

"I think so. I bought him from the butcher back at home. He wouldn't stand still on the round, which was causing quite a problem! He likes to be on the move, does Patch."

"Are we just talking about the horse?" Emmy asked as Patchy nudged her for another scratch, eyes closed and lower lip drooping with pleasure.

Alex laughed. "The truth is we both feel a bit that way, but see how happy he is to be here with you." He turned to her, serious suddenly. "He doesn't want to go anywhere for a while. He's happy not to be travelling."

Now Emmy knew they weren't talking about the horse.

"Good," she said, giving Patchy one final pat. "I'm glad he likes it here."

"I don't think he's ever been happier in his life," Alex replied softly.

They smiled at one another, suddenly shy.

"I was going to make some tea," he said, flushing. "Can I offer you some? Or some lemonade? I have cake too."

"My goodness! A tea party in the woods? Should we be expecting Lady Rivers?" Emmy teased.

Alex pulled a face. "Lord, I hope not. She's a most exacting customer and I can't imagine she would be at all impressed with my modest studio. There certainly aren't any real roses in it, and the choice of backdrop is limited."

"In that case I'd love tea. And I promise I'll do my best not to pull faces and faint!"

"You may pull a face when you see how untidy it is," Alex warned, stepping back and gesturing for her to proceed upwards. "And I'm afraid the chemicals I use for developing can be rather pungent."

Emmy bunched her skirts into her fists and scrambled up to steep steps. Inside, the van was, as Alex had warned, a little chaotic, but it was clean and cosy and she glanced around with pleasure, marvelling at how much could be fitted into such a tiny space. The far end was shielded off with a thick black door which left little room for much else, but somehow Alex had managed to create a home in miniature and already Emmy felt far happier here than she ever had at Rosecraddick Manor, despite its grandeur and beautiful furnishings.

"Please take a seat, ma'am," Alex said with a bow. He hopped in behind her, scooping up a pile of photograph albums from a sagging wickerwork chair, and pulling an egg-yolk yellow cushion from a pile on the floor which he patted into position with great pride.

"There. You'll suit the chair far better than my sample photograph books!"

Emmy sat down while Alex scooted about the tiny space, plumping cushions on his bunk, straightening the bright patchwork quilt. As he placed a kettle on the pot-bellied stove she surveyed her surroundings with fascination. Hats, silk flowers and parasols were strapped to the curved walls with tasselled rope, painted backdrops leaned against the side of the bed and gleaming copper pans were strung up from the roof, which she thought must make quite a clatter when the wagon was in transit – but it was the walls which fascinated her the most, for they were not covered in photographs as she would have expected, but papered instead with exquisite sketches.

"You draw?"

"I do, but not very well, I'm afraid," Alex said over his shoulder while delving into a tiny cupboard and pulling out teacups with a flourish. "Aha! I knew these would come in useful one day, although I must confess I thought they would be props rather than used for entertaining."

Emmy leaned forward and admired at a drawing of a woman in a big straw hat.

"These are wonderful! You don't do yourself justice."

"Ah well, that probably because my scribbling's nothing in comparison to my mother's painting. That's a self-portrait, that sketch you're looking at. Ivy Winter painted portraits and was quite sought after by fashionable society. If she'd lived long enough, I think she would have been very successful." A shadow crossed his face. "I admit I never quite had the heart for painting after Mama passed away. I put all my passion into photography, which is a poor second."

"It certainly is not. You paint with film," Emmy said firmly. "She would be proud of what you've achieved."

Alex smiled at her, a sad smile. "I'd like to think so, but I guess I'll never know. My father was certainly less than impressed with my choice of livelihood."

Emmy thought about Julyan Pendennys, who would want to beat her black and blue if he knew where she was at that particular moment. In her experience parents were difficult creatures to please.

"You took Fate in both hands and made it work for you," she reminded him.

"Yes, I did," he agreed, turning away and carefully spooning leaves into a chipped blue teapot. He lifted up the kettle and poured in hot water, adding, "Apologies for such a maudlin start to your visit to my studio on wheels. Let me show you the darkroom while the tea brews."

The thought of being alone with him in a dark enclosed space made Emmy's heart flutter rather nervously, but Alex, every inch the professional, busied himself showing her the trays, chemicals and plates as well as the lines where he pegged photographs up to dry.

"Here's the one I took of you on the lawn," he said, reaching to unclip it and passing it to her. "I'm rather pleased with it because the light falls beautifully."

Emmy took the print in her hands. How strange it was to see her yesterday self caught in time beneath the cedar tree. She already felt a different person to that girl in the long white dress. That girl had never slipped out of her house and stolen through the woods to meet a handsome man, nor had she stood beside him in a darkroom longing for him to kiss her.

"I love your smile in it," he was saying, tracing the image with a forefinger reverently. "It's just there beneath the surface like a bud ready to burst into bloom. It reminds me of the Mona Lisa, and anyone who sees it will wonder what you were thinking about that day."

'*You*,' thought Emmy. It was unnerving to see her feelings captured for ever in this way. He must surely know how she felt.

"I have lots more to develop." Alex took the picture from her, gently pegging it up once more where it joined others, memories of the garden party strung out like washing to drift with the winds of time. 'One day, people will look at these pictures and wonder who we are,' she thought. The idea made her shiver, along with the realisation that one day nobody would know that the two young men in white with their arms flung around each other's shoulders were Rupert and Kit, or the fat lady with the pug was Lady Kessle, or even that the dour parson with muttonchop sideboards was none other than Killjoy Cutwell. Perhaps somebody might glance at them for a moment and wonder, but then they would be swept away into a box or a drawer to gather dust while the days passed and the images faded. Everything was so fleeting, and the pain of realising this snatched her breath. She pressed her hand against her breastbone and fought to quell a sadness she knew she couldn't articulate. Kit might know how to describe it, she thought as she looked up at the garden party for ever suspended in the late afternoon sunshine, but to her it was just a sharp nostalgia for a world that would somehow slip away without any of them noticing …

"Shall we get some fresh air? It's hot in here and the chemicals are strong," Alex said, seeing her gulp.

Taking her arm, he led Emmy into the living area where he settled her back into the chair and, crouching at her feet, pressed an enamelled mug of water into her hand.

"I'm not feeling faint," Emmy protested as he made her sip it. "It's hard to explain, but it was looking at the pictures. It made me feel …" she paused, struggling for the right word. "As though I was looking at something lost and will never come again. It's beautiful and sad all at once." She pulled a face. "You probably think I'm fanciful."

Alex smiled at her. "Not at all. I know exactly the feeling. The Portuguese have a word for it: *saudade*. It doesn't have an English equivalent, or not in language at least, but it does in photography. I think I feel it a little each time I take a photograph, because that moment in time is gone for ever. There's happiness too, though, because there are so many wonderful moments yet to come." He jumped to his feet. "Like a cup of tea and a slice of the sponge cake I bought in the village this morning."

She loved the way he could understand exactly yet also lighten the mood with a smile and burst of energy. He served cake and strong sweet tea, and as they ate and drank Emmy and Alex chatted easily and as though they had known one another for ever. Living in a quiet place like Rosecraddick, Emmy didn't often meet new people, and she had certainly never met anyone like Alex Winter. He was filled with a zest for life and told wonderful stories of his travels around the Continent and the customers he had met. He was also a good listener, drawing her out and asking thoughtful questions about her own life. As the sun climbed above the clearing and the sponge cake was whittled down to little more than a few crumbs, Emmy told Alex things she had never shared with anyone. In turn she learned that although his father had been disappointed he hadn't chosen the Church, his mother had encouraged him to follow his dreams and not be bound by the rules of class and society.

"She was a wonderful woman," he concluded. "She also had strong opinions, which sometimes gave my father a few headaches! I often think that if she'd been alive now she would have been out and about with Mrs

Pankhurst."

"You approve of women's suffrage?"

"Of course I do," said Alex looking surprised. "And I know my mother would have been all for it. She would have liked you too. You know your own mind and she would have approved of that."

Emmy was pleased to hear this. Henny and Mrs Puckey hadn't been quite so certain that knowing your own mind was a positive attribute. In fact, 'stubborn and wilful' was how her last governess had put it.

Time slipped by as their conversation ebbed and flowed like the tide. There was so much they wanted to say and so much to discover about each other that both of them could have spent days talking without running out of words. Now Emmy understood why Alex Winter was a free spirit, not in thrall to society's expectations, and he understood why she longed to escape and leave behind the weight of the expectations that had been placed on her shoulders. They finished each other's sentences and laughed at the same things, and she knew that he saw the world in a way that made it brighter and more sparkly. And now that Emmy had glimpsed it through Alex's eyes she never wanted to see it any other way. His stories of Paris and Florence filled her mind with images of blue skies, smart boulevards and sun-drenched piazzas, and she didn't need to see his photographs to feel as though she had travelled there with him.

"Memories always stay with you, but photographs can help sharpen them," Alex said finally. He paused and the air between them seemed to thicken, edged with energy like the charged atmosphere of a gathering storm. Slowly, he reached out and took Emmy's hand, weaving his fingers with hers. "I like to take photographs of days and events that mean something to me. Yesterday I did just that. Yesterday is a day I will remember for ever."

His eyes met hers and she knew then everything had changed for him too. He realised, as she did, that the obstacles in their path would be great. His plans had changed in an instant. The path he was taking had diverged and his destination had changed. For Alex, as well as Emmy, that meeting in the studio had set into action a chain of events that would alter everything.

Emmy squeezed his fingers. "May I take a photograph to remind me of this?"

"This? What will your subject be? The broken chair? An empty plate? I would say cake but that seems to have vanished – I can't think where!"

Emmy, who had eaten three slices, grinned.

"The cake was excellent, but I meant this wagon. I want a memory of the day when we were first able to talk properly."

Alex stood up, brushing crumbs from his trousers. "A splendid idea. Let me fetch a camera."

He dived into the darkroom and returned with a tiny box. Intrigued, Emmy watched as he slid out a small box, little bigger than a cigar case.

"My Kodak Vest Pocket camera," he explained, gently teasing out struts and bellows to reveal a lens plate. "It's a wonderful tool and takes good quality pictures."

Used to big cameras and photographers ducking under black cloths, Emmy stared.

"It's tiny."

"Yes, but that's the beauty of it. You can take it anywhere." He passed it to her, his hands gently covering Emmy's as he guided her grip. The leather was warm beneath her fingertips and fitted beautifully in her hands. "Now you look down through there, see? And feel the button beneath your index finger? That will expose the film and take the picture."

"It's that simple?" Emmy asked, peering into the camera, where a ghostly image of the stove waited to be captured for posterity.

"There goes all my mystique," Alex said wryly. "Come on. Time you showed me how it's done."

He jumped down the steps and onto the grass, reaching for her hand. "Don't catch your dress."

In answer, Emmy bunched her skirts into her fists and leapt down too, laughing at the look of surprise on his face.

"I grew up climbing trees and exploring the coves here. Ask Kit or Rupert. When we were small I was forever tagging after them."

"I can't imagine you tagging after anyone," Alex said, shaking his head. "I think it's the rest of us who will struggle to keep up with you. Now, if you'll stand here and turn a little to the left, the sun will be behind and make a nice exposure."

Emmy did as he suggested, cupping the camera in her hand and staring down into the top of it, where a minute wagon floated into sight. Alex's home and workshop, it was also a portal to possibilities and a haven where she could talk freely. Emmy thought that for her it would always represent so much more than just a wagon. It was their own secret world.

She pressed her finger down with a determined click.

"Well done," said Alex, laying his hand over hers and carefully pushing the struts back into place. "That's your first photograph taken."

"I'll treasure it for ever," she said.

"And I will treasure you for ever," he told her softly, so softly that Emmy would have thought she dreamed it if he hadn't been standing right beside her and so close that she could feel the heat of his body and smell his skin. She should have stepped away, but instead she leaned into him and felt his arm slip around her waist, drawing her close.

"I know," she said, raising her hand to touch his face. "I've always known."

Alex leaned in and kissed her, his mouth as soft and as wonderful as she had always known it would be, and Emmy kissed him back, feeling any doubts and fears melt away. And just as the image on the camera had been caught by film like a delicate butterfly in a net, Emmy knew that this moment was caught by her heart where it would be treasured for the rest of her life.

Sketches and Snaps

Rosecraddick

August–December 1913

It wouldn't be true to say Emmy and Alex fell in love over the days following Lady Rivers' garden party since Emmy knew she loved Alex on their very first meeting at the studios and he felt the same, but the weeks and months which followed were a golden and magical time of learning more about each other and snatching as many shared moments as possible. Alex's duties at the manor afforded him little time free and Emmy lived for the hours that they did share, cherishing the memories of each snatched meeting, turning them around and around in her mind like precious jewels.

Alex Winter filled her thoughts from the moment she awoke to the moment her eyelids fluttered closed. When they were together they talked about everything and anything, marvelling in the way that their ideas and thinking were so similar, and delighting in sharing each other's secrets and dreams. Each golden summer's day brimmed with wonder and possibilities, and even when the mellow days of autumn approached, the fields and woods a symphony of ambers and bronzes tinged with plums and olives, Emmy thought the lazy dog days of summer would never end, and felt that this time was more than an interlude suspended between two points in Alex's journey but a voyage all of its own. It was an odyssey with no fixed time of arrival or destination.

If the fact that Alex was a travelling photographer and a minister's son while she was the heir to Pendennys Place were ever dark shadows lurking in the back of her mind, Emmy swept them out of sight just as she'd once seen Rosie brushing dust beneath the drawing room carpet. Her father's heavy drinking, the estate's dwindling finances (Mrs Puckey had lately taken to serving dripping on toast for supper) and the looming prospect of marriage were also all firmly dealt with in Emmy's mental equivalent of Rosie's housemaid skills. Emmy was in love, wonderfully, totally and utterly in love. What could possibly matter more?

If Emmy took far more solitary walks through the woods than before, nobody at Pendennys Place was unduly concerned, although Mrs Puckey did comment on the constant singing which made Julyan growl and bark orders to 'keep the damn noise down'. In the past, when her father's black moods settled over the house like a shroud Emmy had walked on eggshells, hardly daring to breathe, but since Alex's arrival not even those bad tempers could touch her because the whole world was beautiful with Alex in it. The birds sang for her alone, the colours of trees and flowers were one thousand times more vivid and the sunsets were heartbreakingly beautiful as they set the sea alight. Alex Winter allowed her to see Cornwall anew through the lens of his camera, and Emmy thought there had never been such a glorious summer.

On wet days when storms blew in from the sea to strip the world of colour and fill the sky with torn cloud, the soft patter of raindrops on the wagon roof and the merry glow of the stove rendered sheltering from each deluge a cosy delight. If Alex wasn't required at the manor he would work in the darkroom while Emmy curled up in the wicker chair, drowsing in the wood-scented warmth and flicking through one of his many books of photographs, as contented and as happy as she thought it possible for anyone to ever be. On rainy days like these they made toast, drank hot sweet tea and talked for hours, lost in plans of their travels around the world and the life they would lead together, until Emmy suddenly realised how long she had been away from home. Then she would bolt back through the woods, her dragging skirts wet and her thoughts shuttling back and forth as she wove new excuses for her absence.

Yes, the whole world was wonderful. Their love affair was as delicate and as beautiful as the silken spiders' webs which laced the hedges each morning – and equally fragile, for she knew their dreams would be in danger of destruction should they be discovered. They wove plans for the future as they lay hand in hand in the long grass gazing up at fantastical cloud shapes drifting past or when they cocooned themselves in his quilt and listened to the muffled patter of the rain.

"France first," Alex would say, tracing the curve of her cheek and tucking a curl behind her ear. "I want you to see Paris, Emmy. It's so beautiful."

"And where next?" Emmy always asked. She loved to hear him tell her stories of the wonderful adventures they would have and the places they would visit. She would close her eyes as he spoke and see the statues of Florence and the graceful ruins of Rome. If they spoke about these things often enough she felt certain they would come true.

"Down through the lavender fields of Provence and then across the Pyrenees to Spain – if old Patch can make it," was the answer. "Then we'll travel through Spain to the south and across to Africa to see markets and camels and eat spicy food."

"And take pictures of it all," Emmy would prompt, and Alex would laugh and say yes, they would take hundreds of photographs and write a book about their travels.

In between working in the gardens at the manor Alex was teaching Rupert the rudiments of photography. Kit would join in too when he wasn't writing, and Emmy often tagged along on some pretext. The four of them formed a strange band of companions, the Lord of the Manor's dreamer son, the clumsy law student, the skinny and often dishevelled girl, and the travelling photographer who inhabited the strange hinterland between servant and gentleman. Although Emmy suspected Kit had originally been present solely to keep an eye on her, as the weeks passed his relationship with Alex slipped into friendship. The two young men had a great deal in common and would talk at length about art and politics while she and Rupert listened, simply contented to be in their company.

Sometimes the four of them walked past the old church of St Nonna, where the churchyard swelled with sleepers, and down to the rocky cove. Seabirds came and went with solitary purpose, the tide receded and advanced, and the sand was speckled with the prints of birds and glistened in the sunshine before becoming dry once more. While the others discussed composition and light, Emmy would kick off her boots and walk down the tideline to scoop up shells and dip her toes into the mysterious depths of rock pools while her face floated below, pale and trapped. She would turn away with a shiver, reminded of tales of those lost at sea and doomed to walk the shores for ever, and hurry back to the others, her eyes always sliding to rest on Alex and her heart living for the secret looks and smiles they shared.

Alex was a patient teacher, explaining angles and lighting carefully, and Rupert grew in enthusiasm and expertise. Kit said he preferred to use language to create images, but he often accompanied the lessons, notebook and pencil in hand, as he jotted down fragments of verse and snatches of imagery which he stitched into a poem called 'Turning Tide' and handed to her while Alex and Rupert balanced on the rocks with the Vest Pocket Kodak. This was the first poem Kit had shown Emmy since she was a child, and when she read it her eyes filled, for as Kit described oozing sand and impermanent footprints, flat water ripped by the hull of a sailing boat and healed by tide, and the figures on the beach driven inwards by the waves, she knew that he felt as she did: that this moment was fleeting and that a time was coming when they would be scattered. His poet's eye had seen and perfected this moment in time just as Alex's camera did, and reading it filled her with a nostalgia for a time yet to be lost. The poem hinted at a gathering darkness, and she wondered what Kit was alluding to.

"I still don't understand your poems," was all she said, passing the notebook back to him.

Kit sighed. "I don't think I fully understand this one myself. I think I was mourning something when I wrote it. Probably all Pa's gloomy talk of war."

"Does he really think there will be a war?" Emmy asked. She shaded her eyes with her hand and watched Alex rolling up his trousers in order to wade to a high outcrop where, knowing him, there would be a better angle for the frame of the shot. It was the glare that made her blink and her eyes fill, she told herself, not the melancholy poetry.

Kit stared out at the horizon.

"I hope not," he said, eventually. "It's complicated, I think. Pa just wants to take the Germans down a peg or two, but I don't think it'll be quite that simple. Things never are. Look at Troy."

The sun slipped behind a cloud and Emmy shivered. From what she recalled of it, the Iliad was bloody and the war it chronicled long and savage.

"I hope he's wrong."

"So do I," said Kit quietly. "Oh, so do I."

Rupert called them over, waving and demanding they be subjects for his next photograph, and the topic was dropped; but no matter how hard she tried, Emmy couldn't quite forget it. Sometimes she would wake up in the dark, her heart racing and her sheets knotted as her father's night terrors filled the house, wondering what horrors he still suffered and what might lie ahead for them all if Colonel Rivers was right and war did come. It might be selfish, but she hoped and prayed she and Alex would be long gone by then.

Rupert, a keen amateur photographer and a kind-hearted soul, never seemed to mind Emmy tagging along when he had lessons. Sometimes she joined in too, and she soon lost count of how many photographs she took under Alex's expert tutelage. None would ever hold as close a place in her heart as the first one of the wagon, but Emmy was very proud of one she took of Pendennys Place with the horse chestnuts in full glory, and from such a distance that it was impossible to see that the lawns were long and pincushioned with moss or that the pointing in the brickwork was crumbling away. Alex showed her how he loved to break the rules of formal photography, abandoning the standard stiff poses with books and hats, and placing Emmy on the wagon steps, daisies threaded through her loosened hair and with her feet bare and liberated from boots, or curled up on the chair with her chin in her hand and her gaze fixed dreamily on the camera, with her lips tender from his kisses. Emmy loved these photographs most of all and thought she looked like someone else altogether, somebody happy and at ease rather than the girl who once leapt up nervously every time her father shouted and who lived in fear of upsetting him.

"Let me take one of you," she would always plead, but Alex would laugh and say he was far better suited behind the lens of the camera. Once she did manage to persuade him, and the photo she took captured him perfectly. Alex showed her how to develop it and rolled his eyes when she insisted on keeping the finished print. He would have rolled them even more, Emmy thought, if he'd known how often she pressed it to her lips. Aware that Mrs Puckey and Rosie would sift through her belongings while tidying them up for her, Emmy tucked the picture into her Bible and couldn't but smile to think how impressed Reverend Cutwell would have been to see how frequently she opened the good book these days!

Before long the air grew cooler in the mornings and filled with the nostalgic notes of woodsmoke and blackberry. Swifts chattered in the chestnut trees, their leaves yellowed and boughs sagging with the burden of burgeoning conkers, and the harvest was all but gathered in. Patchy was declared sound once more, but Alex thought a little more rest could only do the tendon good and he'd been offered work with the gamekeeper once the shooting season began. It would be foolish to pass up an offer of employment, he said, and there was no need to leave yet. Emmy watched carefully for any signs of fidget in his traveller's soul, but Alex was, as he often assured her, more than content to remain at Rosecraddick, and he promised that when the time came to leave they would depart together.

October nudged September aside, the trees burnished the same deep red as Alex's hair, berries cascading on bushes to turn mouths purple and prompting old wives' warnings of a hard winter to come. Misty's and Patchy's coats grew thicker, Rupert departed from the halt and as Alex and Emmy waved him goodbye seemed far from excited to be off to Oxford for the start of Michaelmas term. Even Kit was dispatched to the London house with Lady Rivers, who found Cornwall in the winter dull. As battalions of leaves cascaded to earth, bonfire smoke billowed and the swallows became an absence, Emmy knew a page had been turned and the golden summer of 1913 was finally at a close. The fields became a mosaic of rich earth and pale stubble, leaves carpeted the lawn, and Rosecraddick's fishermen scanned the horizon and prayed the pilchards would return.

Unlike the swallows and the elusive pilchards, Alex Winter chose to remain in Cornwall. Even when the wind stripped the trees of colour, leaving branches bare against gunmetal skies, and the first frosts hardened the ground his wagon still resided in the clearing. He'd become a part of life at the manor, often glimpsed out with the gamekeeper or loading for the colonel out shooting, and he was always in high demand to take photographs of local families and dignitaries. On the rare occasions when she was now able to escape Pendennys Place, Emmy would weave her way through the woods to the clearing, and her heart would rise if a plume of smoke from the wagon's chimney announced Alex was present. There was never enough time, but what moments they could share were precious, and treasured accordingly.

Alex was granted one day off each fortnight and they lived for the brief time he had free. Sometimes even this was sacrificed in order for him to accept commissions, and to temper her disappointment Emmy had to content herself with the knowledge that every minute lost would be more than compensated by the future they were planning. Filled with impatient energy, she would roam the library searching for books about France and Spain in order to plan their route, but since Julyan's tastes ran to fox hunting and the military rather than art she had to content herself with lugging a heavy atlas up to her bedroom and poring over it by candlelight.

"You'll roast us all alive, Miss, letting them burn so low!" Simmonds often scolded when Emmy brought a collection of candle stubs down to the kitchen for melting. "You're as bad as the master."

Julyan was notorious for slumping onto this desk after several large brandies and knocking his candle over, and Simmonds had on several occasions been required to douse his papers with water. It was a household black joke that he would set the place alight one day.

"Why we can't have gas, I'll never know," Mrs Puckey would complain bitterly, even though she knew exactly why. "The manor even has electricity. Imagine that!"

Emmy would have settled for a fire in her bedroom that didn't belch smoke, but since the chimney sweep had failed to visit that year the winter months meant cold nights spent shivering under damp blankets as the chill seeped through the brick of Pendennys Place and into her bones. Thoughts of Alex and dreams of long sunny days travelling through Provence kept her warm – along with thick socks and at least three layers of clothing – but

Kit, used to the manor with its huge cast iron radiators, was always horrified whenever he came to visit.

The winter of 1913 was long and hard, but later on Emmy would struggle to remember the chilblains, the damp sheets and the nights spent shivering as draughts blasted along the corridors, lifting rugs and sweeping papers to the floor. Julyan was constantly ill with chest infections, and her days were spent helping Mrs Puckey and Simmonds nurse him, a dangerous occupation which involved a great deal of spluttered cursing from the patient and bowls of steaming posset hurled across the sick room; her memories of this would also be patchy. Even the long mud-spattered days spent hunting would be hazy, unless she happened to hack back through the woods or canter along the edge of the fields where the gamekeepers tended the pheasant feeders in the hope of catching a glimpse of the beloved russet head. In years to come when she tried to recollect that time, it was only memories of curling up inside the wagon, drinking tea and weaving dreams that she would recall with any clarity – those, and the snatched hours of daylight when she and Alex would walk hand in hand, boots kicking up jewelled leaves and crunching over frozen plough. On such walks they would talk non-stop, because there never seemed enough time to say it all, and Alex would take pictures of her with his trusty Kodak camera.

"The camera loves you," he said once when she asked why he needed yet another picture of her on the beach or sitting on an ivy-smothered log. He caught her hands and, pulling her close, kissed her and added, "And so do I."

The kisses they exchanged could be as tender and soft as the snowflakes which drifted down in late December or as hot and all-consuming as the fire glowing in the stove. For Emmy the longing to be closer to Alex grew ever stronger, and she would lean into him, feeling the heat of the flame between them as his body pressed against hers. She would tremble then with need and anticipation, and she wanted nothing more than to give in to these feelings. Even so, what they shared was magical. Wonderful. Meant to be. Emmy had felt this way from the moment she had first met Alex Winter; her feelings for him were as instinctive as breathing. Why wait any longer when they were planning to elope and be married?

One goose-grey afternoon, as the rain fell and a busy wind scooped handfuls of leaves and twigs up into whirling eddies, Alex and Emmy lay in front of the stove, wrapped in his quilt and drowsing in the warmth of the fire. Alex stroked her hair from her face and described the places they would visit, and Emmy's eyelids grew heavy. Her limbs felt honeyed, as though she was melting in a pool of longing, and when Alex's lips grazed her neck, flames leapt through Emmy just as they roared through the wood in the stove. She didn't want to wait a moment longer. She couldn't.

Turning, she raised her hand to his cheek and kissed him. Lost in the moment and the pleasure she closed her eyes, ready to give in to this molten pooling of self and sensation. Emmy was ready to belong to Alex Winter in every way possible and she slipped her arms around his neck, drawing him closer and marvelling at the way two such different bodies, two such different lives, could become one so easily.

"Don't stop," she whispered.

Alex pulled away. In the soft glow of the fire his face seemed to melt like wax and shadows danced over them both.

"What's wrong?" Emmy asked. She tried to pull him back down to her quilt nest, kissing his smooth shoulder and tracing the muscles of his back, but Alex shook his head.

"You mean everything to me, Emmy. You must know that?"

"More than photography?"

He laughed. "Yes, even more than photography! Why else would I still be here? But we can't do this. Not yet."

"We can," she said. "I want to."

"No. It isn't the right time." His voice was taut with a resolve she hardly recognised.

"Fine," Emmy said. "I understand."

But she didn't. Not in the slightest. His rejection stung and her hand dropped away. What must he think of her for being so forward? Embarrassed, she struggled to escape the tangled quilts and blankets.

"I should go. Mrs Puckey will send out a search party if I'm not back by dusk."

Alex turned and tugged her back down, wrapping his arms around her and holding her against his heart.

"Lord! I'm messing this up, aren't I? Don't leave in a huff, Em. Of course, I want to make love to you. What man wouldn't? I love you and I can't think of anything I want more right now and it's taking all my control not to. Lord, I'm so much of a saint these days I'm surprised Killjoy Cutwell doesn't stick me in a stained-glass window!"

Emmy couldn't help laughing at this.

"So why ...?" she blushed, unable to say it.

"Why don't we just make love? Why don't I throw all caution to the wind and do what I've wanted to do since the moment I first saw you?" He pushed the long swathes of hair from his face and gave her a look which dusted her skin with goose bumps. "Because, Emmy, I'm trying to say is that I don't want you to do anything you might regret. Or that could cause you shame."

"You could never cause me shame!" she cried, pressing kisses onto his beloved face. "Never!"

"You say that, Emmy, but I haven't anything to offer you except this wagon and a life on the road. I'm not a wealthy gentleman. I'm a jobbing photographer."

"I don't care," she said.

"*I* do," said Alex fiercely. "And I don't ever want to compromise you. When I've saved enough to take care of you, that's when we'll be together in every sense of the word. I want us to be together for ever, Emmy. Don't you see? I don't want loving you to be snatched moments filled with fear of discovery. I want to hold you while you sleep, I want to wake up with you, and I want to take care of you for ever. I want to know nothing can separate us."

She was unable to speak. The passion in his voice made her tremble.

"I want you to be my wife, Emily Pendennys. Once … when …" he flushed, and her heart melted to see him struggle to articulate his conflicted feelings. "When we do, I know I won't want to be apart from you for a single moment. So, until the time comes when I can take care of you for ever, no matter how hard it is, or how much I might want more, I'm not going to do anything that could compromise you. Do you understand?"

She nodded, and tears filled her eyes because she wanted and loved him more now than she had ever thought possible. Alex was a true gentleman.

"It's too hard to let you go as it is," he said softly, kissing her forehead. "I want to be with you for ever."

"Is that a proposal?" Emmy asked.

He smiled. "A terribly clumsy one! I should have been on one knee with a string quartet playing and a ring, shouldn't I? Emmy, I don't have much at all to give you – only my heart and my promise that I will love you every day for the rest of my life. I'll die loving you and with your name on my lips. You're everything to me."

"And you are to me," she replied.

"So, you'll marry me? That's a yes?"

"Of course, I will," Emmy said. "You know that already. As soon as we elope we'll find a church and beg the vicar to marry us!"

"Not Killjoy Cutwell though," he said with a shudder. "He'd send us both packing – me from Rosecraddick and you back home to your father. No, when the day comes we'll go straight to a minister I know. He'll marry us gladly."

"I can't wait!" Emmy said. She felt she would burst with joyful anticipation.

"It won't be long. By next summer I think I'll have enough saved for us both, and the weather will be fair. Then, my love, we'll set off together and we'll never, ever look back."

He kissed her again and it was the sweetest kiss that spoke of promises and hope and the wonderful future which lay at their fingertips. They would not be rich, Alex said, and he could never give her the life that somebody like Kit could offer, but he would love her more than anyone had ever loved before, and Emmy already knew being loved by Alex Winter made her wealthy beyond her wildest dreams.

As she returned to Pendennys Place, Emmy's feet scarcely touched the mossy path and even her father's bad temper and Mrs Puckey's suspicious glances couldn't spoil her mood or stop her from singing. Alex Winter had asked her to marry him and she had said yes because there was never any other answer, never had been since the moment she had first seen him. As soon as they had saved enough Emmy would elope with him and they would be married quietly at a country chapel by the sea. Then they would lie beneath the star-encrusted sky and love one another all night long and for the rest of their lives. They would never be apart again.

A wonderful future lay ahead for them, Emmy told herself as she lay in bed that night, watching her breath huff into the darkness and the ice crystals on the window glitter in the moonlight. Life was wonderful and their future together was destined to be wonderful. There was nothing that could divide them now. Not Julyan's temper. Not money. Not Kit's worried looks. And certainly not her godmother's matchmaking plans.

Nothing could stop Emmy being with Alex Winter.

Absolutely nothing.

Deckchairs and Horses

May 1914

Rosecraddick

The afternoon sun gilded the flowering grasses of the so-called lawn, and the pollen-speckled air was thick and hazy. Kit and Rupert lolled in stripy deckchairs, dutifully working their way through the piles of egg sandwiches Mrs Puckey insisted upon serving, while Alex sat with his back against the knotted trunk of a chestnut tree sketching Emmy and Misty. The boys had their shirtsleeves rolled up and were wearing boaters, but Emmy, in her velvet riding habit, feared she would boil alive and was starting to regret agreeing to Alex's request to sit for him. The sunshine was dazzling, and she scrunched her eyes shut until the lids were scarlet and bright circles of white flared against darkness. Disorientated, she shifted in the saddle, which Misty chose to interpret as his cue to wander off.

Alex glanced up from his sketch pad. "Don't move!

"I'm so hot," Emmy grumbled, fanning her face.

"I'm almost there," he promised, pencil flying across the paper as it cross-hatched and shaded. "Can you keep his head up?"

Emmy picked up the reins and Misty, fed up with standing still when there was a lawn full of grass at his hooves, flattened his ears to make his displeasure clear.

"Don't draw him like that, whatever you do. He looks like a donkey," said Rupert, peering out from under his hat to study the scene.

"He does not," Emmy protested. She patted the horse's neck. Misty had been very patient, standing still for at least fifteen minutes while Alex sketched furiously. "Don't listen to him, boy. I know the flies are biting you."

Rupert scratched the pale ankle between trouser and sock. "They're biting me too. I think it may be time to surrender and find some shade. Emmy, you're turning crimson. It clashes most dreadfully with your habit."

Emmy didn't give a tuppence about the contrast of her face and dress. She was too hot to care about much at all.

"Nearly there," Alex said, sharpening his pencil before holding it up and narrowing his eyes. "A few more minutes. You can do it."

"Yes. One must suffer for art," agreed Rupert.

Emmy decided she wasn't keen on suffering. Sweat trickled between her shoulder blades and the tip of her nose was burning."

"I need to go sea bathing," she said wistfully. "Like you, Kit."

But Kit didn't reply. Staring down at his copy of Keats, he appeared lost in his reading.

"Yes, Kit swims so much I'm amazed he hasn't developed gills and fins," said Rupert. "Or maybe he already has? We see so little of him lately, how would we know?"

It was true that Kit had been noticeably absent in recent weeks. Emmy, who'd made the most of any rare time Alex had to spend it alone with her beloved, hadn't minded in the least – unlike Rupert, who sounded hurt. She supposed he'd missed Kit while he'd been away at Oxford and was hoping to catch up. But now, even when he was with them Kit seemed to be drifting away, and often looked troubled. Emmy suspected his father was putting pressure on him once again to join the army and continue the family's military tradition, an expectation she knew would not sit well with her poetic and sensitive friend. If Kit was seeking time alone this was his business, she felt, and she shot Rupert a warning look; Kit didn't need anyone else to make him feel beholden.

"The weather's been glorious. I don't blame you in the slightest, Kit. If I didn't have to wear woollen bathers and a silly hat, I'd love to swim," she said.

But Kit didn't reply.

"You haven't heard a word I've said, have you?" Rupert waved his hand in front of Kit's face, shaking his head in despairing amusement. "I may as well have been speaking in Mandarin for all the good it's doing me. And your book's upside down!"

Kit started as Rupert reached out and turned his copy of Keats around.

"Sorry, Rupe. I was miles away."

"Anywhere nice?" Emmy asked.

"Just down at the cove," Kit said easily but the sparkle in his eyes piqued Emmy's curiosity; she'd seen that look many times – mostly when she was sitting at the dressing table brushing her hair and thinking about Alex. Was Kit walking out with somebody? If so, she was pleased for him, and it suited her friend because he looked more handsome than ever. His face was tanned, freckles dusted his nose and his hair was bleached white gold by the sun – but it was more than this that lent him a special magic, and an aura of happiness seemed to shimmer around him. Instinct told Emmy that her friend was doing far more than simply swimming and she wondered if he could tell that the same was true of her. Surely it must be obvious to everyone that she was in love with Alex?

Like anyone in love, Emmy wanted the whole world to be as gloriously happy as she was, and she truly was so totally and utterly happy. Alex had worked hard all winter and through the spring and although this had meant she hadn't seen him nearly as often as she would have liked, knowing he had almost saved enough for them to leave and start their new life more than compensated for his absences. Alex thought he would have saved enough by August, and Emmy could scarcely wait to elope. She lay in bed dreaming of spending all night in his arms, of walking hand in hand through the boulevards of Paris and of the wonderful life they would build together. Julyan, the burden of Pendennys Place and her godmother's hints about marriage to Kit, would soon be firmly in the past. Emmy was poised on the threshold of the biggest adventure, teetering on the brink of the rest of her life, and she could scarcely wait.

Sometimes it seemed too much happiness to bear or to deserve, and Emmy feared it would be snatched away from her. Superstitious nonsense? Maybe, but the talk of war she overheard between her father and Reverend Cutwell when he called was a dark cloud on the horizon. Surely it just was academic? And even if it wasn't, as Kit and Rupert seemed to suspect, a war would have no impact on her plans, because Alex wasn't a soldier. She was worrying about nothing. What lay ahead was a wonderful and as sun-drenched as this perfect May afternoon.

Misty pawed the ground and snorted, breaking her train of thought.

"He's had enough," she said, smoothing the grey neck. "And much more of this heat and I'll faint like I did at the studio."

Alex, bent over his sketchbook, looked up in alarm. "I can't have that! One moment more."

"I've no idea why you insist on drawing when you have a camera," Rupert remarked. He was now a passionate devotee of photography, insisting on lessons when he was down from Oxford, and often seeking Alex out for instruction. On more than a couple of occasions Emmy had been forced to hide in the wagon when Rupert came by. She didn't like concealing the truth from her friends but there was little choice. If Kit or Rupert had ever suspected the truth about their love affair they had never said a word, and she and Alex had been careful not to draw attention to their friendship, sometimes even going as far as to ignore one another when all four were together. Before she and Alex eloped, though, Emmy had resolved to tell Rupert and Kit the truth. They were her friends and she owed them that much.

"I enjoy sketching," Alex said simply. His pencil darted back and forth and then he set it down. "If I hadn't been a photographer I think I would have like to have been an artist."

"Like your mother," said Emmy.

"Yes," Alex agreed. "Although I'm nowhere near as good as she was." Kit's quizzical gaze settled on Emmy.

"I don't remember you saying your mother painted, Alex?" he said slowly, and Emmy knew he was wondering how she had come by this knowledge. If Kit was aware of the extent of her relationship with Alex she knew he would hold himself responsible and be terribly worried for her; it was another reason she and Alex had always been careful not to appear too familiar when in company.

"She did indeed, and much better than my poor scribbles," Alex said evenly. His pencil made one final excursion across the paper and then he sprung to his feet, brushing grass seeds from his trousers. "Still, poor or not, I'm finished."

"Let's see what you've done, then!" she said before Kit could probe further, swinging her leg over the pommels and preparing to jump down.

"Here, allow me."

Alex took her hand and helped her slip down from Misty's back. The light fell on his face as he smiled up at her and the love etched there made Emmy's heart turn over. Thank goodness his back was to Kit, for if their friend had glimpsed it he would know everything. Emmy couldn't risk discovery, not when they were so close to leaving, nor did she want to put Kit in an impossible situation where he would be torn between keeping her secret and his duty to protect her honour.

"Very gallant," she teased.

He laughed. "I try my best. Just as I have with this sketch. I hope you like it?"

Alex had drawn her many times and in spite of his protestations he was hugely talented, but this drawing took Emmy's breath away. The stately trees with their waxy white candles and framing the elegant house draped in an ivy mantle spoke of long afternoons spent drowsing on the lawn, and the thoroughbred horse with pricked ears and liquid eyes could have been drawn by Munnings – but it was seeing herself through his eyes in the lines of this slender rider with tumbling curls and secretive smile that made Emmy's breath catch. The curve of her breast beneath the velvet and the lean line of her left thigh against the saddle were sketched with an intimacy and tenderness which leapt from the page, and the meaning of that half-smile was known by him alone. His feelings for her were shouted out by the pencil marks.

"Do you like it?" he asked, and she could only nod. 'Like' was too bland a word. She loved it. The picture was the perfect distillation of this sunny afternoon, and almost before the day was over she was already nostalgic for it and so glad to have this reminder. Memories aren't linear. They fold back on themselves like laundry. They recur, overlay and repeat. But this drawing would, like the shutting of the camera lens, for ever tell the truth about this May afternoon and the love that a young artist had for the poised young woman seated on a dapple-grey horse.

Emmy would treasure this sketch for the rest of her life.

Recruitment, Dickon and the Boys

Rosecraddick 1914

May burgeoned into a verdant and leafy June which melted into a
simmering July. When Emmy turned seventeen her father and Lady Rivers
began to make serious noises about an engagement, and tentative plans for
a summer ball at the manor were put into place, with Alex commissioned to
take the photographs. Time was starting to collapse in on itself and with
talk of dresses and music and menus, Emmy began to fret. Although she
knew Kit would never go along with his mother's plans it felt as though a
noose was tightening.

She attempted to seek Kit out on numerous occasions, but he was
always absent when she visited the manor, leaving Emmy to endure tea and
gossip with Lady Rivers, a trial sustained only by the faint hope of catching
a glimpse of Alex as he hoed flower beds or trundled his wheelbarrow
along the gravelled paths. Rupert, still keen on photography and often to be
found talking to Alex at the wagon while walking his father's dogs, said Kit
was still swimming most days, but Emmy suspected her friend was walking
out with somebody. If it was a secret then she imagined that Kit Rivers had
also fallen in love with somebody his family would regard as unsuitable and,
like her, he wouldn't let this stand in his way. How she wished she could
talk to him!

"We need to leave soon. 'Take charge of Fate before it takes charge of
you', remember?" she said to Alex over and over again, but he protested he
needed to earn more money. He was determined now on setting up his own
studio once they had travelled for a while, and nothing she said could
persuade him otherwise.

"I don't want to make you an improper proposal and compromise you. I
want to marry you, Emmy and offer you more than a life on the road with a

hand-to-mouth wage. I want things to be proper. I want to take care of you and our children," was always his response, and she would roll her eyes.

"I'm not afraid of being poor."

"That's because you've never *been* poor," Alex would point out darkly. "And I never want you to be, either. I want to offer you a future and I'm so nearly there. Just a few months more, my love. It isn't so long now."

Emmy knew Alex was right and she loved him all the more for wanting to do this properly, but she couldn't shake off the sense that as time's sands trickled through an invisible hourglass they were gathering pace. Instead, she asked Rupert to drive her to Truro where she pawned the pearls and silver spoons she'd been given as christening gifts and which had only escaped a similar fate at her father's hands because she had hidden them behind the skirting in her bedroom. Emmy had been proud of her ingenuity, but Alex had been horrified.

"I'll support you," he said fiercely. "I won't hear of you parting with your beautiful things."

"They're only things," Emmy protested.

"They're *your* things. When I said I wanted to marry you and take care of you, Emmy, I meant it. I may not be a rich man and I can't offer you as much as somebody like Kit, but I promise I'll take care of you. You don't need to do this. We'll get them back."

Emmy had never seen Alex so upset, and she realised she'd hurt his pride deeply.

"I'm sorry," she said, and he kissed her hands, smiling at her sadly.

"You never need to be sorry, my love. I just wish I was able to give you more."

Telling Mrs. Puckey she was with her godmother for the day, Emmy met Alex at the halt where they caught the train, stunned by their own daring and holding their breath nearly all the way to Truro in case they were spotted. Once her belongings had been redeemed they had a wonderful afternoon, strolling arm in arm through the twisting cobbled streets which huddled in the shadow of the newly built cathedral as Alex took photographs and explained the intricacies of its architecture. They wandered down narrow alleys, peering into shop windows and weaving dreams of what they would buy when Alex's photographs made their fortune. Emmy admired a beautiful locket she noticed in the window of a tiny jeweller's, Alex picked up some photographic supplies, and they enjoyed afternoon tea before catching the train back to Rosecraddick. For Emmy, walking arm in arm through the city without the shadowy fear of being spotted felt like surfacing for air after a long time holding her breath beneath the water. Here they could breathe and laugh and be like any other courting couple. Their afternoon in Truro was a magical escape from the reality of having to hide away, and she cherished every moment, longing all the more for the day when they would leave this place far behind and be married. Surely that time couldn't be too far away?

But Emmy's dreams were tipped upside down in the summer of 1914 when war was declared. Even before the sun-drenched days had a chance to turn russet around the edges, Emmy already feared she would look back on them with longing. In the blink of an eye the threatening storm clouds had marched over the horizon and Rosecraddick was engulfed in an eruption of patriotism as banners were waved and bunting strung across the village for recruitment drives.

As elsewhere across the nation, Rosecraddick's sons flocked to enlist, and with great excitement as though they were off on an adventure rather than to war. Alex, who'd been commissioned to take photographs of the new recruits at a local recruitment drive, told Emmy how Fore Street was decked out with red, white and blue bunting and a marching band had played. The event enjoyed a carnival air, he said, and the local boys had queued in scores to take the King's shilling. From his fellow gardeners and keepers, from the manor staff to farmhands and fishermen, they were all filled with patriotic zeal and determined to play their part in teaching the Germans a lesson. Reverend Cutwell preached, the recruiting officer delivered a resounding speech about each man playing his part, and Colonel Rivers promised that recognition and glory awaited every man who enlisted.

Thinking of her father, wracked with pain and as far from a glorious return from battle as it was possible to be, Emmy took such rhetoric with a huge pinch of salt, but Alex had been very quiet, shutting himself away in the darkroom for hours. Over the past year he had taught her how to develop film and they often worked together side by side in a harmonious ballet, but this evening Alex said there were so many photographs from the recruitment drive it was easier if he worked alone. Emmy suspected he wanted to collect his thoughts and was deeply conflicted, torn between doing his duty to King and country and keeping his word to marry her. Did he want to enlist? Was he secretly longing to join the other young men? These were questions Emmy didn't dare ask because she was far too afraid of what the answer might be, but they nibbled at her peace of mind like rats. She couldn't bear it if he joined up. She would die without him.

While Alex worked Emmy sat on the wagon steps, hugging her knees tightly to her chest. Alex wouldn't choose war. He couldn't. Not after all the promises he'd made and the careful plans they had been putting together. They were only weeks away from eloping, and he wanted to be with her, she knew he did. Besides, Alex wasn't a soldier. He was a photographer. An artist. There was no role for him in a conflict and, unlike the local lads who were caught up in the thrill of journeying further than Cornwall, he was already well travelled. She was being foolish, worrying about nothing. This was not their war. It would not touch them.

"You won't enlist, will you?" she eventually asked later that evening as, dusk smoking through the trees, they strolled hand in hand along the well-worn path to Pendennys Place. "Nobody can make you, can they?"

Alex didn't reply straight away, and Emmy felt cold to the core. Somebody had opened up her rib cage and poured iced water over her heart. She tugged him to a halt.

"They can't? Can they?"

"They're not conscripting men, Em. It's a free choice," he said.

But the way he said it didn't make it sound like much of a choice.

Alex kissed her goodbye, but his mind seemed far away and as she watched him slip away through the trees it seemed to Emmy that as he melted into the twilight she was already losing him and the future they had dreamed of. Alex might not have joined up but part of him was already drifting to a place she would never be able to follow. It was as though a ghost had run a finger down her spine, and she shivered, rubbing at the goose bumps on her arms.

Emmy turned away from the billowing night and walked towards the warm light of the house, but she couldn't escape a growing sense of dread. The darkness crept in with her and she spent most of the night staring wide-eyed into the deep blackness. Something bad was coming. Something very bad.

"My cousin's lad, Dickon Trehunnist, was the first Rosecraddick lad to sign up," Mrs Puckey boasted over breakfast the following day. "He's a brave lad, all right!"

Emmy knew of the Trehunnists; they were a large farming family with members of the clan dotted just about everywhere in the area. She vaguely recalled Dickon, a brawny youth with thick blond hair and a high sense of his own importance, and it didn't surprise her in the slightest he'd barged his way straight to the front of the queue. His photograph, all square-jawed confidence as he eyeballed the camera, had been one of the first Alex had pegged up to dry.

"My brother enlisted too. He says the army pays much better than fishing," Rosie chipped in, as she took off her boater and unhooked an apron from the back of the door. "He's going to save the wages and buy his own pilchard boat afterwards."

"There won't be anyone left to do a decent day's work at this rate," grumbled Simmonds, who was scowling down at a newspaper. "Damn fools, all of them."

"It'll all be over by Christmas and they'll be back then, you mark my words," Mrs Puckey said. She ladled porridge into a bowl and pushed it towards Emmy. "Eat up, Miss."

Emmy stared at the stodgy mound in front of her and felt her stomach churn. She didn't think she could face a mouthful. 'Over by Christmas' was what everyone was saying, but Alex hadn't thought this likely – nor did Simmonds, judging by the scornful look he threw the housekeeper. Since her father's old batman had seen far more of battle than had Mrs Puckey, Emmy didn't feel cheered. It seemed impossible on such a warm morning, when the sun was already drying the dew on the lawn and the air hung heavy with the scent of wall flowers and honeysuckle, that war lay in wait across the water. Surely it was all no more than a bad dream?

"Christmas my foot," Simmonds scoffed, folding up the newspaper.

"You're a pessimist today, Mr Simmonds. Don't let the master hear talk like that," Mrs Puckey scolded, waving her ladle. "Our boys'll show the Germans what's what! Especially once our Dickon's there. He's a crack shot."

"With a rabbit or two maybe – but they've no idea what's coming," Simmonds said darkly. "It's all very well to be full of it when the band's playing and the sun's out but it's something else again when you're facing the enemy." He rose to his feet, his chair scraping the stone floor in protest, and gestured towards the floor above with his grey head. "And if you don't believe me, ask *him*. Lambs to the bloody slaughter, all of 'em."

Emmy, who had heard Julyan Pendennys crying out in pain many times, didn't want to hear any more. She couldn't bear the thought of all the shiny-faced Rosecraddick boys setting off for war with such high hopes and zeal only to be cut down in their prime or maimed like her father. She shoved her bowl away.

"What's rattled *his* cage?" asked Rosie as Simmonds stomped out of the kitchen, banging the door behind him.

"Jealous because he can't join in, I shouldn't wonder," said Mrs Puckey knowingly. "Most of the older gentleman are itching to go."

But to Emmy, Simmonds hadn't appeared at all envious. If anything, he'd sounded angry. She watched him cross the stable yard, pausing to rub the noses hanging low over the stable doors, and his shoulders seemed more stooped than ever. His words, 'lambs to the bloody slaughter', echoed in her ears, and felt horribly prophetic.

"My sister works at the manor and she says the colonel's pea-green that his boy's enlisted while he's stuck at home missing all the fun," Rosie chipped in. Apron strings tied, she picked up Emmy's bowl and raised her brows. "Not hungry, Miss Emily?"

Emmy barely heard the question. Kit had enlisted? Since when? Spending every spare moment with Alex, she'd scarcely seen him or Rupert for weeks. Were her two friends leaving for the war too?

"Kit Rivers has enlisted?" she asked.

Rosie nodded. "He has, Miss, and he looks very handsome in his uniform, if you don't mind me saying so! You're the envy of all the girls for miles around."

Sometimes Emmy forgot that everyone in Rosecraddick was expecting her to marry Kit. She imagined his blond good looks would cut a dash in uniform, but the very idea of Kit going to fight was at odds with everything she knew about her old friend. Kit wasn't a soldier. He was a poet!

"Mind your station, my girl," sniffed Mrs Puckey, shooing Rosie to the sink, where a pile of pots and pans waited to be scoured. While Rosie clattered and the housekeeper scolded, Emmy slipped from the kitchen and wandered into the garden where a lifetime ago two young men had dozed in deckchairs while another, eyes filled with love, had sketched a girl whose head was filled with dreams. Where were those people now? What would happen to them? Would they ever meet again like this?

It already felt like a memory of another life.

War fever gripped Britain, and with each passing day Emmy berated herself for not having persuaded Alex to elope as soon the winter had passed. If only they had gone when spring had arrived; they would have been far away from England by now, and Alex would be safe. Although he was no soldier, she understood now that didn't matter a jot, for all manner of men were enlisting, from poets to curates to fishermen. Rosie's snippet of gossip was correct; it turned out that Kit had joined his father's old regiment and Colonel Rivers had never seemed prouder of his son.

Emmy saw Kit briefly at a luncheon party her godmother held, but he was distracted, making an excuse to leave the gathering as soon as the meal was over, and she had no chance to speak with him. She sensed he didn't want to talk to anyone, and wondered whether there was a girl he was seeing secretly, as Alex had suspected. If so, Emmy hoped Kit was as happy as she was, even if the dread of harm coming to the one you loved was becoming a terror which woke you with a racing heart and fragmented dreams. She learned from Lady Rivers that Rupert Elmhurst had chosen to join the same regiment as Kit and would serve alongside him, friends for a lifetime who would face war together and look out for one another. Although there was some comfort in this it also filled Emmy with sadness, for Kit was a poet and Rupert an academic. They weren't men for war.

In his role as the local photographer Alex was commissioned for a selection of shots featuring Kit and Rupert in their new uniforms. Most were formal, but several that he had composed and lit in his own style were strikingly different. In these the two friends slung their arms around one another's shoulders as though off up to Oxford for a term rather than leaving to fight in France. Alex's ready lens captured the lifetime of easy friendship between them, and although these pictures weren't formal enough to grace sideboards or mantelpieces in family homes, Emmy thought they were wonderful. Kit was resolute yet so deeply sad, and Rupert stared at the camera as though daring it to say he was afraid, the clenched fists and teeth biting into his top lip revealing how he felt. Alex called this picture 'Friends Conflicted', and put it aside with a pile of others, saying it wasn't good enough to sell.

Emmy liked it best of all, so she took it home and slid it into the leather wallet where she had taken to storing cherished objects. It bulged beneath her mattress, an odd treasure trove packed with Alex's sketches, an assortment of the photographs he had taken of her and the boys that summer, some dried roses he had given her, and a curl of his hair tied with a pink ribbon snipped from the seldom-worn corset. Little more than rubbish to the unknowing eye, but to Emmy they were priceless talismans. If she kept them close maybe that would keep everyone safe? Eventually there were so many treasures that she had to transfer them into a small leather suitcase that had once belonged to her mother. She pushed this under the bed behind the chamber pot and a box of old toys; Rosie was nosey but she was also very lazy, and Emmy felt sure the housemaid wouldn't be bothered to snoop if it required effort.

Emmy was reading in the library one ordinary Tuesday morning when, after a tap on the heavy door, Rosie's frilly-capped head peeped around it.

"Sorry to disturb you, Miss, but there's a young man called to see you."

Emmy put down her book, surprised. Rupert and Kit had been exceedingly busy recently and she wasn't expecting a visitor.

"Who is it, Rosie?"

"The photographer, Mr Winter," Rosie said. She was looking intrigued. "I didn't know you were having your photograph taken, Miss. Shall I send him in?"

"It's just a meeting about a future commission," Emmy improvised. She put her book down and glanced in the mirror above the mantelpiece, relieved to see that she didn't look as surprised as she felt. She smoothed her hair and secured a pin. "No need to send him through. I'll speak to him outside."

"Very well, Miss," Rosie said with a grin. "He's very handsome, isn't he?"

It was terribly forward of a housemaid to speak like this, but Emmy couldn't help being amused. Alex Winter had caused quite a stir among the young ladies of Rosecraddick, and a fair few of the local girls had set their caps at him. Rosie was well known in the village for having an eye for the boys.

"That'll be all, Rosie," she said firmly.

Alex was standing at the foot of the front steps. His face was flushed, as though he had hurried all the way up the drive in the midday sun, and he twisted his cap in his hands.

"I'm sorry to come to the house but I need to talk to you," he said quietly.

"What's wrong?" Emmy didn't care that they might be overheard or that it was most improper for an undergardener to call upon the lady of the house. She closed the door behind her and hurried down the steps, her skirts bunched in her fists as she leapt the final few. "What's happened?"

"Not here," Alex said. "We need to speak properly."

There was a tension in his jaw, and the way he held himself she hadn't seen before. Dread bloomed in her chest.

"The stables," she said. "If anyone asks it's because I want to commission photographs of our horses in their looseboxes. Follow me, as though I'm instructing you where you may set up."

He bowed his head. "Very good, Miss Pendennys."

She turned on her heel and marched past the front of the house, Alex following several steps behind as was his place. Emmy didn't look back, holding her head high and her back straight, every inch the lady. Although Mrs Puckey had departed for the village, and Simmonds was toiling in what remained of the walled vegetable garden, you never knew for sure whose eyes might be watching. Dr Parsons could be making a call on her father, and Rosie was a dreadful gossip.

Emmy crossed the stable yard and drew back the bolt on the farthest loosebox. The familiar smell of hay and horse and dung wrapped itself around her like an embrace. Cobwebs laced the high windows and draped over the hayracks. Nesting swallows had splattered the cobbles. The inside was dusty and dingy, but unless anyone was especially looking for a balding dandy brush or old halter they would be safe here. A stable cat, curled up in the manger, stretched and started at them with bold green eyes, but otherwise they were unseen. As her vision adjusted from the brightness of the sunshine to the gloom, Emmy turned to face Alex. Her heart thumped against her ribs because she knew what he was here to say.

She realised she had always known he would say it. From the day that war had been declared, this moment was as inevitable as the sunrise.

"You've enlisted."

"Yes."

They stared at one another. Emmy thought she hated him at this moment as much as she had ever loved him. How could he have done such a thing, made such a dreadful decision, without even so much as speaking to her first? Had all his promises been false? Were all the plans and dreams nothing to him? Why did these boys race to France and certain death as though it was more important than anything else?

She felt sick. "You didn't even tell me first? You just did it?"

"I have to go, Em. You know I do."

He stepped forward to take her in his arms, but Emmy held up her hand. Hurt made her savage.

"Don't. Just don't."

She hardly recognised this snarl as her own voice. Alex's arms fell to his sides.

"Emmy, please —"

"How could you? After everything we promised one another. 'I want to be with you every moment and for ever', you said. It meant nothing to you, did it? Nothing."

"This isn't about how I feel about you," he said quietly. His eyes were bleak, but there was no hint of regret. "I do love you, Emmy. More than ever, don't doubt that, but I have to do this. I can't stand aside and watch my friends and countrymen fight and know I've not done the same. What kind of man would that make me?"

"One who keeps his word," she shot back. It was cruel and Alex flinched, but Emmy didn't care. All she cared about was changing his mind back again, and if not, then making him feel as hurt as she was.

"Keeps his word but loses his soul?" he said bleakly. "I have to go and fight with the others. There's no choice when it's a question of duty. You must see that. Do you think Kit or Rupert have chosen this?"

Emmy felt her mouth trembling. She dredged her memory for an argument that would keep him by her side.

"You said yourself nobody's been made to join up. They're not conscripting anyone. You're a photographer, not a soldier."

"That's true, I am. But there's a way to be both. I've always believed photography is my calling, my way of telling the truth, and I believe this is what I'm meant to do." He raked a hand through his hair and exhaled wearily. "If I have to go to war – and in all honesty I *must* go to fight along with the rest – then I want my photographs to be a record of it all. I want to be a war photographer, Emmy. My work was never about portraits of well-to-do gentlefolk, you know that. You knew it the first time we met. This is my calling. It's what I'm meant to do."

Emmy had heard Alex and Kit discussing art and truth many times, but such debate was hugely different when it was a philosophical concept, words washing over her as the bees grumbled in the long grass and Rupert was entertaining her with anecdotes about Oxford life. Now that such language was no longer abstract and the man she loved was hurtling towards who only knew what terrible danger, she was appalled.

"Don't dress this up with philosophy. You're choosing to go," she said.

"This isn't a matter of choosing. This war, this calling – *it* chooses *me*. I don't have a choice, Emmy. Do you think for one moment I'd ever leave you if I didn't have to?"

"You wouldn't have enlisted if you loved me!" she cried. "You promised we would run away together and get married. Take charge of Fate, you said! You promised, Alex! How could you break that promise? Maybe you never meant it at all?"

He swallowed. Misery was etched into his beautiful face and his eyes were scooped hollow by it.

"I meant every word. I do love you and I want to marry you. More than you'll ever know."

"So, don't do this. We could go away right *now*." She hurled herself at him, clutching his shirt and clinging to him as though she could tether him through sheer willpower. "Alex! We can go tonight. Please —"

"No."

He peeled her fingers from the shirt and held each tight claw in his own. "I can't do that. I'm not a deserter. I won't be that man, not even for you. Can't you see? It would poison us. If we travelled as far as we could, even to the moon and back, the knowledge of what I'd done would follow me for ever. It would eat me alive. The shame would consume me. I wouldn't be the man you deserved. I'd deserve every white feather that came my way."

She closed her eyes. "I don't care about any of that. I only care that we're together. This isn't our war."

"It *is* our war. It's ours as much as it's Rupert's and Kit's and even Dickon Trehunnist's. Not just ours but thousands, hundreds of thousands, more. This is about our country and our way of life." He increased his hold on her hands. "I would die willingly if I thought it would keep you safe. When I leave I need to know I'm fighting for something precious, that the best part of my life is here and still to come. I want to know that my girl is still here, but if you don't want to wait for me ..." He swallowed and shook his head sadly. "If you find you can't love me any more, then I'll understand. But I *am* going to France and I *will* play my part."

She knew his heart was breaking and she knew too that he would never change his mind. Her anger and fear were so great that she couldn't speak.

"I know I've let you down and you're angry, and I'm sorry for that. Sorrier than you'll ever know," Alex said. "I wish it could be different, Emmy. I love you as much now as I ever did, and I want you to understand that I'll love you for ever."

Fine words indeed, Emmy thought, but she knew Alex wasn't sorry. Not really. Not in his heart. Deep in there she had been supplanted by his 'glorious calling'. His precious photography would always come first. If Alex Winter loved her, truly loved her, he would never leave.

She ripped her hands from his grasp.

"You're not sorry enough to have chosen to stay with me. Not sorry enough to have never enlisted. I don't think you ever loved me at all."

He hung his head and even the bright curls seemed to dim in the gloom.

"No matter how much I love you I can't ignore my duty. So no, I'm not sorry I've joined – but I am sorry it takes me away from you, because I love you so very, very much. I love you more than life."

Unable to bear another word of this, Emmy pushed past him, ducking under his arm and bursting into the courtyard. Her stomach was lurching. She needed air. Alex was leaving her for France. Choosing to throw her aside for his photography. This so-called calling meant more to him than her and all their dreams. He was choosing war above their love, and she hated him for it.

Hated him.

Emmy stood on the cobbles, her hands pressed against her lips and her stomach roiling. She was going to be sick. A metallic rush of terror and loss and betrayal was rising in her throat.

"Emmy, please." Stricken, Alex held out his hand to her, but she backed away.

"Don't. Just don't. Please leave me alone."

Alex's hand dropped.

"I'm so sorry, Emmy, I would never have hurt you for the world."

Emmy closed her eyes. How could such hurt exist? Such fierce betrayal? How could she wave him farewell knowing he had swept her aside for the glory of war? This calling of his? When she opened them, Alex was shutting the door behind him.

"We're leaving for France on Tuesday from the halt," he said quietly. "I know you're angry with me, Em, but it would mean the world if you were there to say goodbye. My God, it would mean everything. I love you, Emily Pendennys. So much. That will never change."

But it already had. Alex had broken her heart.

"You've made your choice, Alex," she choked. "Please take care."

She turned and crossed the stable yard, not looking back but knowing Alex was watching her intently and willing her to stop. She didn't. She couldn't. It would break her to feel his arms around her once more and his soft lips pressing kisses and whispering words of love, for how could she live with the dread of knowing he was leaving for war? Anger was better than fear. Anger would fuel her and keep her strong. Anger would carry her forwards when all she wanted to do was crumple weeping onto the ground and pummel the cobbles until her fists bled.

Emmy swept up the steps and into the house, hand clamped over her mouth as she raced up the stairs. Reaching her safety of the bathroom she jack-knifed over the lavatory and threw up, a rush of pure dread which left her gasping and coughing. She splashed her face with water and rinsed her mouth before crawling into her bed and closing her eyes in despair.

Alex was leaving. He had chosen war over her. The beautiful future was no more.

Tears slid into her hair and soaked into the pillow. The aching emptiness in her stomach was nothing in comparison with the emptiness of a life without Alex Winter. That loss bit deeper than anything Emmy had ever known.

Embarkation and Farewells

1914

"I've come to say goodbye."

It was surprising how a uniform transformed a man. Emmy had known
Rupert all of her life, had watched him grow from Kit's scab-kneed shadow
to tousle-headed youth to studious young man. But this officer, in pristine
khaki with his hat and cane tucked beneath his arm, was a stranger. Gone
was the thick mop of dark hair which always stuck up in all directions as
though at odds with itself, and in its place was a close crop, while a newly
grown moustache traced the line of his top lip. As he stepped into the
library, Emmy couldn't but stare.

"Goodness, Rupert. You look quite different. Very dashing."

"So, it's true then, what they say about girls liking a soldier," he said with
a wry smile. "Much good *that* may do me."

Emmy uncurled herself from the window seat where she had been
trying to read, an impossible task since all she could think about was Alex's
betrayal, and crossed the room for a closer examination. Rupert was not as
tall as Alex or Kit, but the cloth of his jacket accentuated the broadness of
his shoulders and his powerful chest, and she could almost see her face in
his boots. The was no denying that the uniform was wonderful, and he
wore it well.

"You look very smart," she said. "And terribly unlike yourself. I almost
want to salute."

"I think that's the idea. I can't imagine a bookworm with ink-stained
cuffs would inspire the men. The uniform is made for the job, even if I'm
not."

"You'd inspire them anyway. You're the cleverest person I know," she
told him staunchly.

Emmy rang for tea and Rupert settled himself in the winged armchair by the fire as he had a hundred times before. While she poured she studied him thoughtfully from beneath her eyelashes, concluding that it wasn't the change in clothing or his new haircut which made her old friend feel older and removed from the man she knew, but rather the air of acceptance he wore with the unfamiliar garments. Rupert Elmhurst had chosen to step into this new world and accept the challenges it brought, no matter how unwelcome they might be. Emmy, who had railed and wept and stormed her way through the past days, was filled with admiration.

"When do you leave?" she asked, taking the seat opposite.

"Tomorrow. Embarkation is from the halt at noon." The teacup rattled in the saucer and she saw his hands were trembling. Rupert set the china down with a clatter. "Christ. What a thing, Em. It hardly seems real."

"No."

It didn't seem real to Emmy either. Since her fierce words with Alex she had felt as though she was living in a nightmare. Time had crawled by as though maimed, any trace of appetite had fled, and her emotions had veered between rage and despair. Emmy was torn between longing to fling herself into Alex's arms, telling him she was sorry that fear had made her cruel, and wanting to scream and rage at him until her voice was raw. It felt impossible that in a matter of days the wagon would be locked and empty, the stove cold and Alex far away. Even Patchy would be leaving for France, since the army needed horses. The colonel's hunters were already on their way to the Continent, and she feared Misty and Hector would join them before long. Soon the past year, their year of plans and joys and new wonders, would be nothing but a memory …

"This time next week we'll be at the training camp, and by September we'll be in France," Rupert was saying. "Then the rest is in God's hands."

She swallowed. The windows to the library were thrown open and birdsong, light and carefree, came drifting in with the scent of roses. The sea sparkled in its dip, skylarks darted in the vivid blue above the hayfields, and the woods beyond the garden were deep green. On such a beautiful English summer's day it was impossible to comprehend what might lie ahead.

As though following her train of thought, Rupert gazed over her shoulder and into the garden. "Glorious, isn't it? I think I'd die willingly to make sure all this stays the same and the people I love are safe. Everything I love is here. Who wouldn't give his life to keep it safe?"

"Don't talk like that."

"Like what?"

"Like you're not going to come back!"

Rupert picked up his cup again and swirled the tea before replacing the cup as though uncertain what it was for.

"The truth is, Em, I might not make it back. Any one of us could be killed out there. Me. Kit." He paused then said quietly. "Alex."

Her insides contracted. Speaking this possibility aloud felt like the most dreadful curse.

"Don't."

"I must, Em, because there's not much time left. There may never be another time to say the things you want to say or to tell those you love how you feel. And I think you're in love with Alex, aren't you?"

She turned all her attention to dropping sugar lumps in her tea. It was a useless ploy, since Rupert knew she drank hers without sugar.

"What a thing to say. Good Lord, whatever makes you think that?"

"Emmy, stop. I saw you with him at the halt last month. You were waiting for the train. Your faces were lit up like Christmas trees."

Emmy's heart was beating fast and her thoughts were whirling even faster. She couldn't remember seeing Rupert at the time, but she had only ever been able to see Alex when they were together. Little else existed.

"Why didn't you say hello?"

"You didn't want company, not if you were going to Truro with Alex Winter and without a chaperone. I'm not an idiot."

She flushed. "I never thought you were."

Rupert folded his arms and regarded her over the top of his spectacles. "Well, then. What else am I to think?"

"We had afternoon tea. Like I had with you at Mirabelle's. You said yourself the eclairs were to die for."

"Never mind the eclairs! It's totally different to go to Truro with someone like Alex, and well you know it."

"And why's that? Because he's not the same class as you?" Emmy flared. "Or because his father isn't a magistrate? Or maybe it's because he didn't go to Harrow? Is that what you mean by 'someone like Alex'?"

She wanted to say so much more, but stopped herself in time, aware that this excess of words and emotions gave far too much away.

Rupert looked taken aback by her outburst. "Don't be absurd! That isn't what I meant at all. What I meant was that to put your reputation in jeopardy being alone with a man, and one who isn't a gentleman either but an *undergardener*, must mean something significant. Emmy, no matter what we think of Alex, you must know people will talk. It could cause a scandal."

He was right of course. Flustered, Emmy stirred her tea violently. Liquid slopped into the saucer.

"I thought you didn't care about such things. You always say he's clever and talented."

Colour spilled across Rupert's cheekbones. "Stop being so damned difficult. You know what I mean. That's why you're getting in such a tizzy."

"I can't see what the difference is between me spending an afternoon in Truro with him or with you," Emmy said, even though she could see very well what the difference was. Rupert was … well, he was Rupert. Her gentle, reliable, comfort blanket of a friend.

"Come on! Besides the fact that I'm an old family friend? One who's known you all your life? And who would always tell your father exactly where he was taking you?" Rupert asked. "It isn't the same at all. Besides it's always going to be different with someone like me."

"What does that mean?" she demanded, perplexed. "Someone like you?"

"You know what I mean," he said.

Abruptly, she recalled the odd half-conversation she'd had in the car with Kit all those months ago, when he'd alluded to Rupert being different. 'Rupert wouldn't know what a girl was up to if she turned cartwheels and sang the national anthem', Kit had said. Slowly, and as Rupert stared at her as though willing her on, Emmy began to understand. Of course. There had always been clues; Rupert's vehemence that he would never marry, for example, or his quiet admiration of Alex bestowed from afar, or the way he would stay away from matchmaking mamas. Like jigsaw pieces slotting into place, she finally saw the whole picture.

"Oh!" she said.

Rupert smiled, a weary smile.

"Yes, *oh*," he agreed. "So, do you see, Emmy? Being with me would never be like it might be with Alex, in more than one way. Things never could be improper between us, but that doesn't mean I can't see when a girl has a thing for a chap or when he's in love with her."

There was a pause. Her spoon clinked against the china as her hand shook. So much for hiding their love affair.

"Are you in love with Alex?" Rupert asked gently. "If you are, you must tell him. I've never seen him so subdued."

Emmy wanted to deny it, she was so angry with Alex and so hurt, but found she couldn't – even now, her love for Alex was imprinted into her soul. Besides, Rupert was her beloved friend. He was *their* friend. She could trust him with the truth, and she didn't want to hurt him by lying. There are moments when life feels as though it's so finely balanced that events can tip one way or another like dominoes; a seemingly small decision can change the direction of a life for all eternity, and something told Emmy that the answer she gave Rupert would have echoes reaching far beyond this moment in the sunlit library.

"I've loved him since the first time I saw him," she confessed.

Rupert's eyes were wide. "That afternoon at the garden party?"

"No, before that. I met him at the studio. On my birthday." She closed her eyes. It was a scene she had played over and over, especially during the long wintery weeks when rain trickled down the window panes like tears and there was no hope of escaping the house to fall into Alex's arms. How she missed him since they had quarrelled – was it only last week? – and how she wished she hadn't been so quick to anger. "I'd always thought it was utter nonsense, love at first sight, and no more than the kind of idea Kit adores so much. But it's not imaginary, Rupert. It's real, and it's the most powerful thing in the world."

Rupert swallowed. "Yes, I imagine when love is reciprocated, it must be wonderful. A true gift. I'm glad for you."

Bitterness swelled in her chest and she leapt to her feet, pacing to the window with her skirts flying out behind her. The rage and hurt had not abated.

"Don't be, Rupert, because love means nothing to him. Alex promised to marry me. We were planning to marry this summer and now he's chosen to enlist instead! He doesn't love me at all. I never want to see him again!"

Although it was a genuine *cri de cœur*, the words spoken out loud, and to a man in an officer's uniform who was preparing to leave for war, sounded petulant and childish. In the shocked silence that followed she felt hot all over and ashamed.

Rupert was staring at her. She had never seen his merry face so serious.

"Do you really think it's a choice? We've all enlisted, Emmy! We may not have been forced, as such, but we know our duty and we'll do it because it's the right thing. Choice? Christ! What choice? Do you think I have choice? Or Kit? Do *you*?"

She swallowed miserably, knowing in her heart that he was right.

"Alex thinks it's more than that. He thinks he has a calling to tell the truth about war through his photography."

Rupert laughed despairingly. "Dear God, between him and Kit with their verses and pictures, I'll have my work cut out fighting the enemy. Perhaps we shouldn't have all joined the same regiment."

"You're going together?"

"We are indeed. Kit and I have joined Colonel Rivers' regiment, and quite a few of the gardeners and grooms have enlisted alongside us. Alex will be with us. Kit and I will keep an eye on him."

"If he hadn't joined up because of his great calling, you wouldn't need to," she said, bitterly.

"Dearest Em, who are we to judge what a man's calling might be? Or decide whether it's genuine in nature? Maybe you and I are merely called to love and support those who shine more brightly than we do. Or perhaps that's the greatest calling of them all? Whatever the truth of it, I promise I will do my utmost to protect Alex and bring him home to you."

A tear slid down her cheek. Rupert stood up and passed her a handkerchief.

She dabbed her eyes.

"You love him too." It was not a question.

In answer, Rupert kissed her cheek.

"I always said I'd be your knight if you needed me, Em. Remember it always. This is war, and no matter what the newspapers say it won't be over by Christmas. Some of us are never going to come back home. This is the last Cornish summer that many of us will ever know, and when that train pulls away from the halt it may be the last time we see the dear faces we love. This is the end of so much more than the summer. Oh, I know that everyone's very excited right now, and they think the war's a marvellous adventure, but it's easy to sing songs and wave flags. It's the loss and goodbyes that will kill us as much as bullets and cannons, and if you love Alex then don't let him leave thinking he's lost you. Whatever your grievance and your hurt, this is no time to hang onto it. You have a chance to put things right, and if you don't it could be the biggest regret of your life. Believe me, Emmy, it's the things we *don't* say that eat us up in the end. Don't let that happen to you, and don't let Alex go to war thinking you don't love him. That will kill him sooner than any German ever could. Don't waste the precious time you do have. Not if you truly love him."

His words flew like arrows into her heart, and Emmy flung her arms around him. Rupert really was the sweetest, kindest friend anyone could have.

"Thank you," she whispered, and he smiled down at her as wearily as one who'd walked a thousand miles.

"Don't thank me," he said. "Just be at the halt tomorrow."

War Photographs

1914–1916

Later on, Emmy would often reflect that if she had ever owed anyone a debt of gratitude, it was Rupert. How would she have borne what was to lie ahead if she'd allowed Alex to leave believing she no longer loved him? As the news of the war reached Rosecraddick and they learned with horrified disbelief of the drowning mud and choking gas, Emmy's anger and sense of betrayal felt as though it belonged to another life and she knew she would have been racked with remorse had she clung to her hurt pride and refused to say farewell. There was also the growing realisation this might have been the last time she was ever to see Alex, and to know that he had left with words of love and the certainty that she was waiting for him was some kind of comfort to her.

His locket was now Emmy's most treasured possession and she wore it always. Tucked beneath her blouse, its solid weight against her skin was the embodiment of Alex's promise to her and she would touch it a thousand times a day as though it was an anchor that would keep him from drifting away. Inside and resting beneath a whisper of glass, was the treasured picture she had taken of Alex all those months ago when he was teaching her how to use his camera. It was comforting to know that she could spring the catch and look at him whenever she needed to and kiss his dear face and tell him how much she missed him. He rested next to her heart and within it, and she would never, ever, let him go.

Simmonds was right; by Christmas the war showed no signs of being over. As the months trudged by and the seasons turned, the golden days of summer 1914 assumed the semblance of another life. How blessed they had been then, and what Emmy wouldn't have given to open up the glass eye of the longcase clock at the foot of the stairs to wind the hands back to those sun-filled days of white dresses, whispered promises and a future brimming with wonder. Now the days were dark and dreary, young women wore black and spoke with tear-choked voices, and she was Persephone, confined to the underworld and dreaming of a spring which might never come. She scanned the newspaper casualty lists, her blood turning to iced water when she saw row upon row of young men from Alex's regiment listed, and feeling lightheaded with relief when his name was not included. If cowards died a thousand deaths then women with sweethearts and sons at war must die tenfold whenever they scanned the newspaper or saw the telegram boy on his bicycle.

Alex wrote to Emmy when he could, and his letters were peppered with amusing stories and observations of the lowlands of France, but within the spaces of what he didn't overtly write, she learned of the mud and the gas and the carnage in France. He sent photographs too, all taken with the trusty little Kodak, and charged her with keeping them safe until he returned. Emmy stored them in her suitcase and pored over them when she was alone. The light of her candle burned low as she studied each image, simple shots to the untrained eye yet each crammed with meaning and truth. Some were simple shots of his new world, showing soldiers shaving in a trench or playing football, impossibly young and yet to shed the hopefulness of schoolboys aiming to do their best, while others depicted the same young men after battle as they lolled against one another or limped through mud. Bandaged and bloody and with their uniforms ragged, the contrast between these weary men and the earlier pictures snatched the breath away. On each one Alex had written in ghostly white letters with the stylus 'The Boys', but as the sequence progressed youth slipped from their faces until they were melting like wax into haggard old men, their haunted eyes filled with knowledge at odds with their years.

Sometimes Alex sent pictures of Kit and Rupert. Holding rifles with bayonets and surrounded by their men, they stood to attention in a flat sullen landscape and in their uniforms were strangers rather than the boys she had grown up with. There were never any photographs of Alex for he was always behind the lens, and Emmy wasn't sure whether to be saddened by this or grateful for it. At least in her mind he remained exactly as she knew him, clear-eyed, idealistic and so totally convinced of his calling. It would hurt terribly to see his eyes shadowed and his cheekbones even sharper beneath his flesh.

She wrote back to him, long chatty letters which contained anecdotes of life in Rosecraddick and descriptions of the changing seasons. She told him how the wheels of his wagon were hidden now by brambles and nettles, and confessed that she often left herself in and imagined he was there beside her, the quilt thrown over them as they watched the flames dance in the stove and made their plans. Her letters described the changes to the villages, the sacrifice of the flower garden at the manor for vegetable plots, which had upset Lady Rivers dreadfully, and her own endeavours to grow food and knit for the troops. Sometimes he felt so far away, in more than just distance, and Emmy would panic that he was slipping from her grasp. When this dread came upon her she would open up her locket, and Alex's eyes would hold hers and tell her all was well. She never failed to be comforted by this, and often she would pull the suitcase from beneath the bed and study her precious photographs. The wagon. Garden parties. Sunny days. Sketches. Snatched kisses. A lock of hair. This treasure chest of memories filled Alex's memory with colour once more, and her heart would stop racing. He was still kept in there, buried deep and safe, and nothing could ever change that.

Just as Alex omitted details from his letters, so Emmy forbore to tell him about her father's declining health and erratic rages, her humiliation at being refused credit in the grocer's, and how she'd been held back by

Simmonds when the army came to take Misty away. Nor did she tell him how she cried herself to sleep most nights, missing him and worrying for his safety. Instead she wrote of how she loved him and couldn't wait to be his wife when he returned, the two facts of which she was one hundred per cent certain and which sustained her when the hours dragged by and the news from the Western Front was bleak. She reminisced about the wonderful times they had shared and the wonder of their first meeting. It made her happy to describe their conversations and the hours spent in the caravan, and when Alex wrote back he did the same. Their letters and shared memories were the bedrock of their love and the foundations of the future they would build together when the war was over.

But apart from dreams of their future there wasn't a great deal which gave Emmy hope. Happiness often felt as though it too was a distant memory. Rosie's brother, the fisherman with dreams of his own boat, had been killed in the early weeks of the war, along with several other Rosecraddick lads who'd enlisted alongside him and with such high hopes. Several of Mrs Puckey's nephews were listed as missing, Dr Parsons' son had been wounded badly at Ypres, and the entire country was shaken by zeppelin raids on London. Before long the newspapers were filled with patriotic poems about 'playing the game' and 'tackling the fight', as though this war was no more than a rugby match, and more recruits were sought. Emmy wrote of this to Alex who in reply sent her a picture of three lads huddled in a trench, faces screwed up and hands clamped over their ears.

'The noise is unimaginable,' he wrote. 'I cannot photograph it, but I take photographs of the men who are subjected to it day and night. Their eyes are the conduits of such a ceaseless and unbearable assault. Cutwell was wrong; hell isn't hot. It's noisy and filled with gunfire. Even if it stops we will hear it for ever more.'

Emmy, who had read that the gunfire could be heard in Kent, had put his letter aside and wept. Her tears weren't only for Alex. They fell for her father, in more pain and more bitter than ever, and for all the brave boys who'd left Cornwall with such high hopes, and for a way of life that would never ever return. Her tears were for Kit and Rupert, officers in a war they had never dreamed of, and the lost lives they should have all led.

With Julyan's health declining rapidly, Emmy assumed more responsibility for Pendennys Place, and she was alarmed to discover just how greatly in debt the estate was. She spent hours fretting over balance sheets, tugging at her hair and snapping pencil after pencil as she scribbled sums which never seemed to tally, but no matter what she did the figures stayed stubbornly red. There were debts everywhere. They owed the grocer, the butcher, the feed merchant and the wine merchant, and she even feared that the servants had not been paid for some time.

When panic made her hands tingle, she would close them around the locket, and the cool hardness of the silver case would soothe her. Alex loved her. He would return to marry her, and then it wouldn't matter to Emmy whether the Pendennys family no longer possessed a good name and had very bad debts because she would be disinherited anyway, and leaving it all behind. Until then, though, she had bills to pay and accounts to settle, and unless Julyan wanted to sell their land, which she knew he didn't, Emmy wasn't sure what she could do to make ends meet. She put her best dress and hat on and visited the family solicitor who regarded her over his leather-topped desk with the sad eyes of a jowly old bloodhound and said there was nothing he could do. Perhaps she could persuade her father to sell some land? The woods would be attractive to the right client. Or perhaps make a profit on this year's harvest?

There was no chance of either course of action. Julyan wouldn't dream of selling land, and without the village menfolk to work the land it was no longer possible to farm the fields effectively. Being down to only Hector made ploughing almost an impossibility, and most of their fields slumbered beneath weeds and nodding grasses. Simmonds did his best to maintain the land, but it was far too much for one man, no matter how devoted, and the neglected paddocks were pricked with thistles and starred with docks. Fences listed and fell into the gorse. Hedgerows were choked by grasping fingers of ivy. Stone walls, split by elder and lanky saplings, crumbled. Everything was falling apart.

Lacking gamekeepers to manage them, the cock pheasants grew bold and flapped from the woods to peck at the tender plants in Mrs Puckey's vegetable garden and strutted along the drive with their wives in tow with all the arrogant swagger of Henry the Eighth. Emmy watched them from the library and was tempted to unlock the gun cupboard to see whether her aim was still true, for without a good harvest and a steady income, a lean winter beckoned. In the end she caught the train to Truro and pawned her spoons and pearls again, a cold lump of misery settling in her stomach when she passed these treasures over in return for half the amount she had received on the last occasion. Still, at least they could eat. For now, anyway. Emmy didn't know what would happen the next time their creditors refused them. The thought filled her with a sick panic.

The spring of 1915 flamed into summer, the sun climbing impossibly high like a child scaling a tree and calling for admiration, and Emmy divided her time between tending to her ailing father and weeding the vegetable garden. Mrs Puckey had given up long ago fretting about what tasks were suitable for a lady, and Emmy found she enjoyed the repetitive nature of the work. As she weeded the newly created vegetable beds and listened to the droning bees, she would tip her head back and to enjoy the warmth on her skin. If nobody was looking she might even take her straw hat off and risk a few freckles – for who cared now, if her hands were rough or her skin tanned?

On one such late August afternoon, Emmy was alone battling a goose grass invasion in the walled garden. Simmonds was mowing the hayfields with the help of two prisoners of war borrowed from the manor, and Mrs Puckey had an afternoon off to visit her sister, Dickon Trehunnist's mother, a lady with the unenviable status of having lost the most sons of any woman in the neighbourhood. Alone and deep in thought, Emmy was working quietly, and she started when a shadow fell across the earth. Shading her eyes, she looked up, expecting to see Simmonds armed with his hoe rather than this soldier silhouetted against the sunlight and with a kitbag on his shoulder.

A soldier who was both familiar and a stranger.

The trowel fell from her fingers.

"Hello, Emmy," said Alex.

Laughing and crying, Emmy hurled herself into Alex's arms, pressing her face into his neck and holding him tightly. She didn't care whether anyone spotted them from the house, because nothing else mattered except that Alex was home and safe. He held her against his heart and she clung to him.

"Am I dreaming?" she gasped.

Alex's hands slipped from her waist and he stepped back. She gazed up at him and her heart twisted to see the small changes which only one who loved him would notice. He was thinner, his uniform hanging loose on his shoulders, and his once bright eyes were dulled, as though a veil was drawn between the sights they had witnessed and the world he walked through. His hair was hidden beneath his cap and it took her aback not to see the thick auburn curls she had loved so much. The faint lines around his eyes were new too. Yet these things were nothing in comparison to the livid scar which tore from the corner of his left eye to his jaw.

"Shrapnel," he said, seeing her shock.

She traced it with her fingers. The raised flesh was smooth and taut.

"You never told me you'd been injured."

He caught her hand and kissed it.

"It's was just a scratch, Em. Hardly worth even mentioning. I was only in hospital for a few days, not like some of the chaps."

She was horrified. "Why didn't you write and tell me?"

"I wasn't really in a state to write anything when they took me in," Alex confessed. "It was a shell, and the blast knocked me for six. I owe my life to Kit because he dragged me into the dugout so most of it missed me, but some of the others weren't as lucky. My leg and my face were sore for a few weeks, but I think the nurses did a good job of stitching me up. I'm not nearly as ugly as I used to be, and I think a limp makes me distinguished!"

One corner of his mouth lifting in a half smile, he attempted to take the horror out of what he had described, but Emmy felt cold to the bone for how could something like this have happened without her sensing it? While Alex had been bleeding into foreign mud she was planting peas and cutting flowers, and while he had lain in hospital she had been taking tea with her godmother. She always told herself that because she loved Alex so much she would know if anything had happened to him, but now she realised she was only fooling herself. There was nothing special that would keep them safe, and there was no god who favoured young lovers watching over them. There was no magic link and no special dispensation.

"Kit was a hero. He could have been killed diving in like that to knock me aside," Alex said. "I owe him my life."

Emmy was almost overwhelmed with a surge of love for her old friend.

"He's safe? And Rupert?"

"When I left they were, or at least as safe as any man is out there," Alex said quietly. A haunted expression settled over his face and she knew he was no longer present in the garden, holding her and feeling the sunshine on his skin, but hundreds of miles away in the trenches where boys fell in the mud, tangled their limbs on barbed wire and choked to death on gas. She didn't press him for any more details about her friends. Alex was home and he was safe. The rest would unfold.

"I've missed you," she told him. "I can't begin to tell you how much. I can hardly believe you're here."

Alex didn't say another word but drew Emmy into his arms and kissed her. His mouth felt like coming home and she closed her eyes, suddenly as weary as someone who has reached the end of a long and arduous journey. As they held one another the long months of fear and longing melted away. This moment, right now, was all that mattered.

"I've dreamed about this moment since the train pulled away from the halt, and I can't tell you how wonderful it is to see you again. There were times when I was afraid …" Alex shook his head as though shaking away thoughts. "Only knowing you were here waiting for me kept me going."

Emmy's eyes filled with tears and she pressed her face against his jacket, blotting her eyes against the scratchy fabric. She wouldn't cry, not now. This was a happy time. This was what she had been living for.

"I love you," she said. "So much. I was afraid that —"

Alex kissed her tenderly to stop the cascade of fearful words.

"Somebody was watching over me, that's for certain."

She reached for the locket and opened it to show him his picture.

"You watch over me every day."

"That's a dreadful photograph! The light's all wrong. Who took it?" he teased.

"Some amateur," Emmy laughed, closing the locket and tucking it inside her blouse. "Although I blame the subject. I don't think he was a patient sitter at all!"

"The very worst, I should think!"

They smiled at one another, both recalling that afternoon. Alex had wrestled the camera away from her in the end and they'd nestled in the long grass of woods, kissing until they were breathless and the patches of blue sky above the leafy canopy seemed to spin like a merry-go-round.

He picked up his kitbag and held out his hand.

"Shall we see what state the old wagon's in?"

"I've been looking after it. Sometimes I go there to be close to you," she confessed, blushing because the words sounded foolish spoken out loud. Would he laugh, a man who had seen action and fought at the front?

But Alex didn't laugh. He squeezed her hand. "I love that, Em. I can't tell you how many nights I've lain on my pallet and thought about the times that were spent there, or spun my thoughts away from the mud and the guns back to holding you by the fire and listening to the gentle rain. Maybe we were both back there at the same time, one in thought and the other in reality? I like to think that."

Hand in hand they left the walled garden, Emmy's goose grass battle abandoned to be waged another day, and walked along the shady path through the woods. The sun filtering through the dense leaves danced a dappled ballet on the mossy floor and it felt as though they were stepping into a magical world. There were so many wonderful memories here, and as time shimmered Emmy thought she glimpsed their earlier selves deep in conversation and so blissfully unaware of what lay ahead.

They arrived at the clearing, tangled with brambles and thick with ferns now there were no groundsmen and keepers to tame the woods, and Emmy reached behind the wagon steps and pulled out the key.

She passed it to Alex. "You must open the door. It's your home."

In answer he dropped the kitbag and pulled her into his arms, kissing her until she felt giddy.

"*You* are my home, Emily Pendennys. I could travel the whole world, but the only place I want to be is right here and right now, with you. Whatever comes next and whatever the future holds, everything in my life has led me here to you, and I could never, ever, ask for anything more."

"Let's go inside," she said.

The overgrown wagon was filled with greenish light like a sun-caressed rockpool when Emmy opened the curtains. It was a little dusty; with all the work in the garden and her father's latest illness, she hadn't been inside for a few weeks, and so she bustled around sweeping dust aside with her sleeve and plumping cushions while Alex stood in the doorway as though unable to believe he was truly here.

"It's just the same," he said quietly. "How can that even be possible? How can so much have changed yet this is as it always was?"

"Because this is our haven," she said quietly, "and it doesn't belong to anything else but this. Do you see, Alex? This is perfect. This is *right*."

He nodded, glancing around in wonder. "It's exactly as I left it. It feels as it always did. Oh Em, here I feel like myself again."

She crossed the wagon and wrapped her arms around him, holding him as he trembled.

"You *are* yourself, Alex. Never doubt it."

"Those dreams we had, Em? The things we were going to do? They feel like they still could happen now I'm back here. It's all possible, isn't it."

"Of course, it is," she said softly. "We'll do all of it, Alex. You'll see."

Now they were reunited the world was filled with colour, the future brimmed with wonderful adventures and the war was no more significant than a child's half-recollected nightmare.

"I dreamed of this," he said quietly. "When it seemed unbearable, when I wondered whether I'd ever see you again, I thought of being here again. Thinking of you kept me hoping. I know how much I hurt you when I enlisted. Thank you for waiting for me, Emmy."

She looked up at him, her stomach swooping at the red slash of the scar and the web of lines around his eyes. Her body was trembling because everything felt right. Everything had condensed into this moment.

"No more waiting," she said taking his hand and leading him to the quilted nest. "The time for waiting is past."

Emmy ached for Alex. She needed him and she wouldn't spend the rest of her life wondering what it might be like to know him fully. Their time was now and she would not waste a moment because every second was a gift. As Alex kissed her, a deep kiss which spoke of the pain of long months apart and the urgency of knowing there were only days remaining, she knew she couldn't wait a moment longer. This was their time. When Alex lay her back against the quilt she opened herself to him and held him close. This was pure happiness.

This was *everything*.

Alex had been granted seven days of leave, and two them would be spent travelling to and from Cornwall. The five remaining days were precious, and Emmy, no longer caring whether her absence might be noticed or her behaviour attract attention, spent every possible moment with him. In the chaos of a wartime household, where the staff was pared to the bone and the lady of the house was frequently tasked with shopping errands and gardening, it wasn't difficult to go unmissed.

They had five days in which to squeeze a lifetime of loving. Five days to make memories that would last for ever and sustain them through the parting which yawned ahead of this interlude like an evil fairy's curse. Five days to make believe the war wasn't happening to them. It was a time where reality was suspended, and nothing mattered except their love and the magical world they were creating. The war was another life, and as she lay in Alex's arms, drowsy and heavy with bliss, Emmy could almost believe that it was nothing more than a bad dream and they had eloped after all. They were safe in the south of Spain where the skies were boldly blue and the sun a gold disc of heat, and they dined on fat olives and oranges. In these moments when she drifted through the hazy hinterland between sleeping and waking, life felt perfect and right, and she had never been happier. When dark thoughts chilled her, she would bury her face in his shoulder to drink in the scent of him and hold him as tightly as she could. If love alone could keep a man safe, Alex Winter would be invincible. She would give anything to keep him here for ever. How could she bear to let him go again?

Alex never said a great deal about the fighting or burdened Emmy with tales of the horrors he had witnessed. He never spoke of any fears he might have about his return to the front, but sometimes he seemed to drift away from her, and she knew his thoughts were with Kit and Rupert and the others. She tried to understand, but how she wished Alex could escape from the action just for this short time. It was beyond unfair that even when he was here in Cornwall, and safe within the circle of her arms, his thoughts were still mired in mud and death.

One afternoon as they were dozing in the wagon, their heavy limbs entwined beneath the quilt, a shot rang out through the woods. Simmonds shooting a hapless pheasant, Emmy thought lazily – but Alex sprang to his feet, his hands clawing for a gun that wasn't there, his contorted face almost unrecognisable. She realised then that his photographs were not the only evidence of the war Alex had brought home, and as she held him tightly, feeling the drumming of his heart beneath his warm skin, Emmy fought to keep her tears from falling for all the boys like him, so beautiful and brave and so utterly, irrevocably, damaged.

When Alex developed the rolls of film he had brought back with him Emmy watched his hands shake when he opened the jars of chemicals or pegged up prints. In the reversed light and shade of the darkroom his face, looming over the dishes, seemed haggard and aged, as though the merest glimpse of the developing images was enough to drain all joy from him. Although he mixed liquids with his old confidence and moved through the stages of development with his old methodical ease, the red light trickling over him like blood made Emmy shudder. She had always known she could never compete with his love for photography, but she had never dreamed it might lead him into such danger, and she was filled with foreboding. Photography could take Alex from her. He was willing to die for it.

These photographs were vitally important, Alex explained as he worked at the bench, bent over the images swimming up through the chemical baths. Each picture here told the truth of the war in a way that could not be denied or reinvented by the army or the press, he said. But Emmy turned away with a shiver because the horrors appearing slowly through the liquid were the stuff of creeping nightmares. This was Dante's deepest circle of hell. It was a purgatory of mangled flesh and ghastly white bone.

"The army isn't keen on the men having cameras," Alex said, fishing a picture from the solution. "They prefer to arrange shots which tell things their way. But with a camera like the pocket Kodak any Tommy can take a picture. I suspect they'll attempt to ban them soon."

"What will you do then?" Emmy crossed her fingers hoping that Alex might say he would leave and come home to her, impossible as this was because he would never desert or shy away from his duty.

"Keep taking them regardless. I can't imagine it will be possible to keep tabs on who has what. It's mayhem there. I'll send the camera back to you if the worst comes to the worst."

Emmy wasn't certain what 'the worst' meant. Was it having his beloved camera taken away, or death? She shivered.

"I'd keep anything safe for you," she said.

Alex's head, still bent over the trays, nodded.

"I know you will, my love, and when I go back you must keep these pictures safe too. They are my finest work and my legacy. If I don't …" He paused, still intent on his task, before adding softly, "If I don't come home again they're yours, Emmy, and you must decide what to do with them."

'I'd burn them,' she thought with a flash of hatred, "because the taking of them will steal you from me.

She swallowed her revulsion. Alex was right; these harrowing photographs were his best work. They were hateful because they showed the true face of war.

"I'll keep them safe," she promised, and he turned to her and smiled, the very same sweet smile that had made her heart turn to thistledown the very first day they met.

He left the pictures pegged up to dry, and they spent the afternoon in their own magical world beneath the quilt, lost in touch and taste and longing, but when Emmy walked home through the woods the trees seemed bowed as broken limbs and the leaves sighed like dying boys. The war was inescapable, even here in Rosecraddick, and now she had seen those powerful photographs it would haunt her waking hours as well as her dreams. She wondered how she would sleep at night with them stowed beneath her bed.

As Alex's leave raced by there was an unspoken acceptance between them that he might not return. There was nothing to be gained from talking about this, and so Emmy locked her fear away in the deepest and darkest corner of her mind, turning the key to an imaginary vault and walking away from it. She would make every second of the precious remaining time count. When she wasn't with Alex, she was thinking of him and dreaming of their lovemaking. It was a revelation to her, this molten-lava longing and the fire he had lit. It licked through her, slowly at first and a slow burn, before it burst into flames and consumed her. She longed for his touch, reliving over and over the moments they spent together and aching for more. Any fears and misgivings were swept away by sensation, and there was no space to think any further ahead than the minutes they would spend together. They were reckless with passion, speaking a silent and invisible language and reading a book filled with words only they could understand. Crazed by time's racing, Emmy could barely eat or sleep, and just a glimpse of Alex from beneath her lashes was enough to snatch her breath. When his fingers skimmed her flesh she melted, and as one they shared every heartbeat, thought and breath.

It was magical. Wonderful. And terrible.

They walked along the cliffs to watch the marching waves and wandered hand in hand through the woods, retracing the paths they knew so well as they picnicked and reminisced and kissed. They made the wagon theirs again, lighting the fire and curling up beneath the quilt to hold one another tightly and make love, but most of all they talked about their hopes of the wonderful life that lay ahead. It sounded fantastical now, as much a fairy tale as any told in childhood, but Emmy held Alex's thinner frame as he spoke and kissed his brow, murmuring agreement and weaving in more details of the countries they would visit and the sights they would see. She understood that now he needed to cling to hopes of their future more than ever before, just as she clung to him already dreading the parting that lay ahead.

Time had sped up in a way which made nonsense of any rules which might apply to science or physics, and all too soon the day dawned when Alex put away his simple shirts and faded cords, and with them the days of quiet happiness, to don his uniform and shoulder his kitbag. He locked the wagon but didn't hide the key away this time. He passed it to Emmy.

"Keep this safe for me," he said, and she knew he was not speaking about the key alone.

They walked hand in hand to the halt, saying little in words but speaking a thousand promises in tender touches and stolen glances. There was no more left to say now; Emmy knew Alex loved her and he knew she loved him. She would never love another. He was everything and more to her.

Apart from the station master, checking his pocket watch and scarcely noticing yet another Tommy and his sweetheart saying their farewells, the halt was empty. There was no brass band to send Alex off with rousing music today, and the bunting had been pulled down and stuffed into sacks long ago. Emmy tried to recall herself as that hurt and proud girl who had almost missed saying goodbye that day, but that Emmy felt like a character from a story, and one with whom it was impossible for her to identify or sympathise with. How little that girl had understood of how it felt to have your own heart beating in another's breast or to be as close to someone as the air in their lungs. She clung to Alex's hand, faint with the dread of knowing she would soon have to let it go.

Skylarks soared and sang above them in a bold blue sky, and the cascade of joyous notes snatched at Emmy's throat. Life was still beautiful even though across the sea men were falling in scores. She gripped his hand more tightly when a line of smoke smudging the farthest stretches of track announced the approach of the train. Time accelerated once again, and for all her resolve Emmy couldn't contain her grief. The tears she had fought so hard to keep in check spilled over her cheeks.

"Alex, I —"

He turned her gently to face him, looking at her with such love and tenderness that she wept even harder. He brushed away her tears with his fingertips.

"I love you, Emily Pendennys," he murmured. "I did from the very first second I saw you and every moment since. Always know that."

She clung to him, tears falling as her heart broke.

"Don't speak as though you're not coming back," she sobbed.

"Emmy, I want you to know that no matter what happens you've made me happier and luckier than any man ever deserved to be. I'll cherish these days with you for the rest of my life be that ten minutes, or ten years, or until I'm old and grey."

He wrapped his arms around her, holding her close while she cried. As the train drew alongside the platform, she remembered how all those months ago it had seemed like a dragon that would devour all the hopeful boys, and her tears fell even faster.

Alex picked up his kitbag and took her hand. "It's time."

She wiped her eyes with her hand and nodded. She couldn't deny it, because the train was stopping now, and the doors were swinging open. They walked slowly along the platform as some local people alighted and luggage was swung onto the platform. If anyone noticed Emily Pendennys with a humble Tommy they didn't call a greeting or doff their hats, and she was grateful to be cloaked in the steam and confusion. Alex didn't speak when they reached the final carriage and Emmy tried her hardest to gulp back her tears. She must smile. It was her duty. She couldn't let Alex leave for the front with memories of a running nose and red eyes. If he could return to war without falling apart she had to be as courageous as he was. She bit hard on the inside of her cheek. She would be brave for Alex.

The carriage door was open, and Alex paused beside it.

"Remember our trip to Truro?" she said, attempting a smile as she pulled the locket from beneath her dress. "It was where we first saw this."

"I'll never forget it. You'd pawned your jewellery." He shook his head. "What was Rupert thinking, letting you do such a thing?"

"Rupert didn't know," Emmy confessed. "He thought I was in the milliner's shop."

Alex laughed. Then his expression grew serious and he took her hands.

"My love, if anything should happen to me and you need help, promise me you'll ask Rupert. Or Kit. I couldn't bear for you to be alone or frightened."

"I promise," Emmy said, even though at that moment neither Kit nor Rupert featured in her thoughts. "Anyway, you'll be back before you know it, so I won't need to ask them for anything!"

He pressed his lips together and nodded his satisfaction, holding her close once more and kissing her softly while the steam billowed and the station master blew his whistle.

"Time for me to go," he said, releasing her. "I love you, Emmy. Never forget that. I love you."

"I love you too," she whispered. "So much."

He stepped into the carriage. The door clunked shut behind him. Alex pushed down the window and Emmy rose on tiptoe so he could lean down and kiss her one last time. It was the softest, sweetest kiss she had ever known.

The train began to huff, wheels screaming on the track as it began to ease away from the platform. Alex reached his hand to hold hers for one last moment before the guard's whistle shrilled in rebuke and their fingers were wrenched apart. Alex leant out, waving amid the din and clouds of steam and mouthing that he loved her. Emmy ran along the platform but the train was gathering speed and each huff of steam and rattle of wheels carried Alex further out of reach. His waving arm became no more than a blur as the train accelerated. It was carrying her heart and soul away, and Emmy was blinded by tears.

Alex Winter was gone, and she was so dreadfully afraid he might never return.

War Bride and Baby

1915-1916

"It won't help our brave boys if you fade away, Miss. Eat up now."

Mrs Puckey, returning to the kitchen with Julyan's tray, was unimpressed to discover Emmy still picking at her lunch.

"I'm starting to think you don't like my cooking any more," the housekeeper added, a hurt note creeping into her voice,

"Of course I still like your cooking," Emmy said, trying to gulp back the rising nausea which the scent of gravy and pastry was causing to rise in her like a spring tide. She glanced down at her plate and speared a chunk of meat valiantly, but her stomach roiled at the sight of the game pie, shiny with aspic and speckled with congealed fat, and she put her fork down quickly. There was no way she could eat even a mouthful.

"I told Simmonds those pheasants were old and stringy, but there wasn't anything else in the pantry so what's a body to do?" Mrs Puckey grumbled, half to herself and half to Emmy. "Then the damn rain comes along and ruins most of the vegetables, so we're only left with last year's old stuff. The Lord knows I try my best with the meals, but when there's a war on what are we to do?"

She stomped around the kitchen, hurling pans into the sink to make her displeasure clear, although whether this was with the war or with Emmy for not eating her luncheon wasn't entirely clear. Emmy shut her eyes as the housekeeper grumbled on about wicked Germans and the poor dear boys who had been forced to leave home and taken far too soon. It didn't help to point out that, as Alex had said, the enemy was suffering just as greatly, or to remind Mrs Puckey that most of Rosecraddick's boys had left in high spirits and with great excitement. Of course they had been excited; most of them had never been further than Plymouth and had no idea of what was waiting across the English Channel. How could they have known? How could anyone have imagined this?

So, she only said, "Your pie's lovely, Mrs P. I'm not feeling very hungry, that's all."

"You've been saying that for weeks, Miss Emmy." The housekeeper turned from the sink, soapy hands dripping, and scrutinised Emmy with eyes bright as wet currents. "You do look a bit peaky."

Emmy felt peaky, if 'peaky' could be applied to describe this sensation of dragging a millstone about the place.

"I hope you're not sickening for something." Mrs Puckey was worried. "You're dreadfully pale. Maybe we should send for Dr Parsons? Or fetch for some tonic?"

Emmy shook her head. "I'm just a little out of sorts. It's probably the weather."

"I've never known an autumn like it," agreed Mrs Puckey. "We'll all have webbed feet at this rate."

It was bleak and soggy autumn. As though mourning all the fallen men at the front, the ripped clouds were leaden grey, and leaves fell in endless battalions. The skies were bereft of swallows, and each gloomy dawn brought only more rain which trickled down the window pane like tears. The sodden harvest had been poor, and the muddy fields beyond Pendennys Place echoed the quagmires in no man's land. The endless damp seeped through the walls into Emmy's bones; it was hard to rise from bed when your heart was heavy, each day wore leaden boots and the world beyond the window was weeping. She wished she could close her eyes and sleep until the sun shone again and the dreadful war was over.

In his letters Alex told Emmy about the mud. There was nothing he could compare it to, he'd written, for the cloying, choking wetness seeped into everything from your food to your boots to your dreams. Men drowned in it, horses were sucked in hock-deep, and rats the size of dogs squelched through it at night. He described how men's feet rotted in the wet, and the photographs he enclosed for safekeeping turned her stomach. Even his own feet were sore and blistered, and during those few sweet, snatched days Emmy had heated water on the stove and filled a bowl, kneeling beside him to soak each foot in turn, rub in lavender ointment and roll on the soft woollen socks she had knitted. Alex had closed his eyes and dozed, lulled by the fire and the tender touch of her hands. As she had watched him sleep, Emmy's throat had tightened, for it broke her heart to see him so tired and broken. She hated knowing he had seen – and she feared had done – things that haunted him. Dreadful things which made him wake from his sleep with a jolt and tugged him to places where she could never follow.

"What will become of us all I don't know," grumbled Mrs Puckey, still talking even though Emmy hadn't replied. "No men left to work the land – Simmonds hardly counts these days – and all the girls off looking for excitement. Even that good-for-nothing Rosie's a nurse now! Whatever next?"

Emmy didn't imagine that working in a munitions factory or becoming a VAD was necessarily about excitement. Judging from Alex's photographs, Rosie would have a daunting task in the military hospitals. Her pretty face would be a comfort to the men she nursed, men whose mangled limbs and bloodied faces appalled onlookers, and Emmy admired her for playing her part in the war. If Emmy had been older, and the estate had still been Morvan's burden, she would have done exactly the same. It would have been so much better to be doing something useful than drifting around Pendennys Place like a sad phantom.

"I think Rosie will do us all proud," she said firmly, and Mrs Puckey sniffed.

"I'm sure you're right, Miss Emmy. Why don't you sit by the fire and I'll bring you some of that tonic the doctor left for your father? He won't touch it, and it's only going to waste."

They exchanged a look, both knowing that brandy was the only supplement Julyan Pendennys would tolerate.

At this point Simmonds appeared, seeking a slice of pie. He dripped muddy water all over the floor, distracting Mrs Puckey, who shooed him onto the mat and hung his wet coat above the range where it steamed gently and fogged up the windows. The threat of calling the doctor safely forgotten, Emmy slipped from the kitchen and dragged herself along the tiled passage which led to the back of the house, where shuttered windows plunged the house into a gloom which matched the heaviness in her heart. She felt so weary and so sick that rather than sitting by the fire in the library she pulled herself up the stairs to her room where she lay on her bed and listened the incessant rain plopping into pails and drumming against the roof. She curled one hand around the locket and rested the other on her stomach. How Emmy wished she could close her eyes and not wake up until Alex was beside her once more.

She turned her face to the wall, drawing her legs up against her chest and wrapping her arms around them. Alone and frightened, she longed for Alex to hold her and tell her everything would be fine. She wrote to him every day, long letters in which she tried her best to be cheerful, and which she never posted because without telling the truth they were as meaningless as the long days were without him. As soon as Alex read the first line he would know she was keeping something back, and how could she bear to do this to him when they had always been so honest? Yet, how could she be selfish and give him any extra worry? If he was distracted it could prove fatal …

From the day the train had pulled away from the halt, carrying Alex far away from her and back to the front, life for Emmy had adopted a strange and dreamlike quality. She had walked home from the halt, and the hot afternoon had grown heavy and oppressive, the heat pressing down on her like a crushing hand. The thick air was as warm as blood and the sunlight turned a sickly lemon, spilling from bruised purple clouds which billowed in from the sea. Before she reached home a thunderstorm split the uneasy stillness, ripping up clouds and flinging fistfuls of rain onto the parched earth. Emmy thought it fitting that even nature was weeping tears of loss and anger. The good weather had fled from that moment, and premature autumn stole all colour and joy. Emmy wept every day, alone and unseen, until she was exhausted and sick.

At first Emmy had thought that feeling sick and bone-achingly tired was a symptom of heartbreak. The days following Alex's departure were bleak, and she hauled herself through them as though dazed. She couldn't face food, and she didn't want to see or speak to anyone. Diagnosing a chill, courtesy of her drenching, Mrs Puckey packed Emmy off to bed with a hot brick, a hot whisky toddy and strict instructions to stay put for a couple of days. Emmy hadn't argued. She had been grateful to hide away, and a cold was wonderful explanation for her swollen nose and puffy eyes.

She rested her hand on her belly, knowing there was little hope of a cold explaining what was really happening. Tears slid into her hair and ears and soaked her pillow. No wonder Mrs Puckey thought she was looking peaky and wanted to send for the physician. Emmy felt a dizzy dread at the mere notion; if Dr Parsons examined her he would know in an instant what was happening. If only she could just stay up here for ever, staring into the gloom and alone with her thoughts or find a way to pause time until Alex returned and they could be married. How she needed him to hold her and tell her that she and this baby were loved and safe!

A baby. Emmy pressed her hand harder against her belly, unable to believe that beneath the smooth, flat skin was a brand-new person, a unique and glorious mixture of her and the man she loved. Would this little one have his auburn curls? Her green eyes? Would its chin dimple when it laughed, just as his did? It was a mystery and a shock and the biggest wonder she had ever known, all churned up at once into a growing sense of panic. What would happen to her? Would Julyan beat her? Throw her out? Disinherit her? How would she care for her baby then?

Emmy vaguely recalled a servant girl, Betsy, who had been sacked because she was, as Mrs Puckey explained disapprovingly, 'in the family way and a wicked girl'. Emmy had been very young, but she had noticed Betsy's red eyes and heard whispering amongst the servants which stopped abruptly whenever they thought she might be listening in. 'Shame', she had heard Mrs Puckey mutter, and 'a girl like that will say anything'. Morvan had been summoned to the library where Julyan bellowed at him so loudly at him that her own feet had left the floor. Betsy had vanished shortly after all this, and Emmy hadn't thought of her for years. Now she couldn't put the young girl's tear-stained face out of her mind. What had become of Betsy and her baby? Where had she gone? Had she been taken care of by her family, or had they turned their backs on her because she was a wicked girl? And what happened to her baby? Was it taken away from her? Was it given to the parish?

Emmy felt a lurch of panic. She and Alex had never spoken about children, at least not in any other way than the abstract imagining of the little people who might one day accompany them on their travels. Emmy couldn't remember ever feeling the need to coo over babies. She much preferred foals and found the demands of children tiresome when their proud mamas insisted on foisting them on her. This little stowaway was different; it was theirs, and Emmy already knew she would fight anyone who tried to take it from her. This was Alex's child, entrusted to her to keep safe. As she lay on her bed with one hand on her belly and another curled around her locket, Emmy swore she would do everything in her power to protect it.

I'm not Betsy, Emmy told herself firmly. She was an engaged woman. Alex loved her, and if the beastly war hadn't come along they would have been married long ago. There was no shame in loving him, no shame in this child, and the baby was wanted. It was hers. She wasn't a penniless fishergirl from the village. She was Emily Pendennys, the heir to Pendennys Place, and this baby was the next heir. He was part of a story that stretched back to the start of time and reached out into the unwritten future.

He was the future.

He was hope.

Her tears drying, Emmy sat up, filled with resolve. Weeping would not make this situation go away any more than drinking brandy would banish her father's injuries. Julyan Pendennys would be angry, but what could he really do? His temper was fierce, and he drank more than ever these days, but he was also increasingly weak and in recent months had barely left his bed. He was in no state to beat her, and if he disowned her then there would be no one left to inherit. Her mind spun like a child's windmill in the sea breeze as plans and solutions whirled through her thoughts. She could let out her dresses and disguise her changing figure, which would buy her time, and Mrs Puckey's eyes weren't as sharp as they had been in the days of the unfortunate Betsy. There was no need for her father to find out until there was little choice, and by then surely Alex would have returned to marry her. There must be a way of obtaining a special licence, since young couples were marrying at short notice all the time these days; Killjoy Cutwell would have to help them, since it was a matter of mortal sin, and once Emmy was officially Mrs Winter all would be well. And if Julyan still threw her out? Well, let him!

Cheered by having a plan, Emmy hopped off the bed and sloshed some water into the bowl on the washstand. The reflection in the mirror above it was pale, but the green eyes were lit with determination and the stubborn chin tilted firmly upwards. As she splashed her face Emmy felt her stomach grumble and she smiled. Even her appetite was on their side!

"Hungry, little one? Would you like some game pie?"

Her stomach growled again, and Emmy laughed.

"I'll take that as a yes! Shall we see what we can find?"

It was so fast, this falling in love with their child. How was it possible that in less that the beat of her pulse her situation had transformed from being the worst predicament and punishment imaginable to something wonderful and cherished? Alex was still here with her! She was no longer stupefied by fear but was filled with energy and a fierce determination to do whatever she must to protect their child.

This baby was a blessing and a gift. How could she ever have thought otherwise?

There could be no more lying around in bed feeling sorry for herself now, and no more picking at food. Alex had left Emmy with something very precious and she would not let him, or this baby, down. She would do whatever it took, and even if that meant forcing herself to eat stringy pheasant pie, then this was exactly what she would do. The harvest and the garden and the crumbling estate too – all these were no longer just hers but a precious legacy to hand on this little one. It would be his home one day, and his place when she and Alex returned from travelling.

She smiled wonderingly at the girl in the looking-glass.

"You," she said sternly, "are going to be a mother. So, you had better stop lolling around here and get on with things!"

She would write to Alex and tell him about the baby, Emmy decided, as she brushed her hair and pinned it up neatly; but this time it would be a letter filled with joy and love rather than vibrating with loneliness. She would tell him her plan and ask him to speak to Kit to request leave to marry her. Kit would surely agree, Lady Rivers would think what a lucky escape she'd had in escaping a such a daughter-in-law, and all would be well. She'd describe the thousand and one plans suddenly filling her head for improving the estate, clearing their debts and growing food, and Alex would know she was excited and proud and not in the least afraid – well, only the tiniest bit, and Emmy could temper that with the excitement of the life which lay ahead.

Yes, this was exactly what she would do. But first she'd better feed this baby some of Mrs Puckey's finest game pie!

As 1915 limped on, and news from the war grew ever bleaker, the high hopes they'd had back in 1914 that it would all be over by Christmas seemed dreadfully naive. Simmonds liked to mutter that nobody had mentioned *what* Christmas this might be, and the golden days of brass band send-offs felt as though they had happened in another life. Now many women wore black, only old men remained in the village, and the sight of the telegram boy freewheeling through Rosecraddick struck terror into the heart. Rosecraddick became a ghost village, and Emmy began to despair of ever finding anyone to work the land. Short of learning to plough herself, something that would soon be rendered impossible anyhow, she was running out of ideas. The Rivers had taken some Hun prisoners of war to work their farms, but Julyan Pendennys had refused to countenance the idea when Emmy tentatively suggested it to him, and since he was still the master of the house she had no choice but to muddle on with Simmonds.

It was a bleak November afternoon, the sky leeched of colour and scribbled over by chalk clouds, and as Emmy sat by the fire in the drawing room she wondered whether she could smell snow in the air. Would it be cold where Alex was? Did he shiver and long for the sunshine just as she longed for the warmth of his smile? It seemed so long ago now that she had last seen him that sometimes she was frightened he was slipping from her memory once again. She rested her hand on her stomach, taut and hard beneath her loosened skirts, and squeezed her eyes shut as she summoned memories from the treasure trove of her heart. She liked to think that the baby could see them too in some magical way, and that as Alex's child lay deep inside her most secret self it shared her visons of dancing brown eyes and waterfall laughter.

Once the sickness passed Emmy was possessed with a rush of energy in the mornings followed by a bone-deep exhaustion once the hands of the longcase clock passed noon. Her appetite had returned with a vengeance, much to Mrs Puckey's delight, and when she looked in the mirror her rounded cheeks and bright eyes spoke of good health. Emmy hoped this meant the baby was well too. She was walking miles through the woods and along the cliffs each day to drink in the salty air, and at night she slept long and deeply. It was fanciful, but she liked to think that through his baby Alex was taking care of her; he had sent his little helper to ensure she rested and ate properly rather than pining for him and wasting away while longing for his return.

Emmy had written to Alex to tell him about the baby, but as yet there had been no reply. Their letters must have crossed in the post, she realised, for although she had received one in mid-October there was no mention of her momentous news. Much of the page was slashed through with harsh black lines and if there had ever been any photographs enclosed these were all lost, along with the meaning of his sentences.

Emmy had felt a surge of anger towards the unknown censor who'd stolen Alex's words from her. She gleaned as much from them as she could while snatching the odd sunny morning from the grey winter murk, but all she could tell was that the food was awful and something about Kit being promoted for bravery and a vague half-line where he wrote excitedly about 'inside the camera'. The fragment made little sense, but it must have been important to Alex because his pencil had pressed deeply into the paper at this point, and she shook her head as she read, for the camera was always foremost in his thoughts! After this there were descriptions of the bully beef the men ate most days, and a sketch of a horse he had thought looked a bit like Misty, which made Emmy cry a little, but it was his final 'I love you' which she held closest to her heart and carried with her. It was the most perfect sentence in the world, and the essence of everything.

A log shifted in the grate and she blinked, back in the drawing room once more. The gloom was deeper, and the flames hissed like a restless crowd. The wind snatching the piles of leaves Simmonds had raked up was sharp and knife-edged, and although it was not yet three, darkness was already stealing in from the woods as though longing to creep through the warmly lit window. Emmy shivered and pulled her shawl around her shoulders. She ought to see whether her father needed anything but, tired and sleepy, she couldn't face walking along the chilly passageway to his study.

A knock on the door made her jump. The blonde head of Tilly, Rosie's replacement, and according to Mrs Puckey even more useless, peeped around.

"Sorry to disturb you, Miss, but there's a gentleman to see you."

Emmy was surprised. It was a miserable day and she couldn't imagine why anyone would journey out of the village to see her. She smoothed her hair and arranged her dress to fall in loose folds around her, disguising any hint of the little stowaway beneath.

"Show him in, Tilly," she said and rose to her feet as a man in officer's uniform stepped into the library.

"Hello, Emmy," said Rupert.

Emmy was shocked beyond speech – not just to see him so unexpectedly but by the changes in her old friend. Like gazing at a reflection in a misted mirror it was Rupert yet not Rupert. He was lean and his shoulders seemed broader, while his face, once smudged by youthful plumpness, was all angles and planes as though as master sculptor had chipped away the layers to reveal the man beneath the boy. She couldn't imagine this serious-faced officer ever being uncertain of anything and as Rupert stepped forward to kiss her, Emmy realised she was gawping.

"I can't believe you're here," she said, half-laughing and half-sobbing as she threw her arms around him, feeling how thin he was now.

"I can't quite believe it myself. My, God, Emmy. It's good to be home."

"Tilly, would you fetch us some tea? And cake?" Emmy released Rupert and sat back down, gesturing for him to take a seat. "And crumpets, if we have any! You always did like crumpets, Rupert. I remember you once ate six in a row. Kit couldn't keep up."

He stared at her blankly as though she was speaking Mandarin.

"Crumpets. Yes. Well."

Alex had once told Emmy how strange it was for a soldier on leave to exchange mud and guns and death for a world of cricket, afternoon tea and small talk. It jolted one, he'd explained. You became a khakied Odysseus – belonging nowhere and doomed to roam for ever. Rupert's gaze slipped from hers like butter off hot toast.

"Please take a seat," she said, gesturing to the one opposite her, but Rupert didn't move.

"What's wrong?" Emmy asked, concerned.

He twisted his cap as through trying to wring the fabric, and a muscle twitched in his cheek.

"Emmy," he began helplessly. "Oh, God, I don't know how to say this.

It's Alex …"

A cold wash of dread broke over her.

"What is it? Rupert, tell me. What's Alex?"

His mouth twisted, a moue of misery. "I'm sorry, Em. I'm so, so sorry."

Rupert didn't need to say anything more. Emmy knew. This was no social call. He was here in lieu of the telegram boy.

The room spun. Her legs were water. The sea broke free of the cove and crashed over her, rushing in her ears and pulling her under, deeper and deeper, until she was gasping for breath.

"Fetch some brandy and smelling salts," she heard Rupert ordering Tilly, who'd come rattling in with their tea things. "Miss Emily's in shock. Hurry!"

Emmy thought shock was a strange word to describe how she felt. 'Blank' came close, or perhaps blotted out, for everything had gone still and silent inside her mind. She was frozen in a snowy Hades; lost in a whirling blizzard of a life rendered void and empty. If Alex was lost, so was everything else. Their hopes, their dreams, the future she was living for, her baby's safety – it was all drifting away like ash from a bonfire. She was torn into pieces. She was scattered to the winds.

"Alex," Emmy whispered, and his name still tasted as sweet on her lips as his beautiful mouth always had. This couldn't be true. How was it possible that he could be gone without her sensing it? Although she was by the fire Emmy shook with cold. The sun had gone out for ever. She would never feel warm again

"I came to tell you the moment I could," Rupert was saying, kneeling beside her and holding her icy hands. "He had no next of kin and I didn't want to write. I was worried you might have seen his name in the casualty records."

Emmy scarcely heard a word. The room turned cartwheels around her, and her lungs refused to draw in air. She closed her eyes and wished she never had to open them again.

"I don't look at the lists any more," she said, and her voice sounded far away, as though the real Emmy was listening from another room. Scanning the names of the fallen felt like courting the bad fairy from a folk tale, as though by inviting her in you opened yourself up to a curse. If she didn't look she wouldn't see his name, and then Alex would be safe.

She opened her eyes. The drawing room looked the same. The fire was burning cheerfully. Tea and cake were set out on the table. The Stubbs was on the far wall. How was this even possible when everything that mattered was so dreadfully, irrevocably changed?

"When?"

He swallowed. "Three weeks ago."

Three weeks ago? Alex had been dead for three weeks and she'd had no idea? How was it possible that while she dreamed about the baby, read to her father and haggled with the butcher for a better cut of meat, Alex had already been lost?

"Tell me what happened," she whispered.

Rupert closed his eyes and Emmy knew he was struggling, and knew he had loved Alex too, but shock made her merciless. Nothing of Alex should be kept from her.

"Tell me! I need to know."

Rupert's eyelids fluttered open and she saw in his face the grief and unspeakable horror of what he had seen.

"He died a hero. Isn't that enough to know, Emmy?"

Maybe it would be for some women, Emmy thought, and perhaps it was better not to open the Pandora's box of knowledge and have details fly out which would torture you for ever, but she needed to know for her child. Alex's child deserved to know how the father he would never know had died. She would need to make certain that his baby knew everything about him.

"Don't you *dare* try and spare me," she warned. "Alex would have never tried to do that. My God, Rupert, he left those damned photographs with me for safekeeping. I've seen scenes in his work that will haunt me for the rest of my life. His life's calling, remember? Telling the truth about the damned war! This is the truth: death and destruction and despair. Tell me the truth. Tell me!"

He nodded, knowing she was right.

"Always photographs. That camera was never far from his reach. He was using it on his final offensive even though the army's starting to take a dim view of that kind of thing," Rupert recalled. "I have it for you, Em, and the rest of his belongings. I thought you'd want them."

She nodded but her thoughts weren't on Alex's camera. Emmy wouldn't care if she never saw it again. That camera was to blame for taking him away to war. Photography had been the mistress Alex Winter had left her for and in the end had died for. It, and not her, had been the true love of his life.

"He was brave that day. More than brave. Magnificent," Rupert said. "Our regiment was leading an attack on the first of three German trenches. The idea was to take the Germans by surprise and overwhelm them before pressing on to take the next trench and force them back. I'm not sure what went wrong, but something must have alerted the enemy because they were waiting for us."

He took a deep, juddering breath. It was as though he was still there with his men, plunging through mud and confusion as soldiers scattered beneath showers of bullets.

"Men were falling everywhere," he continued, so softly she had to lean forward to catch his words. "Our attack was meant to be a diversion while another division pressed on from the left, or so the CO told me afterwards, but the strategy was a disaster from the start. I lost sight of Kit early on in the confusion, but Alex and I pushed forwards as best we could."

Emmy listened as he described the battle, recognising the hellish scene from those Alex had photographed. She heard shells squeal and rifles pop like demonic fireworks, and watched outnumbered soldiers struggle through mire. The horror hit her like gunfire.

"We needed to draw attention away from the injured men falling back. I led a charge to take the enemy trench and inflict as much damage as possible, but it was pushed back, and we took a lot of casualties. It was utter carnage. Alex should have been retreating too, but somehow he managed to capture a machine gun post and held the Germans off for as long as he could, buying time for the rest of us." He hung his head. "He saved me, Emmy, and lots of others too. We wouldn't have made it back without the cover he gave us."

"What happened to Alex? Did you see?"

He met her gaze without flinching.

"I did. Alex was shot in the back when the enemy recaptured the machine gun. I saw him fall."

Hearing this, Emmy felt as though a bullet was passing through her own heart. But falling wasn't dead, she told herself desperately. He might have been injured, like he was before. He could have been badly injured and unable to write. You heard such things all the time.

"Are you sure he's not in a field hospital?"

Rupert tugged a handkerchief from his pocket and blew his nose loudly.

"I wish that was so with all my heart, but he was killed in action. If I could have taken his place then I would have done so without hesitating."

She gripped his hands. "But are you certain? You don't know for sure. He could have been hurt. He might be in a hospital."

"No, Emmy. I do know for sure. It was a mortal wound. No man would survive a volley of fire like that. I saw Alex fall and he isn't coming back. Do you understand what I'm telling you? He's dead."

There was a buzzing in Emmy's ears. 'Dead' was not a word that should ever be spoken in conjunction with Alex.

"No," she said. "I won't believe it."

"You must believe it, because it's true."

Her friend's fingers were vice-like, tethering her to an ugly truth. Emmy strained to tug them from his grip, but Rupert held fast.

"Alex Winter is dead," he repeated. "He isn't lying in a hospital bed somewhere in France. He's dead and he's gone, and I'm so, so sorry, but that's the truth. He's buried in France, and he isn't coming back to you."

His words were a blunt chisel chipping away any hope. Emmy slumped in the chair. Buried in France. Fallen. Dead.

"I'm so sorry, Emmy," Rupert whispered. "I wish it had been me. It should have been me, because he had you to live for. If I could take his place, I would."

His words had no more meaning now than the cawing of the rooks huddled in the chestnut trees. Nothing held meaning now. How could it when Alex had fallen face first in alien mud, his back peppered with bullets and his life draining away with his blood? He was dead. There was no farewell. No time to compose a last message to her. No words she could hold close and cherish in the long, dark days ahead. No acknowledgement that he ever knew about the baby and was filled with wonder and love. A snowstorm of black dots whirled across her vision.

"He saved my life, Em," Rupert was saying from that faraway place. "He was the bravest man I ever knew, and his photographs are works of genius. You must hold onto all that. Be proud of him."

The room was whirling. *Proud?* Emmy wanted to scream. She wasn't *proud*. She was angry with him! Furious. How could he have left her and their baby? He had promised they would be together.

The old hurt bit deep.

"He left me," she said, and her voice was flat. "How could he have done that if he'd loved me?"

"He did his duty. Alex is a hero." There was steel in Rupert's voice. He released her hands, straightening up and regarding her with a stern expression. "There are mentions in dispatches and there'll be a posthumous medal awarded to him at some point, or so the CO thinks."

But Emmy didn't care about medals or dispatches. What good were these things to her? All she wanted was Alex alive and by her side. Medals and talk of honour and battlefield heroics wouldn't hold her close or make love to her. They wouldn't take care of her and the baby. They were no substitute for the man she loved.

The room dipped and tilted, and she gave in to it, feeling as though she might drift away at any moment. She was bitterly angry, and as she wept her tears were as much from rage with him for leaving her as they were from grief. She wanted to scream at him. She wanted him to have never left her. She wanted this horrible war to have never happened in the first place. But most of all she just wanted Alex. Emmy wept and wept, and Rupert held her until the storm of tears abated.

Rupert poured brandy into a glass.

"Here. For the shock."

She turned her head away. "I can't."

"You're not your father, Em. A few sips will help."

"You don't understand." Her hand slipped to her belly. "I can't."

If Emmy hadn't been so exhausted and heartsick she would have laughed at the suite of expressions which crossed Rupert's face when he realised what she was telling him. His hands rose to tug at hair long since lost to the military haircut.

"Good Lord, Em!"

"Yes," Emmy agreed, thinking to herself that even the good Lord couldn't help her now. Nobody could. She was lost in every way a young woman could be. "Good Lord, indeed."

"Did Alex know?"

"I wrote, but I don't think he ever got the letter." She hoped not anyway. How horrible if he had died knowing he would never see his son. "The only person who knows apart from me is you."

He swirled the brandy. "Do you mind if I have this if you don't want it?"

"Please do," she said, and Rupert knocked it back. Emmy wanted to say more – it was a relief to be able to speak about this at last – but Tilly was back in the library lighting the lamps because all light was gone from the sky. Rupert and Emmy sat quietly while the maid moved around the room, only speaking again once the door had clicked behind her.

"When's the little one due?" Rupert asked eventually.

Emmy thought for a moment. "Sometime in May, I think."

"Forgive me, I don't know much about your condition, but does that mean ..." Rupert flushed. "That is to say that you will, err ..."

She took pity on him. "I'll put on weight which I can hide for a while longer, I think, but some point I'll have to make provision for having the baby."

She felt numb about this now. Before Rupert's visit her plans had only extended as far as telling Alex and finding some way they could marry before she had the baby. Now he was gone, and she was on her own. She couldn't turn her face to the wall and give up, which was what she felt like doing, or walk into the sea until her skirts were heavy and the waves sucked her under, because there was this little one to think of. She would have to speak to Dr Parsons and at some point take Mrs Puckey into her confidence. This idea made her wish she could reach for the brandy.

Rupert's brow furrowed.

"Lord, Em. You *are* in a pickle."

The old childhood expression raised a ghost of a smile because 'a pickle' hardly came close to describing giving birth to an illegitimate child and finding a means to keep it – and for that matter herself, if her father threw her out. 'Shamed, despairing, ruined' sprang far more easily to mind.

"It would seem so," she said. The black cloud of losing Alex grew heavier and darker. If only Rupert would leave so she could plead a headache and be alone. She wanted to cry and cry until there were no more tears. She wanted to be alone to open her locket and look at Alex. Her hand rose to touch its heavy weight where it lay against her heart, and at once she felt comforted, as though she was reaching out to him through it, and taking courage. 'All will be well,' she heard him say. 'I won't leave you alone. Take charge of Fate before it takes charge of you!'

'Easy enough for you to say,' she told him silently.

"There's only one thing for it. You'll have to marry me," Rupert said.

Emmy's mind was in pieces. Nothing made any sense.

"You're asking me to marry you?"

"Yes."

She shook her head, not following. Rupert didn't want to marry anyone. He had always been adamant on this matter and she understood why.

"You don't want to marry me."

"Em, I've always said I don't want to marry at all, but that if I ever did, it would be you."

"You don't love me."

"I do," he said firmly. "I always have. You know that."

"But not in the right way. You're not in love with me."

"Maybe not, but not all of us are lucky enough to find that kind of love, Em. I do love you in my own way. You're like a sister to me and you always have been. Alex loved you as a woman. And I loved him too." He smiled sadly and spread his hands in a hopeless gesture. "He was my friend and I owe my life to him."

She said nothing. They both knew what Rupert was really saying. He was hurting too, and like her was trying to make sense of something so dreadful and so utterly wrong that there was no logic to it and no meaning to be found.

"The biggest honour I could have would be if I could repay Alex by taking care of you and his child," Rupert said quietly. "I know your heart's broken, Em, and I can't hope to mend it any more than you can mine, but please marry me. Let me keep you and your child safe now that Alex can't do so. Let me do that for him."

"You don't have to do this. Alex would have never expected anything in return for what he did," Emmy told him. Alex was selfless and brave and a loyal friend. He would have given his life without hesitation or question.

"I know that, but didn't I always promise I would be your knight in shining armour? Let me be that now, Emmy. Let me take care of you both. If we marry by special licence while I'm on leave nobody will think to question it. Couples are marrying in haste all the time, and we can say the baby's mine. He will be too, in all the ways that he needs to be. I'll love him as my own. I swear on my life I will."

She shook her head. "It's too much."

He knelt down beside her. "Oh, Em, don't you see? I want to do this. It's not entirely selfless. It's for me as much as you. We both know why I'm not the kind of chap to marry, but if I can make things better for you – and yes, repay Alex – then I want nothing more than to marry you. Let me assure you, my parents will be delighted and when they hear there's a baby on the way Mama will be thrilled."

Emmy bit her lip. "She wouldn't be if she knew the truth."

Rupert's expression was set with resolve and she glimpsed the officer he had become.

"The truth is this will be my child and you will be Mrs Elmhurst. Nobody will dare to question it. You'll be the daughter-in-law of the local magistrate, wife to an officer in His Majesty's Army and the heiress of Pendennys Place. If anything should happen to me, then you and the baby will be safe and provided for. Nobody will be able to touch you, and I count your father amongst that number."

Her eyes filled. Rupert was offering her a lifeline. If she married him Emmy would have respectability. She would have a name and a father for her child – things that now Alex was lost would be for ever out of her reach. Shame and ostracisation from society Emily could bear for herself – but for her innocent child? How could she bring Alex's son into a world where he would be despised and seen as a cause for shame? Or even worse, where he might be taken from her? Her hand fluttered to her belly and knew what her answer would be.

She would do whatever it took to protect her baby.

"So, Emily Pendennys, will you consent to be my wife?" Rupert asked.

Emmy's heart was raw. She wanted nothing more than to curl up and grieve for the man she loved. This was not a time to think about marriage and weddings. Yet the baby burrowed beneath her heart, Alex's precious last gift to her meant it was exactly the time to consider these things.

Emmy didn't love the man who was proposing, and he didn't love her, not in the way she knew she could be loved. She would never love anyone again the way she had loved Alex Winter – but Alex was dead, so what did anything really matter? When he had fallen in a shower of bullets her life too had ended. All she had ever hoped to be, everything she had ever dreamed of, had died with him, so what did it matter who the shell of Emily Pendennys married or what name she took? Rupert Elmhurst was kind. He was her friend. He had loved Alex too. If she married him, then her baby, all that she had left of Alex, would be safe.

She took a shaky breath.

"Yes," Emmy told Rupert. "I'll marry you."

The wedding was a low-key affair, as befitted both wartime and the nature of their union. Rupert managed to arrange a special licence and they were married a week before he returned to active service. It was a dank winter's day with billowing sea fret rubbing out the landscape, marooning St Nonna's in a white lake, and it felt fitting to Emmy that the whole world should be subdued and colourless. She couldn't imagine it any other way now that Alex was no longer in it. She had stepped into a void between the loss of the man she loved and the loss of the life they should have lived, and even as she chose flowers and accepted congratulations she was falling, plunging, plummeting into the bottomless canyon of days unlived and a future rendered empty.

During the days leading up to her wedding it seemed to Emmy that she was watching events unfold through a pane of glass, and this dark-haired girl accepting congratulations and tucking her hand through the crook of her officer fiancé's arm was a stranger. Numb with misery, she had little to say when asked by Rupert's mother what flowers she might like or whether shrimp paste sandwiches would be acceptable fare to serve at the small tea party afterwards. Emmy could only shrug and murmur that she didn't mind. What did any of this matter? Alex was gone and nothing would matter ever again.

If Rupert's parents thought her behaviour peculiar for a happy bride-to-be they never said as much, but several times Emmy caught Mr Elmhurst studying her through narrowed eyes, as though trying to solve a puzzle, and when sitting unnoticed in their drawing room she overheard Mrs Elmhurst telling Rupert things were moving too fast.

"We're fond of Emily," she said, "and it's a wonderful match, but why the haste, dear? We haven't time to organise anything much at all."

"War has a funny way of making a chap realise his priorities, Mama, and I want her to be my wife," was Rupert's gentle reply. "I thought you'd be pleased."

"I am pleased, of course I am, I'm just a little surprised. I had no idea you had feelings for her."

"Well, there you go; life is full of surprises," Rupert replied blithely. Mrs Elmhurst hadn't said anything further, although Emmy suspected she must have drawn her own conclusions regarding her son long ago and was as surprised by this hurried wedding as the rest of the neighbourhood.

Lady Rivers was obviously chagrined by the news, but with Kit at the front and the colonel's health failing, she was less upset than Emmy would have expected. She actually offered to provide lilies from her glasshouse for the bridal bouquet and to host a small reception at the manor. Julyan Pendennys said little at all on the matter, but once Rupert had formally asked him for Emmy's hand, it didn't escape her notice that their outstanding bills were paid in the village and that the wine merchant was delivering once again. Mrs Puckey was thrilled – Rupert had long been a favourite of hers – and Tilly chattered non-stop about dresses and hair. The only rumblings of discontent came from Simmonds, who looked at Emmy askance on the day of her wedding.

"This is a rum thing, Miss," he said, sucking the air through his teeth. "A rum thing indeed."

"Enough of you, Mr Simmonds! It's Miss Emily's wedding day," Mrs Puckey scolded. "Help her into the dogcart and stop your mithering!"

Simmonds did as he was told, but as he drove her to the church, the plough horse in its gleaming harness doing its best to take her to St Nonna's in style, he shook his head and tutted.

"Out of the frying pan and into the fire," he said to nobody in particular.

Emmy ignored Simmonds, and his words washed over her like waves on the beach. As Hector's gleaming quarters swayed along the drive she fixed her eyes on the road ahead and huddled into her coat as the dampness hanging on the arched trees above dripped down like tears.

Emmy had no tears left to shed. Numb with grief, she moved through the days in a daze, not recognising the world around her. Something in her had died with Alex, and the girl who had been Emily Pendennys lay buried beside him in cold clay. All was lost and as she grieved for him she also mourned the lonely years of lost love, their unborn children and the woman she should have become. The future had been stolen by a greedy thief, and the time which now yawned between his death and hers was a burden which often felt too heavy to bear. How would she drag herself through them? How could she bear to inhabit a world where there was no Alex Winter? Emmy didn't much care what happened to her now. She would marry Rupert and she would keep her child safe, but there was no more substance to her than this. If it was not for the baby she would have blown away like sea foam, for without Alex she was no more than a sad ghost haunting the lonely years until her own eyes closed for the final time.

Emmy had little interest in the wedding ceremony. Afterwards she looked at the photographs taken that day and wondered where the essence of her had been. When this doppelgänger for Emily Pendennys made her vows and then stood, posed for a photograph, in the church porch with her hand tucked into the crook of her husband's arm, where had her true self been? Far away from Cornwall and in no man's land searching for Alex, she sometimes thought. Or perhaps blissfully entwined with him beneath that dear patchwork quilt, holding one another close as they whispered promises for bullets to rip holes through.

The wedding photo took pride of place in the Elmhursts' elegant house. When she took tea with her in-laws Emmy studied it and tried to place this girl who stood beside the serious-faced young officer. She was every inch the demure bride in the white gown that Lady Rivers had bought her in what seemed like another life, and she clutched a small bouquet of lilies in her gloved hand. The groom was smart in his full-dress uniform, and stared into the lens as though challenging anyone to make a negative comment. Somebody had lent the bride a fur stole to wear inside the stone-cold church, and a lady's maid had woven silk flowers through her hair. The photo was like the wedding of two strangers. The only part of herself Emmy recognised was the gleam of the silver chain around her neck which kept the locket and Alex's face pressed against her heart. She would never take it off, she vowed, never.

"It should have been you, Alex," she would whisper turning away from the ornate photograph frame and curling her hand around her precious locket. "It should have been you. Why did you leave me?"

But there was never any answer, and each day she plummeted deeper into a bottomless well of loss.

Their honeymoon was short: three nights at a hotel in Truro. Emmy, exhausted from misery and pregnancy, slept through most of it while Rupert amused himself reading and walking by the river. Sharing a bedroom with him was less odd than Emmy had feared, since they knew each other well enough not to feel too awkward, and Rupert insisted upon sleeping on the couch so that she wasn't disturbed. Outwardly they looked every bit the dashing officer and his new bride as they ate dinner together in the restaurant and made small talk, but when they were alone Emmy would weep bitterly and Rupert would hold her, stroking her hair away from her damp cheeks with his own tears falling onto her dark hair. Rupert understood her grief and in these bleakest moments of shared and savage loss, Emmy saw her old friend laid bare and glimpsed the seam of golden kindness which ran through him. She knew then she loved Rupert, if not in the way a wife should, then for his pure heart and his quiet companionship. Death and war had laid him open and exposed everything, and in Rupert she saw beauty of heart and soul, and above all she saw selflessness.

Emmy knew she had done the right thing by accepting her old friend's offer of marriage. Alex's child would have the very best of fathers in Rupert Elmhurst, and in return she vowed to be the very best of wives. It was not the life she'd dreamed of, nor was it the life she wanted, but it was the life she must live to keep her son safe. He was all that was left of Alex, and she would do everything to protect their little one. Rupert had gifted her the chance to keep her child, and each time Emmy felt the baby fluttering inside her, she was thankful beyond words.

On the final afternoon of their honeymoon Rupert visited the cathedral to admire the architecture, and Emmy returned to the jeweller's shop where Alex had bought her locket. She thought she glimpsed their former selves just a little ahead of her in the cobbled lane, arm in arm as they chatted and laughed, happy and impossibly naïve. Had she slipped in time, Emmy wondered, as her former self tilted her face up to Alex, a flower seeking light, and he tenderly tucked a lock of hair behind her ear. Did this happy pair sense her presence in the shade of the cathedral spires? Alex whispered something to the long-ago Emmy, who laughed and flushed. They could only see one another and had no idea what lay ahead.

Should she step out of the shadows and warn them?

The baby flickered, a butterfly fluttering beneath her heart, and Emmy sighed. Even if they could see her, how could she dull such happiness? If would be gone soon enough; and it was precious moments like those which sustained her in the darkest days. If she could speak to the Alex and Emily from the past she wouldn't breathe a word of the future but would urge them to be happy now and to live every moment. She would tell them to hold one another close, and she would tell herself not to waste a single moment with petty hurts and perceived slights.

Thank God Rupert had helped her to see sense and say goodbye to Alex on that long-ago day. It was another reason to be thankful for Rupert's friendship, for how could she have lived with herself otherwise?

The smiling young couple melted away as she approached the shop. Emmy took a deep breath and pushed open the door. A bell jangled and an elderly man with mutton-chop whiskers glanced up.

"Good afternoon, Miss. How can I help you?"

It was warm inside the jeweller's shop. A cheerful fire glowed in the grate at the far side, and in the soft lamplight diamonds nestling against black velvet twinkled like stars. Although she wore Rupert's grandmother's emerald beneath a plain wedding band, Emmy yearned to be here with Alex as they excitedly selected an engagement ring.

She pushed the thought away. It hurt too much to countenance now, especially when visiting the shop for such a dreadfully different reason.

"Do you engrave items here?"

The jeweller nodded. "Indeed, we do, Miss. What did you have in mind?"

Emmy pulled off her gloves, unbuttoned the neck of her velvet cape and teased out the locket, slipping it over her neck and laying it out on the counter.

"This."

The old man's watery blue eyes rested on the necklace.

"Ah. A fine piece that," he said. "Just as I told the customer who purchased it."

"You remember selling this locket?"

"I remember every piece which passes through this shop, my dear, and this is one of the finest, just as I told the young gentleman at the time. I confess I didn't imagine he would have sufficient funds and was somewhat surprised when he placed the money on this very counter. He was a photographer, I recall, and he'd sold his best camera to buy the piece because the girl he loved deserved nothing but the best." His gaze slipped to her left hand. "He married you then. I thought he would."

Emmy didn't correct him.

"Young love. There's nothing like it. Even an old fool like me still goes misty-eyed remembering how it felt," he chuckled, picking the locket up and letting the chain trickle through his fingers. He turned it around, examining the smooth silver back of the case. "What would you like engraved? The date of your wedding? That's always a popular choice."

Emmy reached into the bag hanging from her wrist and drew out a piece of notepaper which she placed it in front of him.

"This."

The old man reached for his spectacles and read out loud the words she'd spent hours agonising over. Torn from her soul, as she'd written them down the ink had bled into the paper with her grief and the overwhelming loss. She would ache and long for Alex every day for the rest of her life. In wearing his locket Emmy would keep him close and one day, when their son was twenty-one, she would open it and show the child his birth father's face.

Alex,

Your wings were ready.

My heart was not.

The jeweller slid his glasses from his nose. The watery eyes which met hers brimmed with compassion.

"My dear, I am so sorry. My condolences. I had no idea. What a thing. What a wicked, wicked thing …"

His words died. The clock ticked loudly, and a log shifted in the grate. Emmy struggled not to dissolve. Until this moment she had not been able to speak about Alex to anyone except Rupert and this acknowledgement of her grief breached a dam.

In danger of being overwhelmed by his gentle sympathy, she swallowed her grief down.

"Thank you," she said.

"This damn war, pardon my language, ma'am, but where's it going to end? My grandson's in France and my sister's boys." He shook his head in despair. "How many more will it take from us? How much more can we all bear?"

Emmy blotted her eyes with fingers because there was no answer to this question. Seeing her distress, the jeweller gathered himself visibly.

"Well, now, enough of that. Let's see what I can do for you. The engraving shouldn't take more than a day or two."

"A day or two?" Emmy echoed, crestfallen. She couldn't bear to be apart from her greatest treasure for that long. It was a wrench to have taken it from her neck at all and already she felt a little lost without its familiar weight. "I'd hoped you might be able to do the engraving while I waited?"

"Usually we would, but my grandson's the one who would do the work. Ted's a talent for engraving and there's no one better. My old eyes being not what they were, I'll ask a fellow I know to come in and do the job tomorrow. We can send it to you once it's ready. It won't be more than a few days."

Emmy couldn't let Alex's image out of her sight. That would be unbearable. Opening the locket and looking at his beloved face was the only solace she had.

"Couldn't you do it now? Yourself, I mean?"

He frowned. "Well, yes, ma'am, I suppose I could, but the work might not be up to our usual standard."

"I don't mind about that in the slightest," Emmy said quickly. "Not if I can take it with away with me today. Please? It would mean a great deal to me."

"I can see how much this piece means to you, my dear. Take a seat by the fire and let me see what I can do. I'll ask my wife to bring you some tea while you wait."

Emmy sat down and warmed her hands by the fire, and the jeweller disappeared through a narrow door behind the counter. The warmth and the sonorous ticking of the clock made her eyes grow heavy and her head nodded. It felt like only seconds later that a gentle hand was laid on her shoulder but as her eyes opened she saw the clock's hand had crept around the mother-of -pearl face to past four, and the world outside was dusky.

"All done for you, ma'am."

The locket was laid out on a piece of midnight velvet. Polished and gleaming, it shone in lamplight, and the words she had so carefully chosen were picked out by the leaping flames. The script was beautiful, flowing and elegant, and as timeless as her love for Alex.

"Now, my hand slipped a little there, see? But apart from that I'm rather pleased to find I haven't lost my touch," the old man said, pointing to a flaw so minute Emmy could scarcely make it out.

"It's perfect. Thank you."

She fastened it around her neck and the silver case slipped against her skin, as reassuring a caress as though Alex had taken her hand.

'I'll always stay close to your heart, my beautiful, wonderful Emmy.'

"How much do I owe you?" she asked the jeweller, reaching for her purse.

He waved her question away with a hand as wrinkled and bony as a hen's foot.

"Nothing, my dear. It's the very least I can do to thank young men like your husband and my grandson – the very least – and that's my final word on the matter."

Not wishing to offend him Emmy slid her purse back into her bag.

"That's so kind. I can't thank you enough."

He was smiling at her. A mysterious smile which lifted one side of his mouth and lit his blue eyes. "There is one thing you could do for me. When you pass that locket on to your little one, tell her about the old man who sold it to her father and engraved it for her mother. I'd like to think I'm a small part of its story."

Emmy stared at him. She was wearing a cape and in her winter layers it was impossible he could know from looking at her.

"How —?" she began but the old man tapped his nose with his forefinger.

"I have five children of my own and there's a secret look a woman has about her when a little one is the way. I saw it in my Annie, and I see it in you. God bless you and your little one. I pray she grows up in a kinder world than this."

Outside the street was dark, the lamps lit and the narrow lane thick with shadows. As she walked away from the little shop, Emmy laid her hand against her stomach.

"Is he right?" she said softly. "Have I been getting it all wrong, baby? Are you a little girl, after all?"

The was a flutter as soft as the opening of a butterfly's wings and Emmy's heart swelled with love. This was her baby talking to her. This was a yes!

"Not Alex then, but Alexandra?" she said.

Ivy.

Unbidden, the name popped into her mind and Emmy laughed out loud. Alex's mother, the artist, had been called Ivy. It was a beautiful name. Festive and evergreen and so fitting, for just as ivy weaves its tendrils around trees and winds its way through even the hardest stone, so this surprise baby had coiled its way into her broken heart, binding it back together and filling it with hope. Emmy no longer knew where her love for Alex ended and her love for this little one began. Maybe that was the answer? Love never ended. It never died. Her love for Alex lived on in this brand-new person and would stretch beyond this lifetime, down the years and into infinity. Whispers of his face would appear a hundred years from now, when their names and story was long forgotten. Just as the old jeweller wanted his work to be remembered, so too Emmy wanted her love for Alex to live on and it would, in this child. Their child.

Little baby Ivy.

Rupert returned to the front three days after their wedding. He kissed Emmy on the forehead and whispered that he was at peace. He had taken care of her, Alex's child was safe, and Rupert said he was ready for whatever might follow. As she watched him join his father in the Daimler, Emmy had the strongest conviction she would never see her dear friend again.

Rupert's debt to Alex was paid, and he was free.

Grief, her constant companion now, knotted around Emmy's heart, and it was much as she could do to wave and smile as he hopped into the car. She stood at the top of the steps and watched it pull away and remained standing there long after the car swept through the gates, staring after it and gripped by sadness. That sunny afternoon when Alex had sketched her while Rupert and Kit lazed in deckchairs belonged to another age, one consigned to history and bearing little resemblance now to reality. Those three boys were lost for ever. Alex was dead, sleeping alone in foreign soil, Kit was a dreamy poet no more but a seasoned officer fighting hard in France, and gentle Rupert had sharpened his edges to become the resolute man she had married. The ghosts of who they had been, and the shades of the men they would never become, would haunt Rosecraddick for ever.

She turned away, despair massing in her chest, and shut herself in her bedroom where she wept for them all and for the dreadful waste. Nobody would disturb her. A distraught new bride who had just bid farewell to her soldier husband would be left to cry in peace, and even Mrs Puckey knew to stay away. There were too many partings these days, the housekeeper said, and she didn't know how they would bear it.

"We'll bear it because we must," Simmonds told her sharply. "Bearing it's the least those of us here can do. Bearing it's the easy part, woman."

But Emmy wasn't so certain this was true. She thought waiting and wondering was the hardest thing of all. The front was hell, but it was an active hell as opposed to a hades of inactivity and fretting. In his letters Alex had described how he had been kept so busy that sometimes he fell asleep on his feet. Weeks could pass where he hadn't been able to snatch a moment to put pen to paper, and in the photographs he sent home the faces of the men were white with exhaustion and their eyes scooped out with fatigue. Although she seldom looked at Alex's photographs she was unable to forget what they had shown her. His gift and his calling hadn't been wasted, for they indeed showed the true face of the conflict. One day in the future, once little Ivy was grown up and able to understand everything, Emmy would explain who her father really was, and pass this dark legacy to her daughter. Maybe Ivy, for this was how she now thought of the baby, would wish to do something with Alex's work. A book or an exhibition? This would be her daughter's choice entirely, Emmy decided, since her own preference was to never see these pictures again. It was in his pursuit of them that Alex had chosen to go to war and had died. Emmy hated them but she guarded them fiercely because they were all he had to leave his child. They were Ivy's.

Rupert had brought Alex's few possessions back with him. Before the wedding, Emmy had locked her bedroom door and spread these out on her counterpane to study them. There was precious little to show of a life so filled with such promise: a Princess Mary tin, a Bible, some cigarettes and the Vest Pocket Kodak. The small camera case was more battered than she remembered, and speckled with dull, rusty marks. His blood? Appalled, Emmy hid it away in a small suitcase with the photographs and her treasures. Who knew what atrocities it had seen and what horrors might still lurk on the film curled within? She didn't want to know. Emmy didn't need any more photographs to understand the truth of war.

Her tears drying, Emmy lay on her bed, one hand curled around her locket and the other resting against her stomach, where the baby nestled safe and snug. Her breathing grew calm, and soon it seemed to Emmy every mile which took Rupert further away from Rosecraddick also brought her closer to the strange new future he had built for her. She owed it to her old friend and to her little one to be brave. There would be no more weeping. She splashed water into the bowl and washed her face and repinned her hair before returning downstairs. It was time to focus on the baby.

Since Emmy and Rupert had married at such speed they had not been able to find a house of their own. The Elmhursts had suggested that Emmy remain in situ at Pendennys Place since the estate would become their son's one day. Rupert, catching her eye, said in his opinion the house and land would always belong to his wife.

"Not in law," Mr Elmhurst, ever the magistrate, had said.

Rupert had taken himself off to Bodmin the very next day to have a will drawn up which stated very clearly that in the event of his death everything was to belong to his wife, Mrs Emily Elmhurst, and any heirs of his body. This will, he promised, left no room for dispute.

"You always said you wanted to marry for love, not money," he explained on his return from town. "Emmy, please know our marriage is about love even if it isn't the conventional kind. There's no other reason on my side. I don't want your land and your fortune. I never did. If anything happens to me, you will be an independent and wealthy woman."

Her eyes filled anew at this memory and she wiped her tears away with the heels of her hands. The childish games and sharing of secrets had bound them close, and it made her heart brim with gratitude that Rupert had never forgotten her oldest fear. Love was love, Emmy thought now, and how blessed was she to have known Alex's love and her dear friend's love in one lifetime. Then there was Ivy, too. Emmy felt she was luckier than most, and even if her heart was shattered she could draw strength from her baby.

There were now, to Emmy's estimation at least, just six months until the baby would be born. The time had come to pick up the reins of Pendennys Place and make certain everything was in place for her arrival. If this meant selling what remained of their precious things in order to pay off the loans secured against the property and buy food, then so be it. The Stubbs in the library would fetch a fair sum at auction, and there were several fine Munnings portraits of cherished family horses hung at intervals down the stairs. Her father's study also boasted two Joshua Reynolds pictures of vast-bosomed Pendennys women, which Emmy knew must be valuable. Then there were still some of the fruits of the Grand Tours – in essence, aristocratic shopping sprees – her ancestors had enjoyed around the

Continent, and the house contained some other artefacts she could send to the Truro sale room.

Emmy knew Julyan would rage and rant, but she was determined to overrule him. He was deteriorating and growing more erratic by the day. Several times in recent weeks he had set light to his papers while reading into the small hours, and his drinking was heavier than ever, making the entire household nervous about the candles he insisted upon using. He refused to use oil lamps and had hurled a vase at Simmonds for daring to suggest one. It was becoming dangerous, and now she was a respectable married woman she would take full control of the running of the estate. Alex's child would want for nothing.

As her pregnancy progressed Emmy found herself inhabiting a strange dream world where she slept a great deal and drifted through the days. On others she was filled with great surges of energy and walked miles over the cliffs or strode through the woods. Alex's wagon was still parked in the clearing, but the elements were starting to claim it and it made Emmy desolate to see his beloved mobile studio abandoned and falling apart. It felt as though it embodied the disintegration of all their hopes and dreams. Faded paint flecked from the sides like peeling skin, one of the shutters hung on a rusty nail, and the winter storms had ripped away part of the roof. The once cosy living space was speckled with black mould and, distraught, Emmy had snatched up the quilt and taken it back to the house where she had washed it secretly before storing it away. Sometimes she wrapped herself in it and closed her eyes to make believe she was in Alex's arms as they listened to raindrops pattering on the roof and wove dreams, but the ripping away of this magic when she opened her eyes was too painful to bear and so eventually she locked the quilt away with the camera and the pictures. It would be another heirloom for the baby.

She visited the wagon a couple more times as spring arrived, but it hurt to see the scene of her greatest happiness grow so dilapidated. When tendrils of ivy began to prise the floor boards apart and rats shredded the mattress, Emmy collected the last of Alex's photographs and books to pass to the baby before turning the key for the final time. Then she ordered Simmonds to have it moved and stored in the empty coach house. If he thought this a strange request or wondered why the travelling photographer's wagon would be brought from the Rivers estate to Pendennys Place, he never said as much, and only nodded in his taciturn way before fetching Hector. By the time the wild garlic and bluebells were bursting through the woodland floor only the faint impressions of four wooden wheels and an air of melancholy suggested that a jolly green wagon had once rested there. Simmonds pulled an old sail over the wagon to conceal it and no more was said on the matter, but whenever she passed the stable yard Emmy sighed to know that Alex's hopes and dreams mouldered behind cobwebby windows, entombed in a sailcloth shroud.

Emmy made her condition official in February to the great joy of Rupert's parents and Mrs Puckey's huge excitement. Her father gruffly congratulated her, but he was thinner and weaker than she recalled, and no longer given to violent rages. He slept a lot of the time, and Emmy knew that he was slipping away from them. Dr Parsons became a regular visitor to the house, and no longer able to escape medical scrutiny Emmy gave in to an examination. She fixed her eyes on the ceiling and willed her soul to fly to wherever Alex might be as the doctor prodded and probed and sucked on his teeth.

"Well, my dear," he said, scrubbing his hands in the wash bowl before towelling them rigorously, "it appears that this baby will be arriving a little earlier than we might have thought."

Emmy, slumped against the pillows with the counterpane drawn modestly up to her neck, felt as though she was falling from a tall cliff.

Thank goodness Mrs Puckey, acting as chaperone, had bustled off to fetch tea. Dr Parsons had been the family physician since she was a child. What would he say to her father? What must he think?

Her tongue stuck to the roof of her dry mouth.

"I —"

Doctor Parsons held up a hand.

"I don't need an explanation, my dear. There's a war on and Lord knows people have to snatch what time they are given at times like these. It's not my job to be the judge of such matters. I leave all that to Reverend Cutwell. Matters physical, not spiritual, are my concern."

Emmy stared at him. What was he trying to say?

"Babies are contrary little creatures," the doctor continued, half to himself. "They don't always arrive when expected, and they can come earlier or later than anticipated. Rupert's son will be with us sometime in May, I would wager." He paused and smiled. "It seems he's as impatient as his parents."

Emmy didn't know whether to be relieved or horrified by this remark. The doctor thought she had Rupert must have …that they had …

Well. That. It felt so wrong to think of Rupert in this context that Emmy blushed to the roots of her hair.

"There's not much I haven't seen in my time," the doctor told her, replacing his instruments in his big black bag. "You need to rest more because your blood pressure is raised; and do try to eat more red meat. Liver and spinach too, and Guinness if you can stomach it. You're very pale."

"I will," she said, and then, gratefully. "Thank you, Doctor."

He snapped his bag shut. "There's no need to thank me. Your baby's my priority, Emily."

Mrs Puckey returned at this point bearing refreshments, and the doctor turned his attention to issuing her with a long list of instructions. Emmy closed her eyes and rested her hand on the solid bulk of the locket lying hidden beneath her dress. She would eat all the liver and spinach Mrs Puckey could find, she promised Alex, if it meant their baby arrived safely.

Newspaper Photograph: The Great Fire

May 1916

Ivy Hope Elmhurst was born on a bright sunshiny morning in 1916, a day
when a brisk spring breeze blew across the village, its salty freshness at odds
with the wisps of ash and the scent of burning which it also carried. In
Rosecraddick the village folk looked across to the woods and shook their
heads to see the smoke still rising from the spot where Pendennys House
once stood. The events of the previous night had shocked them all, and
from the grocers to the bakery to the vicarage, the talk was all of the
devastating fire at the big house.

Ivy's arrival heralded the beginning of one era and the definitive ending
of another. A wailing, angry scrap of a person with a fuzz of dark hair and a
screwed-up red face, she screeched her indignation at her abrupt change in
circumstances to the whole wide world, and Emmy, holding the new baby
tightly in her bandaged arms, shared her daughter's shock.

Everything was gone.

Everything.

This morning's newspaper rested beside her on the starched white sheet.
Emmy, alone and recovering in the best bedroom at her in-laws' house,
could scarcely comprehend what she was looking at. The smoke-blackened
carcass in the photograph bore no resemblance to the red brick façade she
knew so well, and the headline description of fire and devastation seemed
more like a story than an event which had happened to her. If it hadn't
been for her blistered hands and the scent of burning, an aroma now
mingling unpleasantly with lavender in a way Emmy suspected would
always bring back nightmarish memories of billowing smoke and leaping
flames, she would have thought the events of the previous night little more
than a bizarre dream.

Oblivious to the high drama taking place in Rosecraddick, the baby slept soundly in Emmy's arms. Her starfish hands were held out as though she sought to clutch at life. Her hair stood on end in outrage, and her fuchsia-bud mouth was popped open by the surprise of being rudely ejected into an upside-down world. Emmy stared down at Alex's daughter and wondered how it was possible to feel so blissfully happy when everything else in your life was lost. How could she feel this contented when her home was no more than a smoking ruin, the man she loved was dead, her husband of not yet a year, had been reported missing at Verdun in March, and her father had been lost in the terrible fire? Yet, holding her sleeping baby, Emmy thought her heart would burst with joy.

What sort of monster was she to feel this way? Surely no feeling person had the right to be happy under such dreadful circumstances, but as she held the baby, marvelling at the rose-petal skin and the unfocused dark eyes, Emmy was happy. Ivy was safe in her arms, and that being so, nothing more mattered. This was pure love distilled. She had never known anything like it in her life and she was drowning in it, willingly drowning, because Emmy would die in a heartbeat for little Ivy. She had loved Alex entirely and perfectly, but these feelings were magnified a thousand times for this new person who was all she had left of him. The dark eyes were his, she thought in wonder, and the dimpled chin too. Would Ivy share his artistic talent? His passion for truth? His stubborn nature?

She kissed the soft head and felt intoxicated with the scent of new skin and milk. One day, when Ivy came of age, Emmy would tell her daughter where all these traits came from. She would open the locket and explain exactly who the man inside was and why she had loved him so very much. Ivy would understand, Emmy knew she would, and then she would open the suitcase, charred now but rescued and intact, and pass Alex's photographic legacy to his only daughter. It would be Ivy's choice and hers alone what became of his work.

But all this was a lifetime away. Ivy was not even a day old, and for now the child was hers, entirely hers. In the circle of her arms, the baby slept safely, and Emmy already wished she could keep her daughter this way for ever. Nobody had ever told her how terrifying love could be. She had felt the chasm of dread each time Alex left for the war, and she felt it now just by imagining a time when Ivy might leave her. She tightened her arms, and the baby wriggled as though she already sought her independence no matter what the risk.

That made Emmy smile; hadn't Alex been exactly the same?

Ivy Elmhurst was a miracle baby, everyone said so. It was also nothing short of miraculous that Emmy had escaped from Pendennys Place with only minor burns to her hands and arms, and lived to deliver her child, pre-term. The local constable told the reporters he would never forget the sight of Mrs Elmhurst staggering through the kitchen door and into the night, clutching a battered old suitcase tightly and with her nightdress charred while sparks fantailed behind her. Dr Parsons said it was no wonder she'd gone into labour that very night – the shock alone of the fire, never mind losing her father in such terrible circumstances, would have been enough to bring the contractions on. Why Emmy had insisted on carrying the suitcase nobody could fathom, but the general consensus was that breeding women were given to strange fancies, and having lost her young husband only weeks before, she couldn't have been in her right mind.

Emmy dropped another kiss onto Ivy's downy head. The truth was somewhat different; she had never thought so clearly in her life. She closed her eyes, drifting back to the previous afternoon, only hours away yet already belonging to an entirely different woman ...

The air was mild. Red campion and willow herb swayed in the hedges and the sky was dotted with puffs of cloud. Emmy, feeling more cumbersome by the day, had walked through the garden and as she trailed her hands through the thigh-high grasses she thought how impossible it seemed that the seasons still turned, and the birds still sang while young men were dying in numbers beyond all comprehension. It was hard not to feel guilty when the sun shone down on your upturned face with benign warmth and fledgling birds yelled at their parents from the hedges, and harder still when your husband of less than six months was among the fallen.

Rupert had been reported missing at Verdun in late March. Although the red-eyed Mrs Elmhurst was admirable in her insistence that until there was a body her son must be alive, everyone knew what 'missing' really meant. Emily had mourned her dear childhood friend deeply from the moment the black-edged telegram had arrived, but she was not surprised by the news. When he'd kissed her farewell, Rupert had already been somewhere she wouldn't be able to follow. In her heart Emmy had known she wouldn't see him again.

Kit, whom Rupert had suspected of reserving his precious letter-writing time for a secret sweetheart, had penned a rare letter to Emmy expressing his condolences and pouring out his raw grief for their dear friend. On a beautiful spring day, a day teeming with new life and optimism, it seemed odd she should feel the need to revisit Kit's letter, but the baby was lying still for once and she felt dreamy and peculiar. It seemed fitting to hear her old friend's voice as she re-read his words beneath the chestnut trees, for how many times had they played there as children or picnicked and lazed in the sun? Today, with the canopy thick with bright green leaves and decorated with white candles, the old trees threw shade onto the lawn in a respite from the warmth making her breath come in short gasps as she crossed the garden.

A stitch in her side, Emmy lowered herself to the ground and groaned with bliss as she slipped her shoes from her swollen feet. She would put this letter away after lunch; tuck it out of sight in the case with Alex's pictures, because the words in it were too sad to revisit often. One day she would pass it to her baby, along with the poem Kit had enclosed with it, 'The Last Summer'. Filled with religious symbolism, the poem compared their final Rosecraddick summer to the Last Supper, and the death of men at the front to the Crucifixion. He had grown as a poet, Emmy thought, and there was a depth to Kit's writing now that had never been there before the war. She supposed the irony was that, like Alex, the one event which had honed his talent to perfection would be the one thing which could cut it short …

No. Not Kit. Emmy wouldn't allow such thoughts, and she pulled Kit's letter from her pocket, smoothing it with her fingers as she read it once more:

The last summer we four spent together, the summer before the war as it will always be known to me, seems to be in the forefront of my mind lately, as an ideal of some golden age when the sun shone more, the air was softer and the world a kinder place. I think of those times often, Emmy, I always see us in the garden, me drowsing with a book and Rupert fiddling with his new camera while Alex sketched and you held us all together with your smiles and laughter. Lord knows there has been precious little to smile about since, but I pray every day for a time when the darkness of this war is over, and the light of peace blesses us once again. There will be shadows of absence, and how we learn to live with those I cannot fathom, but the sun

will shine again. If not, what are we fighting for?

As Emmy re-read the letter, a tear rolled down her cheek, splashing onto the notepaper and feathering the ink. Her hand rested on the tight mound of her abdomen where the baby slept beneath her ribs, and she prayed Kit was right; peace had to come again for this baby and all the other little ones. A war like this must never come again. She returned to the letter, Kit's beautiful script shimmering as she read on:

The Germans planned to bleed France white at Verdun,
and they tell me the artillery there has been incessant. I
have seen the dispatches and I am proud to have been
Rupert's friend. You must be proud to have been his wife,
even for a short time and in these strangest of
circumstances.

Did Rupert tell Kit the truth? Or did her dear friend guess that Rupert had stepped forward to be her knight in shining armour, just as he had always promised? Emmy wiped her eyes with her wrist as she continued to read, knowing she wouldn't have an answer until she saw Kit once again.

He saved his men while holding off the enemy for as long as he could. Even when the battalions on his left and right retired he rallied his own men again and again, leading them forward five times in all. The final time he led all that remained, no more than forty men, and he fell at their head. It was mainly due to his bravery and inspiring leadership that the line was at this point able to check the enemy's advance. They will award him a medal at some point, Emmy, because our Rupert is a war hero. How he would laugh to read that line and how I weep to write it. I would give every line of my poetry as yet unwritten to see him back in a deckchair and with his head full of thoughts, just as I would to see Alex narrow his eyes at the light and move us into a better composition. They were not men for fighting or for war; but how they excelled themselves and how their bravery humbles the rest of us. This world is a poorer place without them.

Kit's gift had always lain in untangling knots of thought with his pen. He was right; the world was a poorer place without Alex and Rupert. The sun still shone but it seemed a little less bright than before and even the stars twinkled with less of a diamond sparkle. The world was diminished, and sometimes Emmy wondered how it would have been possible to keep moving forwards if there hadn't been the baby to think of. She recalled the pitiful end of one fishergirl from Rosecraddick who had read the telegram delivered to her door and placed it on the table before leaving her cottage to walk into the sea with her pockets filled with stones. Some voices in Rosecraddick had rung with shrill condemnation, and Reverend Cutwell had had to be persuaded by his god-daughter, Daisy, to give the body a full Christian burial, but there was also much sympathy amongst the women of the village. Emmy understood only too well how the overwhelming futility of the empty years stretching ahead might drive a person to seek blissful darkness as the cold waves closed for ever over the head.

She folded up the letter and hauled herself to her feet. This baby had saved her just as Rupert had saved her, and she would not let either of them down. The stitch was back and stronger now, slithering through her side in a flare of pain, and she clutched her belly with a gasp of sudden understanding. A gush of warmth between her legs followed by another stitch left no doubt in her mind as to what was taking place.

Alex's baby had not been sleeping but gathering strength to make her journey.

Gasping with surprise, Emmy returned to the house and dragged herself up the stairs to her bedroom. She had to be swift because there were things she needed to do before alerting Mrs Puckey, who would fuss and panic because she would believe the baby was coming long before its time. Childbirth was a dangerous business, and Emmy had to make sure that her precious belongings were kept safe for the baby just in case …

She closed the bedroom door behind her and slid the suitcase out from underneath the bed, clicked the clasps open and threw back the lid. The lining at the bottom of the old case was loose and Emmy knew it could be used to create the perfect hiding place for concealing anything precious from prying eyes. In between the pains, she picked away the final few stitches from the lining with her nails and lifted the frayed edge to create a small opening. Perfect.

She slipped in all the letters Alex had sent to her from the front, letters filled with his words of love and all the promises he longed to keep, and before each one was swallowed by the void between case and lining she kissed the faded envelopes and imagined that her lips were brushing his beautiful mouth again. Kit's letter followed, and several photographs Alex had taken of her during that last golden summer when they walked on the cliffs and picnicked in the woodland. The Emmy in those images was wide-eyed and hopeful, and bore little resemblance to the pinched-faced girl who stared out of the looking-glass these days. She was gone, along with the sunny days and the innocence, lost in the mud alongside Alex and fallen in battle with Rupert.

Using her fingertips, Emmy inched each document through the almost invisible gap in the lining. Unless it was subjected to close scrutiny nobody would ever know where they were concealed. Satisfied, she sat back on her haunches, panting as she rode through another pain. Then she steeled herself for the final task. Once this was complete she would ring for Mrs Puckey and succumb to whatever Nature had in store for her. She reached for the locket, tugging it from beneath her dress, and flipping the catch in a motion that had become as familiar as breathing. Trapped beneath thin glass and forever twenty years old, Alex smiled out at her and her heart melted with love. 'Don't be afraid,' he seemed to say. 'Death isn't the end, Emmy. It's just a new horizon. Love lives on. Now take charge of your own fate!'

"I will," Emmy promised as she kissed his picture. "And I have."

Another pain took the breath from her lungs. The room spun, and shooting stars raced across a night sky. The veil was thinner than she had ever thought possible. Gasping and trembling, Emmy snapped the locket shut, unclasped it from her neck and pushed it beneath the lining to join her secret hoard. It was swallowed up in moments and she exhaled with relief. The quilt, the war photographs, the dried roses, a curl of bright hair, and a picture of an angry-looking young lady in a white dress were all innocent enough to remain in place; if the worst happened to her, then the baby would know nothing more until she was an adult and Kit could speak to her.

Emmy's letter to Kit rested in the case and on top of the quilt. It would only be sent if she didn't survive the labour, for in it she had told Kit everything, from the truth about her marriage to Rupert to the baby's true parentage to her dread of leaving her child alone with Julyan. As her pen had flown over the page Emmy had charged Kit Rivers with telling her child the truth, for the sake of their friendship and for the sake of truth, and asked him to stand as the baby's godfather and guardian. Emmy knew that Kit, her true friend, would honour her wishes, for he had understood from the very beginning that her great love for a humble travelling photographer was not negotiable.

Yes, Kit Rivers the poet would understand that.

Everything was in place. She had taken charge of her own fate and there was nothing more to be done now except to give in to Nature. Emmy pushed the suitcase back under the bed and pulled herself to her feet. It was time to ask Mrs Puckey to send for Dr Parsons.

Mrs Puckey was soon as red-faced and panic-stricken as Emmy had predicted. Filled with gloomy tales about childbirth and 'babes born afore their time' she fussed about with hot bricks and boiling water and blankets, and insisted upon building a fire in the hearth even though the room was oven-hot. Simmonds was sent to fetch Dr Parsons, but returned alone because the good doctor was away from home and since his partner had enlisted there was nobody in Rosecraddick to assist. Emmy, drifting in and out of a twilight world of pain and exhaustion, listened to the hissed conversations between Simmonds and the housekeeper, and quickly realised if she didn't intervene her baby would either be delivered by the local wise woman or her father's old batman who, more used to foaling, would most likely tug little Ivy out with a rope.

"Drive to Bodmin and find a doctor there," she told Simmonds. "Hurry."

Simmonds nodded and Emmy fell back against the pillows, letting the waves of pain break and retreat. Then, amazingly, the pains retreated and she must have dozed for a while because it was growing darker and Mrs Puckey had lit the lamps. Shadows danced. The back door banged shut. Time blurred.

Emmy opened her eyes with a sense of panic. Something was wrong. The curtains weren't drawn, and the sky was dark but lit up in a strange way she couldn't comprehend. Shadows flickered and leapt on the walls and the air smelt acrid. As Emmy struggled to see through the gloom, she saw smoke drifting beneath the door and poking stealthy grey fingers into the bedroom. Mrs Puckey was dozing open-mouthed in a chair pulled up by the bedside and hadn't noticed this silent intruder. Emmy's ears straining above the housekeeper's snuffles and snores, she heard a faint scrunching sound as though somebody downstairs was screwing up fistfuls of paper over and over again.

Emmy shifted her weight onto her elbows and pushed herself up against the pillows. Her heart was pounding as she caught the unmistakable reek of smoke.

Pendennys Place was on fire!

She dug her index finger into the older woman's plump trunk.

"Mrs Puckey! Wake up!"

The housekeeper jolted awake. "Miss Emmy! What's the matter? Is it the baby?"

"The house is on fire! We need to get out!" Emmy was already swinging her legs over the side of the bed, her feet pushing their way into slippers as she struggled to stand.

Mrs Puckey's eyes were wide as she caught sight of the smoke threading its way under the door. The window was now illuminated with a ghastly orange glow. Crossing the room, one hand clutching her side, Emmy pushed up the sash and leaned into the night, and cried out in distress when she saw flames licking upwards from the floor below.

The floor where her father would be, in his study.

She pressed her fingers against her mouth in distress. As she had so often feared, Julyan must have passed out, knocking over his candle and setting fire to his papers and books. His study was stuffed with a hundred piles of such documents, accounts of successful campaigns he'd waged in his military days and scores of old maps; the place would go up like a tinderbox. Usually the faithful Simmonds was on hand to keep a close eye on his master, but this evening he was somewhere on the road between Rosecraddick and Bodmin, and not on hand to check. Petrified, Emmy watched as dead creeper and old ivy acted like a fuse, carrying the snarling flames closer. Fire rained down on the gravel below, hissing and spitting like an angry cat. There was only a matter of minutes before the entire house was engulfed.

She turned to Mrs Puckey.

"There's a suitcase under my bed. Pull it out. We need to go."

"Lord a mercy! We'll roast alive if we leave here!" The older woman was backing away from the door, her eyes wide as grey smoke bloomed from beneath the door.

"We'll roast alive if we *don't*! Now, do as I say!" Emmy ordered.

Fear lent her an authority she'd never had before. Mrs Puckey nodded, kneeling down and pulling out the case, while Emmy flung open her wardrobe and snatched out the white birthday dress. The fine fabric was thin enough to tear with her hands and she pulled it apart, the ripping of the cloth joining in with the hiss and growl of the flames.

"Pour some water into my wash bowl," she said to Mrs Puckey who was staring at her in confusion. "We'll wet this and hold it over our faces."

It was the only plan Emmy could think of, and even as they wrapped sodden strips of cloth over their mouths and noses she didn't know whether it would work. She only recalled Alex's dreadful descriptions of the mustard gas attacks and the way men without masks plunged blinded through the murk unable to think or see their way past death as they coughed up their lungs. Those in masks stood a chance, he said, and it was best to stay low, crawling on the belly through the choking confusion to safety. Emmy and Mrs Puckey didn't have masks, so wet fabric would have to suffice. It was from the dress she'd worn when she'd met Alex, she reflected as she smoothed the makeshift mask over her face. It had brought her luck that day and she could only pray it would do the same now.

'Take control of your own fate, Em!' she heard him say. 'Don't wait a minute longer!'

"We stay low and we crawl along the passage to the back stairs," Emmy told Mrs Puckey. She hoped that it would be in the library and the study that the fire would be raging first, greedily consuming all the paper and wood before turning its forked tongue to lap at all the tasty morsels which lay beyond. If they could make it to the far staircase, the one used in the olden days by the army of Pendennys servants, they might be able to descend to the scullery area and get out into the courtyard. The route was a gamble, for Emmy had no idea which way the flames had turned. They could be walking straight into the heart of the fire for all she knew. But if they stayed here they were certain to perish.

She placed her hand in the small of her back and breathed through another pain. Smoke stripped her throat and she coughed. Labour or not, she had to leave now.

"Ready?"

Mrs Puckey gave a sob which Emmy chose to interpret as an affirmative. She pushed the door open and immediately the room grew thick with smoke. All vision was lost, and her eyes streamed and stung.

"Turn left and crawl. On all fours, Mrs P! Go!"

Mrs Puckey was rooted to the spot.

"I can't, Miss Emmy!"

"You can! I say you can. Leave the case. Just go! *Now!*"

Emmy's order ended in a fit of coughing, but Mrs Puckey fell to the floor and moved away, her swaying rump swallowed in seconds by smoke as she vanished into the passage. Gasping, Emmy sank to her knees and followed, dragging the suitcase with one hand.

Eyes closed against the heat and smoke; she was blinded. She was suffocating, no longer in her house but deep in the quagmire of no man's land and transported into one of Alex's pictures. Was she in the passageway at all, Emmy wondered, as she clawed her way along the worn carpet? Or was she at the front with Kit now, pressing forward into the unknown and facing the grim realisation that each breath could be her last? Her eyes streamed, and even with the damp fabric over her mouth her chest was on fire. How much longer could she keep crawling like this? The contractions had started again, and they were linked now with the rasps of her breath and the fire in her throat. The suitcase was a millstone pulling her beneath the water, and she was thrashing for the surface and desperate to drink in air. She was sinking, fading, drowning. How Emmy longed to surrender to this enemy, to lie down and accept the approach of the darkness! She was so, so tired …

"Keep going, Ems! You're almost through!"

In the swirling smoke she saw Alex just ahead of her, holding out his hands. His dark eyes shone with love, and she was so happy to see him that for a moment Emmy forgot the smothering smoke and the stealthy flames creeping ever closer.

"Alex!" she gasped, stretching her arm towards him. He was just a fingertip's touch away! She was so close. If he took one more step …

"To me! Hurry!"

But with Alex still out of reach, Emmy had no choice but to pull herself along, sideways now, and kicking out like a swimmer to propel her ungainly body down the passageway. Each time she thought she was almost with him the smoke swirled and Alex shifted, but his hand remained stretched out to her and Emmy could no longer think of anything more than feeling his fingers close around hers.

It was funny, she thought dreamily, how quickly his hair had grown back and how the red scar no longer slashed his cheek. She thought about teasing him for wearing such a white shirt in all this ash and soot, but each time she tried to speak he put a finger to his lips.

"Don't speak. Just keep coming towards me," he urged.

Emmy couldn't have stayed away from Alex in a thousand years, and as she inched her way to the end of the passage she wanted to giggle because she was literally crawling through fire to be with the man she loved. How Kit would love that detail! He could weave it into one of his poems. She closed her eyes again, suddenly so tired she could curl up and sleep right there on the floor.

"You're almost there, Emmy. Not far now."

Alex's face swam to her through the massing grey. Her eyes hurt, her nose was blocked, her lungs were aflame, her hands and arms were blistering, but somehow Emmy crawled on – and then wonderfully, miraculously, beautifully, there was air, and the smoke was behind her. Blinking, she realised she had reached the top of the servants' staircase and, mercifully, there were no flames skipping towards her.

"Down you go," said Alex.

Now the smoke was lessening she was no longer able to see him. Emmy paused, rubbing her smarting eyes with her fists. She glanced frantically back along the passageway but there was nothing to see, only smoke swelling like the sail of a boat as it carried the fire towards her.

"Alex? Where are you?" Her voice was hoarse and it hurt to speak. She looked around but there was no sign of him. Where had he gone? She tried again. "Wait for me! I want to be with you."

"Not today, Em, but it's truly only minutes until we're together again, I promise. Minutes. That's all. Now, *go!*"

His voice was behind her and before her and all around her, growing as faint and as wispy as the coils of smoke which were catching her up. Something in the atmosphere shifted and she knew he was gone.

If he had ever been there at all.

Had she dreamed him? Were the shapes shifting in the dancing smoke playing tricks on her senses? Emmy edged her way down the stone staircase. Perhaps the pains in her belly had whisked her to another realm entirely, one between worlds, where only love mattered. And Alex loved her. He loved her so much he would never want to steal a second of her given time. He wanted her to live every moment until they met again.

'Minutes,' Alex had said; to him it was only minutes until they were together again, and as she staggered into the scullery, the suitcase bumping behind her, Emmy knew she would be counting every single one until she felt his arms close around her once again.

She learned later on that day that the flames from Pendennys Place had lit the sky for miles around that night, a crimson glow illuminating the woods as ash fell like tainted snow. When she and Mrs Puckey, singed and burned, emerged spluttering into the courtyard they discovered that the villagers had gathered and were doing their best to battle the blaze. Men too old to fight, with women and open-mouthed children, were passing buckets along a chain in a valiant attempt to douse the inferno, and even Reverend Cutwell was present, his lips mouthing silent prayer.

"Where's my father?" Emmy coughed, but nobody answered her question, nor did they look her in the eye. She tried to turn back to the kitchen, frantic to reach Julyan and drag him to safety, but the heart of the fire was beating hard and flames flared from the ground floor windows. She wanted to look away, but she was mesmerised by the ghastly spectacle.

"Papa!" She sobbed. "Papa!"

"Come away, Miss Emmy. Please!"

Mrs Puckey, her face streaked black and crimson, blood and flame, attempted to shepherd her away from the inferno, but Emily shook her hand away.

"My father," she wept. "We have to get him out. Please."

Somebody draped a coat around her shoulders, and she was given brandy from a hip flask. The alcohol burned her charred throat, her raw palms throbbed against the cold metal, and the spirit generated a new contraction. Even so, she saw Simmonds running to the porch only to be held back by several villagers as the flames leapt higher and the first gable swayed.

"The master!" he sobbed, shoulders shaking and voice breaking. "I shouldn't have left him! He's inside! Get off me, damn you! He's inside!"

But even as he struggled to free himself the fire roared like a beast and masonry tumbled. Roof trusses cracked like thunder and when the far wall fell they all knew the battle was lost. Flames played follow my leader up the curtains, every book in the library was ablaze, the drawing room breathed like a blast furnace. Pendennys Place was a great house no longer but a funeral pyre.

As she watched the house fall Emmy knew this blaze was destroying everything the once great Pendennys family had ever been. It was razing her past and her future to the ground. When the second gable swayed and fell Emmy realised it was only right and fitting that Julyan Pendennys had remained inside; her father would not have wanted to inhabit a world without his family home. Who was he without Pendennys Place? What purpose did he have except brooding over his precious maps and campaign papers, his mind manacled to the past, and his body a slave to his drinking? She tried to imagine him away from his study or his dimly lit bedroom and failed. Julyan Pendennys was Pendennys Place, and it was only right that the grand house should perish with him.

Had she loved her father? Emmy asked herself, as sparks fantailed into the darkness and beams cracked like matchsticks. The answer to this question was far more complicated than a simple yes or no. She had loved the tender father he had once been before disappointment and drink had warped him into something different, and she also thought she understood a little more of how it must have been for him to lose not only his strength and the army but the wife he'd adored and the heir who'd lit up his world. A daughter was a poor substitute, but if he had only let her in Emmy thought he might have found some solace. Choosing not to love was still a choice. Life was made up of labyrinthine decisions, and only the person standing at the heart of the maze could pick which path to follow. Her father had chosen drink and despair when he lost love – but she wouldn't follow in his footsteps. Emmy still had her baby and she still had hope.

She wrapped her arms around her swollen, shifting belly and as if the baby knew her thoughts had turned outwards once more, another pain tore through her side. She jack-knifed, and immediately people were at her side, helping her to a seat and fetching blankets.

"The baby's coming," she heard a woman cry. "The shock must have started her pains."

"It's too soon."

"Somebody call the doctor!"

The scene blurred. Voices rose and fell in time with the whirling ash. There was noise. Weeping. The scrunch of tyres on gravel. Gentle hands helping her to her feet. Dr Parsons with his bag. The Elmhursts in their Daimler. Cool air on her face. Warm water as the smoke was washed away. Stiff clean sheets. A draught of laudanum. Emmy's mind turned inwards. The chaos outside the room became unimportant; her baby was all that mattered now. The baby was all that would ever matter, she realised, and was all that ever had, because this creation of new life was the secret power of women everywhere. It was the sole reason for her own existence and in a floating world where all was impermanence, and where men maimed and killed without reason, it was the wonder of understanding this, rather than the labour pains, which almost overwhelmed her. Everything had led her to this one moment. It was the reason she had been born, and in this child Emmy knew that the chain of life was continuing far beyond anything she could imagine. Suddenly she understood so much more than she had ever believed was possible and the wonder of this snatched her breath as much as the pains.

Her baby was born at sunrise the following morning.

"It's a girl," Dr Parsons said, but Emmy already knew this.

"Ivy," she told him, holding out her arms.

Mrs Elmhurst wrapped the baby in a shawl and passed her to Emmy.

"That was Rupert's christening shawl," she said, her eyes wet. "And now it's his daughter's."

As her arms closed around the baby, Emmy felt a pang of guilt at the deception.

'Don't feel that way,' she thought she heard Rupert whisper into her ear. 'Can't you see, Emmy? This was the last thing I could do for them too. Ivy will be their comfort now. Don't deny them that joy.'

She turned her head but there was nobody beside her. Of course there wasn't. The shock of the fire combined with the exhaustion from her labour and the remains of the laudanum Mrs Puckey had given her had blurred the edges between dreams and reality. Yet Ivy's unfocused eyes, as dark as wet leather, suddenly swam across the room to fix on the very spot the whisper had come from, and although the room was hot Emmy's neck pimpled with gooseflesh.

After a while, once Dr Parsons had declared mother and baby to be healthy and safe, the room cleared and the events of the past few hours had taken on a dreamlike quality. Alone at last with Ivy, Emmy lay awake with the baby in her arms, whispering to her the story of how she had come to be and telling her how very much she was loved and wanted.

Now, hours on from the birth of her baby, and as the sun climbed across the sky and seagulls bickered on the rooftop, Emmy traced the curve of Ivy's soft cheek with a trembling finger and fell deeper and deeper in love with each snuffle of the button nose and every flicker of dark lashes. She would love this precious new person until the final breath left her body and would lay down her life for Ivy if necessary. Emmy would ache for Alex for the rest of her days but as she held his child in her arms she was filled with peace, for no matter how hard the road which had led her to this moment had been, she wouldn't change a single moment of it. Today there was an Ivy Hope Elmhurst in the world, and this already made it the better place Alex and Rupert had died fighting for.

Little Churchlands Farm

July 1916

Emmy pushed the perambulator up the lane. Leaves were thick on the trees, green and thrusting ferns burst from the soil and cow parsley frothed along the banks. Swallows arrowed above, shrill with excitement as they heralded the height of summer. All was lush and fecund and full of new beginnings, and Emmy thought it was fitting that she and Ivy should be a part of all this.

The lane climbed slowly upwards. As she wheeled her daughter along, Emmy raised her face to the early morning sun, loving the warmth on her cheeks and pleased to be out and about once more. The Elmhursts thought it still far too soon for a new mother to be venturing into the world, but they had also disapproved of her visit to Pendennys Place only days after Ivy's birth, and fretted dreadfully when she asked Simmonds to drive her to Bodmin in order to speak with the family solicitor. They doted on Ivy, and Emmy couldn't have asked for kinder in-laws, but, used to making her own decisions, she found their attention suffocating.

It was time to take Fate into her own hands, for her sake and her daughter's. Pausing to catch her breath at a shady bend, Emmy prayed that Ivy's future might be filled with peace and hope. It might not be the future she had dreamed of with Alex, but it would be one which would keep their daughter safe and make a happy home for Ivy as she grew up. The war would surely end one day, and these dark years of loss and sadness would be no more than memories, snapshots in time slumbering in a suitcase, faded lines of poetry jotted onto a page in between offensives. Emmy knew that a way of life and a delicate innocence had ended for ever. Just as in Kit's cherished poem, their last golden summer had slipped into history and the three beautiful, brave boys she had loved so dearly were gone.

The world would never see their like again.

Asleep in the shade of the perambulator's hood, baby Ivy seemed oblivious to sadness. Emmy hoped she would never know such loss, and that when her daughter was a young woman, the misery of war would be no more than a memory. She reached in and stroked the soft baby hair on her daughter's head..

"Are you ready to see your new home, little one?"

Ivy snuffled to herself and Emmy's heart melted. She loved her with such a fierce intensity, and when the baby smiled up at her with Alex's smile she marvelled how such joy could come from such sadness. She adjusted the crocheted blanket, a gift from the adoring Mrs Puckey, and continued up the lane, her thoughts drifting back over the past weeks.

Emmy had visited the ruins of Pendennys Place three days after Ivy's birth. The Elmhursts were worried, fearing the shock might be too much for her, but having lost Alex Emmy knew that the destruction of bricks and mortar was as nothing in comparison. Her father had been lost that night, she pointed out, and she wanted to pay her respects. There was no arguing with this and so Rupert's father had driven Emmy past the manor, then along the sunken lane which flanked the woods and twisted past the wheat fields before arriving at the entrance. He stopped the Daimler short of the gates, when it became clear that the elaborate metalwork served only as an entrance to charred ruins.

"My dear, maybe we shouldn't …"

Emmy was already opening the door and swinging her legs out. With Ivy clutched against her chest, a warm, milky tyrant sleeping for now, she stepped onto the drive and with trembling legs walked towards the blackened emptiness where her home had once stood. Her mind struggled to understand what it was she was staring at, for the old chestnut trees stood just as proudly as they ever had, and only a few days ago she had rested in their shade to re-read Kit's letter. She stared at the scene, struggling to comprehend how life could shift so greatly that while she had become a mother and the grand house had become no more than smouldering ash and blackened brick ribs, the spreading chestnut trees remained the same. The pools of shade they cast on the lawn fell in the same patterns as when Kit and Rupert had sat in their deckchairs while Alex sketched a girl sitting high on her horse, but unlike the trees the people were moved about as pieces in a chess game. The wise old trees could only watch. They had seen kings behead wives and kings lose their own heads. They had looked on as crowns were won and lost. They had seen babies born and age and die, and Emmy found a strange comfort in knowing they were still here when everything else had been razed to the ground. These trees would be standing long after she was gone and maybe even after Ivy too. Who would look on them a hundred years from now? Would anyone even know there had once been a house here? And if they did, would they think of her?

Ivy shifted in her arms and Emmy held her baby against her thudding heart. Each footstep she took carried her deeper into a landscape she no longer recognised. Although the gardens were untouched, the neat rows of newly planted vegetables already turning their faces to the light, and beans climbing vigorously up the poles placed by Simmonds in anticipation of their assault, the kitchens where the produce would have been prepared were nothing but air. The smell of burning filled her nose and snatched her back to those terrifying minutes spent crawling blind along the passageway, and she closed her eyes, overcome with the enormity of it all.

Only the farthest gable remained. Like a sole tooth inside a diseased mouth, it stood, spotted with black patches, its windows empty of glass and blank as blinded eyes. Birds already swooped in and out of them and it would not be long before Nature began to reclaim her own, stealthy green fingers creeping over the sooty brick and tendrils clawing away at plaster. The lower part of the staircase was carved from stone and remained to climb to nowhere, and she wondered whether the spirits of those Munnings horses whose pictures had once graced the damasked walls had galloped free with the smoke and ash. Was Julyan riding one now, young again and filled with vigour as he charged across the Elysian Fields on a leggy thoroughbred? And were the bosomy Reynolds ladies watching him, giggling coyly behind plump beringed fingers and blowing him kisses from their rouged lips? She hoped he was happy in death as he had never truly been in life.

"I'm sorry, Papa," she whispered, but there was no reply, only ash drifting in the breeze.

It was incomprehensible that until three days ago there been a house here. It was impossible to imagine tapestries, chandeliers and paintings furnishing this ruin or to equate the burned detritus littering its footprint with furniture. Emmy's memory attempted to recreate the library from the shell of the house – the oxblood opulence of the seldom-used dining room was over there, surely, and that way the library; but fallen beams scattered like Spillikins confused what she recalled, and the knowledge that her father had perished somewhere beneath it all was just horrible. Hoping he had been unconscious before the smoke had crept beneath the door and stolen into his lungs, she turned away with tears spilling down her cheeks.

Julyan Pendennys had been moody, a heavy drinker and given to bouts of violence, but nobody started life like this. She glanced down at little Ivy, so new and untarnished, and her heart broke to know that her father had also once been just the same. Life had twisted him, disappointment and loss warping him into a different shape from the one that he should have taken, and there was a lesson to be learned from this. She could choose to follow his path and allow bitterness to bend her, or she could take charge of her own Fate, pick up the pieces of the life she had been granted, and make a good future for her daughter.

Emmy knew which path she would choose.

She picked her way through the still warm ruins of her home, making tentative plans. The facts were bleak. She was a widow with a child, and homeless. Her inheritance was in charred ruins and if her father's debts were as bad as she feared there would be no money available to pay off his creditors. Then there was the matter of the family retainers, Mrs Puckey and Simmonds, now homeless and without employment. Mrs Puckey was staying with her sister, the mother of the heroic Dickon Trehunnist, and Simmonds was camping out above the stables at her in-laws' house. Both servants had lost everything, too. So, as the last of the Pendennys clan, a dynasty once so important it had warranted a railway station all of its own, Emmy was determined to do the right thing by those who had stood by her family when it had fallen on hard times. She was the mistress of this house now, and even if all that remained of it was ash she would do her utmost to make use of it.

"Emmy? Come back, my dear. It isn't safe," she heard Mr Elmhurst call, but his words held no meaning. She threaded her way through rubble and fallen masonry towards the place where the stables had been. Ivy held tightly with one arm, she bunched her skirts up in her free hand to avoid pools of sooty water and clambered over the stumps of stalls until she was standing where the coach house had been and where Alex's wagon had slumbered beneath an old sail.

Now even this was ashes. Everything was gone.

Emmy held Ivy tightly and the baby grizzled in protest. Not everything, she thought. The suitcase with Alex's photographs and letters had survived, and his locket was around her neck once more, but most of all there was Ivy now. Their daughter was here, and Alex Winter lived on in her dark brown eyes and stubborn nature. Just as he would risk all for his art, so Ivy would give every scrap of air in her lungs for attention.

Emmy dropped a kiss onto the wispy dark head. Ivy was the best of it all. She was the reason.

The baby wriggled and spluttered, and Emmy wondered whether her little one sensed the melancholy atmosphere. No good would come of staying here, stirring up memories. The future lay ahead. It was only minutes, Alex had said, and Emmy repeated to herself that she did not intend to waste a single one.

"Let's go, my darling," she said to Ivy. "There's nothing here for us now."

The next day, despite the protestations of the Elmhursts and Mrs Puckey, solicitous of her welfare, Emmy sat at a vast oak desk in the office of Marrick and Pemberton, the legal firm which had represented the Pendennys family for generations. Reams of paperwork were spread out before her and as the solicitor explained what it meant, she stared over his shoulder through the bow window and into Fore Street. It was market day, and even in wartime Bodmin was bustling with dogcarts, drays, gigs and motor cars, but Emmy scarcely saw a thing. Her head was spinning.

"May I offer you a drink, Mrs Elmhurst?" Mr Marrick asked. His lined face was filled with concern and Emmy realised she must present a worrying picture indeed, a young widow with bandaged arms, newly delivered of a child and witness to the house fire which had claimed her father's life. If anyone deserved a drink, it was her.

She shook her head. "Thank you, no. I need to keep my thoughts clear."

He cleared his throat a little awkwardly and stared sadly at the balance sheets spread out across the desk.

"I can imagine. There is a great deal to take in. It must be something of a shock."

Emmy didn't find the true extent of her father's debts a shock in the slightest, since for most of her life she had lived with creditors calling and antiques disappearing at regular intervals to settle the bills. The shock was the realisation that without the house itself she would lose everything else too.

"My father has taken out substantial loans against the house," she said quietly. "There are many outstanding bills and also a large amount to repay the bank since there was no insurance on the property. Am I correct?"

My Marrick took off his glasses and polished them.

"That's the sum of it, yes. You are the sole beneficiary of the will, which means you inherit everything – debts as well as assets – once the inquest is complete and probate has taken place. As you'll know, Mr Elmhurst left you a modest military pension, but I'm afraid this won't be nearly enough to cover the debts on the Pendennys Estate."

Emmy laughed out loud at this. Rupert's pension wouldn't pay a single one of Julyan's bills to the wine merchant, never mind the mortgage on the property.

"No. I can't imagine it would."

Mr Marrick regarded her over the paperwork.

"You need to understand that in effect the house belonged to the bank until the loans secured on it were repaid. You will need to sell your other assets to repay that debt."

"By assets you mean the land," Emmy said. This too was no surprise. Hadn't she grown up always knowing that she would be married off to the highest bidder to pay the estate's debts? If she had married Kit as planned then Colonel Rivers would pay off the bills and pocket the land. That had always been the understanding. But Kit was still fighting on the Western Front and his parents were no longer nearly as ambitious as they had once been: Colonel Rivers was said to be very unwell and his wife's whole focus was on nursing him. No, marriage for money was not an option. But then it never had been.

The solicitor was nodding. "Correct. Along with the farms on it, which will have to be sold too. That should fetch enough to settle your father's affairs, and it will leave you with a fair sum to live on."

She nodded. So, this was where it would end for the Pendennys family of Pendennys Place. Some blackened ruins and the sale of their estate. It was an inglorious end, but oddly fitting at a time when young men were falling in their tens of thousands and the shape of the old way of life had changed for ever.

"I shall put the land up for sale as soon as I can," she said. "And I expect a fair market price. I imagine there may have already been interest expressed?"

The solicitor looked a little flustered by her forthright manner. Emmy wondered whether he had been expecting tears.

"Indeed there has, and there are several very interested parties. Would you like me to make further enquiries?"

"Please," she said. "I wish all of it to be sold – and in the meantime, Mr Marrick, I would like a sum released against the value of the assets."

The solicitor nodded and picked up his pen. "How much of a sum will you need? Will five pounds cover any shopping you might require?"

He thought she wanted a new hat or a dress. Emmy's hand rose to touch her locket for courage before she named a figure which made the pen fall from his grip.

"My dear! What can you possibly need such an amount for?"

Emmy looked him in the eye. She was a mother. She was an heiress. She was going to take charge of her own fate.

"I wish to buy a house of my own," she said slowly. "And I know the very place."

Little Churchlands Farm drowsed at the far end of its own meandering lane, more accurately a track no wider than a horse and cart, and with a furry grass spine ridging the centre. As the perambulator bumped along Emmy sang to Ivy and pointed out the birds which rustled in the hedges and called from the trees which met overhead. She loved the way their knotty branched fingers were clasped together to throw pools of deep green shade over the dusty track and keep the sun from her bare forehead. In the winter they would shield her from the rain, too, and already she knew that everything about this place would protect her and Ivy.

"Nearly there," she told the baby. "Not long now, my darling! Almost home!"

To anyone unfamiliar with Rosecraddick this lane would seem to twist and turn to nowhere, but Emmy knew that at the far end, over the dear little bridge over the ha-ha and through the pretty white gate, was the storybook farmhouse. Her pulse quickened because it was her farmhouse. Hers and Ivy's. At last Emmy had found the safe home she had been dreaming of. With twenty acres of land it would be enough to manage with the help of Simmonds, and there was more than enough room for him and Mrs Puckey here. This modest dwelling with white walls bulging like an over-iced wedding cake and its little porch smothered with fat pink fists of rambling roses might not be grand like Pendennys Place, or stately like Rosecraddick Manor, but it was welcoming and warm, and it would be here that Ivy could grow up, surrounded by those who loved her.

Reaching the gate, Emmy paused to contemplate the property, and her heart skipped like a pebble skimmed over the water. Two storeys high plus several little attic rooms that she had already earmarked for Simmonds and Mrs Puckey, it had chunky chimneys at either end, a freshly tiled roof and generous windows which allowed daylight to flood in. The small front garden was filled with roses, foxgloves, honeysuckle and sweet peas, and the bees droning through the blooms seemed drunk on the scent as they tumbled from petals and bounced among the lavender hedges.

Inside was modest: a pretty sitting room and a small dining room at the front, and at the back a large farmhouse kitchen with a temperamental range with which Mrs Puckey was already doing battle. Above were four bedrooms, the biggest of which Emmy had claimed and furnished simply, her precious suitcase stowed beneath the big brass bedframe and filled with the treasures she would pass to Ivy, along with the truth of her birth, on her daughter's twenty-first birthday. There was an indoor bathroom, too – and, an absolute necessity, electricity, because there would be no more candles or lamps and risk of fires. The rear of the farmhouse boasted a barn and a piggery as well as stables, and Emmy thought that one day, when the war was over, she would find herself a horse once more, and a pony for Ivy. Until then, it would be old Hector who pulled their cart and carried her side saddle. Maybe she would even ride astride! After all, who was there to tell her otherwise? Emmy was a mother, a widow and her own woman now.

She touched the locket, safely around her neck.

"I did it, Alex," she whispered. "I took charge of my own fate, and I'll look after Ivy for you. It's only minutes after all, my love, until we meet again, but until then I promise I'll live every single one of them for you."

There was no reply, but it seemed to Emmy that the wind was a little warmer and the flowers nodded their assent, while the bees droned just a little louder, too, by way of reply. She let her hand fall from the locket and back onto the handle of the perambulator. The walk from Rosecraddick was only a couple of miles, but her journey had been far, far longer.

"Ready?" she asked Ivy, and in reply Alex's daughter opened her dark brown eyes and smiled, a deep and joyful smile. Somewhere Emmy thought she heard a camera's shutter closing.

She smiled and lifted the latch. Emily and Ivy Elmhurst were safely home.

Chapter 7

Alison

Cornwall

In wintertime the lane is bare, the last tenacious leaves clinging to the trees and the rain dripping from the branches in a dismal staccato. The grass growing down the middle of the lane and along its edges is sodden; if I lose concentration for just a second the wheels will spin and I'll be stuck until Steve can tow me home. I don't relish the notion, so keep my eyes glued to the track. I hope I don't meet a tractor and have to reverse because the road leads uphill and it's not much wider than my car.

While I swish along the lane towards Churchlands Farm, praying the Cornish hedges don't scratch the car's paintwork or the potholes cause irreparable damage, I decide isolation is all very well if you rock up in the height of summer for a couple of weeks, when the sun is high and fat bees are exploring the roses around the twee porch, or perhaps cosy up by the log burner for a week at Christmas when the snow and the slippery trudge to Rosecraddick is a festive novelty. But to live out here all year round is something else entirely, let alone farm it alone and in an age before mechanisation, and I'm filled with admiration for my great-grandmother, Emily Pendennys. She didn't allow circumstances to break her. No matter what was thrown at her, from an unplanned out-of-wedlock pregnancy to widowhood to near destitution, she refused to give up, and against all the odds managed to make a home at this smallholding for herself and her daughter. A happy home, too, judging by the photographs of haymaking and little girls holding chickens or riding ponies.

I slow down to round a corner, not wanting to ground the car, and suddenly there it is – the farmhouse from the photograph, and the very same building whose bill of sale is tucked into the folder on my passenger seat. My heart flutters with the strangest sensation, a mixture of fear and excitement, because now I am seeing for myself somewhere Emily knew and loved. This is the place where she raised Alex's precious daughter with love, and where she took charge of her own fate, just as she'd promised him. Unlike Pendennys Place, razed to the ground and achingly empty except for swooping birds and stealthy weeds, this pretty farmhouse has barely changed since Emmy's time. I pull up the handbrake and kill the engine, half-expecting the door to open and my great-grandmother, young again, to step out into the garden with Ivy toddling after her.

Rain trickles down the windscreen. Each drop appears to fall at random yet tracks its own particular course down the glass. Is this chance or predestination, I wonder? Is anything written in the stars, or do we truly have the power to set our own destiny? Did my great-grandmother take a step away from the life laid out for her, or was it always written that she would meet and fall in love with a handsome travelling photographer? Either way, if it hadn't been for her choice to choose love there wouldn't be a middle-aged woman sitting in her car right here today to stare through rain and tears at the farmhouse. I am beginning my journey today at the end of my great-grandmother's, and it feels right to be here, where her letters and pictures finish, before turning around and meeting Matt at the manor where so much of her story took place.

Resting on the empty passenger seat beside me is the folder containing all the letters Matt found inside the camera as well as the newspaper cuttings and pictures the suitcase yielded. I had read them all late into the night, long after a yawning Steve had kissed my cheek and headed to bed, and once I was finished I sat in the stillness watching the fire dwindle to a red glow and listening to owls call from the woods, once home to a pretty wagon with red wheels where two young lovers met in secret. Pale fingers of daylight were scratching away the darkness by the time I joined my husband, but I couldn't sleep and eventually crept downstairs once more to brew more coffee and relight the fire. As the flames caught in the logburner I was transported to the warmth of the wagon where a merry little fire danced in a pot-bellied stove, before the scene shifted to a blazing building and heavily pregnant girl crawling on hands and knees through smoke and dragging a suitcase behind her.

Now I understand why Matt and Pippa are caught between two worlds; the landscape of 1914 overlays the present, and as the two merge and blur it becomes hard to tell where one ends and the other begins. Perhaps there is no end and no beginning at all, but they run parallel just like the railway tracks once laid outside my house?

While I sit in the car, my breath fogging the windows and my hand closed around the locket, just through the most gossamer of veils I know Emmy is wheeling Ivy in her pram while Simmonds digs over the vegetable beds and Mrs Puckey hangs out the washing. I understand now how for Matt Enys the world of Kit Rivers and First World War Rosecraddick is as tangible as the present. I have heard my great-grandmother's voice and those of Alex and Rupert and Kit, and that last summer of 1914 has become vivid for me, no longer sepia-faded and decade-dusty, but colourful and immediate. The boys' faces are fresh, and their voices echo down the years. Love and fear and death and war are timeless. Who knows this better than the mothers and wives of those who serve? The dread which gripped Emmy when she spotted the telegram boy riding along on his bicycle and the pain of parting, an agony she felt in the very place where I kissed my Jamie goodbye, will never age. These emotions are sliced into us by love's blade, and we bleed regardless of epoch when our dear ones face danger.

I don't need to read the letters sent to the front to know what my great-grandmother had kept hidden for so long. I'd known long before Matt's frantic suitcase-saving dash to me at the halt, with those curled-up letters. Now I can even understand why my grandmother, Ivy, fell out with her own mother and had such an aversion to discussing family history. Our family past had been locked for over a hundred years, but the moment I opened my great-grandmother's locket I'd understood everything.

My own son is the key.

I no longer require Matt Enys to piece together our family's history. There is no need for me to visit the Imperial War Museum and see Rupert Elmhurst's medal. I don't even have to pore over the letters my great-grandmother so carefully secreted away in the suitcase lining. All it took was one glimpse of the image inside the locket to understand it all. The photograph might have been over one hundred years old, and the young man smiling out at me long dead, but I recognised him instantly. The image might be sepia-tinted, but I know that the young man's eyes were as dark as the rich Cornish soil and that they sparkled like the sea when the sun shone over Rosecraddick Bay. I know that dimples danced in his left cheek when he smiled, and that he brimmed with energy and enthusiasm for life. I know that his hair was the same deep red as beech leaves in the rain, and it curled in soft waves to his shoulders when left unmolested. He loved to laugh and tease and joke, and when he did his eyes would crease up and his nose crinkle. When he sketched or took pictures a frown of concentration would ripple his forehead and the tip of his pink tongue would poke from the corner of his mouth. He was steadfast and true and rare and wonderful.

I know this boy, this Alex, whose wings had been granted far too soon. Alex is Jamie and Jamie is Alex. This young man, so dreadfully young and with everything stretching ahead of him is my own son one hundred years before Jamie chose to don a uniform and leave our home soil for conflict under a foreign sun. Like my son, Alex was artistic and creative. Like my son, he was principled and determined, and when he gave his heart he gave all of himself and for all time.

Alex, like Jamie, was ready to die fighting for what he believed in. He had a calling and he chose to answer it no matter what the cost.

My heart shivers and I open the locket slowly, inhaling sharply, because the shock of seeing my son's face, a traveller in time, hasn't lessened. Jamie's conflict is played out in heat and dust and with IEDs rather than with mud and mustard gas and bayonets, but his steadfast belief in his calling is the same. Jamie says little of this to me, but he has seen his comrades die yet he fights on, serving his country and doing his duty. And like the kind man who lent his name to my family for a generation as well as the man whose blood flows in his veins, my son is a hero. My son and his great-grandfather Alex are one and the same. The links in the chain have held true for over one hundred years, even when we didn't see them or even know they were there, keeping us connected.

"Do you know your greatest legacy was much more than pictures?" I ask the handsome boy beneath the glass. "Your life's calling was here all along, Alex. Do you see that now, wherever you are?" But there's no answer, only the pattering rain and sighing wind to remind me that it all passed a long time ago.

Alex had indeed received Emmy's letter where she had poured her heart out about the baby, because it was curled up with all the others he had kept close as he marched through mud and death. He must have fallen in action before finding the opportunity to write back, or maybe his letter contained more pictures and was censored. Was he pleased to be an expectant father? Frightened for Emmy? Desperate to return to Cornwall and sweep her into his arms to hold her close and protect her? I study his open face, thinking of my own son, so tall and strong yet tender and loving, and feel certain Alex Winter would have felt all of these emotions. He had loved her. They were soulmates.

What a dreadful, awful waste.

Overwhelmed with sadness, I click the locket shut and tuck it underneath my jumper. It's hard to explain how a loss that happened so long ago can be so raw, but after reading his replies to my great-grandmother's letters, Alex and Emmy are no longer distant names from the past but have become my friends. Along with Mrs Puckey and Simmonds, the fearsome yet pitiful Julyan, and the ghost of a once great house, they are only a thought away. There's Kit Rivers, whose own words tell part of the story, and the gentle Rupert Elmhurst, both of whom loved my great-grandparents and who I will never forget.

There are many ways of being a hero, I reflect while wind buffets my little car. Protecting your mother from worry is one, as is wanting to tell the truth through writing or art; and saving a young woman's reputation and safeguarding her child by offering your name is no less heroic. I think I'm moved most of all by the quiet courage of Rupert Elmhurst. A hero for far more than his bravery in battle: in putting his unrequited love and grief aside and marrying my great-grandmother, he showed a selfless nature and great love for both Emmy and Alex.

Little Churchlands Farm wobbles through the rainy windscreen and my tears. Without Rupert, what would have become of Emmy and her child? Would she have been forced to give Ivy up? Perhaps a life of hardship and poverty would have been her lot, because her world was not kind to unmarried mothers. Without Rupert's name to protect Ivy, what would have become of my mother? Or myself, and Jamie? Would we even exist? The possibilities seem endless, one parallel universe after another splitting away into infinity, but there is one thing I know for certain – Rupert's part in my family story will not be put to one side. He will be remembered.

"Did you know about this, Mum?" I whisper. "Did Grandma Ivy tell you? Is this why she fell out with Emmy?"

The rain grows heavier and I take this drumming as confirmation. The letters and photographs were Ivy's legacy from the father she had never known. Last night as I sat by the fire and read into the early morning, my thoughts had turned from Alex and Emmy's beautiful and doomed love affair to their daughter, my grandmother. Only a handful of photographs remain. They are my grandmother's chrysalis, charting her metamorphosis from chubby baby to dimpled toddler to smiling girl on a pony and finally butterfly young woman in 1930s fashion. There is no trace of the austere old woman I dimly recall from my own childhood. There is no evidence here of the woman who seldom spoke to her own mother and wanted nothing to do with her family's past.

I'd fanned the pictures and the letters out on the coffee table, feeling desperately sad about this estrangement, because the great love Emmy bore for Ivy is palpable in everything. It shines in her letters to Alex and Kit. It's there in her marriage to Rupert. It's proven by the home bought and the hard life she led to farm it and provide for her daughter. Love pours from every picture she saved, and every cherished memento. Yet nothing remains to tell me much more about Emmy's life after she bought the farmhouse. Matt Enys had said to me, when I visited the manor to give him the artefacts, that history is a mosaic made up of facts and snippets of evidence and a little guesswork. His job, Matt had said with a smile, was to piece all these together. If I did the same for Grandma Ivy, where might it leave me?

The hard evidence I have is that Ivy Hope Elmhurst donated Rupert's military cross to the Imperial War Museum when she was twenty-one and spent the rest of her life estranged from her mother. My guess is that this falling out occurred when Emmy told Ivy the truth about her birth on her coming of age. Raised to believe she was the daughter of a war hero and the granddaughter of the local magistrate and proud of these things, Ivy would have felt hurt and betrayed. Perhaps she was shocked? Or disgusted by her mother's behaviour? That would explain a great deal, for young people can be harsh in their judgement of their parents, and often swift to condemn. From what I did remember of my grandmother she was never the most forgiving woman. Could Alex and Emmy's determined natures have crystallised into unyielding stubbornness in their only child? It's also a fact that Grandma Ivy had hated speaking about her family. How much of that might have come from fear of discovery at first? And how much, later on, might have come from guilt once Emmy had died? That was in the fifties, and there's no record of Emmy being buried in the graveyard at St Nonna's. The only clue I have of my great-grandmother's final resting place is in the picture of my grandmother at a graveside in France. Was Emmy laid to rest as near to her beloved Alex as their daughter could manage? Might this have been Ivy's way of atoning for a near-lifetime of bitterness?

The problem with family history, I'm realising, is the way it poses questions which can never be answered without the key players. I have facts to build on which I have to interpret myself, since Ivy is no longer here to ask. She kept Alex's photographs, his finest work and her legacy, and at some point she may have sorted them into the tin. Did she kept them out of respect for Alex but, unable to face the truth of her birth, hide them away rather than celebrating them? Or did she toy with the notion of destroying them, and with each image the truth of her birth, but falter at the last moment, unable to destroy work which was so powerful and so hard won? Ivy kept her mother's letters and photographs too, as well as the locket containing her father's image. Perhaps a part of her revisited the past in secret and wanted the truth to be told once she was gone. Did she confide in her own daughter? If so, my mother didn't choose to share the secret with me. Had Mum planned to tell me when the right time arose, never dreaming that Alzheimer's would nibble her memories to sawdust before that day dawned?

I have so many questions, and as I try to seek the answers I miss my mum more than ever. The void created by the loss of a parent is never filled; life expands around it, but the absence is always vast and sometimes the loss still steals my breath. Would Mum smile and explain how the women of my family have guarded the story of Emmy and Alex through the years, the locket and the photographs passed on from mother to daughter and the family secret held close? Or did she have no idea, believing Emmy's cherished belongings no more than bric-à-brac which she'd boxed up after Ivy died with the intention of sorting through them one day?

I'll never know the answers to any of this. I have to piece together the facts with my own guesses and create a mosaic of my past because this family secret belongs to me now. It is mine to keep or to share. I watch the chasing raindrops and wonder what might be the right thing to do. Is it time for Alex's work to be seen and his story to be heard? His name doesn't appear on the war memorial because he wasn't from Rosecraddick, and I have no idea where he is buried. The powerful pictures he paid such a high price to take have never been seen except by me and Matt, and it hurts my heart to think he's been brushed out of history. Yet my grandmother never breathed a word, and her anger with her own mother lasted a lifetime. Is this really my story to tell?

'She's a proud woman', I remember my mother once complaining to a friend on the telephone, curly flex stretched across the hall to the sitting room so she could talk in comfort. "She never likes to admit she's made a mistake or to ask for help.' Ivy was just like Julyan Pendennys, I realise with a jolt. Two people who never met yet who shared the same DNA were both stubborn, lonely and proud, choosing to isolate themselves from those who loved them and losing themselves in other distractions – drink for

Julyan and good works for my grandmother. It's strange to recognise unconscious patterns repeating themselves, and a stark reminder that none of us are perhaps as free as we might believe. Jamie's artistic talents and his conviction to do the right thing are from Alex just as my determination to support him and survive until he returns have echoes of Emmy as she waited for Alex.

The rain falls, the wind sighs and I sigh too, wondering whether any of us are truly ever just ourselves. Do we really take charge of our own Fate, or is that merely an illusion? What should I do now?

My mobile, resting by the handbrake, vibrates. *Matt E* lights up the screen. Not quite ready to talk, I let it ring through to voicemail. After reading Emmy's letters to Alex, Matt is also party to my family's secret. When I'd called him earlier, my eyes itching with exhaustion and my mouth rough from strong coffee, he was adamant that the destiny of Emmy and Alex's story lay with me.

"But it's Kit's story too," I pointed out. "People will want to know these details about him."

The Kit of Emmy's letters has made a huge impression on me; he's no longer a flat literary figure but as real as Jamie and his lanky contemporaries, lazing like them under trees and falling in love during an endless summer before the conflict changed everything. I picture Kit, his blond fringe falling into his eyes as he scrawls lines on a page or frowning when he realises that in helping Alex and Emmy he has set them all on a course of action which nobody could control, and my heart squeezes with affection. He was a loyal friend, and this side of him should be celebrated just as much as his poetry.

"Kit's poem and his association with Emmy are already in the public domain. People have speculated about the fate of 'The Last Summer' for years, and that he sent it to her is a wonderful twist. The rest is your family's history and your call," Matt said gently when I pressed for his opinion. "I can't decide for you, Alison, because this isn't my tale to tell."

"Okay, so in an ideal world what would you like me to decide?" I badgered, and Matt laughed.

"On a purely selfish note as a historian there's nothing I want more than to be able to use all this material. It gives far more depth to Kit's story and the context of his work as well as being exceptional in its own right. But I appreciate it's sensitive and you need to think hard about whether you want this in the public domain. It could hurt any remaining relatives Rupert has."

"Ivy was the last of the line, and Rupert was an only child, so any living relatives would be distant cousins," I said. "I don't know why she never wanted to do anything with Alex's work. She should have been proud of his talent."

"She was twenty-one when she gave Rupert's medal away. That's young, even if at the time it feels like the height of being an adult. Goodness, when I look back on myself at that age …" I heard the smile in his voice as he recollected his earlier self. "We all do daft stuff at that age. And we feel things more acutely, I think, because all of our emotions are so new."

"I was in love with Simon le Bon," I confessed.

"Well, there you are! No offence to Simon, but I imagine you've moved on since then?"

"You've met my Steve," I laughed.

"Rosecraddick's answer to Simon," Matt said diplomatically. "So, let's imagine Emmy tells Ivy the truth on her twenty-first birthday. She's shocked and hurt by what Emmy tells her, rather than intrigued and excited, because she has grown up believing she's the granddaughter of the local magistrate and the daughter of a war hero, both of whom hold great sway in local society. She must have been angry with Emmy for keeping such a secret, and horrified that her real father was a mere low-born travelling photographer. If she was courting, there would be no way she would have wanted this secret to be out. Village gossip would have been as bad then as it is now – and, trust me, that's bad."

I'd flushed, glad Matt was on the phone and couldn't see me. How many times had I listened to Pippa or the girls in the local Londis gossiping about *him*?

"Now add to this anger a conflict of identity, alongside the shame associated with being born out of wedlock in that era, and you can begin to see why there was an estrangement," he continued. "Ivy must have been very unhappy, and I feel this would have stayed with her for the rest of her life and made her bitter. There would be no way she would want to open a can of worms by putting Alex's photographs into the public domain, even if she felt she ought to. Would this make sense from what you remember of her?"

I tried to recall what I'd known of Ivy, but struggled to equate the chubby, cherished baby, born of such love and hope, with the stern churchgoing woman of my childhood. Baby Ivy, with her red crumpled face and shock of dark hair, has become more real to me than the grown-up version I had known.

"She died in the early eighties, Matt. I barely knew her. Grandma Ivy left everything to my mum, who passed away, too, a while back. I have no idea what Mum would have made of this, or even if she knew of it. I suspect she didn't have a clue."

"It seems a shame if she didn't. It's such a moving story, and a powerful photographic legacy."

"Grandma used to say that delving in the past never did anyone any good, and now I think we know why. Mum was a gentle soul who probably took after her father. She was the kind to take all things on board and not question too much. She simply left all Grandma's bits to me by default, because they were with her belongings when she died."

"Which leaves you as the custodian," Matt said. "Ivy's legacy of the war photographs and the true story is yours now. Only you can decide what to do with it."

I'd not known what I wanted to do then, and as I sit in the car now outside Emmy's farmhouse I'm still torn. Is the story really mine to tell? My reason for visiting this peaceful place, which Emmy made her home, is that it might provide some clarity. Am I hoping for a whisper from the past to guide me? Faint shadows of my great-grandparents drifting in the mist and granting me their blessing? A voice in the wind offering absolution?

Good Lord. I watch far too many films!

Nobody's in residence on such a bleak January day. Not a soul's about to wonder why this middle-aged woman abandons her car in the lane, walks over the bridge across the ha-ha and stands at the gate. There's nobody to question why she's here or to notice the tears falling down her face and mingling with the soft Cornish mizzle. She is alone.

This is where Emily Pendennys' story ends and Emily Elmhurst's begins. It's here that my great-grandmother built a new life as a smallholder and took the first step on the road to beginning my own family's journey. I lean on the gate and hope she felt the same peace as I do, listening to the steady patter of rain and inhaling the scent of wet earth and salty air. I hope she lay in her bed, warm and snug, and listened to her child's steady breathing in the darkness. Perhaps she opened the locket, just as I do now, and her heart filled with love to see Alex's dear face smiling up at her.

'It's only minutes.'

I spin around to see who's standing at my shoulder but there's nobody. I'm alone. The voice wasn't real. Then I glance at the open locket and Alex's eyes hold mine questioningly, as though asking how anyone can ever know what is and isn't real.

"You're my great-grandfather," I say softly. "And that's as real as anything I've ever known. You're not forgotten, Alex. You *did* live on and so does your work. Nothing is ever forgotten."

The rain seems to lessen, just the softest of mizzles now, and the wind drops away.

I run my finger over the glass, wiping away the drops that have formed from the mist.

"I think you'd be proud of Jamie. He's you and Emmy and himself too. He's the best of us all. Will you watch over him for me, wherever you are? Will you bring him safely home?"

There's no reply, of course, but the mizzle stops and lemony sunlight frills the torn clouds. One ray reaches down and strokes the locket tenderly, turning the glass guarding Alex's picture to pure gold, and as it shines brightly I know this is Alex's promise to me; Jamie will return safe and sound to Cornwall. I will hold my beloved son in my arms again.

My great-grandfather is watching over him. Maybe Alex always has.

"Thank you," I whisper. "Thank you."

I close the locket and let it fall. The weight is my anchor to past and present. It holds me close to family long gone, still living and yet unborn. This locket is more than a necklace; it is part of something bigger and the symbol of a greater love than anything I could ever have hoped to find.

The wind rises again and in its soft breath I think I hear it remind me that nothing is ever lost. Nothing is ever forgotten.

Alex and Emmy's love affair, his life's calling and his powerful photographs, Kit's friendship, Rupert's selfless generosity – none of these things are lost. They will live on and the faces from the past will be remembered. Alex's work will tell the truth of that conflict to a world which seems to have learned so little. And his great love for a headstrong girl with dark curly hair will no longer be consigned to the shadows.

I press my hand against the silver case and laugh out loud because my heart feels so light. Love always lives on, Jamie will return safely, and the way ahead is clear.

It's time to call Matthew Enys.

I have made my decision.

Epilogue

Alison

Loos-en-Gohelle, France

June is beautiful this year. A soft wind lifts the leaves of the lime trees which edge this small churchyard, and the air is sweet with the scent of newly mown grass. Wisps of gauzy cloud drift across a sky of softest duck-egg blue, and when I lift my face to the sun the warmth feels like a blessing. This churchyard, deep in the French countryside, is a haven of nodding grasses and wildflowers where bees bumble and butterflies, their lives as beautiful and brief as those of the young men who fought and died not far from here, flicker through petals.

Impossible to think the landscape here was once pockmarked with craters and shattered from conflict or the air split with the endless roar of guns. Today the only sounds are the droning of insects, the song of invisible birds and the faraway grumble of a tractor tilling the soil. The iron harvest here is still plentiful, or so I hear, and as I listen to the distant engine I wonder whether the earth will yield more appalling fruits today. These flat green fields were once gouged with trenches and this rich soil was the final resting place of over twenty thousand young men.

Somewhere near here Alex Winter fell on an October day in 1915. Even if the sky had been blue then, too, the trees would have been burned skeletons and there would have been no neatly sown crops; only the deep and unforgiving mud. Today poppies sway and the battle-ravaged land has healed itself. The broken villages are long rebuilt, broken dwellings patched and new stone time-soothed, while the torn landscape has healed until only the faintest scars betray the horrors of the past. At the side of a busy ruler-straight road a walled memorial guards the memory of the twenty thousand who fell at Loos and whose bodies were never recovered from unmarked graves. Lines of simple white lozenges stand to attention to commemorate each lost man, and on tables attached to high walls at the rear each soldier's name is carved with honour and pride.

Among these is that of Alex Winter, my great-grandfather.

It's impossible not to be moved by the sight of the row upon row of simple headstones. Inconceivable not to feel appalled by the realisation that each one represents tens of men fallen too soon, and for what? A war which made little sense then and even less now, and a conflict that will always be infamous for carnage and mud and gas. It's the war which poets such Kit Rivers ensured will never be forgotten through their haunting verse and which photographers like Alex Winter captured for ever in stark and terrible pictures which haunt dreams and shadow wakefulness.

I find Alex's name amid the list of the fallen and as I stand back it's swallowed by the thousands and thousands of others. One of countless thousands, he fell in action and gave his life for generations not yet born, and I weep to think of him dying so far from Emmy and for the terrible waste of it all. His body was never recovered. This is the closest he has to a grave, this solemn and stately monument beside a busy French road, but if I'd thought I would find him today I was wrong. Alex Winter isn't here. This isn't his memorial. Instead, it's the young man who stands beside me, red head bowed to pay his respects, and it's the photographs that have become Alex's legacy.

As the traffic swishes by and the sunlight glances from the stark white marble, I touch the locket at my neck and offer a silent prayer of thanks that my son has come safely home. His great-grandfather had watched over him, as I had known he would, and Jamie returned from his tour of duty with a quiet new maturity that spoke of experience and of military decisions he would have to make his own peace with. When he hugged me, I felt new strength in his arms and although his deep brown eyes still crinkled with mirth there was a sadness in them that was new. Like Alex, Rupert and Kit before him, and all the young men whose names were carved here, Jamie had faced conflict with courage and honour. As I'd told Alex all those months ago when I stood outside Emmy's house searching my heart for the right course of action, Jamie truly is the best of all of us and Alex's greatest legacy.

Jamie lays his wreath and as he pays his own silent tribute to the fallen, I know he's grown into a man that his great-grandparents would be proud of. With curling red hair, the same hue as beech woods and the golden light playing over the sharp planes of my son's face, Alex Winter is no longer a faded picture behind glass but lives on in his great-great-grandson. My son is the man Alex Winter might have become if history had been written differently. Whenever Jamie is with Cally and their family I see the love and tenderness Alex had for Emmy; Alex's eye for composition lives on my son's new civilian career as an art teacher, and Jamie's commitment to the young people he teaches reminds me of Alex's dedication to his own calling.

Are there traces of Emmy in my son too? Perhaps, because Jamie loves animals and now that he lives in Rosecraddick he's often to be found walking through the woods or showing his son the shy sea creatures in the rockpools. Emmy's strong survival instincts have stood Jamie in good stead on his tours of duty, and I sometimes think his stubbornness has echoes of her single-minded determination. There must be other attributes I don't know about, too, little nuances of speech or an inherited gesture which have echoed through the years. Like ripples on a pond the people they were have influenced those of us who have come after them; we are all a shifting kaleidoscope of chance, beads shifting and settling into a picture of bright genetic inheritance even when we don't realise it.

That rainy day at the farmhouse, I didn't phone Matt back but drove straight to the manor. My head was filled with ideas and I was buoyed by a sense of purpose that couldn't be constrained by a telephone conversation. While I talked myself to a standstill, Matt listened intently, and I could tell by his expression he was as excited as me.

"I really think we can make this work," he said, jumping up from his seat and starting to pace his office. "Let me make some calls to my contact at the Imperial War Museum and then my publisher. I'm sure they'll be enthusiastic."

Matt was right, although 'enthusiastic' was underplaying the response he received. 'Ecstatic' would have been closer. The lost poem and newly discovered images of Kit Rivers at the front caused a surge of excitement which took the literary world by storm and brought even more coachloads of visitors to Rosecraddick. Pippa's till rang in the shop all day long and the manor's exhibitions expanded and developed as Kit's story continued to capture the imagination of the nation.

Yet it was the war photography of Alex Winter which caused the biggest surge of interest across the globe. I loaned everything I had of Alex's to the Imperial War Museum, and a big exhibition of his work opened the following year. Alex's photographs were hailed as powerful and visionary, and their intrinsic links with Kit's poetry brought them even greater attention. If he had wanted to tell the world the truth about the First World War, Alex Winter was granted his wish, and his legacy was protected for posterity.

Matt had understood why I wanted to keep the personal parts of this discovery under wraps until Jamie returned from his tour of duty. These were family matters and I wanted my son to hear the whole story from me. Then and only then, I said, would we decide as a family what we would do next. If Jamie was happy to share the story of his great-great-grandparents then that was what we would do, but until that point Alex's identity would remain as no more a soldier and an artist. Nothing more would be disclosed. Steve agreed with me and, although it was hard, we didn't even tell Pip the whole story. I think she has just about forgiven us, although whether she was more cross with me for keeping such a big story from her or for having a far more interesting family history than her, I'm not sure …

Jamie always chose not to speak to us when away and even when he was back at base it was hard to talk for more than a few snatched minutes. Almost ready to burst, I waited until he arrived at the halt for his leave, and just as I was poised to tell him everything, Cally broke her news and we were all swept away by the happiness of an imminent new family member. How she had kept that secret was a wonder, but like Emmy before her she was a slender young woman and very resourceful. It seemed I wasn't the only one with big news to give my son on his return!

As Steve poured champagne and teased me about becoming a granny it felt even more important to share the family's secret with Jamie now he was to be a father. This new baby was the latest thread which stitched past and present together, a continuation of Alex and Emmy's story. So I took out the locket and showed him the photo.

"Wow! Cally told me he looked like me, but this is *freaky*," he breathed, studying Alex's face. "I'm not sure what to say.'

"Don't say anything. Just read these." I gave Jamie the letters, the personal pictures and the copies I'd taken of the war photos. "This is your family and your story."

Jamie took the letters to his room and he and Cally shut themselves away for the afternoon. When they emerged both of them were red-eyed.

"Poor guy," was all Jamie said.

"Poor all of them," Cally added. "And how awful nobody ever saw his work and he was forgotten. What a waste."

"But it wasn't a waste. I'm here, and Jamie," I pointed out. "And while we remember him and as long as his work exists, Alex Winter lives on in that too."

"We have to tell the whole story, Mum," Jamie said. "I'm cool with it. I think it's right that people should know just how much Alex loved Emmy and how brave they all were in spite of everything." He dropped a kiss onto Cally's temple and pulled her close, laying his hand on what I now saw was a rounded and very pregnant tummy lurking beneath the baggy sweater. "It reminds all of us how bloody lucky we are to live in peacetime. We must never forget how men like Alex and Rupert and Kit fought for that privilege – I've seen what it's like when it's taken away."

The clouds came over his eyes and I knew my boy was far away, where the roads were dusty tracks and people cowered in bombed-out buildings, their lives as shattered as their cities. I'd hugged him, and then called Matt to tell him our family history was in his hands. It was up to him now to make sure nothing was forgotten.

With the lost summer of 1914, a doomed love affair, a famous poet, unrequited love and a dash of Downton Abbey glamour added to the mix, there was huge interest in Alex and Emmy's story. It made the national press alongside the discovery of 'The Last Summer'. Next month an auction will take place for the rights to a book containing Alex's work, and Jamie wants to give any money it makes to charities supporting injured servicemen. That feels right, and in keeping. I feel sure his great-great-grandparents would approve.

The locket stayed with me; I couldn't part with it, and I wear it close to my heart. In it is Alex's picture and in the other side I've slipped a copy of the photograph he took of Emmy at the garden party, the one where she's smiling to herself, and I love knowing that her face will look at him for ever.

Jamie and I are in a small churchyard, less than a mile from the grand memorial cemetery. Rather than ribbons of graves threaded through a galaxy of loss one simple headstone drowses here in the shade of a spreading lime tree. It's a peaceful place, the smooth grass kept so neat by the villagers it's as though a green counterpane has tucked up the sleeper beneath. I step forward with tears rolling down my cheeks. I have travelled a long way to find her, and now that I have at last, I know her final resting place is perfect.

Emily Pendennys Elmhurst
July 16th 1897–August 24th 1957
Beloved wife and mother
'Your wings and heart were always ready'

Grandma Ivy had loved her mother after all. She must have done to have gone to the great trouble of making certain Emmy was buried as close as possible to the final known resting place of the man she'd loved her whole lifetime – Ivy's father, Alex Winter.

There was no record of Emily Elmhurst in St Nonna's churchyard, and I'd had to enlist the help of Matt once more to locate my great-grandmother's grave. I was moved and amazed to learn that far from being buried in Cornwall with the generations of the Pendennys family, Emmy sleeps in this tiny churchyard in Pas de Calais. I'll never really know what happened between mother and daughter, but I think – I hope – that Grandma Ivy finally made her peace with the past. That she made sure her parents rested near each other tells me that she did.

Rupert Elmhurst, having fallen at Verdun, is remembered on the memorial there as well as on the clifftop memorial at Rosecraddick. I often pause beside it when I walk the cliffs with Waffles and tell Rupert how much he did for our family, how we remember him still and how his name lives on in Alex Rupert, my chubby little grandson who sometimes comes with me, when I can summon up the energy to strap him into my backpack and heave him up the cliff path. I lay my hand on the worn granite and recite the names aloud, the Gems and Ruperts and Kits, and hope they know how grateful I am to them for their sacrifice. Little Alex Rupert can sleep safely in his cot because of young men like these, and he will grow up in a world which has, I can only pray, learned from the dreadful waste of their war.

So now, in this quiet French churchyard when the sun slants low across the velvety grass and the cornflowers and poppies sway, I lay my simple posy and step back. On a small card tucked into the greenery I've written *'It's only minutes'*, and it truly is, I'm sure. Somewhere Emmy and Alex are together once more, lying in one another's arms in the little wagon as they weave their dreams, and I feel certain that they know about, and are proud of, the wonderful family they have made. Rupert is there too, sitting in a deckchair reading, and Kit is composing a poem in the shade of the chestnut tree while dreaming of his secret love. All four are together again and forever young in the land that is always summer, and which is only minutes away.

My hand slips inside my jacket and my heart lifts as my fingers close around the locket.

"Thank you," I say softly.

My words are for them all. Is the gentle rustle of leaves in the spreading lime trees an acknowledgement that they know they are remembered and that nothing is ever truly forgotten? I'd like to think so.

Then I tuck my hand in the crook of Jamie's arm and we turn for the churchyard gate where Cally and little Alex Rupert wait for us. It's time for the next chapter in Emmy and Alex's story to be written.

THE END

I really hope you have enjoyed reading this book. If you did, I would really appreciate a review on Amazon. It makes all the difference for a writer.

Amazon UK

Amazon.com

You might also enjoy my other books:

The Promise

The Last Card

The Letter

The Island Legacy

Chances

Runaway Summer: Polwenna Bay 1

A Time for Living: Polwenna Bay 2

Winter Wishes: Polwenna Bay 3

Treasure of the Heart: Polwenna Bay 4

Recipe for Love: Polwenna Bay 5

Rhythm of the Tide: Polwenna Bay 6

Catching Hearts: Polwenna Bay 7

Magic in the Mist: Polwenna Bay novella

Cornwall for Christmas: Polwenna Bay novella

Escape for the Summer

Escape for Christmas

Hobb's Cottage

Weight Till Christmas

The Wedding Countdown

Dead Romantic

Katy Carter Wants a Hero

Katy Carter Keeps a Secret

Ellie Andrews Has Second Thoughts

Amber Scott is Starting Over

Pen Name Books

Writing as Jessica Fox

The One That Got Away

Eastern Promise

Hard to Get

Unlucky in Love

Always the Bride

Writing as Holly Cavendish

Looking for Fireworks

Writing as Georgie Carter

The Perfect Christmas

Ruth Saberton is the bestselling author of *The Letter, Katy Carter Wants a Hero* and *Escape for the Summer*. She also writes upmarket commercial fiction under the pen names Jessica Fox, Georgie Carter and Holly Cavendish.

Born in London, Ruth now lives in beautiful Cornwall. She has travelled to many places, but nothing compares to the rugged beauty of the Cornish coast which never fails to provide her with inspiration for her writing. Ruth loves to chat with readers so please follow her author pages on Instagram and Facebook You can also follow her on Twitter.

Twitter: @ruthsaberton

Facebook: Ruth Saberton Author

Instagram: Ruth Saberton Instagram

Head over to Ruth's website for more information about her and her writing. You can also sign up for her newsletter where you'll receive updates on any new releases and other exciting items.

Web: www.ruthsaberton.com

Made in the USA
Monee, IL
04 September 2020